Una-Mary Parker lives in Knightsbridge, ~~~~~~~~~~~ extensively on her background as a former social editor of *Tatler* and prominent member of the social scene, Una-Mary Parker has written a stunning new novel of romantic suspense. Her previous international bestsellers, *Riches, Scandals, Temptations, Enticements* and *The Palace Affair* are all available from Headline and have been widely praised:

'A compulsive romantic thriller' *Sunday Express*

'Deliciously entertaining' *Sunday Telegraph*

'I shall pop *The Palace Affair* into my overnight bag when I am invited to Balmoral for a weekend' *The Sunday Times*

'Scandal . . . saucy sex and suspense' *Daily Express*

'The novel has everything – intrigue, romance, ambition, lust and the royals' *Daily Mail*

Forbidden Feelings

Una-Mary Parker

HEADLINE

First published in 1993
by HEADLINE BOOK PUBLISHING PLC

First published in paperback in 1993
by HEADLINE BOOK PUBLISHING PLC

10 9 8 7 6 5 4 3 2 1

ISBN 0 7472 4000 0

Printed and bound in Great Britain by
HarperCollins Manufacturing, Glasgow

HEADLINE BOOK PUBLISHING PLC
Headline House
79 Great Titchfield Street
London W1P 7FN

This is dedicated to my late father, Hugh Power Nepean Gubbins, who returned to his Highland roots to seek peace and quiet, but whose subsequent experiences inspired this book.

Prologue

SUMMER

The old mansion looked deserted, as if no one had breathed life into its solid grey stone walls for years. Even the garden seemed to be abandoned, the air so still that dust motes hovered almost motionless in the hot rays of sun that slanted down between the trees on either side of the long winding drive.

Where was everyone? Surely Edith was around? And the kennel maid? They must be somewhere because the dogs couldn't be left for long, those silky grinning Alsatians that Edith had been breeding for years and which usually clamoured noisily whenever anyone visited Creagnach.

Camilla pushed open the gate and started walking up the drive, her handmade leather boots crunching with startling loudness on the gravel. She felt uneasy at the silence, and quickening her pace tried to ignore the closed windows, the sense of desolation, the forlorn mantle that seemed to drape itself over the sturdy eaves and around the massive porch, where the solid front door looked as if it had been sealed to all comers for a very long time.

Perhaps she'd been foolish in thinking she could drop in on Edith, she reflected; after all they'd never been close, and now that Malcolm was gone . . .

Camilla rounded the side of the old house, seeing in the distance beyond the lawn that sloped down to the Firth of Lorne the mountains of Bhreach, smoky blue in the afternoon heat. This was the first summer for a long time that Scotland had been hit by a drought, and for as far as she could see the landscape lay parched and dusty, the bracken a brittle dull gold, the heather shrivelled, offering no nectar for the bees.

Suddenly, Camilla felt as if Creagnach was a brooding presence, its shuttered face that of a blind person whose other senses had been sharpened by loss of sight, the stillness a listening silence, the airlessness a holding of breath. Something's happened here, she thought. Something so terrible it has left an imprint on the atmosphere, an indelible mark of such blackness that it could not be obliterated even by the pleasant afternoon sunshine.

It was at exactly that moment that it occurred to her the dogs should be barking at her approach. The air usually rang out with their wild warning when anyone neared the kennels, their acute hearing picking up the faintest footfall from a hundred yards.

Tense now, her heart hammering so that she could hardly breathe, she walked slowly round to the back of the building to where the kennels stood.

Then she saw it; a scene so appalling, so utterly tragic, that her cry of anguish became caught in a throat constricted by horror, and she had to lean against the warm stone walls of Creagnach as the strength drained from her body and she was unable to go any further.

Chapter One

THE PREVIOUS YEAR
It began with the arrival of Malcolm's letter. Camilla liked to speak to her father on the phone at least once a week, but in spite of this Malcolm Elliott was of a generation who believed letter writing was part of civilised behaviour. Ever since he'd gone to live in Scotland six months before, with his new wife Edith, he'd penned witty and entertaining descriptions of his new life in the remote Highland village of Ardachie. For a retired merchant banker of seventy-two, he'd lost none of his zest for living and his accounts of dealing with the local village people were sometimes hilarious.

In one letter he'd told Camilla how their new gardener, Jock, had insisted on mowing the lawn at five o'clock one morning, which had resulted in zig-zag stripes 'wavy enough to make you seasick, because he'd been indulging in a "wee dram" in the tool-shed. The wee dram turned out to be a whole bottle of whisky which Jock eventually slept off, curled up on a pile of old sacks . . . and to add insult to injury, it so happened that the bottle of whisky was one of mine! The bastard!'

Today, though, the tenor of Malcolm's letter was different. He sounded deeply disturbed. '. . . I hope we haven't made a mistake by coming to live up here,' he wrote. 'Things are not working out as we'd hoped but we've sunk so much money into this place we can't afford to up sticks and go . . . We certainly weren't prepared for the animosity our presence is generating in the village . . .'

Camilla frowned. This was unlike her father, whose indomitable spirit, a refusal to acknowledge adversity, was something she'd always admired. Never in her life had she heard him complain or grumble or feel sorry for himself, not even when her mother had died eight years ago. In fact, he'd insisted on carrying on alone in the big London house they'd always lived in, until, to everyone's surprise, he'd announced his intention of remarrying. Camilla had been thrilled for him at the time, but dismay had followed when she heard he was thinking of starting a new life in Scotland, helping Edith to build up her business of breeding Alsatians.

'But you don't know anything about dogs, Daddy,' she'd protested. Malcolm had been cheerfully adamant.

'I need a change and a challenge,' he'd replied stoutly, his white moustache bristling, his grey eyes sparkling with enthusiasm. 'Sitting on my backside in a bank all my life has made me long for a bit of fresh air, and anyway Edith's set her heart on living up north.'

Now it seemed the idyll was disintegrating and what, Camilla wondered, did he mean by their presence in Ardachie causing animosity? She glanced at her watch. It was eight-fifteen. In a few minutes the chauffeur would come to take her to the office, and she hadn't even had breakfast yet. Slipping her father's letter into her handbag, she hurried out of her bedroom on the first floor of the elegant Wilton Crescent house and down the wide curving stairs. Dazzling sunshine flooded through the half-landing window, transforming the blue stair carpet into a sea of brilliant sapphire, filling the hall below with reflected light. Unaware of the beautiful morning with so many worries on her mind, she reached the bottom and then paused.

At that moment the heavy mottled glass and wrought-iron front door opened slowly and a slim waif-like figure in a misshapen T-shirt, black leggings and heavy black lace-up shoes entered the hall and flung a grubby army surplus bag on to the immaculately polished marble floor. Her exquisite elfin features were lost beneath her post-Punk makeup, a lurid *maquil-*

4

lage of purple eye shadow, black kohl and deep plum lips that contrasted crudely with her white foundation. Her expression as she looked up the stairs was sulkily defiant.

'Poppy! Oh my God, darling, I've been frantic! I've told you a hundred times to phone me if you're going to be late. Where on earth have you been?'

'I'm sixteen. I can do as I like.'

Mother and daughter stood looking at each other: Camilla worried and upset, Poppy cool and composed. This was the first week of the summer holidays and Poppy, who was at a fashionable London day school, was obviously catching up on her social life. At moments like this, Camilla wondered if she'd made the right decision in sending Poppy to Sloane House; at a school based in town it was impossible to keep tabs on who her friends were and what she was doing. On the other hand, Poppy being her only child, Camilla couldn't bear the thought of her being away for eight months of the year.

'Poppy, you can't do as you like. It's not safe for one thing. There are such nutters about. Anything could happen to you. I get desperately worried when I don't know where you are, imagining all kinds of horrors that could have happened to you.' She'd said it all a hundred times before. Poppy seemed to switch off, gazing sullenly into the middle distance as if she'd gone suddenly deaf. 'Where were you anyway, darling?' Camilla continued. 'Staying with Rosemary? I nearly called her mother to see if you were there.'

Poppy looked balefully at her mother. 'Rosemary's a drag. We're not friends any more.'

'Then where were you?'

'Just out,' she replied shortly, then stalked in her cumbersome shoes into the dining-room. Stifling a sigh, Camilla followed.

Maitland, the manservant who had been with them for years, stepped forward and placed a grapefruit in a crystal bowl in front of Camilla. Chubby and jovial-looking, he nevertheless moved with quiet respect, as if someone were asleep in the next

5

room. Behind his restrained manner, though, Camilla had always noticed the hint of hidden laughter; the twinkle in the slightly bulging blue eyes, the air of unspoken merriment.

'Coffee, madam?' He came forward with a silver coffee pot on a round silver tray.

'Thank you, Maitland.' Camilla watched distractedly as Poppy sauntered over to the sideboard where she proceeded to pull a banana from an exquisite pyramid of fruit Maitland had arranged earlier.

'Coffee, Miss Poppy?' he enquired.

She shook her head, her long blond hair falling into untidy wisps and tendrils round her face. 'I'll have a Coke.'

Her mother looked at her with disquiet and a faint feeling of sadness. What had happened to the sweet-natured girl whom everyone had loved? At first Camilla had thought Poppy had coped very well with David's death three years ago. She'd seemed to take the tragedy of the helicopter crash in her stride, although of course she'd been heartbroken at losing her father. In her own grief, Camilla had been thankful for her daughter's philosophical attitude. Then, last year, Poppy seemed to change completely. Almost overnight she became rebellious and difficult. She refused to study and for the first time her school reports showed poor work. At this rate the likelihood of her getting any GCSEs was remote. Instead she grew increasingly petulant, fault finding with everything.

Nothing was right. Their house was too big and too grand, so that suddenly she said it was embarrassing to ask her friends back. Her mother was too busy, too Establishment, and too old-fashioned. Their lifestyle was boring, pointless, too affluent and shallow. Grumbling constantly, she drove Camilla mad as she insisted on trying to emulate the anti-Establishment Punk youth movement of the late seventies. Only her grandfather seemed to understand.

'It's delayed shock and grief at losing her father,' Malcolm told Camilla. 'Be thankful she's not sticking safety pins through her nose! She probably looks upon that era as a time when she felt secure and happy at about nine years old, and wants to recapture it. All young people go through some phase or other, you know,' he added comfortingly.

'But was I ever like that, Daddy?' asked Camilla, appalled.

'Times were different then, sweetheart. You didn't get the opportunity to kick over the traces or misbehave. The permissive society hadn't arrived, thank God.'

Camilla watched Poppy now as she ate her banana. 'You can't have Coca-Cola for breakfast,' she protested.

'I've got news for you,' Poppy retorted. 'I can have what I like.' Defiantly she flipped the banana skin into a silver wine cooler on the sideboard, looking insolently at Maitland as she did so. Then, with great deliberation, she wiped her fingers on her leggings.

The butler's eyes seemed to blaze for a moment, and it occurred to Camilla that if he'd been Poppy's father he'd probably have clouted her. Instead he turned sharply away and left the room. She wants people to be angry with her, Camilla thought with sudden insight. She is deliberately trying to goad both Maitland and me into losing our temper. Instead Camilla calmly helped herself to some toast, smiled warmly and said: 'I'm coming home early this evening and I thought we might get a video to watch and have a cosy supper together.'

There was a pause before Poppy answered, 'If I'm here.'

'What do you mean . . . if you're here?'

'It means,' Poppy replied with a theatrical air of patience, 'that I'm probably going out.'

'Where to?'

'With friends.'

'Which friends? What time are you going out?'

Poppy leapt to her feet, her face flushed with anger. 'For Christ's sake, what *is* this? The Spanish Inquisition?'

Camilla looked across the dining table, determined not to lose her temper. 'There's no need to be rude. I meant, if you're going out I could order dinner earlier than usual so we could have it together.'

Poppy sauntered to the door, her slight frame undulating sexily as she moved. Camilla, watching, wondered why she had to ruin her looks with hideous clothes and weird makeup. What did she think she looked like? Her delicate features were all but obliterated by eye shadow and the darkness of her lipstick against the youthful texture of her skin gave her an extraordinary look of juvenile decadence.

'If I'm not doing anything else I'll be here,' Poppy grudgingly conceded. Then, through the open doorway, Camilla watched her go up the stairs to her room, her back a ramrod-stiff study in mutiny.

'See that you are,' Camilla called out after her, and instantly regretted it. This was not the way to deal with a rebellious daughter. She glanced at her watch again. It was eight-thirty.

Pausing in the hall to gather up her handbag and briefcase, she caught sight of herself in the full-length gilt-framed mirror and for a split second wondered who the sharply dressed executive woman was who stared back at her so coldly and disapprovingly. The dark blond hair was pulled back severely into a chignon from the fine-featured beautiful face that seemed this morning to be too immaculately made up, too perfectly poised. Camilla found it hard to recognise herself. Of course she recognised the tall slender frame and long slim legs; of course she recognised the large grey eyes that changed from blue to the soft green of the Aegean Sea in some lights; but what she couldn't find in the reflection was herself.

I've changed, she thought with a pang that amounted almost to panic. I've changed from the woman I was only four years ago. Where, now, was the warm, friendly-looking woman who used to exist? The wife and mother? The smiling hostess of this elegant house in the most fashionable part of London? The woman who loved to romp with her only child? The lover who turned to David in the night, trembling with passion? Where, too, had the youth and the laughter gone?

Camilla turned hurriedly away, not wishing to confront herself as she was today; not wishing to acknowledge herself as chairman of the large advertising agency whose name she bore, Eaton & Eaton. The company had been founded by David's father in 1934, and then run by David himself until he'd been killed. That was when she had taken over. Now she ran a huge operation with a staff of sixty, and they handled several dozen major accounts that ranged from brand-named mineral water and perfume to frozen fast foods and life assurance. Every time she turned on the television there was another commercial Eaton & Eaton had commissioned on behalf of a client. In every newspaper and magazine there were pages of adverts proclaiming their clients' products. It was an exciting, fast-paced profession, and highly competitive. But she'd grown to love it, and during the past three years it had helped her recover from the shock and grief of David's death. And she'd succeeded beyond her wildest dreams, turning herself from the boss's wife into the boss.

Camilla glanced fleetingly into the mirror once more. No matter that it reflected a tough-looking woman in her early forties! If she'd been a weak type she wouldn't have survived at all. There were times, of course, when she wondered if she'd ever been a retiring malleable creature, content with her role of The Little Wife. Hadn't there perhaps always lurked a stronger woman inside her? Squaring her shoulders she hurried to the front door which Maitland was holding open for her. The only remaining legacy of the past was the beautiful silvery grey stone house in Wilton Crescent where David had brought her as a bride and where she now lived as his widow.

Ferris the chauffeur, who had been with the Eatons for fourteen years, was waiting for her by the latest model of Mercedes.

'Good morning, Ferris,' she greeted him smilingly, as she did every morning.

'Good morning, madam,' he replied, touching his cap.

Camilla Eaton, chairman, settled herself with her briefcase on her knee, so that she could go through some papers on her way to the offices of Eaton & Eaton in Upper Grosvenor Street.

From now until six o'clock she'd be immersed in her work, all thoughts of a private life put on the back burner.

Poppy lay face down on the bed, unconcerned that her black shoes were leaving streaks of mud on the wistaria-patterned chintz quilt, or that her makeup was coming off on the collection of little white broderie anglaise pillows that were piled up at the head of her four-poster.

Last night had been mind-blowing, she reflected, her young body still aroused by Danny's love-making . . . if you could call it love-making. Poppy smiled to herself. Danny had called it fucking, but whatever it was she had only to remember what it had been like as she pressed herself against the mattress for the exquisite echo of an orgasm to surge and swell and burst again, bud-like, in her hot young loins. Danny was her first lover but she was sure he was unique. Surely no one else could make love like that? Surely no one could maintain an erection for so long, or probe her very being so deeply, or bring her to climax after climax until she was screaming with ecstasy?

Poppy rolled on to her side, her small breasts still tingling with desire, her insides still aching to be filled again. Would Danny be at the King's Arms tonight? He'd been brusque when she'd left him this morning, saying he'd be busy addressing another meeting this evening, but he hadn't said where and so she could only presume it would be in the usual place where his band of Class Warriors held their meetings, in a room above the pub in Whitechapel. That's where she'd met him when her new friend Liz, whom she'd first met in a bus queue, had taken her one night the previous week.

'This is Danny Fox, our leader,' Liz had said, taking her over to a tall broad-shouldered man of indeterminate age with a strong square-jawed face, short spiky-cut fair hair, and penetrating pale blue eyes, clear as glass marbles.

Danny regarded Poppy speculatively. 'How y'doing?' he mumbled. 'Come to join the meeting, have you?' He spoke with a strong Cockney accent.

'Yes,' she replied promptly, although she was not sure what she was letting herself in for. Danny continued to regard her curiously for a few more moments, then he turned away to talk to a tall black man who had just arrived. Poppy watched him with fascination. He seemed so in control of the situation and everyone seemed to hold him in such awe, that she realised 'our leader' was a very apt title. Without being at all charming he was charismatic, not wooing his followers but directing and leading them whichever way he wanted them to go. Dictators are made of such stuff, she reflected, wondering what the meeting was going to be about.

When Danny eventually got up to make a speech, standing at one end of the smoky crowded room, she listened for a few minutes and gathered he was head of an organisation who called themselves Class Warriors. Phrases drifted across her consciousness: '. . . a state of urban anarchy is needed . . .', 'bring chaos to the country . . .', 'annihilate the aristocracy . . .', but after a few minutes she found she wasn't listening any more. Instead, she was watching, mesmerised by this rugged-looking man with large powerful hands and thighs that bulged with strong muscles. He stood with feet apart, as if manning some imaginary barricade, one arm raised from time to time when he wanted to stress a point, head at an arrogant angle.

Danny was clever too, Poppy realised. His audience was sitting enthralled, listening to every word he said, drinking in his beliefs, his ideals, his vision of a country where 'the workers will rule', and 'all traces of the Establishment will be wiped out'.

Suddenly Poppy realised she was filled with desire. Danny was turning her on in a way she'd never been before. She looked at his strongly defined mouth and sharp jawline. Her gaze dropped lower and rested on the bulge in his jeans. When, at the end of the meeting, he signalled to her to stay on after the others had left, she waited spellbound, barely even able to murmur goodbye to Liz.

Finally Danny sauntered over to her, zipping up the fastenings of his black leather jacket.

11

'Want something to eat?'

Poppy's heart constricted with excitement. 'I'd love that.'

'Oh, you'd love that, would you?' His smile was mocking as he imitated her upper-class accent, but it was not done unkindly.

Poppy turned scarlet. 'Well, sure, why not?' She tried to sound mid-Atlantic and sophisticated. 'Got any smokes? I've run out.'

He shook his head, amusement glinting suddenly in his pale eyes. 'Bad for the health, kiddo. Come on, let's go and eat. There's a good cafe that does vegetarian food nearby.'

Then he led the way out of the King's Arms and pushed unceremoniously through the crowds that still loitered on the pavement outside. Like a pet dog scurrying at his heels, Poppy followed him up Whitechapel High Street until they reached Ripe Season, an all-green restaurant with a display of pulses in earthenware bowls in the window.

Looking back, she had no recollection of what he talked about; the evening was a blur of curried lentils and warm beer, anger at the rich and raging against the government, and it wasn't until they got back to his rented room in a rundown semi-detached house that everything became sharply focused with a clarity she would remember for the rest of her life.

'Do you like horses?' he asked as he pulled her down beside him on his bed.

'Horses?' Startled, Poppy thought of gymkhanas and polo matches and race meetings at Ascot.

'Stallions.' He started kissing her, running his large hands over her small breasts. Then he thrust his thigh between her legs. 'Stallions,' he repeated. 'Ever seen a stallion's cock? Ever seen a stallion fuck? Jesus, it's a wonderful sight.' He was pulling off her T-shirt and tugging at the zip of her jeans, and as he talked he started rocking his pelvis back and forth, although he was still fully dressed.

Kissing her neck, her breasts and her stomach, his eyes closed, he continued to talk as if he were in a dream.

'Stallions have cocks a foot long; more than a foot long, sometimes. When they mount the mare they're so excited they can't always get it in. The mare is screaming, the stallion is snorting and stamping, and he's almost choking he's so demented with desire. And then they connect . . .' Danny undid his trousers and pushed them down, pinning Poppy beneath him, forcing her legs apart. 'Do you like this?' he demanded, crushing her in his arms. 'Shall I be a stallion? And fuck you . . . and fuck you . . . until you're screaming like a mare? Shall I put my cock inside you . . . like this? Oh, oh, and deep like this . . .'

She felt a sharp pain rip through her, but then only pleasure. For all Danny's rough talk, he was exquisitely gentle and tender.

Poppy moaned. 'Yes, yes.'

'Stallions love fucking, love dipping their great cocks into a mare, love coming . . . and coming.' Danny's face was contorted with passion as he looked down at himself, watching as he lunged forward repeatedly, gasping for breath, completely transported into his own private world of fantasy.

'Oh, yes!' he yelled suddenly. 'Oh, yes! Now, now, now!' In a frenzy, sweat dripping off his face, eyes blinded by passion, he heaved and thrust and plunged wildly until he climaxed in an explosion of inarticulate cries.

Now, as Poppy lay on her bed thinking about him, she realised she was in love, really in love for the first time in her life. To hell with the well-spoken refined young men her mother wanted her to know; young men who were arrogantly unaware of any existence outside Eton or Oxford. To hell with the social scene with its banal chatter and endless stupid parties. All she wanted now was Danny, to fill her days and nights, to be her life. And if that meant becoming a member of Class Warriors, so be it.

It was nearly lunchtime and Camilla's morning had been packed with meetings. At last she turned to her secretary Jean with an exhausted sigh.

'God, what a morning! I thought it would never end!' A stream of clients had been in and out of her office since nine o'clock, discussing a variety of projects. 'We've nothing on this afternoon, have we?'

Jean, who had originally been David's secretary and PA, smiled sympathetically. She was a good-looking woman in her late thirties, dedicated to her work. Neat, with short brown hair and long-lashed brown eyes, she exuded efficiency as she bustled around the office. It was Jean who had been responsible for showing Camilla the ropes when she'd first taken over Eaton & Eaton. It was Jean also who had covered up Camilla's initial mistakes when dealing with space-buying in the beginning. Over the last three years they had developed a strong business rapport, and Camilla always knew she could rely on her.

'You've got lunch with the Chairman of Royal Scottish Airways,' Jean reminded her now, gathering up papers from the large round table that stood at one end of Camilla's office.

'Don't I know it,' she replied. Royal Scottish was a newly formed airline that had approached Eaton & Eaton to undertake their advertising campaign. Budgets had not yet been discussed but it would be a big account and a personal coup for her if she landed it. It had long been Camilla's ambition to break into the travel industry; if she could announce they had taken on Royal Scottish, it would open the door for even greater expansion.

In the washroom adjoining her office, unchanged since David's day except that she'd had the colour scheme altered from dark blue to a sunny shade of yellow, she was touching up her makeup when Jean knocked on the door.

'I'm sorry to disturb you, Mrs Eaton,' she called out, 'but there's a call for you from someone who says she's an old friend. Her name is Lucy Hamilton.'

'Lucy!' Camilla exclaimed in delight. 'Really? Oh, tell her I'll be there in a second.' Stuffing her cosmetics back into her beauty bag she tried to remember when she'd last seen Lucy. Ten years ago? Twelve? Lucy and Anthony and their four children had been posted to Hong Kong where Anthony worked for an investment company, and they hadn't been home since. They'd kept in touch, though. Having been friends since the age of five when they'd met at kindergarten, they'd been débutantes the same year, had both married at twenty, and no matter that they did not see each other regularly, time and geographical separation had made no difference to the warmth they felt for each other.

Camilla strode across her spacious modern office, furnished in black leather and glittering chrome with glossy white walls, and grabbed the phone.

'Lucy?'

'Camilla?'

They both burst out laughing as if they'd just shared a joke.

'Where are you?' Camilla demanded.

'Here, in London, and you'll never guess! We're home for good! Anthony has been transferred and I'm about to start house-hunting, and put Charlotte and Reggie into new boarding-schools, and God knows what else!'

She sounded just as Camilla remembered her, a lively down-to-earth woman who adored Anthony in a quiet way but whose life was centred on her children.

'We must meet,' Camilla said instantly. 'Why don't you come to dinner?'

'Are you sure, my dear? Philip and Henrietta are here too, you know. Anthony's company have found us a furnished apartment for the time being and we can hardly move, we're so squashed. Are you really sure you want six of us for dinner?'

'Of course I do. Are you free tomorrow night?'

'My dear, we're free every night at the moment . . . we've been here only two days, you know. You're the first person I rang. I haven't even got over my jet-lag yet.' Lucy chuckled. 'I don't know if, apart from you, we even have any friends in England any more.'

'We'll soon rectify that. I'll throw a party for you as soon as you're settled,' Camilla promised. 'Meanwhile, come at seven-thirty and we'll catch up on all the news.'

'That would be great. I'm longing to see you again, my dear. It must have been so awful for you when David died, but you've been wonderfully brave taking over the running of his company and everything.' Although Lucy spoke in a matter-of-fact way there was a deep undercurrent of sympathy in her voice.

'There's nothing brave about it. I had no choice,' Camilla replied candidly. 'When a boat capsizes you automatically swim for the shore, don't you?'

'Or drown.'

'Or drown,' Camilla repeated. 'But with Poppy, I couldn't allow myself that luxury.' In spite of the flippancy of her words there was still an edge of pain in her voice.

'I'm longing to see her again. She was only five or six the last time I saw her, wasn't she? Is she as pretty as ever?'

Camilla spoke drily. 'She's pretty, but she's going through a phase of trying to make herself look as hideous as possible.'

Lucy chuckled understandingly. 'My dear, I've been through it all with Henrietta who, thank God, has reverted to being ordinary and normal again. Wouldn't it be great if we could get Poppy and Philip together? He's nearly twenty-four and the pride and joy of my life.' She roared with laughter. 'I can't think how I came to have such a handsome son!'

'He's obviously taken after Anthony,' Camilla teased. 'Tomorrow night, then?'

'As ever is,' Lucy replied enthusiastically.

Poppy was sprawled on the drawing-room sofa, watching television, when Camilla got home that evening. Glancing up at her mother she flicked the remote control from channel to channel until, with an exclamation of disgust, she switched off.

'What a load of shit!'

Camilla, kicking off her shoes and sinking into an armchair, remonstrated. 'Don't talk like that, Poppy. I had a letter from Grandpa this morning, by the way.'

'So?'

'So I thought you'd like to read it,' Camilla replied reason-

16

ably. Poppy and Malcolm had been close ever since she'd been small, but now even a letter from him seemed to bore her.

'What does he say?' she asked in a flat voice.

'He thinks he may have made a mistake in moving up to Ardachie.'

'Why?'

'Read the letter for yourself and you'll see. I hope he's wrong. Creagnach is such a beautiful house.'

'Utterly ruined by those God-awful kennels they've built round the back,' Poppy retorted.

'But Edith breeds Alsatians. They had to have kennels made.'

'Grandpa didn't have to marry her and get involved.'

She's jealous, Camilla thought with a touch of pity. She's jealous because she's lost both the men in her life, her father in an accident and her grandfather to a new wife. More gently, she continued: 'Why don't you go up and stay with him for a few days? He always loves to see you and maybe you could find out what's troubling him.'

Poppy shrugged. 'I've other things to do,' she replied, but nevertheless picked up the letter and started reading it.

'I wish I could get away and go myself, but we're so busy in the office at the moment it's impossible,' Camilla remarked, almost as if she were speaking to herself.

'You could if you wanted to. You don't have to work so hard.'

'I do, darling, if I'm going to do the job properly. Don't you remember how hard Daddy worked?'

Poppy retreated into silence. Then she dropped Malcolm's letter casually on to the floor before uncurling herself and standing up.

'I'm off now.'

Her mother looked startled. 'Aren't you staying in for dinner?'

'Nope.' She sauntered towards the door.

'But, Poppy!' Camilla sighed loudly. 'Well, you must be in tomorrow night whatever happens. Lucy and her family are coming to dinner. Her son Philip is twenty-three now and she's longing for him to meet you.'

17

Poppy cast her eyes to heaven, tossing her long blond hair to one side so that it cascaded over her right shoulder.

'Christ, how awful!' she exclaimed. 'I can't think of anything worse. Count me out.'

Camilla looked at her angrily. 'I insist you're in, Poppy. They are my oldest friends and Lucy is your godmother. It would be terribly rude if you weren't here.'

Poppy looked at her mother insolently. 'I might be in for a drink beforehand,' she conceded, 'but I definitely won't be in for dinner.'

It was eight o'clock the following evening and a meeting of Class Warriors was taking place at a Catford pub called the Nag's Head. Danny Fox had gathered together an even larger following of supporters than on previous evenings and they were all crammed into a first-floor room that stank of stale tobacco and beer. The bare wooden floor was heavily stained in places and a sticky coating of nicotine had made the walls a sickly shade of burnt umber. Outside the traffic still thundered past on its way through the outskirts of London, but Danny's voice, soft yet penetrating, rose above the rumble, binding his audience to him as if they were hypnotised.

'We must bring down the government. We must wipe away all traces of the capitalist system, all traces of greed, all traces of unfair privilege.' His rhetoric was as fluent as any politician's, his control of his followers absolute.

'When the time is right we will form blockades round housing estates and confiscate them for people who have no homes!' He paused in his diatribe, his voice bitter. 'Two hundred – I repeat two hundred – millionaires live in this country, wallowing in their self-seeking greed, whilst others live in cardboard boxes, have to beg for food, have to live in conditions a dog shouldn't have to live in!'

There was a murmur of agreement round the room. A nodding of heads. A clenching of fists. Danny shifted his weight and took a deep breath.

'Comrades, we must put a stop to it! We must stand united against the government! We must eliminate the rich! We must fight for what is right!'

There was a stillness about him, as he stood in faded jeans and a grey T-shirt, that added to the power of his speech; an immobility of hand and face that was disturbing in its very calmness; a quietness of voice that was more deadly than a shout. Behind him, the light from the window shone through the tufted fairness of his hair, outlining his skull. A two-day stubble spread across the lower half of his face.

Danny knew exactly how to manipulate people and he never made the mistake of being too dramatic at the beginning. Warm them up gently, that was his motto. Start by using persuasive reason, capture their interest, hold them spellbound, and then, only then, bring them slowly and relentlessly to the boil. Only when he held an audience in the palm of his hand did he incite them to violence; that was the moment for fist thumping and talk of rivers of blood. But in the meantime they had to be taught to listen to him, and believe in him, and trust him so he could be sure of their loyalty.

Only when that had happened would he exhort the various unions in the country and galvanise them into action. Only then would he tell his followers to ignore the dictates of law and order by attacking the police, setting fire to public buildings and storming radio and television stations.

Danny repeated one of his favourite lines. 'We will bring about a state of urban anarchy!'

'Yeah!' chorused his audience, and a slender girl sitting on the floor in the front row gazed up at him in adoration.

'We will rid this country of the ruling classes. They are all scum,' he intoned with mounting intensity.

'Yeah . . . yeah!' The listeners shouted. 'Down with the ruling classes!' And the girl briefly closed her eyes as if in ecstasy.

Danny looked down at her for a moment and their eyes locked; hers so full of passion, his blazing with desire. Then his gaze swept over the people who squatted on the floor or sat

19

on hard wooden chairs or leaned against the discoloured walls. They were of every race. There were swarthy Mediterraneans and red-haired Scots; there were Indians, Afro-Caribbeans and Asians; but the majority were white and Danny was the whitest of them all.

When the meeting came to an end the others drifted in twos and threes down to the bar below to drink 'snakebites', a favourite concoction, half beer, half cider. Only Danny remained in the room, and with him the girl with the passionate eyes. She moved towards him now, her lips parted, a look of shameless longing on her face. Then she raised her denim skirt and he saw she was naked beneath.

Danny's hard mouth tugged down at the corners with desire as he reached out and at arm's length grabbed her between the legs, squeezing her with his strong hand, twisting the hair, already wet, round and round his fingers. Then he rammed two fingers hard up inside her and pulled her towards him.

'Dirty bitch,' he muttered ardently.

Poppy looked at him wantonly. 'Oh, take me, Danny. Please take me,' she pleaded.

'I'm sorry Poppy couldn't stay for dinner. She seems such a sweet child,' Lucy remarked, as Maitland and his wife, who acted as cook-housekeeper for Camilla, served dinner in the candlelit dining-room.

'There'll be lots of other occasions, now you're back in England for good,' Camilla replied hastily.

The Hamilton family regarded her with warm expectancy; Lucy, plumper than ever, with greying hair cut short and an expression of tranquil benignity; Anthony, red-faced and jolly and a trifle too hearty. And then there were the young ones: Charlotte and Reggie were still in their teens, their charming faces so far devoid of character, their manners politely subdued for the occasion. Henrietta was a pretty twenty-two year old, resembling her mother in every way, except that she had inherited her vivacious personality from her father. Philip, the eldest, was the best-looking of them all, with dark hair and hazel eyes that seemed to twinkle with good humour even when he was being serious. His mouth was attractive too, strongly carved in a lean tanned face that gave a strong hint of laughter, as if he was constantly amused by life.

'Isn't he gorgeous?' Lucy had whispered to Camilla when they were drinking champagne in the drawing-room before dinner. 'I can't help wishing the girls had his looks. And, my dear, he really is the nicest person on earth.'

Camilla smiled, amused by Lucy's open admiration of her son. 'What does he do?'

'He's going to be an architect. He starts his training in a couple of months' time and he's going to get a small flat of his own. They need to be independent at that age, don't they. Don't you think he'd be perfect for Poppy? He hasn't got a girlfriend at the moment.'

'Yes, I do,' Camilla agreed drily, glancing over at her daughter, who had condescended to join them for a drink before going out 'somewhere'. She had her back turned to Philip as if studiously avoiding him, and Camilla thought she looked a fright in a minuscule denim skirt, a leather jerkin, masses of ethnic bangles on her wrists, and her hair a mess. Her makeup as usual was as gaudy as a clown's.

'She's at a difficult age,' Camilla whispered, embarrassed for her daughter as much as for herself.

Lucy nodded. 'Best to ignore it until it passes,' she advised.

'It's not easy.'

'That's because she's the only one you've got. When you have four children, my dear, you don't have time to worry about how they look.'

Poppy had left a few minutes later, without even saying goodbye, and now, looking around the dining table, Camilla wished she'd stayed. It would have done her good to have seen the interaction of a close-knit family, the camaraderie and teasing, and most of all the laughter.

At that moment Maitland came hurrying into the dining-room.

He went up to Camilla and spoke quietly.

'I'm sorry to disturb you, madam,' he said in conciliatory tones, 'but there is a phone call for you.'

She looked up at him anxiously. 'What is it?'

'It's Mr Elliott. I told him you were having a dinner party but he says he must speak to you. He says it's very urgent.'

Chapter Two

'What do you mean, your mail's being tampered with, Daddy?'
Camilla sat perched on the arm of the dark red leather Chesterfield
sofa in the study, listening to Malcolm's account of how his post
was going astray. 'Have you complained to the post office?'

'Of course I have,' her father replied robustly, 'but they're
pretending there hasn't been any post for me in the last few
weeks. That's absurd. I said to them, then why are all the household bills getting through, and circulars selling everything from
life assurance to double glazing? Why has my tax demand
arrived if there was no post for me?'

'What else were you expecting?' Camilla reached for the bell
by the fireplace as she spoke. Her father obviously had a lot to
get off his chest so she might as well ask Maitland to bring her
a glass of wine.

Malcolm snorted at the other end of the line. 'Stud fees for
a start. Enquiries for puppies. Orders for young dogs and bitches.
You know . . . all the stuff that goes with breeding dogs. It's
serious, Camilla. We're losing money and Edith's very upset.'

'Why do you think it's happening?' From the dining-room
she could hear the Hamiltons laughing and talking animatedly.
She didn't want to cut her father off in mid-stream, but she'd
have to get back to her guests in a minute.

'I think our mail is being pinched.'

'Who by?' She sounded startled. 'Who would want to steal
a lot of enquiries about dogs? Unless, of course, they hoped your
mail contained money?'

'I don't think it's as simple as that.' Malcolm sounded deeply troubled. 'The reason I'm phoning you, darling, is to ask you and Poppy to send me a few letters that look like enquiries about dogs, and we'll see if they reach me. Make them all look different, if you can, and post them in different areas, so they don't all have the same postmark.'

'All right.' Camilla sounded doubtful. 'Have you complained to the sorting office in Glasgow?'

'I've written to them twice, but when I phoned them today they said they hadn't received *my* letters.'

'So someone is meddling with both your outgoing and incoming post?'

'Exactly, and bloody angry I am about it too.'

'Daddy, don't get so worked up,' she said, trying to soothe him. 'I'm sure there must be a perfectly reasonable explanation.'

'I'm sure there is, like the village wanting to put us out of business. By the way, don't mention any of this in the letters you send me, in case they open them. I want to get evidence so I can sue the post office for loss of earnings. It'll be difficult if they know I'm on to them, though.'

'They can hardly think you're *not* on to them,' she remarked reasonably as she waved her thanks to Maitland who had come into the study with her wine. 'How many letters do you think have gone missing?'

'Twenty, thirty, maybe thirty-five,' he said, his rich voice, usually warm as brown velvet, sounding tired and strained.

'*What*!' She jumped to her feet. 'Are you serious?'

'Absolutely. We know because dozens of people have been phoning us wanting to know why we haven't replied to their enquiries. Edith has been asking people to settle their stud fees, too, only to be told cheques went off six weeks ago. It's very serious, Camilla. That's why I want you to send me off a batch of phoney enquiries, the point of the exercise being to see how many reach us.'

They talked for a few minutes longer and when she returned to the dining-room, it was with a feeling of disquiet. It was unlike

24

her father to get in a state over anything and she'd never heard him sound so worried before.

When Malcolm and Edith Elliott had first moved to the remote village of Ardachie, they'd been thrilled. Creagnach overlooked the Firth of Lorne, a stretch of water on the western coast which led into Loch Linnhe, and, Malcolm boasted, on a clear day you could see the beautiful island of Mull. Ardachie was the only village for miles, built around a busy little harbour that was tucked into an inlet of the rugged granite coastline. There, life seemed to have stood still for the past fifty years. Lobster pots and fishing nets adorned the quayside in picturesque profusion, and the smell of herring and mackerel pervaded the air whenever the fishing boats returned from the North Sea.

'It's like taking a step back in time,' Malcolm had written in one of his long letters to Camilla. 'None of the houses has any of the things we take for granted, like deep freezes or microwave ovens. Some people still burn peat in winter, and a big day out amounts to a trip to Glasgow, which is a hundred miles away.'

Creagnach stood facing the west, a square-built grey stone mansion, combining the faded grandeur of the past with every modern convenience added by the previous owners. It hadn't taken Malcolm and Edith long to decide that this was where they wanted to live. Kennels and a large run for the Alsatians were built on a stretch of land behind the house, and the furniture from the previous homes of both of them installed. That had been six months ago.

Lucy looked up as Camilla hurried back into the room.

'Everything all right with your father?' she enquired.

'He's fine, except for complaints that his post is going astray,' she replied. 'I didn't say so but I have a feeling that he and Edith are resented in the village because they're newcomers – and English as well! I think the local post office is trying to ruin their dog-breeding business in the hope they'll leave.'

'Who lived at Creagnach before?'

'Hamish McVean of McVean of that Ilk, or something.' She

giggled. 'Scottish titles are so different from English. I think he was the laird. Could that be right?'

Lucy nodded. 'Yes, a laird is simply a northern form of lord – a landed proprietor. Perhaps he was Chieftain of the Clan McVean?'

Anthony chortled from the other end of the table. 'It all sounds a bit feudal to me.' He drained his glass of claret and looked hopefully at Maitland to serve him more.

Camilla grinned at him. 'According to my father they are all very clannish.'

Philip leaned forward, his handsome face alert with interest. 'The Feudal System goes back to the Middle Ages, you know. If the village people feel strongly about their rightful Clan Chieftain's position being usurped by a "Sassenach", living in Creagnach, they could be very resentful.'

'What's a Sassenach?' piped up Reggie who at fourteen was going through a stage of being curious about everything.

'An English person,' Philip replied.

Camilla looked thoughtful. 'I'll have to go and visit them as soon as I can get away.'

'You mean you haven't been?' Lucy sounded astonished. 'Haven't you seen their new house?'

'The company keeps me pretty busy, you know.' Camilla wondered why she felt so defensive, as if she were ashamed of working so hard. 'I flew up when Daddy and Edith first moved in and thought Creagnach was lovely, but I haven't had time since.'

'I imagine running Eaton & Eaton is a frightful responsibility,' said Anthony understandingly.

'It is hard at times,' she agreed, 'but David set such store by the company I felt I must keep it going when he died, and now I'm glad I did. It's very exciting at times, and very rewarding.'

'But do you actually enjoy it?' Lucy's tone was blunt. 'You never worked when you were married, did you? Don't you miss being at home with Poppy?'

'Poppy's at school still, and after all, she's no longer a child.

26

She's got a life of her own and I probably wouldn't see any more of her if I did stay at home.'

Lucy didn't reply and Camilla thought she could detect a hint of disapproval and even disbelief in her manner.

'Anyway, you didn't have much of a choice, did you, Camilla?' Anthony remarked.

'I could have sold out, but David would have hated that.'

'Exactly.' He nodded sympathetically.

'It does keep the pennies rolling in,' she added lightly, 'and God knows, we all need as many of them as we can get.'

'Are you sure you posted seven letters?' Malcolm demanded fretfully.

'Yes, Daddy. Some went from the office, some from our local post box, and Maitland posted a couple in Kensington,' Camilla assured him. 'How many have you received?'

'One. I tell you, my post is being tampered with. There's no other explanation. Wait until I get on to the central office in Glasgow. I'm going to give them hell!'

'Do you think it's because the village resent you and Edith moving into Creagnach?'

'They probably do, but that's no reason to cut off our livelihood,' he boomed angrily.

Camilla tried to mollify him. 'But breeding dogs isn't actually your livelihood. It's Edith's hobby. No one's going to imagine you live in a house like Creagnach on the profits from stud fees.'

'That's got nothing to do with it! It's a criminal offence to tamper with Her Majesty's mail, don't you know that?'

'Of course I know it, Daddy.' Sometimes her father made her feel like a child again, and a rather stupid one at that. 'I just don't want you to get so het up about it.' It worried her that at seventy-two Malcolm should be fretting over something which, though serious, was not a matter of life or death. 'Is there anything I can do? Between us we should be able to bring pressure to bear on your local post office.'

27

'That's sweet of you, darling.' He sounded calmer. 'It's Edith, you know. The dogs are her life and she's getting terribly upset, losing out on orders for puppies.'

'I know, Daddy.' She could visualise her father, upright and still with an elegant air in spite of his age, his thick white hair and white moustache enhancing his distinguished looks. Suddenly she ached with longing to see him again. Before he'd left to live in Scotland she'd seen him at least twice a week, and he'd been incredibly supportive when David had died. Now she realised what an enormous gap his absence from London had left in her life. 'I wish I could get away to see you.'

'I wish you could too, sweetheart. Never mind. Maybe you and Poppy can come up for a week or so in the summer, by which time I hope we can sort out this lot up here.'

'Poppy's being very difficult at the moment. I don't know what to do about her.'

'Most girls go through a tricky stage.'

'But not like this, Daddy. I never stayed out all night and refused to tell you where I'd been, did I?'

'You didn't get the chance!'

'I know. Do you think I'm too lenient? She used to be such an easy girl. I can't believe she's changed so much.'

'She's missing having a father, that's the trouble. The sooner she has a boyfriend who will help replace David, the sooner she'll revert to being her usual sweet self.'

'I think she misses you as much as I do,' Camilla admitted sadly. 'You're so wise, Daddy.'

'Not wise enough,' he said drily.

When she hung up a few minutes later, she wondered what he was referring to with that last remark.

Maitland and his wife always had Thursday and Sunday afternoons off and their routine never varied. On Thursdays they went to the cinema and then on to some little restaurant for supper, and on Sundays they would take a bus to Kew Bridge and walk from there along the side of the river until they came to a small redbrick bungalow in which lived Mrs Maitland's mother. Here they would have a cup of tea, followed later by supper, which in the summer they ate in the garden. Then they would catch the last bus back to Knightsbridge.

On this particular Sunday, Maitland, having served luncheon to Camilla and three guests, cleared the table, helped load the dishwasher, and then with loving care wrapped the silver in green baize bags. It was always kept in the pantry adjoining the kitchen in the basement of the house.

With a sigh of satisfaction, he then locked the pantry door and walked back into the kitchen.

'We'll be in good time for Mother's,' Mrs Maitland observed, putting on her gold wristwatch.

Maitland nodded. 'That's right. Everything's put away so we can be off.'

'Where's Miss Poppy?' Mrs Maitland had adored Poppy ever since she'd joined the Eaton household as cook when Poppy had been five, and she worried about her these days almost as if she had been her own daughter. It wasn't right, her being out all night with God knows who. Nor was the way she looked, all got up like a tart. There was no knowing where it would end, she confided darkly to her husband. A young lady like that should lead a more respectable life. It was a wonder Mrs Eaton allowed it. Mrs Maitland sniffed loudly and pursed thin lips.

'She went out early this morning,' Maitland replied, checking he'd put the pantry door key behind the fuse box on the wall where he always kept it. He thought Poppy was a spoilt little brat, himself; very wayward these days.

Mrs Maitland looked at him, surprised. 'I thought I heard her come in a little while ago.'

'No. God knows where she's got to. Come on or we'll miss our bus.'

Together they left the house in Wilton Crescent, to the sound of laughter coming from the drawing-room where Camilla was still entertaining her guests. It was half-past two.

* * *

Poppy emerged from her room on the second floor and stood on the landing listening. A few minutes ago Camilla and her friends had left the house, locking the front door behind them, and through the heavy net curtains of her window Poppy had watched them drive off in the direction of Hyde Park. She'd already heard the Maitlands go out half an hour before. She had the house to herself now.

Going back into her room, she reached up to the top of her hanging closet where, on a shelf, a canvas travelling bag lay squashed against suitcases, tennis racquets and snorkelling gear. Hurrying down the staircase, the travelling bag tucked under her arm, she arrived in the hall and then continued down the stairs to the basement. It was dark and silent in the gloomy old fashioned kitchen quarters and she remembered how scared she'd been there as a child, convinced every nook and cranny held unknown terrors.

Without pausing, she went to the fuse box and slipped her hand behind it. Her fingers touched something cold, and in triumph she drew out the key to the pantry.

Once inside, she closed the door carefully behind her and turned on the light. Hundred watt bulbs blazed down on the white-tiled walls and scrubbed wooden table where Maitland always sat to clean the silver, but only after he had carefully spread some American cloth and old newspapers on it first. There was something antiseptic about the pantry; it might have been a room in a hospital – clinical and spotlessly clean.

Without hesitation Poppy dumped the travelling bag on the floor and, opening the silver cupboard, started feeling the green baize bundles, being careful not to disturb anything. Candlesticks were easy to make out through the soft fabric, as were teapots and hot water jugs, salvers, trays and sugar basins. What she wanted to find were articles which were rarely used. She felt the things on the top shelf: bundles of cutlery, cream jugs, more candlesticks, salt cellars. Reaching for things at the back of the shelves she realised she could remove quite a lot without it being obvious.

Working with feverish swiftness, although she was sure her mother would be out for at least another hour or so and the Maitlands wouldn't be back until late, she stuffed various items, still in their baize wrappings, into the travelling bag. At last it was almost full and yet the shelves didn't look as if anything had been disturbed. Then she closed the cupboard doors carefully again, turned off the light and crept out of the pantry. The house was silent. Even the street outside seemed deserted. Knightsbridge on a Sunday afternoon was as usual quiet as a graveyard.

Locking the door, she slipped the key back into its hiding-place and then, with an unbelievable sense of relief, charged up the stairs, taking the steps two at a time until she reached her bedroom. She allowed herself to flop down, exhausted by nervous tension, on to her bed. But only after first hiding the travelling bag carefully under it.

Camilla was getting ready for the office the next morning when the phone rang. It was Malcolm, and he seemed to be talking in codes.

'Camilla, is that you?' he barked. 'I still haven't received your request for a bitch, and we can't discuss it now because I've got someone here with me, but I just wanted you to know I'm dealing with the matter.'

'But, Daddy . . .'

'I'll be in touch with you in a couple of days,' he cut in hurriedly. 'I think I'll have something to report then.'

'I see,' she replied slowly, guessing he was unable to talk. But in that case why ring her? Who was with him? 'If I ask you questions, can you answer "Yes" or "No"?' she asked.

'I'm afraid that's impossible, and don't ring me back as I can't talk just now. But don't worry, I'll see that you get a really nice bitch.' Then there was a click and the line went dead.

'WELL!' Camilla looked at the silent receiver in astonishment. Intrigued, and frustrated at not being able to find out more, she hurried downstairs to breakfast. And why couldn't she phone her father back? Who was in the house that made speaking to him impossible?

Maitland was waiting to serve her with her usual chilled grapefruit. There was no sign of Poppy and she didn't like to show her ignorance by asking the butler if he knew her whereabouts.

As it was, there was something else she wanted to discuss with him. 'I'm planning to give a dinner party next Friday, Maitland, for sixteen to eighteen guests. Will you ask Mrs Maitland to suggest a nice menu? And get in plenty of candles and order the flowers, please.' She looked around the exquisitely decorated dining-room with its wallpaper patterned with dark green leaves and red camellias, and the matching dark green silk curtains trimmed with red. Mirrors and crystal chandeliers added their own sparkle, but for dinner parties she preferred to dine by the light of dark red candles.

'Certainly, madam. Were you thinking of three courses?'

'Yes, and we'll offer a selection of cheeses as well. If necessary, put in an order for more wine, and lots of mineral water too.'

'Yes, madam.' Maitland poured the coffee, strong and fragrant, into her cup. He enjoyed it when there were dinner parties. It reminded him of the old days when Mr Eaton had been alive. They'd entertained a great deal then. 'I'll also check on the table linen, madam,' he continued, 'and make sure all the silver's clean.'

'Thank you. This is going to be a business dinner and I want to impress some new clients.'

'I'll see to it, madam.'

Camilla smiled at him. Over the years he'd become a vital contributor to the smooth running of the house, knowing exactly how to organise everything from supper for a few close friends to an impressive formal dinner for twenty.

Maitland, respectful and gracious as ever, smiled back. He knew his place but was grateful that his employer allowed him a free hand when it came to making the household arrangements.

'Will you and Miss Poppy be in for dinner tonight, madam?'

Camilla raised her eyebrows and gave the barest hint of a shrug. 'I think we'd better count her out. She can always cook herself an egg if she turns up.'

'Very well, madam.'

Too many evenings had been spoilt, Camilla reflected, and too many of Mrs Maitland's delicious dishes had been ruined, waiting for Poppy.

Poppy had spent the night at home, but had got up at dawn and slipped out of the house before anyone was awake. Carrying the travelling bag, which was so heavy she had to keep changing it from shoulder to shoulder, she walked the short distance to the Underground station at Hyde Park Corner where she boarded a train for Chalk Farm. The journey would take her forty minutes, she reckoned, providing there was no delay when she changed trains at St Pancras. The address she'd been told to go to was a few minutes' walk from Chalk Farm station.

Placing the bag between her feet, she sat in the railway carriage and wondered how much the contents were worth. Hundreds of pounds? Thousands? Her knowledge of silver was limited to knowing that if something was stamped with a hallmark bearing a lion, then it must be genuine. But genuine what? William and Mary? George III? Late Victorian? It was all the same to her and she couldn't think why her mother liked the stuff so much. When Camilla gave a dinner party, the long dining-room blazed with silver, and the sideboard was laden with dishes and trays, candlesticks and platters. Maitland seemed to spend half his time lovingly polishing it, too, even intricate pieces like the two-foot-high centrepiece of cupids and bunches of grapes and twirly vine leaves.

Poppy reckoned, though, that what she had taken must be worth a bit, even if some of the items were small like salt cellars and butter dishes, and she hoped Danny would be pleased. The organisation needed money, he'd told them at one of the meetings. They had to print leaflets about their cause, get T-shirts stamped with their slogan 'Class Warriors', and buy weapons. What sort of weapons he hadn't specified, and no one had asked.

'Raise money any way you can,' he exhorted them.

Of course Danny had no idea where she lived or that she'd been brought up surrounded by priceless antiques and paintings. She'd told him she shared a squat in Victoria with a bunch of friends, and thank God he'd never asked her to take him back. He was going to wonder where she'd got all this silver from, though. Pity most of it bore the family crest. Her heart lurched uncomfortably for a moment . . . crested silver could be traced quite easily. But then she shrugged. What the hell! Danny would look after her and protect her, just as her father had done before he'd died.

Resentment caused Poppy to tighten her lips and narrow her heavily made-up eyes. How she missed her father! He should never have learned to pilot his own helicopter; it was stupid and irresponsible of him when he had a family. And what was her mother thinking of letting him fly around in the first place? It sometimes seemed to her that neither of them could have cared for her very much or they would never have allowed the accident to happen. Tears smarted in her eyes as she thought about him and she hoped none of the other train passengers would notice. And then, to cap it all, Grandfather had gone to live in Scotland! So far away they were unlikely to see him more than once or twice a year. Did nobody care for her or how she felt? Were they all so taken up with their own lives that they were blind to the fact she was unhappy? Well, fuck the lot of them! If her mother thought she could be consoled with party frocks and going out all the time, she was mistaken. What she needed was to feel that she belonged . . . to someone or something.

Suddenly she leaned forward and heaved the heavy bag on to her lap. Then she put her arms around it and held it close, hugging it to her chest. At least, thank God, she had Danny. And she was going to make sure he was always there, because she couldn't live without him now. The problem was that sometimes he was all over her and then suddenly he'd be cold and not even seem to notice she was there. She couldn't bear that. It made her hurt inside so she couldn't stop the tears welling up. That was why she'd taken the silver. It would prove to Danny how much she loved him, and then he'd never be cold to her again. Never shut her out while he went off with his friends who were all much older than her. He'd realise she was the best thing in his life and he'd stay with her forever. And he'd always be tender when they were alone, and loving, and kind.

Danny looked impressed as he picked over the silver, squinting at hallmarks and examining the Eaton family crest.

'Where did you get all this stuff?' he asked wonderingly.

Poppy shrugged and tried to play it cool. 'I nicked it, of course. But don't worry, it'll be ages before anyone discovers it's missing.'

They were sitting in the kitchen of the house where he'd asked her to meet him. It was, she gathered, the headquarters of the organisation, and it seemed to be full of people, including a very large woman called Marge, two tall black men, a Swedish student, and a camp young man everyone seemed to call Doris.

Danny packed the silver back into Poppy's holdall.

'Good girl,' he said approvingly. 'Any chance of getting any more where this came from?'

She hesitated. 'I can try.' Then, seeing his look of disappointment, she continued rashly: 'Yup. I'm sure I can get hold of some more.'

She slid her hand up his thigh and looked at him with longing. 'I might be able to get some jewellery, too,' she said in a small voice.

'Good. I know a fence who can get rid of it for us. Give us a good price as well.'

Poppy slid her hand higher and moved closer to him.

'Not here, Pops!' he remonstrated, removing it. 'Not in the bleedin' headquarters.' He glanced over towards the kitchen door. 'You never know who's coming in and out.'

'Can't we go to your place then?' she begged. She was aching for him to take her in his arms, to reward her for bringing him all the silver, to tell her he loved her.

'Maybe. Later.' Then he rose and looked out of the window, his broad leather-clad shoulders throwing a shadow across the kitchen table.

'What are you looking at?'

'Bloody council,' he grumbled, sticking his hands into the pockets of his jeans.

'What council?'

'The local council, that's what. See those flats over the road?' Danny pointed to a hideous high-rise block made of slabs of concrete. 'They've just put up the rents. It isn't right, making people pay all that money. What we're going to do when we take over the country is house people in some of those swanky properties in Mayfair and Knightsbridge and Kensington.'

Poppy averted her eyes as Danny swung round to face her.

'Do you realise,' he continued, 'the injustice that's going on? Sometimes only two or three people are occupying a house that has ten or fifteen rooms! Six families could be put up in one of them! And all the while more and more people are having to live in cardboard boxes!' His voice rose angrily. 'Some haven't even got enough to eat, while the privileged classes sit with their bums in the butter.'

She nodded silently, still not looking at him, her cheeks reddening.

'We've got to do something about it before it's too late. If I had my way I'd get rid of the Royal Family for a start.' He was warming to the subject now. 'It's disgusting the way they ponce about, costing us, the people of this country, millions of pounds just to keep them there. What good are they doing anyway? Unveiling bloody plaques all the time, dressed in their fancy clothes! Jesus!' He clenched his fists as if he was going to hit someone. 'I can't wait for the time when we can strike out and eliminate the lot of them! Have you any friends you could recruit to join Class Warriors? We need to swell our numbers.'

Poppy thought about her school friends. There was Lady Davina Coventry, daughter of an Earl, and Vanessa Rees whose parents were multi-millionaires. Then there was the Honourable Charlotte Murphy whose father was an equerry to the Queen ... God, none of them would be any good. They were the most unlikely bunch of candidates for an army of Class Warriors one could imagine. She sat silent and embarrassed. She couldn't think of a single soul she could ask.

'I'll look around,' she said quickly.

'With your posh accent you must know quite a few big cheeses,' he remarked shrewdly. 'What about your family?'

'I don't talk to them any more. Anyway, my father's dead.'

At that moment a voice bellowed from the narrow hallway of the house. 'I'm going out now.' It was the large woman, shouting as far as Poppy could make out to no one in particular. Danny didn't answer but a few minutes after they heard the front door slam the house settled into quietness and slowly he came over to where Poppy sat, his feet planted wide, pelvis thrust forward, inches from her face.

'Want it?' he asked softly.

For an answer Poppy wound her thin arms around his hips and buried her face in his crotch.

'Okay. Up on the table then.' With strong hands, his voice suddenly thickened with desire, he half lifted her until she lay on the table. Then he pushed up her short skirt and buried his face in her as he licked and sucked her with infinite tenderness.

Poppy gasped as waves of pleasure engulfed her, and resolved to bring some more silver with her next time.

Chapter Three

'Why don't I fly up to Scotland, Camilla, and do a feature on
your father being victimised because he's an English newcomer
to the village? It would make a great story: ELDERLY COUPLE
HOUNDED IN FEUD OVER LAIRD'S HOUSE. I can just see
it! Do you think your father would agree to be interviewed?'
Geoffrey Hennessy leaned forward eagerly, his dark beard
jutting as he talked, reminding Camilla of a Frans Hals portrait.
They had been friends for a long time and Geoffrey had been
one of the few journalists David had trusted.

Camilla smiled at him warmly. 'I didn't ask you to lunch in
order to get publicity for my father,' she laughed. Then she
became serious. 'Listen, Geoffrey, I'm not sure the trouble is
about Creagnach and my father moving into it, but I would be
grateful to have someone find out what's going on.'

She had invited Geoffrey to lunch at the Savoy because she
wanted him to write an article on Royal Scottish Airways to go
with the publicity campaign she'd organised, but somehow
they'd got talking about their families and she'd found herself
telling him about Malcolm.

'Look at this,' she said, delving into her handbag and produc-
ing the most recent letter she'd received.

Geoffrey took it from her, his eyes skimming the neatly
written pages. At the end of the letter Malcolm had stated:

I am having to register this and do not be surprised at the
postmark as it is no longer safe to use the local post

office. I shall have to drive to another village to mail it.

Geoffrey looked up, his dark eyes alert. 'Has he been to the police?'

'I don't know. The last time we spoke he was talking in riddles, and told me not to ring back.' She gave a fretful sigh. 'I wish to God I knew what was going on, but even this letter doesn't say much, does it? Merely that he thinks his phone is being tapped as well as his letters intercepted. But the question is – why?' She glanced at the envelope that lay on the table between them. It was postmarked Glasgow. 'Glasgow's a hundred miles away,' she observed, 'and yet he says he's going to another village to mail it.'

'Perhaps something happened which made him think Glasgow would be the safest.' Geoffrey sipped appreciatively at the excellent Riesling she'd ordered, and did his best to sound reassuring. 'Try not to be alarmed. Funny things happen in isolated villages, you know. Feelings can run high over issues that we would think were trivial. Jealousy can take over whole communities, and wreck the goodwill.'

'You really think this is all to do with Daddy moving into the old laird's house and being resented because he's new?'

'And rich. And English,' Geoffrey continued. 'I covered a story a few years ago in which a titled member of the landed gentry left his estate to his chauffeur instead of his family. The entire village revolted, especially when the chauffeur refused to do repairs to their houses. Barns were burnt to the ground, trucks were driven into buildings in order to make them unsafe, and eventually the electricity was cut off.'

'By the villagers?'

'The damage was done by both sides. The chauffeur wanted everyone out of their rented cottages so he could do them up and sell them at a vast profit, and the villagers were prepared to do anything, bar actually bumping him off, to prevent such a thing happening. Mutual terror reigned as each side tried to destroy the other.'

Camilla looked at him in astonishment. 'When did this happen? It sounds medieval!'

Geoffrey shrugged, remembering the feud and the excellent feature it had made. 'About six years ago. I never did hear how it was resolved, but your father's situation is probably similar. Maybe the people of·Ardachie are afraid he is going to buy up local property and turn the whole place into some sort of commercial dog-breeding centre. There can be a great distrust of outsiders' motives in a case like this. Your father may have to win them over.'

'You believe that a newspaper feature would help?' She sounded doubtful.

Geoffrey carefully dabbed his bearded mouth with his napkin. 'If I put across your father's bewilderment, his inability to understand what he's done wrong, his side of the case in fact, I think it might clear the air. I'll take a photographer up with me, too. I'd like to get a shot of your father with Creagnach in the background.'

'When will you go?' Camilla signalled to the waiter that they'd finished lunch. 'I feel desperate not knowing what's going on.'

'Early next week. I've got to do a highly topical feature for the *Globe* in the next two days, and then I think I'll fly up to Glasgow on Monday and hire a car to take me to Ardachie.'

Camilla looked wistful. 'I wish I could go with you, but I'm up to my eyes in work at the moment.'

'Ah, yes.' Geoffrey remembered the purpose of their lunch. 'You'd better give me all the details on Royal Scottish Airways and I'll do a feature on them. Is there anything else I can do in the way of publicity to help you or any of your clients?'

'Why don't you have done with it and join Eaton & Eaton?' she said with a teasing smile. 'You're doing so much for me, you might as well be on the payroll.'

He cast his eyes to heaven, his bearded face as merry as the Laughing Cavalier's. 'I can't think of anything more delight-ful, my dear Camilla,' he rejoined, 'than being linked with you in any way I can.'

'Would you ever consider marrying again?' Lucy asked. She and Anthony were dining with Camilla again that evening, this time on their own, without any of the children. Catching up, as Lucy expressed it, on grown-up conversation.

'I can't see it happening, although I don't like the idea of being on my own for the rest of my life, either,' she admitted.

'At forty-four you're too young to be on your own,' Anthony protested. 'You should think of marrying again, or at least having someone in your life.'

Camilla smiled, sensing what he was really getting at – how could she do without sex? So many of her friends had edged round the same question in the past four years, unable to contemplate being celibate themselves and therefore assuming she felt the same. For a moment she toyed with her hem-stitched linen table-napkin, wondering which words to use to describe how she felt.

'I was so much in love with David,' she said at last, 'that when he died I simply couldn't bring myself to go to bed with anyone else. It would have felt like the grossest act of disloyalty and . . .'

'But David has *gone* . . .' Anthony began before Lucy silenced him with a look.

'Yes, I know he's gone,' Camilla replied, 'but I couldn't just go out and replace him as one replaces a beloved dog when it dies. I would have felt like an adulteress. The guilt would have been terrible then.'

'And now?' Lucy probed gently.

'In the past couple of years I've had a few flings, fairly silly casual affairs of which I'm not proud. But I missed the mental and emotional side of things. Sex without love isn't worth having.' Camilla's voice had hardened as she spoke and there was pain in her eyes. Then she gave one of her dazzling smiles, the smile that won Eaton & Eaton new accounts, charmed clients and made people warm to her. 'So far I haven't found anyone who combined both,' she said lightly. 'I'm not making the mistake of looking for another David either. That would be fatal.'

'You're right,' Lucy agreed. 'But still, you must get lonely at times. Poppy seems to be out a great deal.'

'No, I'm not lonely, because I don't have time,' Camilla declared stoutly. 'Most evenings I'm glad to slide into bed and read or watch television. I'm up to my neck in work most of the time and that's the best way of focusing one's mind and forgetting the sadness of the past.'

'I suppose Poppy has loads of friends?'

'I'm sure she does, but she never tells me anything these days. She used to be in with a really nice bunch of girls she was at school with, and a lot of them have charming brothers, but I've rather lost track of who she sees these days. Actually, I shall be glad when the summer holidays are over and she's back at school again.'

'You just have to trust them, don't you?' Anthony remarked. 'So far we've been lucky with all of ours, and Henrietta has a nice boyfriend at the moment, though God knows how long it will last!' He chuckled indulgently. 'Philip is the one I envy!'

Lucy turned to stare at her husband. 'Why?'

'Why?' Anthony repeated. 'Why d'you think? He's young, good-looking, and we give him a private income, even if it is a small one, while he studies.' He looked at Camilla for support. 'Added to which he's got his own flat, and he's bought himself a car with some of his grandmother's legacy. And she asks me why I envy him!' Anthony threw up his hands in mock despair.

Lucy giggled, exchanging amused looks with Camilla while Anthony continued: 'He's got the pick of the girls in this town and the wherewithal to have a good time. I ask you! I'm as jealous as hell!'

'Oh, darling, you can have a good time with me,' Lucy laughed, reaching out to squeeze his hand.

'Promises, promises,' he quipped back, and Camilla smiled as she watched them rib each other. They shared the same understanding as she had enjoyed with David.

'Philip's fine and I want him to get to know Poppy properly, but what we have to do now is find a lovely man for Camilla.' Lucy sounded complacent. Having been happy with Anthony for more than twenty-five years, she thought everyone ought to be married. To her, a single woman was only half a woman, and a life that was not shared only half a life.

They were still talking in the drawing-room an hour later, lingering over coffee and brandy served in crystal balloons, when the front door slammed so loudly they all started. Lucy and Anthony looked at Camilla.

'What on earth . . .?' Anthony half rose from the depths of an armchair. 'Shall I go and see?'

Camilla glanced at her watch. At that moment the drawing-room door burst open and Poppy came bounding into the room in jogging shorts, the usual grubby T-shirt, and trainers with the laces undone. Her makeup was, if anything, more vivid than usual, but what Camilla noticed with concern was the wanton look in her eyes and the bruised mouth, rimmed purple as if she'd been eating raspberries.

Mother and daughter regarded each other silently for a moment, Camilla temporarily bereft of words, Poppy annoyed to find there were guests.

'Oh, hi,' she said ungraciously, hovering in the doorway as if she was about to bolt again.

'How lovely to see you, darling,' Lucy said sweetly. 'Come and sit down and tell us what you've been doing. Have you been to a nice party?' She patted the sofa beside her. 'I'm longing to hear what you're doing these days.'

Poppy shot her mother a defiant look and then reluctantly dropped down on to the sofa.

'Nothing much,' she replied, her tone defensive.

Her godmother was not to be put off. 'What about your future plans? Have you any career ideas? Henrietta is doing secretarial work at the moment, but she wants to get into the Foreign Office as soon as we're settled. What about you?'

Poppy shrugged and stayed rudely silent.

44

'I think one of the problems young people face today,' Camilla cut in with embarrassment, 'is that there is almost too much of a choice. When we were girls, Lucy, opportunities were limited by comparison.'

'I agree,' she replied. 'Basically they boiled down to: Are you going to get married or are you going to get married?'

Anthony laughed uproariously. 'What's wrong with that? Do you want to get married, Poppy?' he asked jokingly.

For the first time the girl's face softened a fraction and there was a hint of a blush showing through the heavy makeup.

'One day, maybe. Perhaps,' she said in a quiet voice.

Camilla looked at her sharply but the eyes were veiled, giving nothing away. If she was in love she was not going to admit it.

Lucy made a further attempt at engaging Poppy in conversation.

'What would you really like to do?' she asked coaxingly.

Poppy looked straight at Lucy for the first time. 'Right now I'd like to go to my fucking bed. I'm exhausted,' she said insolently. Then she rose and sauntered to the door.

'Poppy!' Camilla looked after her, her mouth open with shock, her expression aghast.

Lucy raised her hand to stop Camilla saying anything further. 'Goodnight, Poppy darling. Sleep well,' she called after her in a motherly voice.

When the drawing-room door had slammed shut they all looked at each other.

'I'm so sorry,' said Camilla. 'I don't know what's the matter with her these days.'

'It's best not to take any notice,' Lucy remarked wisely.

'What am I supposed to do? Let her get away with being rude and insufferable? I'm at my wits' end. You can see how it is.' There was no point in trying to defend Poppy now.

'She'll get over it,' Anthony said. 'Mind if I help myself to another brandy?'

'Please do, and you can fill up my glass, too. How about you, Lucy?'

Lucy shook her head, swirling the remains of her drink round and round in the exquisite balloon. 'No thanks. Honestly, Camilla, don't worry about Poppy too much. She's rebelling against everything at the moment and I've no doubt it stems from David's death. The mind works in funny ways, you know. She could even feel guilty at being alive, and having all this,' she gestured with her hands at the beautiful room, 'while her father is dead and not here to enjoy life any more. She may blame herself; children sometimes do. There could be any number of reasons why she's behaving badly. The great thing is to be supportive, and give her as much love and attention as you can. I'm sure she'll grow out of it in time.'

'I hope you're right. I feel so helpless, Lucy. I just don't know what to do any more. I've tried talking to her, getting her to explain to me what's wrong, but she pays no attention. I'm desperate.'

Lucy spoke bluntly. 'Why do you have to work so hard, Camilla? You can't really need the money? David must have left you a packet, surely?'

Camilla hesitated before answering. The reasons she worked were complex and not easy to explain. 'I need to have something to do,' she began, wondering why she was having to defend her actions. 'After David was killed, I had time on my hands and it drove me crazy. I had time to think, and that was fatal.' She shook her head, remembering how she'd awakened at dawn each morning, unable to go back to sleep, her mind racked with misery and loneliness. The only answer had been to get up and do something to fill the long hours that stretched ahead, before she could go back to bed again and seek refuge in oblivion. That was when she'd decided to take over the running of Eaton & Eaton. Gradually she'd got so involved in the work and it had proved so therapeutic, she couldn't give it up. It was like a drug, addictive and compelling. The perfect excuse to stop herself from dwelling on the parts of her life that were now empty and sterile. It had become more than that, too, as the years passed. Now she actually loved what she was doing. It was a daily challenge. There was also the companionship of her colleagues. She'd miss that dreadfully if she were to stay at home now.

'I love what I do, you see,' she explained. 'As you say, it isn't the money, though I enjoy that part too, but it's the cut and thrust of business that I enjoy. The pitching for a new account; the rivalry with other advertising agencies; the thrill of achievement when we land a new client.' Camilla knew she wasn't explaining herself very well, but it was hard to describe what she meant to someone who had never held down a job in her life.

'But supposing you got ill? Who would run the company then?' Lucy interjected.

'The deputy chairman, Leslie Forbes. He was managing director at the time David died, but I promoted him last year and he's first-rate. If anything happened, he'd take over.' She spoke confidently. David had thought highly of Leslie, and so did she.

'Will you ever let him?'

'What . . . take over?'

'Yes.'

Camilla shrugged. 'Not in the foreseeable future,' she replied. 'I like being in the driving seat and that's where I intend to remain.' There was a touch of ruthlessness in the way she spoke that chilled Lucy. How she's changed, she thought. The Camilla of the old days had been soft and yielding, always laughing, always warm. Poppy isn't the only one who has lost her way since David's death, Lucy reflected sadly.

Camilla spoke, cutting into Lucy's thoughts. 'You think I should spend more time with Poppy, don't you?' she asked directly.

Lucy glanced at Anthony as if for support, and then looked back at Camilla again. 'That's up to you, of course, my dear,' she said gently. 'You know what's best for Poppy, and you also know what you want to do with your life. No one else can make those sort of decisions for you. It's just that I feel

47

Poppy maybe needs you more than you realise.'

When they had gone Camilla sat for a while on her own, thinking about what her friend had said. Maybe she should be more understanding with Poppy? Maybe some of the fault lay with her? I'll try to be patient, she said to herself, as she went up to bed. I'll make a real effort, and perhaps, if Poppy responds, we can have the close relationship we enjoyed a few years ago.

The next morning, however, her good resolutions vanished when Poppy came flying into her bedroom while she was dressing, her face filled with resentment.

'You could have warned me those dreadful people were going to be here when I got back last night!' she burst out without even saying good morning. 'I don't know what you see in them. They're nothing but capitalistic fascists!'

Camilla regarded her with genuine astonishment. 'What are you talking about? Lucy and Anthony have very liberal views. They're neither capitalists nor fascists.'

'Rubbish!' Poppy retorted. 'You're all the same, so busy making money to feather your own precious nest that you don't give a damn for the underprivileged or how they're suffering.'

'You haven't exactly disliked having a privileged life yourself,' Camilla remarked drily as she clipped on her gilt and pearl earrings.

'I've had no choice,' Poppy flashed back. 'You made me go to a smart private school. You've made me live in this ridiculously flash house in a flash neighbourhood.' She sounded as bitter as if her mother had tried to turn her into a whore.

'Thank Christ I've found out before it's too late what real values in life are all about, and what real people feel and think.'

Camilla resisted the desire to laugh. Instead she said mildly: 'Grandpa, who is very wise, once said to me that if someone isn't a socialist when they're twenty, they have no heart; but if they're still a socialist at forty, then they have no head.'

Poppy pounced on the platitude with the venom of a cat pouncing on a mouse. 'How typical! How bloody typical! It's all very well for you to be smug, with your designer clothes and chauffeur-driven Mercedes and glitzy lifestyle, but have you any idea what it's like to be homeless? Hungry? Destitute?'

'No, Poppy. Have you?'

The barb struck home and Poppy flushed. 'I do know people who have, though. Unlike you I mix with real people, not a bunch of money-grubbing businessmen who are only motivated by greed. I know what's going on while you live in a fantasy world of expense account lunches.'

Suddenly Camilla's temper snapped. 'That's enough, Poppy. I have better things to do than listen to your rubbish. You seem to forget we're rich because your father worked hard. Now I'm working hard to maintain that standard of living. We could all be on the dole if we chose to.'

'You'd rather die than be on the dole.'

'You're right, I would. Why should the taxpayer support me when I've got my health and wits about me? Life doesn't owe us a living, Poppy, and if we're not prepared to fend for ourselves then we've only ourselves to blame if we sink to the bottom of the heap.'

Poppy gestured theatrically. 'Oh, for Christ's sake, spare me the Thatcherite philosophy.' Then she marched angrily out of the room, banging the door behind her.

Camilla, who hated arguments, felt shaken as she put the finishing touches to her makeup and sprayed a little Claude Montana at her throat. She and Poppy shouldn't be fighting like this. They needed each other now that David was gone. The sound of the front door being slammed, sending a tremor through the old house, told her Poppy had gone out.

Maitland met her in the hall, hovering by the dining-room door, his normally rubicund face bleached to a sickly white. Thinking he must be shocked by Poppy's turbulent departure, she smiled reassuringly at him.

'Good morning, Maitland.'

'Can I have a word with you, madam?'

'If it's about Miss Poppy, don't worry. She'll calm down in time.'

His bulging eyes looked dark with misery and his hands were shaking. 'It's not that, madam.'

Camilla looked at him sharply. 'Then what is it, Maitland? Is Mrs Maitland ill?'

'No, madam. It's something terribly serious, I'm afraid.'

A cold wave of apprehension swept through her while her mind tried to grapple with potential disasters. Before she could say anything, he continued: 'While I was in the pantry just now, making a final check to see that everything was clean and in order for your big dinner party on Friday, I made a terrible discovery.'

'What sort of discovery?' she asked, mystified.

Maitland took a deep tremulous breath. 'I'm very sorry to have to tell you, madam, that a great deal of silver is missing. All the George III pieces, the William and Mary salt cellars, and a great deal more besides.'

'There's a call for you, Mrs Eaton,' Jean informed her. It was later the same day and after Camilla had spent the morning at home being questioned by the police about the robbery.

'Who is it, Jean?' she asked distractedly. Way behind schedule with the campaign to launch Krispy Krunch, a new brand of chocolate bar, she didn't want to talk to anyone unless it was strictly necessary.

'Geoffrey Hennessy.'

'Okay. Put him through.' She laid down the visuals for a poster that would soon be on every street hoarding and grabbed the phone.

'Geoffrey?'

'How are you, Camilla?'

'I won't even begin to tell you! It's been a disastrous day so far. What can I do for you?'

'What kind of disastrous? Business problems?' His voice was warm with concern.

'No. I've had a great deal of silver stolen, and so far the police have no idea how it happened.' As she spoke she sifted through the various designs on her desk, looking at them from different angles.

'Stolen from your house? Have you had a break-in?'

'That's the whole problem, Geoffrey. There's been no forced entry. Nothing. The police had the audacity to suggest it was an inside job! I was furious because I've had the Maitlands with me for years and would trust them with my life. The same for Lisa.' Camilla spoke vehemently.

'Who's Lisa?'

'My Portuguese cleaning lady. She comes to the house every day, and she's been working for me for years, too. None of them would steal a pin from me, so it must have been someone like a window-cleaner or the man who comes to read the electric meter.'

'I'm so sorry, Camilla. This is the last thing you need when you're already anxious about your father.' Geoffrey's tone was sympathetic. 'I was ringing you up, actually, to tell you I'm off to Ardachie in the morning.'

'Are you? Oh, that's wonderful, Geoffrey. I can't wait to hear how you get on. Where are you staying?'

'As there's no hotel in Ardachie itself and Jim, my photographer, and I don't relish the idea of staying in a Bed and Breakfast, we've got rooms in a hotel in Oban. You haven't told Malcolm we're coming, have you?'

'I haven't even spoken to him for a week, Geoffrey.'

He sounded relieved. 'Good. I want to scout around the village and find out what I can before I approach him. You think he'll co-operate, though?'

'Of course he will, especially if you say you're a friend of mine.'

'That's great. As soon as I get back I'll give you a ring. Perhaps we could have dinner?' His voice was tinged with hope.

'Yes, that would be lovely,' she replied, suddenly finding herself looking forward to the idea of spending an evening with him. She and David had first met Geoffrey through mutual friends at a time when he was going through a tricky divorce.

He was a great companion, witty, cultured, and with a wealth of interesting anecdotes which he told with relish.

'Good. Then we'll be in touch, Camilla.'

'Yes. Talk to you soon.' She hung up thoughtfully. If Geoffrey could expose the petty vindictiveness that seemed to be rife in Ardachie, spoiling her father's retirement years and causing him anxiety, she would be eternally grateful.

When she returned to Wilton Crescent that evening, the police were still probing about, examining door and window locks. They had even been on the roof to see if anyone could have got in by the skylight that led into the loft. Maitland still looked pale and grim, blaming himself for having let it happen.

'It's not your fault,' Camilla assured him. 'I know how careful you are, Maitland. Someone must have got hold of a set of keys, that's the only answer. And then they must have let themselves in when the house was empty, helped themselves to the silver, and let themselves out again. If it's anybody's fault, it's mine. I should have had an alarm system put in years ago. I don't know why I didn't . . . I suppose because the house is hardly ever empty.'

Maitland shook his head, his usual ebullience quenched. 'It will probably have been melted down by now, especially as it bore the Eaton family crest,' he said sorrowfully. 'Whoever stole it can have had no feeling for beauty. They were exquisite pieces of silver, madam. The William and Mary salt cellars were worthy of being in a museum.'

'I know, Maitland, I know.' Camilla's voice was full of regret. 'It's a terrible shame. I suppose we should be thankful they didn't take it all!'

'That's what I've been thinking, madam. Why take only some of it . . . selected, almost at random, from the various shelves?'

'Perhaps they couldn't carry any more?'

'Maybe.' Maitland sounded doubtful. Then trying to suppress his anger, he added: 'I'd like to horsewhip whoever took it!'

Camilla nodded silently. Those were her sentiments exactly.

Some people became deeply distressed by being burgled, feeling their property had been besmirched by strangers. Camilla felt only anger, righteous fury that anyone should dare to enter her house and steal her possessions.

'The assessors from the insurance company are coming tomorrow, but I'm having an alarm system fitted in any case,' she informed him. 'Do you think we should have the pantry door reinforced . . . and have extra locks added?' She smiled ruefully. 'I know it's rather like shutting the stable door after the horse has bolted, but I feel I must do all I can to prevent it happening again.'

Maitland regarded her unsmilingly. 'No doubt the insurance company will advise you, madam.' To him the loss was a major tragedy. He'd cared for the silver as if it had belonged to him personally, and now some of the most valuable pieces had gone. If a pet cat or dog had died, he could not have been more upset.

'Oh yes, I'm sure they will,' she replied drily. They would no doubt tell her also, she reflected, that she had been very cavalier in her care of such valuable items, which would force them to increase her insurance premium in future years.

As there was no sign of Poppy, Camilla dined alone on a tray in the study, reading the newspapers and then watching the nine o'clock news on television. Nothing of world shattering importance had taken place and she was just about to turn it off and go to bed when the telephone rang. It was Malcolm.

'Daddy,' she greeted him. 'How lovely to hear from you. How are you?' She'd already decided not to worry him by telling him about the burglary.

'I'm all right but something terrible has happened here.' Malcolm sounded strained and tired.

Camilla instantly thought of her stepmother, Edith. 'What's happened?' She had visions of an accident, a heart attack. What her father said next took her completely aback.

'It's the puppies, my dear.'

'The puppies?'

'Yes.' Malcolm's voice sank to a note of despair.

53

'What's happened to the puppies?'

'They've been poisoned.'

'Oh, my God. How?'

'We think something must have been thrown into their run. You know we've had problems with the village boys, creeping into the grounds at night and teasing the dogs? Edith thinks it must be them.'

'But that's appalling, Daddy. Surely they wouldn't put down poison! How many puppies have died?'

'Eighteen, all aged between three and five months. They were all sired by Prince, our top stud dog, and formed the best of our breeding stock for the season. It's a tragedy. Edith is heartbroken.'

Camilla frowned. 'And you're sure they were poisoned?' she persisted. 'What does the vet say? Don't puppies often die of distemper or some such thing?' She'd only had one dog when she'd been small, a Cavalier King Charles Spaniel called Max, so her knowledge of dogs was limited.

'I'm at the vet's house now,' Malcolm replied. 'I asked him if I could use his phone because I can't ring you from Creagnach.'

'Is the phone out of order?'

'No.' He spoke succinctly. 'The line is being tapped.'

Camilla ran her hand through her hair. What had started as resentment in the village towards an English newcomer now seemed to be escalating to criminal proportions. And yet . . .

'Daddy, are you sure?' she asked incredulously.

'Absolutely certain. That's why I couldn't talk to you properly the other day when I phoned you. I believe my calls are being monitored.' He sounded less tired now, as if telling her what was happening had in some way energised him. 'This is the last straw. Hector Ross the local vet, a charming fellow, says the puppies have been given something pretty lethal. He didn't have a chance of saving any of them.'

'I'm so sorry, Daddy. Give my love to Edith and say that I think it's too awful for words. Don't you think you should consider leaving Ardachie now? They might have a go at some of your other dogs?'

'Leave?' Malcolm sounded scandalised. 'Certainly not. I've never given way to bully boy tactics in my life and I don't intend to start now.'

Camilla hesitated, wondering if she should tell him about Geoffrey Hennessy's impending visit after all but then she thought better of it. Let Geoffrey do his investigative work, finding out all he could, before anyone knew he was a newspaper reporter.

'Will you ring me again?' she asked anxiously.

Malcolm almost sounded like his old self once more. 'Of course I will, my dear, providing good old Hector doesn't mind.' He appeared to turn away to ask his host something before saying to Camilla: 'Hector says I can use his phone any time I like. He's a generous fellow.' Malcolm chuckled. 'He's even put a very large scotch in my hand.'

'Then take care, Daddy. I'll write to you in a few days, if you're phone's bugged.'

'Be sure to send it by registered post, though,' he admonished her. 'Until these silly buggers stop their antics we'll have to be careful.'

When Camilla replaced the receiver, she couldn't help smiling to herself. They always say an Englishman's home is his castle, she reflected, and that certainly seemed to be what was motivating her father to stay put, refusing to be intimidated by his new Scottish neighbours. Nevertheless, when they started killing dogs! She reached for the phone again, knowing that Geoffrey rarely went to bed before midnight.

He greeted her with pleased surprise. 'What can I do for you at this late hour?' he enquired amiably.

Briefly she outlined what Malcolm had just told her.

'Humph. Interesting.' Geoffrey digested the details. 'I might drop in on this vet. What's his name – Hector Ross? Get a quote from him. This is serious stuff, Camilla. It could make a big feature.'

'Will you call me as soon as you find out what's going on? Right now I feel like dropping everything and coming with you, but we're in the middle of a big Krispy Krunch campaign and life is frantic.'

'Don't worry, I'll keep you posted, and thanks for letting me know the latest,' he said. 'Meanwhile, don't get fat on Krispy Krunch.'

Camilla giggled, suddenly cheered by talking to Geoffrey. 'Thank God my brief doesn't include actually having to eat the damned things,' she exclaimed. 'It's enough having to make them appear so attractive they'll sell by the ton.'

Chapter Four

Poppy had stayed away from home for two days now, sleeping at Danny's place near the Whitechapel Road and helping him write the material for the Class Warriors' leaflets he was getting printed.

'Know anyone in advertising?' he suddenly demanded as he read the blurb he'd just written.

She started. Surely there was no way he could have found out her mother was the chairman of Eaton & Eaton?

'No . . . no one,' she said, flustered. 'Why?'

'It wouldn't be a bad idea to have someone in business take a look at this,' he replied. 'Copy-writers have a knack of putting things down in a way people can easily understand. I don't know . . .' He cocked his head to one side. 'What d'you think?'

Poppy took the foolscap sheet of paper from him and started reading what he'd written in his tiny, barely legible handwriting. It extolled the virtues of the organisation, pointing out that the aims were to annihilate the aristrocracy, rid the country of the Royal Family, and do away with capitalism in all its evil forms.

'It's great,' she exclaimed enthusiastically. 'When is all this going to happen?'

Danny regarded her cautiously. 'When the time's ready,' he replied guardedly.

'What are you waiting for?' Beneath the thick and lurid makeup her expression bore traces of childlike excitement, and her eyes seemed to sparkle.

'In a hurry, aren't you?' He had no intention of telling her what his plans were. Girls, in his opinion, could not be trusted with secrets.

'Yes . . . well, no, not really. Just interested.' Her bony hands twisted the collection of ethnic bangles on her right wrist. Talking politics could be very boring. What she wanted was to see some action. Something to show that the ruling classes were really on their way out while the homeless and jobless were provided for. Then she and Danny would lead the new movement, seeking total equality for everyone. At least, she corrected herself mentally, though it was more tempting to stay with her original fantasy, Danny would lead the new movement and she'd be by his side, with any luck, providing he didn't tire of her. She'd overheard one of the female 'followers' mutter something like 'I wonder how long she'll last?' Of course they might not have been referring to her, but she was pretty certain they were. Somehow she had to hold Danny's attention, do things that would win his approval, make herself indispensable.

'Did you get much for the silver?' she asked with forced casualness, curling herself up in the battered armchair so that she resembled a very blond, very feminine kitten.

Danny glanced over at her, taking in the skin-tight skirt and sleeveless top that showed an edge of tender young breast when she moved her arms. 'Not bad,' he said grudgingly. 'Don't get any more though. It was difficult to unload, being crested and all that, and I don't want the fuzz's attention drawn to us.'

Poppy kept her face composed, her eyes blank. Thank Christ the 'robbery' hadn't been reported in the newspapers although at one time she'd thought it was going to be. No one had suspected her of taking the stuff either. Well, they wouldn't, would they? she reasoned. You didn't steal from yourself. That is . . . again she had mentally to re-write the fantasy . . . most people didn't steal silver from their own family. Then she was struck by another thought. If Danny didn't want any more silver, what else could she get for him? Jewellery, she'd discovered, would be difficult; her mother kept most of hers in a safe

58

at the offices of Eaton & Eaton, only taking out special pieces when she was going to a party. What about paintings? No, that was no use. Blank spaces on the walls would be noticed instantly. Then she remembered something, something so wonderful she couldn't believe why she hadn't thought of it before. Going over to where he lay on the bed, with his arms behind his head and the pad of paper resting on his stomach, she snuggled down beside him, tucking her head on to his shoulder, winding her arms around his neck. He lay silent, staring straight ahead as if she didn't exist.

'Danny?' Poppy spoke in a small voice.

'D'you want to fuck then?'

'No, er . . . yes, I mean yes, of course, but there's something I wanted to say first.'

With slow deliberation he removed the writing pad from his stomach and placed it on the floor beside the bed.

'Yeah? What is it?' he asked, sliding his hand under her skirt, feeling her nakedness immediately.

'Well, I was wondering . . .' Now she resembled the kitten who has found the bowl is full of cream after all, her eyes wide and eager, her mouth parted in anticipation.

'Yeah?' he asked impatiently. Once he thought about having sex he wanted to get on with it straight away, and already his large fingers were probing her, lifting her, manipulating her so that she would be ready to receive him. 'What is it?'

'It would help if I could get you a large amount of cash, wouldn't it?' she whispered, closing her eyes in rapture at what he was doing.

Camilla had spent most of the week on the Krispy Krunch campaign and the client was delighted with Eaton & Eaton's whole presentation package, from the outline of the thirty-second television commercial to the colour advertisements that would appear in selected women's magazines. The slogan 'Get Slim with Krispy Krunch' had gone down well too. Who had ever heard of a chocolate that made you lose weight? A beautiful blonde headed up the campaign, wearing a clinging satin slip with pearls wound round her neck, branding the product 'classy' at a glance.

'Krispy Krunch will stop your craving,' the copy suggested seductively. 'A bar of Krispy Krunch can take the place of a meal, causing you to lose weight . . . in the most delicious way.' And in the television commercial the model slithered on to a grand canopied bed, licking the chocolate dreamily while her fingers fiddled with her pearls.

Camilla was delighted with the concept, most of which had been her own idea, including the pearls. Grateful that the client's brief had allowed her a free hand in deciding how best to create an up-market image for the chocolate, she now went to work on studying her art department's visuals for another product. This time it was a new brand of perfume, called Fantasy, by Luigi Romolo. Eaton & Eaton already handled the cosmetic and beauty care range from Romolo's, and the plan was to expand on the existing image rather than create something different.

Immersed in her work, she did not at first hear Jean come into her office.

'Mrs Eaton?' she began tentatively. All the staff knew Camilla hated being disturbed when she was concentrating on something, and so they were inclined to leave her quietly alone while messages piled up.

Camilla glanced up. Then she rose, stretching, glad of a break. She'd been at the office since eight-forty-five this morning and it was now noon.

'What is it, Jean?'

'I'm sorry to disturb you but Mr Hennessy has been waiting in reception for the past half hour, hoping to see you, and I thought perhaps as it's nearly lunchtime . . .?' Her voice trailed off.

'Mr Hennessy? Geoffrey Hennessy?' Camilla queried. 'But he can't be back from Scotland already. What day is it? Thursday? He only went up there on Monday.' As she talked she hurried through to the hall of the eighteenth-century build-

60

ing in Upper Grosvenor Street which had housed Eaton & Eaton since 1934. Originally the home of a nobleman, the hall walls were carved panelling, bleached pale with age, and from the moulded ceiling a crystal chandelier glittered with dazzling light. While Camilla's own office was all modern chrome and leather and lucite, the reception area remained as it had done when David's father had founded the company. Antique carved chairs were placed on either side of the white marble mantelpiece, brocade curtains hung at the windows which overlooked the American Embassy, and today a magnificent arrangement of lilies, delphiniums and peonies stood on a gilt console table.

Geoffrey Hennessy was standing with his back to the fireplace, a sturdy figure, not very tall but exuding an aura of strength and reliability.

'Geoffrey!' Camilla hurried across the deep burgundy carpet to greet him. 'How wonderful to see you. I didn't expect you back for ages.' She kissed him on both cheeks and her expression was full of anticipation. 'How did you get on? How is my father?'

Geoffrey's expression was guarded as he returned her kiss, but he smiled genially, his hands on her shoulders, and when he spoke his tone was light.

'Steady on! I can't answer all your questions at once. What about a spot of lunch? Can you tear yourself away from Krispy Krunch or whatever?'

'Yes, okay.' She looked at him uncertainly. 'There's nothing wrong, is there?' she asked intuitively.

He seemed to hesitate, and then he patted her on the back gently and affectionately, as if he'd decided to wait before speaking. 'I've got a lot to tell you and wouldn't it be nicer to do it over a glass of wine rather than standing in your lobby here?'

'Of course. I'll just get my bag.' Then she turned to look him straight in the face. 'Daddy's all right, isn't he?'

Geoffrey nodded briefly. 'I can promise you one thing,' he said, 'your father's not in any danger.'

Camilla gave a little sigh of relief. 'I'll be right with you.'

'I've booked a table at Wheeler's,' he called after her, as she hurried back to her office.

It wasn't until they were seated in a discreet corner table in the fashionable fish restaurant in South Molton Street, drinking champagne while they waited for their order of Whitstable oysters to be served, that Camilla, unable to contain her curiosity any longer, asked him again how he'd got on in Scotland. 'I'm dying to know what happened,' she added.

'How long is it since you've actually seen your father?' he began carefully.

She looked surprised and gave a little shrug. 'Five, maybe six months. Why?'

'I just wondered.'

'What's wrong, Geoffrey?'

'Let me begin from the beginning.' He took a long sip of Bollinger as if to fortify himself. 'Jim and I hired a car when we arrived in Glasgow on Monday and drove straight to Ardachie. My plan as you know was to ferret around finding out what I could, pretending to be a tourist until I got a general picture of what life is like in this remote village. It's very isolated, isn't it? There's nothing around for miles except mountains and beaches and wild countryside.'

'I know,' she agreed, watching him closely, noticing still the non-committal look in his dark intelligent eyes.

'Jim and I pretended we were on a motoring holiday. It was a perfect reason for asking all sorts of questions, especially as neither of us had ever been to that part of Scotland before. We talked to the people who run the tiny local post office-cum-general store, and we talked to local fishermen, and a crofter who was minding a whole lot of sheep. We also talked to a few of the village people themselves; Jim even went so far as to say he was getting married soon and was looking for a cottage to buy in the area! He pretended he was going to be living in Glasgow where he worked as an electrician, but wanted a little place for weekends and holidays.' Geoffrey chuckled as he recollected the yarns they'd spun to the inhabitants of Ardachie as they enjoyed several 'wee drams' of whisky at the one village pub.

'And?' Camilla asked desperately. 'What happened?'

'That's the whole point. Nothing happened.'

'How do you mean?'

'Everyone we talked to, without exception, was absolutely charming. They couldn't have been friendlier or more helpful. Jim made it plain he was English, but they welcomed the idea of him buying a cottage with open arms. The man who runs the inn, Alex McTavish by name, even joked about Jim getting employment in the village. I can't impersonate a Scottish accent, but he said something to the effect of: "You'd be kept a wee mite busy if ye opened an electrical shop here aboots."'

Camilla looked perplexed. 'I don't get it. If they resent my father living there, why didn't they object to the idea of Jim? Is it because he bought the old laird's place? Is that the root of the trouble?'

Geoffrey took another sip of his drink and seemed to be pondering before saying slowly: 'I don't think they do object to your father living at Creagnach.'

'But . . .'

'We went to see your father and his wife after we'd done our bit of socialising in the village pub, and we talked to him, and then had a talk to Edith while she showed us the dogs and the kennels. They've got dozens of Alsatians, you know, and it's a very professional outfit. She told me that apart from breeding dogs for private individuals they also supply them as guard dogs. Apparently their hearing is amazingly acute.'

'I know.' Camilla couldn't help sounding impatient. 'But what did Daddy say?'

The guarded look which had faded while he talked about the dogs came back stronger than ever. 'Much the same sort of thing as he's been telling you.'

'So are you going to do a feature about him being victimised? About his post being confiscated and his phone tapped?'

'As I said, I also talked to his wife,' Geoffrey continued, and a sudden look of sympathy filled his eyes. 'Things are not quite as you've been led to believe.'

'I don't understand. What are you talking about?'

He leaned across the table and placed his hand firmly over hers, looking into her eyes intently.

'Camilla, I think your father's ill.'

Alarm filled every plane of her face, drawing the blood away from her skin, widening her eyes. 'You mean the strain of what he's had to put up with in the past few months is beginning to show?'

'He's not physically ill. He's a fine figure of a man for his age. No, I mean that perhaps . . . maybe he is getting old . . . and maybe a little senile,' he said gently.

Bewilderment replaced anxiety in her face. 'Senile? No, that can't be the reason. I speak to him on the phone at least once a week. He's no more senile than I am.'

Geoffrey took a deep breath and looked at her squarely. 'But none of what he's told you has actually happened.'

There was a stunned silence and then Camilla shook her head, confused. 'But his post? All those letters that have gone missing? All but one of the letters I sent him about the dogs? *Of course* everything he's told me is true. He didn't imagine it!'

She was flushed now, hot and upset, but most of all burning with an unknown fear. She signalled to the waiter to bring her a glass of water.

'That's the whole point, my dear Camilla,' Geoffrey was saying. 'I'm terribly sorry to have to say this but none of it is true. He's imagined it all. Everything. It's as if he's suffering from a persecution mania.'

'I don't believe it,' she cut in. 'I'm sorry, Geoffrey, I'm not doubting your word but I know my father. I'd know if something was wrong. What makes you think he's dreamed up this whole thing? You didn't expect the local post office to admit to you that dozens of letters had gone astray, did you? You didn't expect anyone to come forward and tell you they'd bugged his telephone?'

'No,' he agreed, squeezing her hand, showing her how he understood her feelings of scepticism, 'but why, if all that is true, did his wife tell me to leave him alone and stop questioning him about this affair because, to use her own words, he's "suffering from paranoid delusions"?'

In the shocked silence that followed, the waiter placed a dozen oysters in front of each of them and hovered with the various accoutrements.

'Edith said that?' Camilla's voice was a hoarse whisper.

Geoffrey nodded sympathetically. 'I'm very much afraid so, my dear. That was why she took me round the kennels. It was just an excuse to get away from your father for a few minutes so she could explain the true situation to me.'

'I can't grasp this . . . for one thing I don't believe it for a moment. My father is as sane as I am. But supposing it were true, why hasn't Edith told me? How come I don't know. Surely her first duty would have been to inform me if he was ill?' There was a mixture of hurt and frustration in her voice. Supposing it was true? Supposing her father really was suffering from the first signs of senile dementia? From what little she had learned of the disease she knew that sufferers imagined things and often thought people were persecuting them. Racking her brains to recall recent telephone conversations with Malcolm, she tried to pin-point statements he'd made, signs that would convince her he was normal. Then she remembered something. The last time they'd talked he'd phoned her from the vet's house. Relief flooded over her as the full implication of that call sank in.

'There's one thing he couldn't have imagined,' she declared triumphantly, 'and that is the death of eighteen puppies! He actually phoned me from the vet's house, just after it had happened. The vet was there in the room with him, too, offering him a glass of whisky. That proves Daddy hasn't imagined all this trouble!'

Geoffrey spoke slowly, twirling his champagne glass by the

stem so that the bubbles rose softly to the surface. 'Ah, yes. Hector Ross the vet. A delightful chap with a broad Scots accent and a penchant for malt whisky.'

Camilla beamed. 'Right! Daddy said he was very nice.'

Geoffrey nodded. 'He only has a small practice, mostly looking after farm animals, but he says it gives him a living.'

She leaned forward eagerly. 'And he must have told you about the puppies dying?'

Geoffrey's brow puckered with discomfiture. 'The trouble is, Camilla,' he said ponderously, 'Hector Ross told me that none of your father's dogs has even been ill since he arrived in Ardachie six months ago.'

Poppy arrived at the King's Arms just before Danny was due to hold one of his meetings. Stuffed into the purse on her body belt was a thick roll of fifty-pound notes held by a rubber band. It amounted to three thousand pounds and there was plenty more where that came from, she thought with delight. It had been easy to get it, too. The bank clerk had done no more than glance at the cheque, being too intent on making sure there were sufficient funds in the account to scrutinise the signatures. One of them was bona fide, of course. Her own. This was an account her father had opened for her many years ago, funded from the interest on a trust set up when she'd been born. But the other signature, that of her mother, she'd forged, copying Camilla's large rounded scrawl so perfectly she doubted anyone would query its authenticity.

Danny was deep in conversation with a rough-looking man as Poppy sidled up to him, her precious burden half hidden by the hands she clasped to her waist. She tried to hear what they were saying.

''E's due over 'ere in July, ain't 'e?' The man had a rasping cockney voice. He was grizzled-looking, with a ragged beard and unwashed hair to his shoulders.

'Either July or next March,' Danny whispered back, 'but we ought to be ready in case it's July,' he added.

'Oh, we'll be good an' ready!' There was venom in the reply. Neither of them noticed Poppy standing in the shadows behind Danny, and she craned forward to hear more.

Danny spoke next. 'It's all got to be properly planned, you know.'

'I know that. We don't want no fucking cock-ups, do we? D'you think we'll get the lot of 'em, that night?' He sounded full of relish as if he was looking forward to what was going to happen.

'Don't talk so bleeding loud!' Danny snarled. 'It's too soon to announce our plans. No one must know what we're up to.'

'Whatever you say.' Sullenly the man moved away, leaving in his wake a drift of stale body odour that escaped from the confines of his heavy black leather breeches and jacket. Poppy swayed for a second, closing her eyes in revulsion, and at that moment Danny realised she was standing at his elbow.

'What are you doing?' he demanded, his semi-shaven jaw stuck forward belligerently, his eyes blazing furiously.

She flinched, suddenly tears stinging her eyes. She couldn't bear it when Danny was angry with her. He was her life, everything she cared for, and all she wanted was his love and approval.

'Nothing,' she replied brightly, fighting back the tears. Danny hated it when she cried. 'I've . . . I've brought something for you,' she blurted out excitedly.

'What is it?' He frowned impatiently, glancing round the room, not looking at her. There were always a few newcomers each week and he liked to keep tabs on who attended. From Chalk Farm to the Oval, from Wembley where he had a lot of Asian support to Whitechapel, he attracted a motley crowd, and tonight, he thought, was no exception. Of course the day he was really longing for, the ultimate day, was when he mustered all these groups together in one great united roaring hurricane of fury and frustration directed at the highest in the land. Then he would stage a riot to end all riots.

'Go and sit down.' Danny spoke dismissively. 'We're about to start.'

Cowed, like an exuberant puppy that has been scolded, she crept over to the other side of the room, nursing her present for him. Next to her, sitting cross-legged on the floor, was a clean-faced youth she'd seen before. He was reading something in a newspaper which he quickly closed as soon as he saw her looking. She gave him a wobbly smile and he nodded back affably.

'How yer doin'?' he asked. His white T-shirt, emblazoned with their 'Class Warriors' slogan, was spotlessly clean, and his straight blond hair glinted glossily in the dim light.

'What were you reading?' Poppy asked after a few banal exchanges.

He looked at her quizzically. 'You spyin' for the leader? You're his girlfriend, aren't you?'

Poppy looked quite shocked, eyeliner smudged where the tears had trickled down her cheeks. 'Of course I'm not a spy!'

The youth looked sheepish. 'I have to get myself psyched up like, before a meeting. I'm not really too bothered about class differences . . .'

'Then why are you here?'

He glanced at her slyly out of the corner of his eye. 'Same reason as you, I expect. See that girl over there? The one with long black hair? She's my girlfriend. I come because she comes.'

'So what were you reading?' Poppy asked curiously.

He leaned over to whisper in her ear. 'The *Tatler*.'

'The *Tat* . . .? She stopped, astonished. Her mother always read the *Tatler*, for God's sake, and so did all her mother's dreadful friends. 'But it's nothing but page after page of people going to parties,' she protested. 'Débutantes and titled people, and the whole ghastly scene. What do you want to read that sort of junk for?'

'It helps to wind me up, reminds me that we're all here to get rid of people like that – lot of useless Hooray Henrys and chinless morons.' As he spoke, he became increasingly aggressive in tone.

Poppy warmed to him, cheered by the thought of someone

reading the *Tatler* in order to wind themselves up to a pitch of social resentment.

The meeting began and Danny slipped into his persona of leader, dictating what they should think, telling them how they should feel, his rhetoric designed to stir them to righteous anger, his paternalistic style that of someone who knows what is best for his followers.

As Poppy sat listening, his words washing over her like the cool soft waters of a stream, flowing deep and fast, she realised it was just as well she'd had to wait until after the meeting to give him the money. She'd planned to hand it to him when she'd first arrived – gold and myrrh and frankincense for a king – but after the meeting they'd be alone which would be much better. Her eyes grew dreamy thinking of his pleasure at receiving it . . . thinking how wonderful he'd say she was . . .

The meeting ended at last and Poppy said goodbye to the youth with the *Tatler* which he'd rolled up inside a copy of the *News of the World*. Then she went over to where Danny stood, his hands in the pockets of his jeans, his white emblazoned T-shirt clinging to his muscular chest. It seemed an age before all the others departed and they were alone. Then she smiled at him impishly, patting the body belt at her waist as she did so.

'Guess what's in here?' she asked teasingly.

Danny's eyes darted over her and suddenly he was filled with rage, his face scarlet, his eyes blazing.

'You fucking stupid cow!' he bellowed, so loud she was sure the people drinking in the pub below could hear him.

Stricken, she drew back as if he'd hit her. 'What's the matter?' she gasped.

'How could you be so fucking stupid?' he roared. 'Well, you're on your own, kiddo. Don't expect me to have anything to do with it.' He grabbed his leather jacket from where it hung over the back off a chair, and made for the door.

'But, Danny . . .' she wailed, running after him. 'You don't understand! Danny! Stop!'

He was charging down the urine-smelling stairs of the pub

and Poppy was trying to keep up with him, her breath coming in desperate sobs as she clutched the money bag.

'You don't understand! Wait . . .' But he was gone, charging out into the street, and all that was left was the echo of his words lingering in the air around her: 'Fucking stupid cow.'

'Try not to worry, my dear.' Geoffrey kissed Camilla goodbye, outside the offices of Eaton & Eaton. She was still looking very upset, and he wished he could have taken her somewhere quiet for the afternoon so that he could have comforted her more.

'How about driving out to Kew Gardens?' he'd suggested as they finished lunch. 'You love looking at all the flowers, don't you?'

For a moment he had detected a fleeting glimpse of longing in her finely featured face, but then she took a deep breath and replied resolutely, 'It's a lovely idea, Geoffrey, but I really have to get on with a huge pile of work. Another time perhaps. Maybe one weekend.'

'You work too hard, you know,' he observed, as he signed the bill and slipped his gold American Express card back into his wallet. 'You should give yourself a break sometimes.'

She smiled tightly, her face drawn with the shock of what he'd told her about her father. 'I know, but somehow the days rush past and it's the weekend again, and I look in my diary and see I've got another helluva week coming up. It never seems to end.'

Looking at her, Geoffrey remembered how she'd been when he'd first met her and David at a friend's house. He thought he'd never seen a more lovely woman; tall, with long slender legs and the face of a Dresden china figurine, so delicate was the bone structure, so fair the skin. What had struck him most, though, was that she laughed a lot. She seemed to be a person who enjoyed life and relished every moment of it. They had made such a handsome couple, too, she and David. Everyone had liked them. His success in business, and hers as the perfect wife and mother, had made them amongst the most popular couples in

London. No party was complete without them, and when they entertained in their exquisite Wilton Crescent house, Camilla was a thoughtful and hardworking hostess, ensuring that every detail was right.

And then the tragedy had happened. Camilla had been incredibly brave and in due course had taken over the running of David's company, but looking at her now, Geoffrey could see the immense price she'd paid for her bravery. It was as if she'd grown a protective layer to shield her from the toughness of her new life. She was alone now, working to maintain a standard of living so that Poppy would have the sort of upbringing David had wanted for his only child, but, buried in her work, the joyous light had vanished from her eyes. She seemed burdened, heavily so, Geoffrey reflected, and he wished with all his heart that she would allow him to lift away some of the weight from her shoulders.

'Thank you for lunch . . . and for everything,' she said, smiling at him before turning to enter her office building. 'I'm very grateful, Geoffrey, even if I didn't like what you had to tell me.' The smile became wistful and for a moment he had an intense longing to take her in his arms, but then she was gone with a little wave, and only a waft of her perfume, Claude Montana, lingered on the air.

Camilla spent the afternoon trying to contact Malcolm, but every time the phone gave the engaged signal. Who on earth could he be talking to all this time, she reflected, or had he taken the phone off the hook? Worried and confused and wondering what to believe, she asked Jean to keep on trying the number.

'Check with the operator, too, in case there's a fault on the line,' she added. There was a stack of work on her desk to be attended to and she had a meeting with Leslie Forbes, but although she tried to concentrate her thoughts kept drifting back to her father and what Geoffrey had said about him. If anyone else had suggested Malcolm was suffering from paranoid delusions she'd have said it was they who were mentally sick. Her friendship with Geoffrey over the years, though, convinced her he would never say such a thing if he didn't believe it to be true. What would his motive be for saying otherwise? Yet she was equally convinced that her father was far from senile. He had never shown tendencies to paranoia in his life and as far as she was aware wasn't showing them now. She thought back again to his phone call from the vet's house, telling her eighteen of his puppies had died from poisoning. How could he have said that if it had been a blatant lie, when Hector Ross was in the room offering him a glass of whisky at the same time? Unless, of course . . . Creeping doubts kept slithering into her mind like dark shadows. Unless the vet had merely been humouring him!

'Oh, my God,' she muttered aloud, looking at her watch. If it were possible, if she could only drop the huge workload that burdened her desk, she'd catch the next flight and go and see for herself what the hell was going on.

Desperately in need of someone to talk it over with, she put through a call to Lucy, the one person she had known all her life who also knew Malcolm.

'Come to supper,' Lucy said immediately when Camilla had told her about Geoffrey's visit to Scotland. 'You'll have to take pot luck because for once I'm on my own and I'd planned to have an egg.'

Camilla laughed, reassured by Lucy's practical and sensible manner. 'An egg will suit me fine, too. What's happened to your vast family? I can't believe you're really on your own!'

'Bliss, isn't it? Though I'd go mad if they were away for long. Anthony's going to a men-only reunion dinner at his club; Philip has moved into his new flat; Henrietta's off to a dance, and of course Reggie and Charlotte are now at their new boarding school. We can have a wonderful talk, my dear. I'm sure you've no need to worry about Malcolm,' she added reassuringly.

'I hope not,' Camilla said doubtfully, 'but Geoffrey is such a reliable person. Why should he make up something like this?'

When she'd finished at the office and Ferris had driven her home, she went straight to her bedroom to change out of her executive-looking black suit. Then, loosening her chignon so that her long fair hair fell softly to her shoulders, she put on a comfortable white wool jersey dress. The transformation took ten years off her. In a few minutes she'd changed from a smart mature businesswoman into someone much younger, much more gentle; more the woman she'd been when David was alive, she thought, looking at her reflection in the full-length bedroom mirror.

Then she dialled Malcolm's number again. It still gave the busy signal. The operator had told Jean there was a fault on the line, but Camilla reasoned the 'fault' could well be caused by her father leaving the phone off the hook. Whatever it was, she felt depressed at not being able to talk to him. Supposing . . .? She dismissed the thought instantly, knowing her father to be an honest straightforward man who would never shirk issues. Yet supposing . . . supposing he'd taken his phone off the hook because he didn't want to speak to her? Was, in fact, trying to avoid her, because he'd guessed that Geoffrey would have told her by now that he'd been spinning yarns of ridiculous magnitude? No. She shook her head violently. That type of behaviour was totally out of keeping with the way Malcolm behaved . . . unless of course his state of mind was causing him to behave otherwise? Did people suffering from senile dementia realise they were ill? ·

Confused and distressed, she went down to the study. It was too early to leave for Lucy's and she suddenly felt lonely and at a loose end. Where was Poppy? If Poppy was only more co-operative she could fly up to see her grandfather and find out how he was. Camilla rang the bell by the fireplace to summon Maitland. He appeared a moment later.

'Good evening, madam. Is there anything I can get you?' he asked. He'd recovered from the blow of finding some of the silver missing and his bulbous blue eyes were twinkling again.

'I wondered if you'd seen Miss Poppy? If you knew if she'd

be in later?' Camilla hated to have to ask the servants where her daughter was, but what with being at the office since early morning and Poppy being so elusive, she had no alternative.

Maitland looked as disapproving as he dared. 'Miss Poppy wasn't at home last night, madam, and she hasn't been in today. Shall I give her a message if I see her?' he added primly.

Camilla frowned. How humiliating not to know where your own child was! It showed how little control she had over Poppy, too. Her mouth tightened, making her look older again.

'Tell her, Maitland, that I'm anxious about her grandfather and would like her to go up to Scotland to see him as soon as possible as I can't get away,' she said.

'Yes, madam.' He inclined his head understandingly.

At that moment the phone rang on the pedestal desk in the window, a soft 'brupp-brupp' noise like the rhythmic purring of a large cat.

'I'll take it,' she said.

'Very well, madam.' Maitland withdrew silently as Camilla lifted the receiver.

'Hello?'

'Is that you, Camilla?'

'Edith! I've been trying to get hold of you and Daddy all day but your line's been busy.' Camilla slumped into the desk chair with relief.

Edith sounded nervy and jumpy. 'You should never have sent that newspaper reporter up to see us,' she said immediately. 'Never do anything like that again.'

'Hey, wait a minute . . .' Camilla's head was spinning. 'He's a friend of mine, and he was going to do a very sympathetic article about you and Daddy being victimised by the village for . . .'

'Thank God,' Edith broke in, 'no one apart from Hector Ross and ourselves realised he was a reporter, but you had no right to get anyone, friend or not, to go snooping around asking questions.'

'Why not? What *is* it, Edith? Geoffrey doesn't snoop in any case,' she added heatedly.

'He was asking a lot of questions. It was very wrong of you to get him to come here. It's difficult enough as it is. This has made things worse.' Edith had always been a highly-strung woman, Camilla reflected, but now she seemed to be edging towards hysteria.

'Edith, I'd like to talk to my father.'

'That's not possible.'

'Why not?'

'He's talking to Hector Ross. We're at Hector's house now, you see, using his phone,' Edith replied.

'Is your own phone really out of order, then? I've been trying to contact you all day . . .'

Edith wasn't listening. Sounding highly nervous she continued: 'You made a great mistake, Camilla. Why didn't you speak to me first before sending that reporter up here? He even brought a photographer, you know! And your father's so trusting. I nearly died when I heard him telling your friend all about our post going astray . . . and the puppies dying . . . and everything! I did what I could to put him off the scent, but I'm desperately worried he'll write something. Do you think he will?' Her voice quavered and broke.

'He's got nothing to write about!' Camilla burst out explosively. 'What the hell's going on, Edith?' Then a sudden thought, an inkling of how Edith might have tried to divert Geoffrey's interest away from the village of Ardachie, crossed her mind. 'Did you tell him Daddy was ill and had imagined the whole thing?' she asked sharply.

'I had to, Camilla. I had to. There was no other way. There was your father telling him everything that had happened . . . I asked your friend to come and see the kennels, and then I told him he was not to believe a word Malcolm said because he was senile. I'm sorry, Camilla, but it was all I could think of.'

She was torn between an overwhelming sense of relief at finding out that her father was all right and a deepening frustration at not knowing what was happening.

'So why couldn't you let Geoffrey write about what's going

on?' she demanded. 'If people are stealing your letters and poisoning your dogs, surely they should be exposed? And how could you have said Daddy was paranoid? That was a dreadful thing to do.'

'No, it wasn't.' If Edith sounded agitated, she also appeared to be sticking to her guns. 'It was far better,' she continued, 'to let your friend think your father had imagined everything than to let him know the truth. You've put us in great danger by sending that man here.'

The dark clouds that had hung over Camilla and had briefly abated when she'd heard her father wasn't senile gathered again, and this time they were oppressive, ominous.

'Danger?' she asked, her heart lurching uncomfortably. 'What danger?'

'I can't possibly tell you over the phone, Camilla. We can only hope Hector's phone isn't being tapped as well. He says he thinks it's all right . . . but you must never let your father tell you anything over our phone. That has definitely been bugged.'

'But can't anything be done? I mean . . . this is a ridiculous situation, Edith! What are you afraid of? Why don't you go to the police if something is seriously wrong?' Camilla demanded.

Edith seemed to ignore her words. 'The situation is far more serious than you imagine, and far more dangerous too. For God's sake don't come up here, Camilla. It isn't safe!'

Chapter Five

Poppy walked the short distance from the pub to the house in Wyvel Street where Danny lived. The bell had a piece of cardboard taped over it with 'Broken' scrawled in red crayon, so she banged the rusty knocker and waited. After what seemed an age a tall thin black man with dreadlocks and gold earrings opened the door.

'What d'you want?' he asked impatiently.

'I've come to see Danny,' Poppy said in a small voice. Her face was tear-stained and she was breathless as if she'd been running.

'He ain't here.' The man was just about to slam the door shut again but she grabbed the lintel and looked up at him.

'I know he's not in. I'm meeting him here in a few minutes,' she lied. 'We've been to the pub and he told me to . . . well, to go ahead. He won't be long.'

The man hesitated for a moment, his eyes black as coal, his expression suspicious. In the evening light his earrings gleamed richly against the dark lustre of his skin. Then he spoke, shrugging as he did so.

'Come in if you want, then.' Poppy recognised the accent as Jamaican.

'I'm his girlfriend,' she said as she stepped into the tiny hallway, but he wasn't listening. Turning abruptly away he loped off down the dim passageway to the kitchen at the rear of the house where she could hear a furious argument in progress.

'What the hell you doin', shit-head?' a man was yelling, above the din of pots and pans being banged about.

'Don' you talk to me like that, you motherfucker!' screamed another man. 'What the fuck you want?'

The smell of frying chips, Poppy noticed, was mingled with a strong cloying aroma of curry. It clung damply in the atmosphere like an enveloping miasma. Dashing up the stairs two at a time, Poppy arrived on the second floor landing just as she heard agonised shrieks, followed by a terrible clattering noise. Pressing herself against the wall, she held her breath as the sound of pounding feet raced along the passageway below, making the building shudder. 'NO!' A man's voice echoed through the house, terrible in its intensity. 'I'll get you,' bellowed another voice. Then the front door slammed and she heard two sets of footsteps racing away down the street until they became lost in the distant roar of the traffic.

Afraid they would come back Poppy hurried up to the floor above, to the dimly lit landing outside Danny's room. He never locked his door. Hastily, she turned the handle and entered.

The curtains were drawn and in the shadows she could see the unmade bed in the corner and the scattering of clothes around the room. Feeling like an intruder, she looked around slowly, taking it all in. Then she went to the window and drew back the cheap cotton curtains and looked out. The sky was indigo, tinged with violet, and the one solitary tree left standing by the local council when they erected the block of flats opposite now stood etched like black lace against the evening shadows. Through each square window of the block she could see into its rooms, see the dozens of separate existences being lived out in this soulless setting. It reminded her of the old wasps' nest her father had shown her in their loft when she'd been a child. He'd taken a bread knife and sliced into the intricately made construction, revealing floor upon floor of living quarters, supported by pillars, like a miniature multi-storey carpark. The view opposite was not dissimilar.

Encapsulated each in their own little section, people were going about their business unaware of the proximity of others.

A family eating supper in their kitchen did not know a couple were making love right above their heads. Next to them, in the adjoining flat, an elderly woman watched television, eating sweets out of a bag, while below a father cuffed his son for some misdemeanour. Higher up, a man and woman were decorating a room, and through another window Poppy could see a girl getting dressed. Little people in little boxes; isolated, unconnected, and remote from each other.

Absorbed in watching like some Peeping Tom the intimate lives of others, she waited and wondered how long it would be before Danny returned. How stupid she'd been in accidentally giving him the impression she was pregnant! And how nasty he'd been when he believed that she was! That hurt more than anything.

It grew darker and the sky had turned to a murky grey, bled of all other colour. The one street light down below did little to brighten Wyvel Street. The smell of curry from the kitchen had given way to the aroma of cooking fish. Not sure by now whether she felt hungry or nauseated, Poppy curled up on the bed, wishing Danny would come soon. Ten minutes later she was fast asleep.

The bedroom door being flung open noisily some time much later made her wake with a start.

'This is it,' she heard Danny say, and opening her eyes saw him standing in the doorway with a dark-haired girl. She was scrawny and several years older than Poppy, and her tight-fitting lurex dress glinted as Danny switched on the central light. When she saw Poppy she gave a shriek of alarm.

''Ere!' She rounded on Danny. 'You never said you was into threesomes!'

Danny looked at the girl lying huddled on her side, her face flushed from sleep. 'Poppy!' he exclaimed as if he were surprised to see her.

'Danny . . . you've made a mistake,' she began urgently, but before she could explain he retorted with sudden anger:

'You're bleedin' right I've made a mistake.' Then he strode

over to the window and jerked the curtains roughly together before turning on her with savage fury. 'I should never have got caught up with you in the first place. Now, get out. Me and my friend here want some privacy.'

Poppy looked at the girl. She was standing at the foot of the bed, her narrow face and thin lips twisted into an expression of insolence. Completely devoid of makeup, her face looked curiously naked beside the glittery dress and gilt baubles that hung from her ears.

'Yes, we want our privacy,' she repeated. 'We don't want no one else here.'

Suddenly Poppy was consumed with anger. Who did this cheap tart think she was? Rising from the bed she faced the girl squarely.

'Neither do I,' she said grandly, her accent unconsciously reverting to pure cut glass Knightsbridge. Then she turned to look at Danny. 'For your information I'm not pregnant either. I'm not that bloody stupid, you know.'

He looked nonplussed and the girl shifted her weight to the other hip, watching them uneasily.

'So what the hell . . .?' Danny demanded.

Poppy shrugged tantalisingly. 'Just something I got for you,' she replied casually.

'What is it?'

'I'll tell you when we're on our own,' she replied pointedly.

'You want me to go?' the girl asked after an astounded pause. ''Ere, she's got a bleeding nerve, Danny. Get 'er out.' She waved a skinny arm in the direction of the door.

'I'm not going,' Poppy declared. 'It's you who's leaving.'

''Oo d'you think you are – Lady Muck? Don't you go ordering me about. 'Oo is she, Danny? What's she doin' 'ere?'

Danny remained silent.

'I've more right to be here than you have. I'm Danny's girlfriend,' Poppy said coldly.

'Ha! Girlfriend nothing!'

'Get out!' Poppy's wispy blond hair clung to her forehead

80

in damp tendrils and her cheeks flamed with anger. 'You've no right to be here!'

'What's she mean, Danny? What's she mean? I've as much right to be 'ere as you 'ave, you stuck up little bitch.'

Poppy sprang across the room, eyes flashing. 'Tart!' she flared back.

''Ere, who're you calling a tart?' Infuriated, the girl tried to grab hold of Poppy's arm but her hand slipped and a moment later Poppy had pushed her over so that she landed hard on the bed. 'What the fuck are you doin'?' she shrieked, arms and legs flaying. 'Danny . . . stop her!'

Poppy had a grip on the girl's hair now and was twisting it with one hand while trying to protect her own body with the other. Nothing like this ever happened at Sloane House! The aristocratic girls who went there wouldn't even know how to fight. Quarrels were of a vocal nature when they took place, but there had been a lecture last term on the practice of self-defence and for a fleeting moment Poppy was glad that her expensive education had at least taught her something useful.

'Bloody bitch!' the girl was yelling, trying to punch Poppy in the face. Poppy had her pinned to the bed now as she knelt with all her weight on the girl's chest and stomach. Then her opponent heaved herself up, jack knifing her feet against the wall at the foot of the bed, and in a tumbling, jabbing, struggling mass of limbs and legs the two of them rolled around before sliding off the bed on to the floor.

Danny, who was rapidly becoming aroused by the sight of pale thighs writhing against each other, and the grunts and muttered oaths of the two girls as they slugged it out, stood with his hands on his hips, watching.

At that moment the other girl tugged at Poppy's belt and the money-bag burst open. Before anyone could see the roll of notes that fell out Poppy threw herself on top of the money, hiding it with her body while she kicked out at the girl with her heavy black Doc Martins. There was a yowl of pain and it was then that Danny decided to intervene. With a strength that Poppy found erotic he put his hands around the girl's waist, heaved her to her feet as if she'd been a rag doll, and then half pushed, half carried her to the door.

'Out you go, my lovely,' he said unceremoniously, 'and don't bother coming back.'

The girl protested in a series of yelps and shrieks, cursing and swearing and calling him every name she could think of, but Danny pushed her away and then slammed the bedroom door shut. The next thing they heard was the clatter of her spiky heels on the uncarpeted stairs and her threats to call the police.

Danny turned back to look at Poppy and then stood mesmerised as she writhed on the floor, one hand between her legs, arching her back and rocking her hips, her eyes closed as if in ecstasy. He licked his lips, watching her with growing desire, so turned on by the sight of her playing with herself that he reached for the zip of his trousers, wondering how long he could hold on before climaxing himself.

Suddenly she laughed, a triumphant peal of merriment. Startled, he watched as with a flourish she raised her hand and held it out to him.

'What the hell?'

Her face was flushed as she looked up at him, amused by her own bit of play-acting. '*This* is what I had for you,' she said breathlessly. She held out the three thousand pounds. Dazed, he took it from her. Then, as he examined the crisp roll of notes, he let out a long low whistle and gave her a look that was the nearest he would ever get to admiration.

'Come here, you marvellous little cow,' he said, his voice thick with desire.

Poppy heaved herself back on to the bed, smiling. Then she opened her arms in welcome.

Geoffrey Hennessy looked at Camilla with growing perplexity. Although it was late she'd asked him to come round for a drink so she could tell him about her conversation with Edith, and as they sat in her comfortable book-lined study, drinking brandy, his bewilderment increased as he listened to her.

'But this is crazy, Camilla,' he said at last. 'Christ, I haven't been a journalist all these years without sensing a story when I come upon one and I'd swear there's nothing going on at Ardachie.'

'There *must* be,' Camilla argued. 'Edith and my father can't both be mistaken or suffering from delusions. She told me the situation was really serious – and dangerous.'

'What situation? That's the point.' Geoffrey rubbed his bearded face in a gesture of frustration. 'I couldn't find anything that wasn't utterly normal to the point of being boring about Ardachie! As I told you, it's a tiny little fishing village filled with ordinary people going about their every day business. What is your father suggesting?'

Camilla spread her hands in a gesture of helplessness. It was nearly midnight and she was tired now, and Geoffrey was asking more questions than there were answers to.

'I don't know what he thinks is going on, apart from the obvious fact that the villagers want them to leave. But why? If it isn't because they resent his living in the old laird's house then I'm as much in the dark as you are. Perhaps they don't like the kennels? Perhaps they find the dogs a nuisance? Maybe their barking keeps people awake at night?'

Geoffrey shook his head, his hands cupping the crystal brandy balloon.

'Then it follows,' he said slowly, 'that if the dogs are barking at night, something is disturbing them. Dogs don't bark for no reason. Edith told me most of them are bred as guard dogs and that their hearing is acute. It could be that they're disturbing someone's nocturnal activities and that's why the people in the village want them out of the way.'

'But there are less violent ways of getting rid of dogs than by poisoning them,' Camilla reasoned. 'Daddy was given permission to build the kennels by the local council. Why didn't people complain to the council if they didn't like it? What they're doing is barbaric.'

Geoffrey hesitated in answering, and she could see he was not wholly convinced. Leaning towards him as he sat on the matching leather sofa on the other side of the fireplace, she spoke earnestly.

'Don't you believe what I've told you . . . now that Edith has explained why she said Daddy was senile?'

His expression as he looked back at her was gentle and affectionate. Placing his glass on the large coffee table that stood between them, he said carefully: 'I believe *you*, Camilla, but I don't pretend to understand what's going on. Why did everybody I spoke to give me a totally different impression of life in Ardachie? *Why did the vet say none of your father's dogs had even been ill?*'

'Perhaps there are two vets in the vicinity and you spoke to the wrong one?' Camilla felt as if she were clutching at straws but there had to be a reasonable explanation for what was happening.

'I checked,' he said succinctly. 'The next nearest vet is in Oban, thirty miles away. I phoned him up actually to ask if he had ever been called to cases in the Ardachie area, but he said he hadn't.'

There was silence in the softly lit room. Someone is lying, Camilla thought. She was sure it wasn't her father, but she was certain it wasn't Geoffrey either.

'What shall I do now?' she asked, distressed. 'I'm worried sick about Daddy. Perhaps I should go to the police and ask them to investigate?'

Geoffrey sighed heavily. 'You could do,' he said doubtfully, 'but what are you going to tell them? That your father says his post has been confiscated and his phone tapped . . . by the little old lady in a shawl who runs the local post office with the help of her daughter? That eighteen of his dogs have died, when the vet totally denies there's been anything wrong with them?'

'I'm sure they'd believe my father if he told them what had happened,' Camilla pointed out. 'Although . . .' she faltered for a second before continuing '. . . although you didn't!'

'I would have done if I could have substantiated any of it, sweetheart,' he said, and then he paused and a deep flush spread over his features. It was the first time in all the years he'd known her that he'd ever used an endearment when talking to her. Camilla looked away, startled, avoiding his gaze, embarrassed for a moment.

There was an awkward pause and then he reached for his glass and took a gulp of brandy.

'If I were you,' he said, trying to sound matter-of-fact, 'I'd leave things as they are for a few days. Maybe you'll get a chance to talk to your father again, and try to get him to tell you why he's so worried. He must know why the locals want him out.'

'Oh, I think he knows all right,' Camilla replied. She found, once the initial shock of Geoffrey's endearment had sunk in, that she was rather pleased. It had occurred to her, in a vague way, that if she were ever to get seriously involved with anyone again Geoffrey would be the right person. He was not only a dear and trusted friend of long standing, but there was something undeniably attractive about his strong burly looks and laughing bearded face. She also liked his down-to-earth manner and quick wit. He was such a reliable man too, a veritable Rock of Gibraltar, she reflected, someone who would always be supportive, kind and generous. Someone who would always be there. This was the first time, though, she'd realised he might regard her as something more than David's widow, a woman he had always liked and respected. Excitement raced through her veins and she realised she hadn't been listening to what he was saying.

'I'm sorry . . . what was that?' she asked.

'I was saying, if Malcolm knows what's going on, why can't he tell you?' As he looked at her, their eyes locked in a moment of intimacy that made her heart lurch uncomfortably.

'Edith said it was too dangerous,' she replied, feeling suddenly breathless, 'I think I should fly up to see them actually.'

Geoffrey nodded slowly. 'Perhaps that would be a good

idea. I wish I could go with you but I'm snowed under with work . . .'

'Oh, don't worry,' Camilla said, a touch too quickly, to hide what she was feeling. This discovery, that she and Geoffrey might have a future together, had left her dazed. It was as if a delicate and fragile bubble had suddenly enclosed them within its richly hued film, and to move too fast or too boldly might burst it.

'I'll rework my schedule and fly up next weekend,' she continued, as steadily as her voice would allow. 'I might get Poppy to come with me. Daddy adores her and she always manages to cheer him up.'

'That's a good idea.' Geoffrey nodded again in agreement, his intelligent dark eyes never leaving Camilla's face.

At that moment Maitland came into the room to collect the coffee cups, and the spell was broken. They started talking about inconsequential things and Camilla felt a sense of relief. She wasn't quite ready yet for another intense relationship . . . and that was what it would be if she got involved with Geoffrey. It was something she wanted, but not yet. Not until she had gathered her thoughts and feelings together and got everything into perspective.

At last he rose to leave. It was nearly midnight and she'd enjoyed every minute of his company.

'I'll call you when I get back from seeing Daddy, and tell you how I got on,' she remarked as they walked into the hall and she opened the heavy glass and wrought-iron front door. A silvery moon was pouring its light down on to the curve of grey stone houses that formed Wilton Crescent, giving it an unreal air, like a stage set. Camilla stood on the black and white marble front steps, a woman of great beauty and elegance with her fair hair flowing loose around her shoulders tonight and her face glowing with a happiness that had not been there for a long time.

'Perhaps we could have dinner?' Geoffrey asked, his gaze lingering for a moment on the fullness of her mouth.

'That would be lovely.' She gave a little laugh. 'Perhaps by then I will have unravelled the mystery of Ardachie!'

'Perhaps they've got their own version of the Loch Ness monster!' he joked. 'Perhaps the whole thing is the work of ghoulies and ghosties and long-leggety beasties and things that go bump in the night!'

'I'm getting to the stage when nothing would surprise me,' she replied, amused.

Then he leaned towards her and she could smell the fragrance of his after-shave. 'Thank you for a wonderful evening,' he said softly, kissing her cheek near the corner of her mouth. It was a light, almost tender kiss, and as she kissed him back the silkiness of his beard was soft against her face.

'Goodnight, Geoffrey,' she whispered.

'Take care of yourself in Scotland.'

'I will.'

'I'll see you when you get back.'

Then he was gone, striding along the Crescent in the moonlight, his broad shoulders looking powerful enough to carry the cares of the world.

The next morning the post delivered the most disturbing letter yet from Malcolm. Ripping it open as she dressed for breakfast, Camilla's disquiet increased, making her more determined than ever to fly up to Scotland.

I am most awfully sorry that your friend was unable to write about what is happening here and I gather Edith put him off the scent. I was all for going ahead, publish and be damned and all that sort of thing, but we have been threatened, and so perhaps for the time being it is just as well. However, I refuse to be subjected to blackmail. Our only friend here is Hector Ross, but he says that even he is in danger now. We may yet be forced to sell up and leave, but I hope not. The people here have strong links with Glasgow and possibly London too. Just keep your eyes skinned whenever you go out alone although I doubt you are in much danger as yet.

The ravings of a lunatic? The delusions of senility? Or had Malcolm really stumbled on something deeply dangerous?

As soon as Camilla reached her office, she hurried to her desk, calling for her secretary.

'Jean,' she began without preamble, 'I want you to book me on the Saturday morning shuttle flight to Glasgow, and arrange for a self-drive car to be waiting for me. I'll be returning Sunday afternoon.'

Jean consulted the office diary. Today was Tuesday; there should be no problem booking a flight for four days ahead.

'Very well, Mrs Eaton. I'll see to it right away. Just for one, is it?'

Camilla hadn't even seen Poppy for two days and she had no idea where she was. 'Just for one, Jean,' she replied with a touch of sadness.

Work kept her busy all day, but she found it hard to concentrate and at last, unable to bear the strain any more, put through a call to her father early in the afternoon. He answered the phone almost immediately.

'Oh, Camilla.' He didn't sound at all like himself in the guarded way he spoke. 'I can't talk now, I'm just off to get supplies for the dogs from Oban. Meat, that sort of thing, you know.'

'I just wanted to say I'm coming up to see you this weekend, only for a short visit. I'm —'

'DON'T DO THAT!'

'What? Why? I haven't seen you for ages.'

'On no account must you come and visit here.' Malcolm sounded fiercely adamant.

'But I want to see you.'

'No, Camilla. I forbid it! I can't talk now, I want to get back before it gets dark, although I know the road well. I'll try and phone you later, maybe from Oban. Goodbye for now.' There was a click and he'd hung up.

Silently, Camilla replaced the receiver. She suddenly realised her hands were shaking. Whatever was wrong, be it real or imaginary, her father sounded more agitated than she'd ever heard him before. For a moment she wondered if she ought to take a doctor up to Scotland with her, but then she remembered Edith saying he was perfectly well in spite of what she'd told Geoffrey. But something was desperately wrong, there was no doubt about that.

Poppy ambled back to Wilton Crescent for a change of clothes, arriving shortly after Camilla had returned from Eaton & Eaton.

'Oh, Poppy, I'm glad to see you,' Camilla said, ignoring the dreadful beaded sweater she wore over a minuscule black mini-skirt, and the usual weird makeup. 'I'm going up to see Grandpa on Saturday because I'm really worried about him. I suppose there's no chance of you coming with me?'

'No chance.' Poppy chucked her army surplus bag on to the floor and then sank into an armchair. 'If there's anything wrong with Grandpa you can blame that witch he married,' she added tartly.

Camilla looked startled. 'What do you mean?' Poppy had shown no surprise when Camilla had told her earlier about Edith's actions regarding Malcolm's conversation with Geoffrey.

Poppy shrugged. 'What do you think I mean? She only married him for his money anyway. Then she forced him to go and live in Scotland, as far away from us as she could, and now she's driving him crazy. On purpose, if you ask me. She'd be a rich woman with him out of the way!'

'Poppy!' Deeply shocked, Camilla stared at her daughter, horrified at how plausible Poppy had made her theory seem. 'How can you say such a thing? Edith adores Grandpa.'

'It's her dogs she adores, you mean. She's one of those people who prefers animals to people.' Poppy sounded scathing in her judgment.

'Yes, she does like the dogs,' Camilla admitted, 'but so does Grandpa, now he's got used to them. You can't go around suggesting that she's behind all the trouble.'

Poppy sauntered over to the drinks tray and helped herself to a Coke. 'It figures, if you ask me.'

'How?' Camilla felt genuinely bewildered.

'Edith could have pinched the post herself. That would have been easy. All she'd have to do was get up early before Grandpa came down and hide the letters she didn't want him to see. As to the phone tapping . . . it probably isn't even true! She's probably put the idea into his head by saying she thinks the line's being tapped.'

'But she wouldn't have poisoned her own puppies. Don't be absurd, Poppy.'

Her daughter spun round to look at her, and through the thick black eye-liner and mascara Camilla discerned the acute intelligence of her eyes.

'According to you, Geoffrey Hennessy said the vet had told him none of the puppies *had* been poisoned.'

'Yes, I know.'

'You even said Geoffrey thought Grandpa was senile, suffering from paranoia!' Poppy added accusingly.

'But he isn't,' Camilla protested.

'*We* know he isn't, but if Edith is spreading those sort of rumours around, mud sticks, doesn't it? Everything he says will be in doubt now. Don't you see? She's angling to have him put away so she can have Creagnach to herself! Haven't you ever seen *Gaslight*?'

Camilla looked nonplussed. 'Gaslight?'

'You know, that old film,' said Poppy impatiently. 'A husband tries to drive his rich wife insane by playing all sorts of tricks on her, so that he can get her money. In the end she has a sort of breakdown, believing she *is* mad. That's what's happening at Creagnach. Grandpa will soon be wondering what's real and what he's imagined.'

In spite of being worried, Camilla smiled. Poppy spoke with the typical simplicity of the very young, where black is black and white is white and there is no such thing as a grey area of doubt. As far as she was concerned she'd solved the mystery, and her step-grandmother was the culprit.

'Well, I'll find out the truth at the weekend. Are you sure you won't come with me? Grandpa would love to see you . . .' Then she paused, remembering Malcolm's words earlier. Don't come on any account. What was she supposed to do? Ignore his warning and go? Allow herself to get caught up in the melo-drama?

'What's the matter?' Poppy asked.

Camilla decided not to say anything. 'Oh, nothing. What will you be doing with yourself at the weekend, then?'

Poppy shrugged again. 'Oh, I'll be busy,' she said vaguely. Then she rose and headed for the door. 'I'm going out again. I just came back to change.'

'Poppy?' Camilla's voice was suddenly filled with longing and regret.

'Yup?'

'I wish . . . I wish we could be better friends,' she said awkwardly. 'We were so close when you were younger.'

Poppy's eyes became cold, blank, and she seemed to look straight through Camilla. 'Yeah, well, things change, don't they?' she said evasively.

Then she turned and left the room.

The constant ringing of the phone penetrated Camilla's sleep so that she thought she was dreaming, but then suddenly she was wide awake reaching for the bedside light, grabbing the receiver, her heart pounding uncomfortably.

'Hello?'

'Camilla, is that you?'

She sat bolt upright, every nerve straining, every part of her crying out to deny what she knew in her bones had happened.

'Yes,' she replied, trying to keep her voice steady. 'What is it, Edith?'

'It's your father . . .' Edith was sobbing, hardly able to speak. 'There's been an accident. His car ran off the road on the way back from Oban. The police have just been . . .'

Oh, please God, no . . . NO, said a voice in her head.

'He's dead, Camilla. They found him lying dead in the wreckage.'

Chapter Six

A large crowd gathered outside the chapel of the crematorium in Glasgow, waiting for the moment when the hearse would arrive, bringing with it the body of Malcolm Elliott.

'I'm so sorry,' the mourners murmured to Camilla as she moved among them, her face composed in rigid lines as she struggled for control. Most of them had flown up from London that morning, friends and distant relatives, fellow bankers and business colleagues, many older than Malcolm. He had been a popular man and the fact that all these people had come so far for his funeral touched her deeply.

'Thank you for coming. Daddy would have appreciated it,' she murmured back, shaking hands, nodding, going through all the rituals of modern civilised behaviour as her upbringing dictated, while inside her heart was breaking. She still couldn't accept the fact that Malcolm was gone; that she would never see him again, or hear his rich golden voice, or feel the warmth and strength of his arms around her. For over forty years she had loved her father so deeply, and with such an unconditional love, that to realise she'd never see him again brought a pain she couldn't yet acknowledge. At any moment he'd surely phone her up and say it had all been a big mistake, and that he was fit and well. At any minute, surely, she'd see him among the people who thronged here today, tall and elegant still, with thick white hair and merry grey eyes.

Poppy, who had flown up to Glasgow with her, was hanging back, Camilla noticed, not wanting to talk to anyone. She looked childlike and vulnerable in a skimpy black dress and her face for once devoid of makeup. Her rebellious nature, though, had not been entirely quenched for on her head she wore a large black hat with a bedraggled feather she'd bought at an Oxfam shop. With it she was wearing long silver earrings which trembled and glinted in the pale morning sunlight.

Earlier, with Lucy and Anthony, as they were getting ready at the nearby Belhevie Hotel where they'd all spent the previous night, Camilla had stared in horror at Poppy's hat. It gave her, she thought, the rakish look of Eliza Doolittle before she'd been transformed.

'Poppy, you can't wear that thing, darling,' she protested, adjusting her own small black straw with its fine veil.

Her daughter's mouth assumed stubborn lines, however, and she refused to take it off. It was Lucy who prevented an argument by drawing Camilla tactfully aside, saying in her usual matter-of-fact way: 'Listen, my dear, don't worry about it. At least she's not wearing a skirt short enough to show off her crotch!'

Now, as Camilla saw Poppy standing disconsolately on her own, a damp handkerchief clutched in her hand, she felt a pang of remorse at having been cross with her earlier. Going over, she put an arm round her shoulders and said with forced cheerfulness: 'All right, darling?'

Poppy barely responded, her small face pinched and woebegone with grief.

'Shouldn't Edith be here by now?' Anthony asked, coming up to join them.

'Yes, she should,' Camilla replied, looking around distractedly. 'She should have been here ages ago.'

'She's coming direct from Ardachie, isn't she?'

Camilla nodded. 'Her sister is staying with her at the moment, and they've got a car with a driver to bring them here today.'

'Oh, my God,' they all heard Poppy say and, following her anguished gaze, looked towards the entrance gates of the crematorium where the hearse was slowly turning in to come up the drive. Poppy gave an involuntary sob. 'I don't think I can bear this.' Camilla's arm tightened around her.

A clergyman appeared from out of the shadows of the chapel, prayer book in hand, an expression of carefully composed sympathy on his face. He seemed about to say something but Camilla intervened.

'My stepmother hasn't arrived yet. We'll have to wait.'

He looked at his watch, and she knew what he was thinking. As with all crematoria there was a constant flow of funerals, one lot of mourners appearing before the previous lot had even departed, and so they would not be able to delay for long.

'I'm sure she'll be here in a minute,' she said desperately.

'Here she is now,' Poppy announced in a tight voice.

Edith's car came sweeping up to the chapel at that moment and she got out, a bent little woman, looking much older than her sixty-two years. Moving forward, Camilla kissed her and their black-gloved hands touched momentarily. Then, remembering she'd not come alone, Camilla turned to greet Edith's sister but found herself instead looking at a small thin young man with reddish hair. Hollow cheeks carved twin scoops out of his white face, and through his gilt-rimmed glasses foxy eyes regarded her curiously. Then, without a word, he gripped Edith by the arm and steered her firmly into the chapel.

Camilla followed, wondering who he was, but they were taking their seats and the service was beginning, and there was no opportunity to say anything further.

The next half hour was the hardest Camilla had ever had to bear, bringing back memories of David's funeral, still fresh in her memory, compounding the pain of her more recent loss. It took tremendous control on her part not to break down completely. Beside her, though, Poppy sobbed with childlike abandon, her thin shoulders shaking, the drooping feather in her hat quivering.

At last the coffin slid out of sight and the dark blue velvet curtains closed again, hiding its destination; a final hymn was sung and the Blessing spoken. The ordeal was over, and much relieved Camilla left the chapel with all the others, out into the sunshine where the floral tributes were arranged on the grass lawn. Edith, in their midst, scarcely seemed to notice what was going on, her eyes registering nothing as she gazed at the wreaths and sprays that lay in profusion on the ground.

'If there's anything I can do . . .' Camilla began, laying her hand gently on her stepmother's arm, but before Edith could respond the young man had tightened his grip on her other arm and was drawing her determinedly away.

'Come along,' he said unceremoniously. 'The car's waiting.'

Unprotestingly, Edith went with him, allowing him to almost push her into the back of the limousine.

'We have to go.' The young man flung the words over his shoulder as he jumped in after her, and then he slammed the door and looking straight ahead ordered the chauffeur to drive off.

Stunned, Camilla watched as the car swung out of the crematorium grounds and vanished through the large gates. 'What an extraordinary thing,' she murmured, almost to herself.

'Who was that she was with?' asked Lucy, who had been watching the proceedings with amazement. 'His manner was a bit high-handed, wasn't it? Is he her son?'

'Edith doesn't have any children,' Camilla replied slowly, still looking in the direction the car had gone. 'I've no idea who he was, but what a strange way to behave!'

'What did I tell you?' Poppy whispered. She seemed calmer now the funeral was over. 'I'm sure Edith's behind Grandpa's death, and that was probably her accomplice.'

'Poppy!' Lucy protested, not sure whether she was making a sick joke or not. 'That's a terrible thing to say.' She looked at Camilla. 'There's nothing suspicious about Malcolm's death, is there?'

Camilla looked suddenly tired and as if she couldn't take much more. 'No, he had a stroke while he was driving, and the car ran off the road,' she said wearily. 'We'd better be getting back to the Belhevie Hotel before everyone else turns up.'

All the guests had been invited to a reception. Jean had flown up with them the previous day to make all the arrangements.

Lucy slipped her arm through Camilla's in a comforting gesture. 'Edith's probably gone straight to the hotel. I expect she was too upset to talk to anyone right after the funeral.'

But when they arrived there was no sign of Malcolm's widow, or of her unknown companion. Tea and sandwiches and whisky were served, and for the next hour and a half Camilla circulated around the room talking to everyone, longing for this dreadful day to be over and wondering what on earth had happened to her stepmother.

'We've got to leave in ten minutes to catch our flight back to London,' Jean informed her at half-past three. 'The luggage is already in the car.'

'Thank you, Jean,' Camilla replied gratefully. 'I don't know what I would have done without you. I'm worried about Edith, though. I wonder if she's driven straight back to Ardachie? I suppose she must have done.'

'Is it far?' Jean asked.

'Over a hundred miles. I doubt if she'll be there yet, though, the roads are so winding it can take ages.'

Jean smiled sympathetically. 'Why don't you phone her when you get back to London?'

'Why bother?' remarked Poppy, showing signs of her old sparky self once more. 'We don't have to have anything more to do with her now, do we?'

'I think you're being very brave,' Geoffrey remarked a few nights later. He'd taken Camilla to dine at The Ivy, hoping it would amuse her to see the many show-biz celebrities who frequented the restaurant.

'Thank you,' she said simply. 'It's a case of life has to go on, isn't it?' She ran her fingers through the long ropes of pearls that hung around her neck, as if their cool touch was reassuring. 'It has been a hellish week but I suppose the worst is over.'

'How is your stepmother coping?'

Briefly, as the waiter served their first course of *quenelles de rouget au basilic*, Camilla told him about the strange young man who'd been at the funeral.

'I've spoken to her once since but she seemed disinclined to talk,' she explained. 'In a way, I can understand. I remind her of Daddy just when she's trying to get her life together again, and I think she finds it too painful.'

'What did she say?'

After a moment Camilla said thoughtfully: 'It wasn't so much what she said as the way she sounded – as if she didn't want to talk. Apparently the young man was a neighbour who offered to accompany her to the funeral because her sister couldn't come to stay after all.'

'No more talk of being persecuted? Or strange happenings?'

'No, she didn't mention anything like that. She just said, rather quietly, that she was managing the dogs with the help of the kennel maid, Doris, whom they took on three months ago, and that I wasn't to worry.' She shrugged. 'Easier said than done.'

'You've got to try and put the whole ghastly business out of your mind,' he said. Then he put his hand over hers for a moment and squeezed it gently. It was a comforting gesture, and she smiled at him gratefully.

'I know. I am trying, but it's so hard to become reconciled to the situation when nothing adds up, Geoffrey. I'm as much in the dark about what's going on in Ardachie as I was before Daddy was killed. Was he, as Poppy is so sure, pushed to breaking point by Edith because she was after his money? Or was he in reality suffering from senility and perhaps heading for the stroke that finally killed him?' She paused and took a deep breath. 'Or is there something going on up there, something really sinister, that is at the root of everything?'

'You'll never know now so why not leave it?' he replied, as if to dissuade her. 'You'll only upset yourself.'

'I'm not so sure . . .' Her voice trailed off uncertainly. 'I think it's *not* knowing that's driving me crazy; the wondering and the guessing. What was Daddy really talking about when he said the situation was so dangerous I mustn't go up and stay with them? Why couldn't he tell me outright what was wrong? Who was blackmailing him into silence?' Suddenly she drew herself up, squaring her shoulders as if she'd come to a decision. 'I can't let it rest there, Geoffrey. I must find out what's going on. It's my duty to get to the bottom of this, if only for his sake.'

'But it doesn't sound, from what you've said, that there's anything to worry about now. If Edith's managing the kennels with the help of a girl, and seems to have everything under control, there can't be anything wrong, can there?'

Camilla frowned. 'You don't want me to go ferreting around finding out what's happened, do you? Why not?'

He looked at her earnestly. 'Sweetheart, I think it will be a harrowing experience. It's too soon. Give yourself time to get over your father's death before you go charging off on some wild goose chase.'

Camilla looked at him almost angrily. 'Firstly, I don't believe it will be "a wild goose chase", and secondly, if I leave it for too long any evidence of him being persecuted will have been destroyed.' They looked at each other and a silence hung between them.

Then Geoffrey shrugged. 'Very well,' he said peaceably, 'but take someone with you. Don't go on your own or it really will depress you.'

'Do you want to come?' she asked bluntly.

'I wish I could.' His smile was wistful. 'Believe me, if there's anything strange to uncover I'd like to help you do it, but I know my editor wants me to do a series of articles on Lloyd's and all the financial problems that are happening there.'

'I shall miss you,' she said involuntarily. Then her cheeks flushed and she looked down.

He took her hand again. 'Will you?' he asked softly.

She looked at him, her eyes green tonight in the soft restaurant lighting. 'Yes,' she said simply.

'I shall miss you too.' There was yearning in his voice, and desire in his eyes. 'I think I'm falling in love with you, Camilla.' His eyes bored into hers with an intensity that sent rippling waves of longing surging through her body. She could imagine him in bed, experienced, skilful, deeply considerate. He was the type of man, she was sure, who would be a very unselfish lover, reaping pleasure from being able to satisfy a woman. His thighs would be strong, his arms muscular; his hands she already loved. Capable hands with well-kept nails. Hands she could imagine stroking her breasts and her belly, probing her, entering her . . .

'Maybe I'm falling a little in love, too,' she whispered tremulously.

'I want you to be sure, darling. I don't want to rush you into something you're not certain about.'

'You're thinking I might be vulnerable at this moment? Because of all the dreadful things that have happened?'

'Now that your father's gone, Camilla, you're bound to feel more on your own than ever. I'm always here if you need me, as a friend. But I'm also here as someone who loves you, if you ever feel like returning that love.'

'Thank you.' She placed her other hand on top of his, so that she held him between her palms.

'I won't rush you, sweetheart. But I'll be waiting for you whenever you want.' His eyes glowed with love now, ready to offer her everything he had, including himself.

'I won't forget,' she whispered back and her heart was hammering wildly.

At that moment the waiter came up to take their order for pudding and so the moment passed; but she was content. As Geoffrey had said, when she was ready he would be there for her. Somehow she didn't think it would be long.

Lucy, when Camilla telephoned her the next day, gave a crow of delight.

'My dear, of course I'll go to Scotland with you. You couldn't have chosen a better time either. Anthony is going to be away for the next ten days on a fishing trip, Reggie and Charlotte are at school, and Henrietta's going to be with her godmother in Paris for a couple of weeks. For once, I'm free as a bird.'

'That's wonderful. I thought we'd go up on Friday afternoon. Is that all right?'

'That's perfect. I say,' Lucy gave a fat chuckle, 'you and I going on a trip together will be like old times, won't it? Remember that excursion we made to Penzance, when we were eighteen? I can't imagine what we were doing but I do recall we had a great time. Anyway, are we flying to Glasgow or going by car?'

'I'd rather go by car, but it is an awfully long drive. What do you think?'

There was a moment's pause, and then Lucy gave another little crow. 'I've got the most wonderful idea!' she said excitedly. 'Philip doesn't start his course at the Architectural Association until September and I know he's got nothing particular on right now. Why don't we get him to come with us? He can drive the car, make himself generally useful, and if there's any unpleasantness in Ardachie, he'll be there to look after us.'

'But will he really want to be saddled with two old women like us?' Camilla asked. 'Won't he be dreadfully bored?'

'Of course he won't, and who are you calling old?' Lucy demanded. 'In my book, forty-four is merely mature, Camilla, and don't you forget it!'

'All right! All right!' she laughed. 'If he'd really like to come, I'd be delighted. You've no idea, Lucy, how much I appreciate this.'

'My dear, what are friends for? Why don't you get Poppy to come along too? Now that really *is* a good idea! It would be the most perfect opportunity for her and Philip to get to know each other, wouldn't it?'

'I've already suggested it to Poppy, but she says she's doing other things.'

'Nonsense! You must persuade her, Camilla. I'm sure Philip would adore her if he got to know her, and he hasn't got a girlfriend at the moment. It would be perfect!' Lucy was fired with enthusiasm at the thought.

Camilla laughed. 'I'll try and persuade her, but no promises. You know what Poppy's like these days.'

When Camilla broached the subject again that night Poppy remained adamant. There was nothing she'd hate more, she vowed, than being cooped up in a car all the way to Scotland with Lucy and her son.

The silence of Philip's small Pimlico flat was broken by the screaming wail of a passing police car, awakening him from a deep sleep. Rolling over, he stretched and glanced at his wrist watch. Hell! It was only seven o'clock. He rolled back on to his side but, accustomed to getting up early, he was now too alert to go back to sleep. For a while he lay there, enjoying the knowledge he was having a two-month break from studying. It seemed as if he'd been killing himself with work for years now; first at Harrow, and then three years at Cambridge where he'd obtained a BA in Architecture before spending a year in Florence, studying classical architecture. Vacations had either been spent on flying visits to his parents in Hong Kong or getting practical experience in an architect's office. Now, for the first time in eleven years, he had two whole months to do as he liked and the prospect was enticing. Two months before he began a two-year course at the Architectural Association before taking his finals. And then? He liked to think that then the world would be his oyster, and he'd be able to design the most innovative buildings that had ever been seen. Buildings that people would marvel at, constructions that would revolutionise people's attitude. In short, he wanted to tread new ground while using his classical training as an inspiration. One day, magnificent examples of his work would stand around the world: concert halls and museums, office blocks and television studios, shopping complexes and hotels, houses and flats.

At that moment he remembered he'd promised his mother he'd drive up to Scotland with her and Camilla. The trip sounded quite a lark, especially when his mother told him it would involve a bit of sleuthing. He clambered out of bed now, all thought of going back to sleep gone. The story his mother had told him about Malcolm Elliott had been intriguing, and although he wasn't at all sure what Camilla hoped to find when they got there, he welcomed the opportunity of visiting Scotland for the first time. There were some wonderful old buildings he'd like to look over, not to mention some amazing castles.

Naked, his broad-shouldered muscular body still tanned as the result of several weeks he'd spent in Greece with his ex-girlfriend, Fiona, he went over to the shelves in his small, simply furnished living-room, and, searching among the hundreds of books that were jammed there higgledy-piggledy, gave a satisfied exclamation as he found what he was looking for. Then he padded to the kitchen, which was bathed in the clean fresh light of a summer's dawn, and put on some coffee. Perched on a stool, bare feet resting on a nearby chair, he opened the book at the first page and was instantly absorbed.

'Like Rome,' the paragraph began, 'Edinburgh was built on seven hills.'

The trip to Scotland, he reflected as he poured himself some coffee a little later, was going to be fascinating.

Poppy was looking forward to her mother's departure on Friday because then she could come and go as she liked without being questioned. There were always Maitland and Mrs Maitland, of course, but she knew how to get round them – by lying through her teeth! On the nights she was with Danny she'd pretend to be staying with various old school friends, and they'd be none the wiser. Not that her private life was any of their business anyway.

Things were hotting up on the Class Warriors front too. Danny had plans for something in July, and although he refused to give her any details she knew he was working hard to co-ordinate the various groups he had been addressing during the past few months, in pubs around London.

'Are you planning a rally, a sort of march through the streets protesting against the injustice of the present system?' Poppy asked as they lay on his bed that evening, having spent the entire afternoon making love.

'A rally? What d'you think we are?' Danny demanded scathingly. 'The Women's Institute complaining about the rise in the cost of bread? Grow up, Pops, for Christ's sake. We want to change everything . . . do away with private medicine, private schools, capitalism and all it stands for, and rid the country of the greatest scourge of all, the Royal Family. They're a useless bunch of layabouts who cost the country a fortune and perpetuate the whole concept of aristocracy. There will never be equality until . . .'

'I have listened to all your speeches, you know,' Poppy interrupted. 'I know what Class Warriors is all about, but I'm still waiting for something to happen. Giving money isn't enough,' she added with a hint of largesse. 'I want to know how I can help? What do you want me to do?'

Danny's grin was Machiavellian. 'Just stay close to me, Pops. Just stay close to me. That's all you have to do.'

She snuggled into his side. 'I'll do that in any case, but I really want to help, Danny. What date in July are you going to . . .'

He turned on her furiously. 'For fuck's sake, don't mention July to anyone, d'you hear me? If it gets out we'll have to call the whole thing off. How do you know about July anyway? No one is supposed to know.'

Poppy looked sullen. 'I heard you talk about it yourself, to that man in the pub. The one you're always talking to.'

'Well, shut up about it now,' he said sharply. 'We may not do anything in July anyway.'

She knew he was lying to put her off the scent. July had been whispered several times between Danny and the coarse leather-clad man he called his friend, and although the following April had been mooted, July had been mentioned more than once as the likely date. But for what? she wondered. If they weren't organising a rally or a march, what were they planning?

The car was loaded up and Maitland stood on the pavement listening intently as Camilla gave him final instructions.

'Have a good trip, madam,' he said at last. 'Mrs Maitland and I will look after everything, and you'll let us know when to expect you back?'

'We're going to see she gets a jolly good rest and stays away as long as possible,' Lucy said firmly. 'Expect us when you see us, Maitland.'

His eyes twinkled and he permitted himself a prim little smile. 'Very well, madam.'

'Would you like me to drive, Camilla?' Philip asked.

They were using the Mercedes she went to work in every day. She'd given Ferris a week's leave.

'Yes, please, Philip,' she replied gratefully.

'He's a very good driver, very steady. You sit in the front with him, Camilla, while I get in the back,' said Lucy, checking they'd left nothing behind.

Camilla started to protest but Lucy was in one of her organising moods today, and so Camilla settled herself beside Philip.

'I wish Poppy was coming with us,' she remarked regretfully as the car glided forward and they waved to Maitland who had been joined by his wife on the doorstep.

'I wish she was too,' Lucy agreed, signalling pointedly in Philip's direction. 'It would have been such a perfect opportunity, you know. It's such a pity you couldn't persuade her.'

Camilla smiled at Lucy's transparent matchmaking as she observed Philip out of the corner of her eye, trying to remember what his mother had told her about him. She knew he'd been to Cambridge, and besides a year in Florence had travelled extensively during his vacations.

'He's so sophisticated, my dear,' Lucy had confided. 'He's had a string of girlfriends. Fiona, the last one, was very sweet but not too intelligent, I fear. If Philip has a fault it's that he doesn't suffer fools gladly. But then, neither do I!' she added, laughing.

'Young men have changed since our day, haven't they?' Camilla reflected with a touch of wistfulness. 'They're not sexist for a start, and they're not afraid to show their emotions.'

'Ummm.' Lucy was thoughtful. 'Women today can have a far better time than we did, but is it good for them?'

Camilla's eyes widened. 'There's no turning the clock back, thank God. And personally, I think it's wonderful.'

She looked over at Philip now, observing his strong tanned hands on the steering wheel and the outline of his evenly featured profile. Camilla wished he was Poppy's boyfriend. He was eminently suitable in every way: intelligent, funny, profoundly honest, and above all devastatingly good-looking.

'We are taking the M1, aren't we?' Philip asked, breaking into her thoughts.

Camilla nodded. 'It shouldn't take more than five or six hours. I'm glad we're spending tonight in a civilised hotel just over the Border, though.'

Lucy leaned forward from her position behind Philip. 'Are you implying that once we reach Ardachie we'll be slumming it in some wee crofter's cottage, with outside sanitation and black pudding and haggis for supper?'

Camilla laughed. 'Not as bad as that, but I don't expect we'll find five-star hotels every hundred yards along the way! What I really meant,' she explained, serious again, 'is that it will be nice to have a night's comfortable stopover before we face whatever has to be faced in Ardachie tomorrow.'

'Are you really expecting to find a problem, then?' Philip inquired.

'Not exactly,' Camilla said slowly, wondering how much, if anything, Lucy had told him about the situation. 'Let's just say it could be rather stressful.'

They left the Hamilton House Hotel in Appleby, Cumbria, after breakfast the next morning, and headed for Glasgow. In fine spirits after a delicious dinner the previous evening, and refreshed by a good night's sleep, they aimed to reach Ardachie by early afternoon. Philip was at the wheel again, enjoying his first sight of the Highlands, and Lucy sat beside him while Camilla, in the back, explained in detail for Philip's benefit the strange happenings Malcolm had talked about before he'd died.

'So you're looking for proof that what he told you is accurate?' he asked finally.

Camilla gazed out of the car window at the mountainous landscape, rugged and magnificent under a clear dome of blue which was marbled with faint white veins of cloud whipped up by the high winds. The sun was shining brightly on dew-soaked bracken and in the distance a torrent of sparkling water fell splashing over rocks into a ravine. For some reason she was unable to account for a feeling of deep melancholy that had enveloped her, and for a moment she wished she'd never come. A presentiment that she would have done better to leave things alone came strongly into her mind but now was not the time to express the grave doubts she felt. In a couple of hours they would be arriving at Creagnach and although Camilla had decided not to tell Edith to expect a visit from her, there could be no turning back now. For one thing, alongside her dread of visiting her father's house, was the knowledge that she would also bitterly regret it if she didn't.

'I suppose I want to reassure myself that everything is all right, Philip,' she replied, trying not to sound dramatic. 'There are so many loose ends that need tying together.'

'But you think your father was right in insisting that something strange was going on?' he persisted.

'Darling, do stop worrying Camilla with your questions,' Lucy intervened in a mild voice.

'No, he's a right to ask me questions,' Camilla argued. 'After all, he is being kind enough to drive us all this way when he could probably have been relaxing in London, having a good time. The least I can do is put him in the picture as much as I can.'

'Believe me, I'm delighted to be here,' said Philip. 'I've nothing to do until I begin my studies, and if I can help to unravel a mystery and lend a hand in any way, then that's great,' he added enthusiastically.

'Well, I'm very grateful,' said Camilla.

By lunchtime they reached Fort Augustus, a small town at the mouth of Loch Lomond, and here they stopped briefly for coffee and sandwiches. Having got this far Camilla was now anxious to get on to reach their destination and talk to Edith.

'Let's go,' she urged, as soon as Lucy had finished her coffee.

Her friend looked at her with surprise. 'What's the rush? My dear, you haven't even finished your chicken sandwich!'

'I'm not hungry any more,' Camilla replied briefly. 'Philip, have you worked out the rest of the route?'

He was poring over a map, and with a pang Camilla remembered that on her previous visit her father had insisted on meeting her himself at Glasgow Airport. He'd known the way by heart, and she'd hardly noticed the landmarks as he manoeuvred the twisting roads.

'Yup,' Philip replied, looking up and smiling. 'From here we head for Tarbet, Tyndrum, Dalmally, Oban, and then down to Loch Feochan, which we have to drive around the edge of until we reach Ardachie.'

'There!' Lucy sounded triumphant. 'Wasn't it a good idea of mine to bring him along?'

Camilla laughed. 'Brilliant, my dear. If I'd been doing the driving we'd be at John o'Groats by now, with nothing ahead of us but the North Sea!'

Once past Loch Lomond, which Camilla remembered someone had once described as the foyer to the Highlands, the scenery became wilder and more magnificent as they followed the winding roads that led them through dense forests and between towering mountains, across windswept moors and along the banks of shimmering lochs.

'It's awesome to think all this has been here since the Norsemen transported their galleys across the Isthmus when they invaded Scotland,' Philip remarked, driving as fast as he dared.

'This must have been the scene of clan battles and fierce fighting in the Middle Ages, too.'

'What about the famous skirmish between the MacGregors and the Colquhouns at Glen Fruin?' Lucy reminded him.

'Nothing was as mad as the Massacre of Glencoe though, when the Campbells, having accepted hospitality from the MacDonald clan, got up at five-thirty in the morning to murder thirty-nine of their hosts,' commented Camilla, remembering her father telling her the story which she'd long forgotten from school days. 'And to add insult to injury, the Campbells left immediately afterwards, taking two hundred horses, nine hundred cattle and hundreds of sheep and goats with them as well!'

'Charming lot,' Philip remarked. 'It's not surprising that to this day the MacDonalds and the Campbells are sworn enemies and never speak to each other.'

'You think there's something like that going on at Ardachie, don't you, Camilla?' said Lucy. 'Some local feud in which your father became unwittingly involved!'

'He did buy the old laird's house. The locals are sure to feel it should have gone to a member of their clan, and that might be what's behind all the trouble.'

'Why did they allow an Englishman to buy it in that case?'

'When the laird died, his niece inherited the property, but as she lived in Cornwall and didn't want to go north, she put it on the market. I expect it was also more than any of the locals could afford. The laird had spent a fortune doing it up over the past ten years, hoping his niece would live there, and when she decided to sell she was out for all she could get. My father paid three hundred thousand for Creagnach and the surrounding land!'

Philip looked impressed. 'It must be quite a place.'

When they arrived at the imposing entrance, two hours later, he was not disappointed. The previous owner had turned a house of decaying elegance into a splendid mansion with pavilions at either side, giving an appearance of perfect symmetry.

Built of granite, the walls had a silvery sheen in the strong afternoon sunshine, contrasting with the lush foliage of the surrounding garden. On the terrace stone urns placed at regular intervals overflowed with summer flowers, and on either side of the massive porch carved lions lay crouched as if guarding the property.

Camilla got out of the car and walked to the imposing wrought-iron gates. For a long moment she stood looking through them up the long drive, and then turned and went slowly back to the car.

'Lucy, would you mind if I went in alone?' she asked. 'I don't know how Edith's going to be. Perhaps I should have told her I was coming, but it might be easier if I saw her on my own initially.'

'My dear, of course,' Lucy replied understandingly. 'Why don't Philip and I go and find somewhere for us all to stay and we'll come back for you later?'

'Is that really all right?' Camilla looked relieved. 'You don't mind?'

'Of course not,' Philip assured her, while his mother added:

'It'll give me a chance to put my feet up and have a cup of tea. Don't worry about a thing, Camilla. We'll book into an hotel and come back for you in an hour? Two hours? How long do you want to stay talking to Edith?'

'An hour would be fine. Thanks. I really appreciate it.' She waved to them as the car pulled away, and then she turned to look at Creagnach again. At that moment it struck her that everything was strangely quiet and that the house had a deserted air.

Uneasily, she opened the gate and started walking up the drive, straining to hear a dog bark or the hum of a lawnmower, or a footfall other than her own on the gravel paths. There was nothing. The silence was so total, the place so utterly bleak that, frowning, she quickened her pace, feeling the heat of the sun through her linen dress, wishing there was a breath of wind to lighten the sultry air.

Where was everyone? Edith should be around, unless of course she'd gone shopping in Oban in which case they must have passed each other unknowingly on the road. The kennel maid should be around too because the dogs couldn't be left for long. And weren't there gardeners to tend the grounds, and cleaning women to look after the house?

With dismay, it suddenly struck her that she might have come all this way only to find Edith had shut up the house, dismissed the servants and gone to stay with her sister. But wouldn't Edith have told her first? Camilla reflected, then remembered that Edith didn't know she was coming. If she'd gone away, what had she done with all the dogs? According to Daddy they'd had several dozen bitches, three or four stud dogs and endless litters of puppies!

She tried the front door first but it was unyielding, and when she rang the bell it pealed in the nether distance with the hollow ring of an empty house.

The silence now was heavy, almost palpably so, and with an increasing sense of urgency Camilla hurried down the front steps, past the crouching lions, and then for a moment stood looking up at the building. Creagnach looked back at her with dead eyes, the soul departed, all signs of life gone.

Ignoring the right-hand pavilion, with its ornamental arches that disguised a garage, she walked briskly towards the matching pavilion on the other side of the house. She knew she could get round the back this way, through a small door set deep into the granite archway. Her father had kept all the gardening tools in here and it was also a short cut to the kennels. Camilla tried to turn the handle but the door was tightly locked. Trickles of fear darted through her now, making her heart beat faster, giving a new edge to her awareness. Something's happened here! she thought. Something so terrible it has left an imprint on the atmosphere, an indelible mark of such intensity even the pleasant afternoon sunshine can't obliterate it.

Wishing now she'd asked Lucy and Philip to stay, she skirted the pavilion, forced to take the long route to the back door, crossing the smooth lawns and passing the herbaceous borders which glowed with the brilliant colours of summer flowers. Rounding the house, she reached the terrace at the back and, seeing the kennels, understood at once the cause of the uneasiness that permeated the air, the sense of suffering that overwhelmed the place, and the tragedy that now lay before her.

The scene that met her appalled gaze was one of carnage and devastation. Over forty dogs, from fully grown silky creatures to small golden puppies, lay strewn and scattered, legs stiff from rigor mortis, bodies twisted and distorted as if from the last writhing throes of excruciating pain, mouths open in a final dreadful parody of grinning.

Chapter Seven

By the next morning the weather had broken, the sultry calm of the previous afternoon giving way to a wild storminess that cloaked the horizon in grey veils, making the mountains loom with sombre grandeur through the swirling mists and the normally still waters of the Firth of Lorne froth turbulently.

Camilla, staying with Lucy and Philip in the comfortable surroundings of the Ballageich Hotel, fifteen miles away from Creagnach in Kilninver, awoke with a start from a restless sleep, still seeing in her mind's eye the terrible scene she had come upon the previous afternoon. Again and again the vivid mental image swung into focus, like watching endless repeats on a television screen, and each time she saw it her heart plunged in remembered horror as if she was in a lift that had suddenly dropped.

When Lucy and Philip had returned to collect her from what they imagined was a pleasant visit to Edith, they had found her sitting on the broad front doorstep, shaking all over, unable to control the vibrations that sent tremors through her limbs.

'Christ! You look green,' Lucy exclaimed unceremoniously. She'd changed into a comfortable pair of trousers and a loose shirt, and as she clambered out of the car she looked plumper and more motherly than ever. 'What's wrong?'

'Are you all right?' Philip added anxiously.

Briefly Camilla told them what she'd found. 'Whatever you do, don't go round the back,' she warned them shakily.

'We must call the police!' Lucy exclaimed.

Philip craned his neck, looking up at the shuttered windows. 'Is there no one here?'

Camilla shook her head. 'The place is deserted. I think Edith must have gone away, but Doris the kennel maid should have been here to look after the dogs.'

Lucy looked at her sharply. 'You don't think they've starved to death, do you?'

'I have a feeling they've been poisoned. In fact, I'm sure of it.' For a moment Camilla closed her eyes as another wave of nausea threatened to engulf her.

Lucy put a steadying hand on her shoulder. 'You look done in, my dear. We've got to get you a glass of water. Philip!' She looked at her son. 'Do you think you could . . .'

He nodded briefly. 'It may mean breaking into the house.' He glanced up at it again.

'That's all right,' Camilla said, straightening her shoulders and taking a deep breath. 'We've got to get in anyway, if only to ring the police.'

'Right.' There was an air of competence about him as he strode off in the direction of the right-hand pavilion, which Camilla had told him led through the garage to the kitchen door down the side of the building.

'He'll find a way,' Lucy observed placidly. 'I'm glad he's here. He's very good in an emergency. If he can't get into the house, then we'll just drive into the village and find the police station.' Ardachie, she'd discovered, was only five minutes away.

As Philip's footsteps faded away, a heavy silence fell about them like an invisible pall, oppressive, malevolent, the atmosphere charged with tension. Not even a note of birdsong coming from the tall trees that lined the drive or the hum of a lazy summer's bee broke the awful stillness.

Suddenly Lucy drew in her breath sharply. 'You don't think . . .?' Her eyes registered alarm.

'That something's happened to Edith?' Camilla finished the sentence for her. 'That's just what I was thinking, but where are all the others? The gardeners and servants? Doris?'

'They can't all have been bumped off,' Lucy interjected sensibly. 'There must be an explanation for this!'

'But who could have killed all those beautiful creatures? It's barbaric. If you'd seen them, Lucy . . .' She shook her head in distress. 'It would have broken your heart.'

'I'm very glad I didn't,' Lucy responded briskly. 'No one could accuse me of being wet, but when it comes to animals I fall apart. On the other hand, Camilla, I don't think we should jump to conclusions. Maybe they died of distemper or they caught a virus or something.'

'They looked as if they'd died in agony,' Camilla replied grimly.

At that moment, the front door swung open and, startled, she spun round from her position on the steps. It was Philip, his trousers smeared with grime, his hair ruffled. He smiled sheepishly. 'I had to climb up a drainpipe to get in through the top half of the pantry window,' he explained, brushing his knees with his hands. 'There's not a soul about,' he added unnecessarily. Then he looked at Camilla. 'I see what you mean about the dogs. It's a terrible sight.'

'Let's phone the police.' Stiffly she rose to her feet and, entering the house, looked around. She'd forgotten how beautiful the hall was with its panelled walls and polished floors strewn with rugs. Malcolm had bought most of the previous owner's furniture when he'd acquired Creagnach, and Jacobean carved tables and chests and chairs gleamed with the soft patina of hundreds of years. In the deeply recessed stone fireplace, large logs lay propped on an iron grate, while through the one high window on the far side the sparkling waters of the Firth of Lorne lay like a band of silver separating the distant mountains.

Camilla turned to Philip, her face still pale and drawn.

'Did you look in any of the rooms?'

'I put my head round a couple of doors.' He indicated the drawing-room and library. 'Nothing seems to be disturbed. Fantastic house, isn't it?'

'Where's the phone?' Lucy asked.

'I think there's one in the library and another in the kitchen. I'm going to look upstairs.'

'Are you sure you're up to it?' her friend asked anxiously. 'Why don't you sit down and let Philip have a look round while I phone for the police?'

'I'm fine,' Camilla protested.

'I'll come with you,' Philip insisted.

Together they climbed the stairs, Camilla holding on to the banister because in spite of what she said she felt dizzily weak, and her legs as if they had been filled with lead.

'Where shall we start?' he asked when they got to the top. A long carpeted corridor ran the length of the house with doors leading off it.

'Let's start with my father and Edith's room,' she replied, crossing the landing and grasping the brass handle of the door facing them. 'I feel as if I'm intruding but we've no choice. Let's get it over with.' She opened the door and led the way into a large airy room overlooking the Firth of Lorne. It was fussily decorated with swagged and draped chintz curtains and bed canopy, and a dressing table in the window with a frilled skirt. It was not to Camilla's taste, nor to Malcolm's, but she remembered that Edith adored very feminine decor and had a predilection for pink walls and rose-patterned soft furnishings. In this room she'd really gone to town. But then Camilla paused in the middle, looking around, knowing there was something wrong.

Philip looked at her. 'What's the matter?'

'I'm not sure,' she said slowly. Then she looked more closely at the room, noticing there were no personal possessions anywhere. No hairbrushes or makeup or bottles of perfume on the dressing table, no jewellery or trinkets lying in the open leather jewel case on top of the chest of drawers. Bracing herself, Camilla went over to the old-fashioned wardrobe and opened the doors.

'Everything's gone!' she gasped. 'All Edith's clothes . . . shoes, everything.' Bewildered, she rushed towards the adjoining room. 'My father kept his things in here. I wonder if they've gone too!'

Malcolm's dressing room was smaller, with a single bed in one corner which she was sure he had never used. A military chest stood in the window and built-in cupboards lined one wall. Slowly she opened the doors, one by one, seeing rows of highly polished shoes arranged in neat rows and hanging from the brass rail all his tweed jackets and carefully pressed trousers. Nothing had been touched. On a shelf a pile of made-to-measure shirts looked as if they'd just come back from the laundry. Hot tears sprang to her eyes as she caught a waft of his favourite after-shave. Stretching out her hand, she stroked a stack of sweaters. There was even a fragment of heather stuck to the arm of a pale blue one. Carefully she pulled it away, rolling the brittle bloom between her fingers until it disintegrated.

'I'm so sorry,' she heard Philip say. He had waited in the doorway of the dressing-room, sensing perhaps she wanted to be alone in her father's room for a moment.

Camilla looked up, an expression of vague surprise on her face. For a moment she'd forgotten he was there. Wiping the tears from her cheeks, she said with a bleak little smile: 'Thanks. This room suddenly brought back everything, and I wasn't quite prepared.'

'I understand. Look, why don't you go downstairs and find Mum? Get her to make you a cup of tea or something. I'll search the rest of the house although I don't think we're going to find anything.'

'Thanks,' she said again, going back on to the landing. 'This floor is all bedrooms and bathrooms. Daddy never used the attics. I don't think you need to look up there.'

'I'll check anyway.'

Lucy was coming out of the library as Camilla reached the bottom of the staircase. Seeing her friend's tearstained face she spoke with robust cheerfulness.

'They may not have the Flying Squad up here, but at least they're sending someone along in a few minutes. No doubt he'll

117

resemble Mr Plod and say: "'ullo, 'ullo, 'ullo, and wot do we 'ave 'ere?'"

Camilla smiled wanly at her friend's attempted cockney accent. 'Surely he'll be a Scot?'

Lucy slid into a perfect imitation of Glaswegian: 'Och the noo! D'yer ken a wee spot of trouble then?'

They were still laughing, teetering dangerously on the edge of nervous hysteria, when Philip reappeared. He looked from one to the other anxiously.

'Is everything all right?'

Lucy paused for a second to look at him and then dissolved into silent laughter again. Camilla, dabbing her eyes, torn between laughing and crying, tried to pull herself together.

'The police are on their way,' she said in a quavering voice.

'Good. There's no sign of anything having been disturbed upstairs,' he replied. 'I've been all over but there's nothing. Are there any cellars I should check?'

'Yes. Daddy keeps . . . I mean,' she corrected herself, 'Daddy used to keep his wine in the cellar. There's a door which leads down to it by the kitchen. But do you think you need to search it?'

'Probably not, but I'd like to make sure everything's all right indoors, even if it's not outside.' He indicated the garden with a nod of his head. Then he turned back into the hall, heading for the cellar door.

'Let's have a drink,' Lucy suggested. 'Not tea, something stronger.'

'There should be some brandy in the dining-room. I'll go and get it.'

When Camilla returned, a few moments later, she was carrying a silver tray on which she'd placed three brandy balloons and a half-filled cut glass decanter her father had always liked.

'That's more like it,' Lucy remarked appreciatively. 'I think we all need this. I was so afraid you and Philip were going to find a body upstairs, or something.'

'So was I,' Camilla admitted.

Philip came back at that moment. 'All clear,' he announced. 'Your father laid down a magnificent collection of wine, by the way.'

'I know. He was quite a connoisseur. Can I give you some brandy?' She picked up the decanter again and reached for a glass.

'Yes, thanks. So what do we do now?' He sank into an armchair as if suddenly tired. 'It looks as if your stepmother has packed her bags and gone, doesn't it?'

'I suppose so.' Camilla sounded doubtful. 'She must have sacked all the servants, too!'

'But surely she'd never have left the dogs behind?' Lucy intervened.

'No, that would have been unthinkable,' Camilla admitted. Holding her brandy glass carefully, she sat down on the sofa, kicking off her shoes and tucking her feet under her. 'D'you know what I think happened? I think she came down one morning, maybe several days ago . . . we don't know how long the dogs have been dead, do we?' Involuntarily Camilla shut her eyes for a moment, trying to blot out the sight of all those carcasses, their limbs sticking out at odd angles – twenty, thirty, forty of them, some collapsed on top of each other, while large blue flies buzzed around the bodies, swooping angrily. She quickly took a large gulp of brandy. 'I think,' she began again, 'that as soon as Edith saw what had happened she decided to get rid of the kennel maid and all the servants, and then she packed her bags and left. Remember, this wasn't the first time her dogs had been poisoned! I think she wanted to get away . . . turn her back on the whole horrific scene.'

'Poor woman,' Lucy said softly. 'What a ghastly shock it must have been for her, especially coming so soon after Malcolm's death.'

'That's what I think happened,' Camilla said cautiously.

'It would explain everything: the house locked up, all her clothes gone, no one around,' Philip agreed. 'There's only one thing, though. Wouldn't she have let you know if she was going away?'

'We've never been close, Philip. I liked her, and I think she liked me, but we weren't close. She probably thought that now my father was dead the dogs were her responsibility, and she might not have wanted to worry me. I'm sure she's still in shock from Daddy's death.'

'Of course,' Lucy pointed out, 'she may have tried to contact you during the past twenty-four hours but couldn't get hold of you. Why don't you have a mobile phone in your car?'

'My car is the one place where I do not want to suffer the intrusion of a phone,' Camilla replied. 'I know my directors think I'm mad and they nag me to get one, but I really don't want to.'

'I must say, they are one of the bugbears of modern living,' Philip agreed.

'I'll ring Jean at the office and ask her . . . Oh, damn!' Camilla exclaimed, suddenly remembering. 'I suppose you've dropped off all the luggage? Where are we staying by the way?'

'The Ballageich Hotel,' Lucy replied promptly. 'It's about fifteen miles from here, at a place called Kilninver. It was the nicest hotel we could find in the vicinity. Why? What do you want? Philip can always nip back and pick anything up for you, can't you, darling?' She addressed her son with fond assurance, making Camilla wonder how on earth Poppy would have reacted if she'd been asked to drive fifteen miles to collect something for somebody else.

'It can wait,' Camilla replied firmly. 'My address book is in my case and I've got the number of Edith's sister in Sussex. I'll ring her later to check if Edith's gone to stay with her.'

'That sounds likely,' Lucy agreed. 'What could be more natural, under the circumstances, than for her to shut up this great house and go to her sister's?'

'I hate to mention this,' Philip sounded reluctant, 'but what are we going to do about the dogs? I mean, I don't think the police will, er . . .'

'Bury them?' his mother prompted bluntly.

'Exactly.'

Camilla rose, slipped on her shoes again, and headed for the hall.

'Where are you going?' Lucy asked anxiously.

'There's a call I want to make,' she replied, hurrying in the direction of the library. On Malcolm's handsome pedestal desk stood the phone. She was just about to ring Enquiries for the number she wanted when she saw propped against the brass table-lamp a white card covered with her father's neat handwriting. The sight of it brought back a similar throb of pain to the one she'd felt when she'd found all his clothes, but this time she wasn't caught so unawares. She skimmed the list of phone numbers he'd listed, and there, between 'Plumber' and 'Gas Board' was the one she was looking for. 'Hector Ross. Vet.'

A man answered the phone. 'Veterinary Surgery. Can I help you?' He had an educated voice with a Scottish intonation.

'Is that Hector Ross, please?'

'Mr Ross is out. This is Alastair, his son. Can I help you?'

'This is Camilla Eaton. Malcolm Elliott's daughter.'

There was a moment's pause, and then Alastair spoke again, his tone softly sympathetic. 'Ah, Mrs Eaton. May I offer you my deepest sympathy? That was a tragic accident to happen to your father. Everyone around here is going to miss him very much. He was a great character. A fine man.'

'Thank you,' Camilla replied, touched. 'I believe your father was very kind to him and I know he appreciated it.'

'It was nothing.' Alastair Ross's tone was deprecating. 'We were all very fond of him. We were merely neighbourly.'

'I'm very grateful nevertheless. I was wondering, actually, if your father could come and see me?'

He sounded surprised. 'Oh, I'm not sure that's possible. I mean, I'm sure he'd like to meet you, but he never goes to London. He's too busy up here and he hates city life.'

Quickly Camilla explained she was at Creagnach.

'You're at Creagnach? Now?' He sounded stunned.

'Yes. I came to visit my stepmother, but apparently she's gone

121

away. Something has happened, though, something terrible. I need to see your father urgently.'

'What sort of thing?'

She hesitated as at that moment all her father had told her about not being able to talk on the phone, because he feared it was being tapped, came back to her. It was even possible that the person who had poisoned the dogs was listening to her conversation with Alastair Ross at this minute.

'I can't talk about it now,' she said, 'but I would be most grateful if you could tell your father I'm at Creagnach and ask him to come here as soon as possible!'

'Yes, of course, Mrs Eaton, but I'm not sure when he'll be back. He's at a farm some distance from here, tending a herd of sick cattle.'

Camilla thought quickly. She didn't want to hang about if the vet was going to take a long time to get to Creagnach.

'As soon as he returns,' she said, 'could you ask him to ring me at the Ballageich Hotel, please? I'm staying there with some friends and I can explain everything to him then.'

'Yes, that'll be fine, but is there anything I can do in the meantime?' Alastair sounded anxious to be helpful. 'We're only at the other end of the village, you know.'

'Are you a vet?'

He gave a rueful chuckle. 'Alas, no. In that department I'm afraid I'd be of no use to you.'

As Camilla thanked him and hung up, the front-door bell pealed loudly, echoing in the deserted hall. The police had arrived.

Poppy was up before dawn, insisting on making Danny a cup of tea before he left for the television studios. At this hour the kitchen of the house on Wyvel Street was empty and she was glad to have a few minutes to herself to try to sort out her feelings. Danny had been so nasty to her last night, humiliating her in front of a group of his friends by imitating her educated accent and saying she didn't know what the hell she was talking about anyway. Deeply hurt, she'd started to cry, but then he'd whisked her back to Wyvel Street and made love to her with such sweet gentleness, she was completely confused. Did he love her or not? The thought had tormented her all night as she lay awake after he'd gone to sleep. The way he blew hot and cold, nice one minute, nasty the next, made her deeply unhappy, increasing her desire to please him. When they were alone he was so wonderful to her. Why couldn't he be like that in public? He has to love me, she said to herself over and over again, as the kettle started to sing. He has to. He has to. I shall die if he doesn't love me. But no answer came to her in the dimly lit kitchen. All she could do was try to please him and hope that he would grow to care for her more.

The kettle boiled. She made two mugs of strong tea, lacing his with three teaspoons of sugar the way he liked, and then she carried them safely up the stairs, back to his room.

Danny had been invited to appear on *First Thing*, the popular breakfast television show. A researcher for the programme had phoned him two days before, saying she'd been given his name as the leader of the Class Warriors movement and would he like to join a discussion on Class in Great Britain: Does it Still Exist? Danny had jumped at the chance of airing his views to fifteen million viewers and looked upon this opportunity as the perfect vehicle to promote the cause.

Poppy, however, looked upon it differently. To her it was the start of a glittering career for Danny. The media would love him because he spoke fluently and intelligently, and the public would adore him because he was so charismatic. Women would find him sexually attractive, which always helped in politics, and men would admire his strength of purpose. With his black leather gear and spiky blond hair, his 'street cred' would be high too.

Weaving fantasies which always included herself at Danny's side, she entered his room and found him already dressed, waiting for the car the studios had said they'd send for him.

'You look great,' she remarked, handing him the mug. He didn't acknowledge her.

'Where's the bleeding car?' Fretfully he peered out of the window again. A chilly dawn, seemingly devoid of hope, was creeping over the desolate streets, silent at this hour except for the occasional bark of an anxious dog. Danny looked at his watch again, although he'd looked at it only thirty seconds before.

'It'll be here soon,' Poppy said soothingly. 'Are you nervous?'

He spun on her viciously. 'Why the fuck should I be nervous? Lots of telly parasites, they can't scare me! Overpaid bums, that's what they are. Overpaid, overprivileged bastards.'

Poppy watched as he psyched himself up for his television appearance and was reminded of the young man who read the *Tatler* for the same purpose. As if unaware of her presence, Danny's eyes became glassy as he continued his diatribe to an imaginary audience.

'Wait until I tell them what life's *really* all about, and that it isn't poncing in front of a camera, earning three hundred thousand pounds a year, like some of those presenters . . .'

What points Danny scored for rhetoric, Poppy thought, he lost in his inability to articulate his vowels correctly. Pronouncing it pa-ounds, he said it with particular malice.

'. . . they get paid a fortune to sit on their fat arses,' he continued, 'asking stupid fucking questions that *anyone* could ask. That *I* could ask! But would they pay three hundred thousand pa-ounds a year to someone like me, to be a presenter? Like fuck they would, 'coz they'd say I was the wrong bleeding class, wouldn't they? And I'd been to the wrong fucking school! It's time there was *real* equality in this country. A chance for everyone to get the plum jobs and the plum positions!'

'Of course you're right, but there's no need to get so angry about it,' Poppy begged him in a voice so mild it irritated him even more.

'Angry?' he repeated. 'Angry? I'm fucking pissed off with the way this country is run. Class! Class! Class! That's what it's all about. If you're the "right" class . . .'

'I know.' Even though she had heard all this a hundred times before, she still hated it when he grew aggressive. 'You'll be wonderful on the box, Danny. Will you come straight back here afterwards?'

'I dunno.'

Her smile deepened as she patted the bed on which she was sitting. 'I'll be waiting for you. Right here.'

Sex had become like a drug to Poppy, something to be repeated over and over, her body endlessly yearning for Danny's touch, no matter how badly he treated her. Like an addict she was obsessed with the thing she desired most, and yet, once satisfied, was instantly filled with renewed longing. It was as if she could never have enough of him. Day and night she thought about Danny, counting the minutes until she could be with him again, tormented by her quest for gratification, and yet once gratified, consumed by fresh desire. Sometimes, even while they were having sex, she would cry out: 'We can do it again in a few minutes, can't we, Danny? We must do it again.'

At last, exhausted, they would fall asleep wrapped in each other's arms; but the first thought that entered Poppy's head when she awoke was that they must have sex again, and so her small hands would reach for him with urgency and her eyes would look at him with ill-concealed lust.

'Proper little sex-pot' he called her, when he was in a good mood, but when he was tired and angry he would hurl insults at her, calling her names and wounding her deeply; but in hurting her he only increased her desire for him so that, perversely, she wanted him all the more.

At that moment Danny, still looking out of the window, gave an exclamation of triumph.

'At last! Bleeding late, too!' Then he turned and strode out of the room, picking up his leather jacket and flinging it over his shoulder.

Suddenly he stopped in his tracks, turned back, and, coming over to her, took her in his arms and kissed her passionately on the mouth. Clinging to him, she kissed him back. When he released her, he hurried from the room without a backward

125

glance. Clattering heavily down the narrow uncarpeted stairs, he opened the front door and slammed it violently shut behind him.

A Jamaican voice somewhere from the floor below, yelled: 'Shut that fuckin' noise, man! There are folks here who wanna sleep, y'know.'

Poppy turned on the television set, keeping the sound low, and then she climbed into bed. She could hardly wait to see Danny make his TV debut.

It was at the precise moment that Geoffrey picked up the phone to put through a call to the Ministry of Defence, for a feature he was writing on ballistic missiles, that he remembered Camilla would have reached Creagnach the previous day. What had made him suddenly think of her? He had to admit to a feeling of unease when she'd told him she was going, because he feared the trip would be deeply stressful. It was too soon after her father's death for her to go back to Scotland. There would be painful memories and emotional moments seeing her stepmother again, and for the hundredth time he wished he could have gone with her instead of having to spend his days in the city, doing research at Lloyds and reporting on what looked like the worst insurance losses for three hundred years.

Perhaps he should call her now, just to check she was all right? It was reassuring to know she had Lucy with her but, nevertheless, he wished she hadn't gone. He got the number from Directory Enquiries, but when he dialled, all he heard was a whistling bleep telling him the number was unobtainable.

'Damn,' he swore quietly. What a time for the phone to be out of order! Copying the number into his diary, he decided to try again later. No doubt, with her usual efficiency, Camilla would get it fixed within the next couple of days.

Thinking about her made him realise with a jolt that he was missing her. When had he actually fallen in love? He couldn't be sure because it had been a gradual thing, gradual and gentle. Always fond of her, he'd come to realise that he loved her and then that love had grown into desire. In his eyes, she was the perfect woman. Warm, witty, intelligent, and stunningly beautiful in a mature way. He wished he'd done something about it before, but maybe she hadn't been ready. David's death had devastated her, while his divorce had left him feeling free and liberated. But now he had the feeling that it wouldn't be long before they made some sort of a commitment to each other. She'd said she thought she loved him and he hoped she'd meant it. God knows, he loved her with all his heart.

The Ballageich Hotel in Kilninver had originally been a Scottish manse, built along the lines of Creagnach but converted into a hotel some fifteen years ago. Beautifully furnished, it offered guests all the comforts of a well-run home. Log fires crackled cheerfully in all the fireplaces, even in summer, the rooms were large with breathtaking views of the Firth of Lorne, and the owners did all the catering themselves, providing simple but beautifully cooked local produce. Last night there had been lobster, oysters and crayfish on the menu, with a selection of home grown vegetables and fruit which included asparagus and raspberries.

When Camilla came down the next morning she found Lucy already in the lobby reading *The Times* and drinking coffee.

'Want some, my dear?' Lucy asked after they had greeted each other.

'No thanks. I've already had breakfast in my room,' Camilla replied, joining her on the sofa.

The lobby was deserted at this hour, save for a young girl behind the reception desk who was talking on the phone. She was giggling a lot and Camilla and Lucy exchanged amused glances.

'Obviously talking to the boyfriend,' Lucy mouthed. Then in a normal voice, she said: 'How did you sleep?'

Camilla frowned. 'Sort of okay, but I feel shattered. Perhaps I will have some more coffee, it might wake me up.' She rose to press the bell by the fireplace that had a little brass plaque above it, saying 'Please ring for service'.

'What are your plans for today?' Lucy asked. 'I must say I feel terribly deflated by the police reaction yesterday. It was as if we were panicking over nothing, wasn't it?'

Camilla nodded. 'They did make me feel foolish,' she admitted. 'I suppose, on the face of it, nothing suspicious *has* happened. Edith shutting up the house and going away isn't odd except that she never told me her plans.'

'It was their attitude that annoyed me. Talk about being obdurate, my dear! I've always heard the Scots were dour but that sergeant, or whatever he was, was absolutely *moribund*! I had the feeling he thought we were two hysterical women making a drama out of nothing. Remember the way he asked if the house had been broken into? And anything stolen? And when we said no, except for Philip climbing in through the pantry window, he looked at us as if we were raving lunatics!' Lucy folded *The Times* with an impatient gesture.

'They showed no interest in the dead dogs either, did they?'

'I don't understand it,' said Lucy vehemently. A good night's sleep had done much to restore her natural ebullience and she was obviously rattled by the reaction of the local constabulary. 'To my way of thinking,' she continued, 'something is terribly wrong when the owner of the house mysteriously vanishes, leaving over forty murdered dogs in the kennels. How can they say there's nothing amiss as far as they're concerned?'

At that moment Philip joined them, a relaxed figure in beige cotton trousers and a blue and white striped shirt, open at the neck. He looked fresh and alert as he greeted his mother and Camilla before sitting on a nearby chair.

'How is everyone this morning?' he enquired cheerfully. 'What are we going to do today?'

'I've got to make some calls,' Camilla remarked. 'I want to check with the office that there are no dramas there, and I want to try again to get hold of Edith's sister as there was no reply last night. Once I've spoken to her, or Edith if she's staying there, no doubt everything will become clear.

Meanwhile, I'll phone the vet. It's a nuisance he never contacted us last night.'

'Why don't we arrange to meet him at Creagnach this morning?' Philip suggested.

Camilla rose briskly to her feet, clutching her Filofax which contained all the relevant phone numbers. 'You're right. I'll get on to him now to arrange it.'

When she'd gone over to the telephone booth in the far corner of the lobby, Philip turned to Lucy. 'What do you really think's going on, Mum?'

Lucy looked thoughtful. 'If I didn't know Camilla so well I'd say this whole thing was a storm in a teacup, and that there is probably a perfectly plausible explanation for everything, but frankly it's not like her or Malcolm to let their imagination run away with them.'

'Yet the police pooh-poohed everything last night, didn't they? They said the two gardeners Malcolm had employed had been laid off and were now out of work, so that explains why they aren't around. The same goes for the cleaning women who apparently live in the village. Nothing suspicious there. Edith obviously planned to shut up the house a couple of weeks ago. As for the kennel maid . . . what was her name?'

'Doris,' Lucy volunteered.

'Right. Doris. According to the police she came from Glasgow. If Edith gave her the sack she's probably gone back home. It all sounds very plausible, I must say.'

'Except for the dogs.'

'Yes, the dogs,' Philip agreed. 'No doubt we'll know the answer to that when the vet has examined the carcasses.'

It was several minutes before Camilla returned, and when she did she looked harassed.

'What is it?' Lucy enquired.

'I've been talking to Harriet. She hasn't seen Edith for months.'

'What?'

'She says Edith told her not to come to Daddy's funeral

because it was for the immediate family only, and she hasn't heard from her since.'

Lucy and Philip sat in stunned silence.

'Harriet has no idea where Edith can be,' Camilla continued grimly. 'She's promised to ring several friends to ask if they've heard from her, but it seems that although they were sisters they were never close. Harriet said they'd always had different sets of friends and different interests. I've left her my number here and in London, and she says she'll get back to me if she hears anything.'

'Then who was it that came to the funeral with Edith?' Lucy asked.

'God knows! I asked Harriet just now if she knew who it could be, but she said she'd no idea.'

'Did you get through to the vet?' Philip asked.

Camilla nodded. 'Yes, we're meeting him at Creagnach at noon.'

'Well. Thank goodness for that!' Lucy exclaimed. 'At least there's a chance we'll get something sorted out.'

130

Chapter Eight

Hector Ross had an untidy face, the mouth charmingly crooked when he smiled, the vague and rather dreamy eyes embedded in random wrinkles and folds of weathered skin. His hair was untidy too, an unruly mass of white curls that sprang up from his head and made him look as if he'd been standing in a high wind. In a suit a size too small for him, and a collar half a size too large, he shambled amiably from the direction of the kennels at Creagnach to greet Camilla and the others as they got out of the car. Camilla glanced at her watch. It was still only ten-thirty.

'Mrs Eaton?' he said softly. His voice was richly whisky-laden and he spoke with a Scottish burr. 'How very pleasant to meet you. I was very fond of your old father.' He nodded his head in the direction of the kennels. 'It's a sad sight you have there.'

Camilla shook his hand and introduced Lucy and Philip.

'I hope we haven't kept you waiting?' She looked puzzled. 'I thought we were meeting here at noon?'

'Aye, we were, we were, but I got through my work this morning faster than I expected, and so I came along here. I thought I'd have a wee look at the dogs before you arrived, too.'

A pained expression at the mention of the dead Alsatians crossed Camilla's face. 'Have you discovered how they died?' she asked in a low voice.

'Och aye, 'tis distemper they died of. It's highly contagious, you know, and there's been a lot of it in these parts recently.' His tone was complacent as he withdrew a pipe from his jacket

131

pocket and, having tapped it on the heel of his boot, then proceeded to fill the bowl with tobacco from a brown leather purse, tamping it gently down before leisurely lighting it. The others watched him in silence. Then he spoke again. 'We've nearly finished removing them so there's no need for you to worry any further. If you were thinking of having any more dogs, though, those kennels ought to be fumigated first.'

Camilla looked startled. 'You're removing them already? My goodness, that's quick.' She shot Lucy a covert glance. 'How are you removing them, Mr Ross?'

'Hector, m'dear, Hector,' he remonstrated gently, smiling at her. 'My assistant is round the back with the van. He's loading them up now. We'll soon have them out of your way.' He spoke with no more feeling than if he'd been shifting sacks of potatoes, and it struck Camilla that living in the countryside must harden people to the life cycle of animals.

'You don't think it's necessary to have any tests carried out?' Camilla queried. 'How can you be sure they died of distemper?'

Hector Ross looked faintly offended. 'I would like you to know, Mrs Eaton, that I have been a vet for nearly forty years,' he said with cold dignity. 'I can recognise a fatal case of distemper when I see one.'

'Of course. I'm sorry,' Camilla said apologetically. 'Why don't we go into the house while your assistant . . . while . . . Perhaps you'd like a drink?' she added in desperation.

His faded eyes lit up, and his charming crooked smile spread over his face again. 'That would be vurry vurry nice.'

'Let's go into the house then.' The previous afternoon Camilla had found a spare set of keys in Malcolm's study, and she now hurried up the front doorsteps to open the front door.

'Lucy, could you take Mr Ross into the drawing-room while Philip and I get the drinks?' Camilla asked.

Lucy looked at her in surprise. 'Why don't I get the drinks while you . . .'

Camilla gripped her elbow and gave her a little push. 'No,

it's all right.' Her tone was light. 'You look after Mr Ross. I'll only be a minute.'

'Oh! Oh, yes. Right. Fine.' She led the way to the drawing-room, while Camilla, catching Philip's eye, indicated they should go into the dining-room next door.

'Will you do something for me?' she whispered, closing the door quietly behind them.

'Yes, of course. What is it?'

She covered her mouth with her hand for a moment, her eyes troubled. 'I don't know how to ask you this but . . .'

'What?' He stood in front of her looking down at her face, and he sounded so earnest and anxious to help that she was touched. Nevertheless, what she was going to ask him to do required courage. She took a deep breath.

'Philip, I'd like you to get hold of two of the dogs, maybe a fully grown one and a young one, and put their bodies in the boot of my car, without Hector Ross or his assistant knowing.'

He blanched. 'All right. But what's the idea?'

She held on to the back of one of the dining-room chairs, feeling the smooth carving beneath her hand, solid and reas-suring. 'I think Hector Ross is lying,' she said flatly. 'I don't believe the dogs died of distemper. I'm still convinced they were poisoned but there's only one way to find out and that's to have a post-mortem carried out by another vet. We need an inde-pendent opinion and this is the only way we can hope to get that without causing suspicion.' She looked up at him, her eyes pleading. 'I know it's a terrible thing to ask you to do, Philip . . .'

'Consider it done,' he said firmly. 'I think you're right to get someone else to examine the dogs. Have you any . . .' He looked round the room, as if searching for something.

'Any?'

'Anything I can wrap them in?' His embarrassment made him inarticulate.

'Of course.' Briskly she led the way from the dining-room to the kitchen, remembering the utility room that led off it. She knew this was where her father kept the canvas sacks in which they brought firewood into the house.

'Will these do?'

'Yup.'

'Go and invite the assistant to join us for a drink,' Camilla suggested. 'Then, as soon as he's in the house . . .'

'Okay.' He touched her arm in a gesture of understanding. 'Don't worry about a thing.'

'Thank you, Philip. I'm really grateful, and I'm sorry to have to ask you to . . .'

'That's why I'm here . . . to make myself useful,' he said reassuringly, and she liked the openness of his face and eyes, knowing she could trust him.

In the drawing-room Lucy was listening to a long tale about a calf which had swallowed a length of wire, and Camilla, as she walked into the room with a tray of drinks, could see that Hector Ross was boring her friend to death.

'Would you like some whisky?' she asked, forcing her voice to be light and cheerful.

'Thank you vurry much.' He had settled himself at one end of the sofa, his pipe clamped between his teeth, while little puffs of acrid smoke rose above his head fouling the atmosphere.

After Camilla had poured the drinks, she sat down beside the vet. 'I'd like to thank you very much for all the kindness you showed my father,' she began, 'and now that I'm here, and we can talk, can you tell me what it was all about?'

Hector sipped appreciatively at his drink. 'You mean his missing mail? And the phone tapping?'

'Yes.' She leaned forward, eager to hear what he had to say. 'He was being threatened, wasn't he? And what about all the puppies that died of poisoning?'

He looked at her benignly, his lined face folding back into a smile of understanding. 'Is that what made you think those dogs in the kennels today had also been poisoned?'

'Of course.' She thought about Philip carrying out his grisly task as they spoke. 'Are you sure they weren't poisoned?'

'Quite sure,' he said quietly.

'How can you be so certain?' Lucy demanded.

Hector Ross tamped down the tobacco in the bowl of his pipe again with the side of his box of matches. 'Because the puppies died of distemper too. They weren't poisoned.'

Camilla felt her head spinning. This is what he'd told Geoffrey, but he was an investigative journalist. She was Malcolm's daughter. Edith had told her they'd spun Geoffrey a web of fabrication because the truth, if it got out, would put them in greater danger than ever. But surely she could be trusted to be discreet?

'You can be straight with me, Mr Ross. I know something was going on. You can trust me, and you can trust my lifelong friend, Mrs Hamilton. What I want to know is, who was victimising my father and Edith, and why?'

He looked at her with an expression she couldn't quite fathom. It was a mixture of wariness, coupled with pity, as if he had something terrible to tell her but wasn't sure how she would react.

'I'll leave you on your own if you'd prefer it,' Lucy offered, half rising from her chair.

The vet waved his pipe in her direction. 'There's no need, dear lady,' he protested. 'There are no secrets, no mysteries, nothing that can't be talked about openly.'

'I don't understand,' said Camilla.

'There's nothing to understand. Your father suffered from dementia; he was showing all the first signs of senility, including paranoia. He thought everyone was after him.' He shook his head.

'But Edith told me he was perfectly all right; that she only told my friend, Geoffrey Hennessy, he was senile to put him off the scent. My father said you were his friend, someone he could trust.' There was accusation in her voice now, and hurt.

Hector smiled benignly. 'I was his friend, Mrs Eaton. I did all I could to protect him from realising what was happening to his mind. When he first moved up here he was fine. A sprightly man with all his wits about him. After a while, though, he started to get fussed about trivia; then he thought people were tampering with his post. It's a progressive disease, you know. He was perfectly fit in the physical sense, but his mind . . . well . . .' His voice drifted off, filled with regret. 'His mind started to play tricks on him. He believed he was being persecuted. He thought there was danger in every shadow and a threat around every corner. It was vurry vurry sad to see him become so confused and full of unfounded fear.'

Camilla, listening, nevertheless heard his voice coming as if from a great distance, and it seemed as if it was someone else he was talking about, not her father. Not Malcolm. She'd spoken to him shortly before his accident, and she would have sworn he was as sane as she was. And yet . . . had Geoffrey been right all along?

'Why wasn't I told?' she asked, in a small voice.

'That was his dear wife's wish,' Hector replied. 'She was afraid that if you knew you'd say something to your father about it, and I think she was right. If he'd realised what was wrong he'd have been deeply upset. Much better to humour him, and that's what we did. He never knew he was ill. And then the hospital said he'd had a stroke while driving on his own back from Oban, so in the end it was perhaps just as well. He died, my dear, having no idea there was anything wrong with him.'

Lucy, who had been sitting quietly, leaned forward suddenly. 'Excuse me, but don't you think that was taking rather a lot on yourselves?' she asked bluntly. 'Camilla is his only child, his only blood relative. Don't you think, under the circumstances, she should have been the first person to be informed if he was ill?'

'It was Edith's idea, dear lady,' he pointed out mildly. 'I was only a neighbour. It wasn't up to me to interfere in a family matter. I gave support where I thought it was needed. I had a great admiration for Malcolm Elliott, and I naturally didn't want to see him upset.'

'Where is Edith?' Camilla asked. 'I spoke to her sister this morning, but she didn't know where she'd gone.'

Hector Ross shrugged his shoulders in his ill-fitting suit. 'I'm afraid I can't help you there. I've been so busy I haven't seen her for a couple of weeks.'

Lucy spoke again. 'The dogs hadn't been ill then? She hadn't asked you to come and see them?'

'Distemper can start very suddenly, and spread like wildfire,' Hector explained. 'If she didn't spot something wrong in the early stages, it would have been too late to save them.'

'Yet this is supposed to be someone who has bred Alsatians all her life, and presumably knows a lot about them,' Lucy pointed out drily.

'Something must have happened,' said Camilla, almost to herself. She felt completely confused now, but further conversation was halted by the arrival of the vet's assistant, a burly young man with a sullen red face. He was followed by Philip.

'This is Jock. Sorry we've been so long. We had to have a good wash after we'd . . . er . . . finished,' Philip explained.

Camilla tried to gauge whether he'd been successful in retrieving any of the carcasses, but he was pointedly looking away as he poured drinks for himself and Hector's assistant and so she couldn't catch his eye.

Jock said nothing but stood awkwardly, glass in hand, large feet planted wide.

'Did you help him then?' Hector Ross asked Philip wonderingly. 'That was surely vurry good of you.'

'I thought we'd get it done more quickly if there were two of us,' Philip replied simply.

Hector drained his glass with relish. 'Drink up, lad,' he commanded Jock. 'We've got a busy day ahead of us.'

Camilla didn't ask what he was going to do with the bodies of the Alsatians. Presumably he had an arrangement with a slaughterhouse where they would be incinerated. In silence, feeling guilty now that she had not been gracious to this elderly man who had befriended her father and been kind to him, she led the way to the front door. The van, she saw, had been brought round to the front drive, parked behind the vet's car and alongside her own. Trying not to look at it, she shook hands with Hector Ross.

'Thank you for everything,' she said gravely, wishing she could warm towards this rangy man with his irregular features and slovenly appearance. The trouble was she found it hard to imagine her father getting on with him. What did they have in common? A taste for whisky wouldn't have been sufficient reason for Malcolm to befriend a neighbour. The fact that Edith bred dogs and Hector was the local vet was hardly grounds for a close regard. Background, intellect, culture and life experience put Malcolm and Hector at opposite ends of the social scale, and yet Malcolm had confessed to Camilla his liking for Hector, and the fact that he trusted him.

'How long will you be staying up here?' the vet asked, as he got into his car.

'A few days, I expect. If you should hear from Edith will you tell her I'm at the Ballageich Hotel?' Camilla asked.

'Certainly I will. Now goodbye, dear lady. Have a safe trip home.'

In convoy, Hector and Jock drove off, and as soon as they'd got half way down the drive Camilla looked questioningly at Philip.

'Yes, I got them,' he replied, indicating the boot of her car. 'While I was helping Jock, I managed to slip two into your car.'

'Two *what*?' asked Lucy in an appalled voice.

'You've guessed it,' Camilla replied succinctly. 'I want an independent post-mortem carried out because, in spite of everything, I didn't believe a word Hector Ross said.'

Danny didn't come back to the house in Wyvel Street that day. Poppy, having watched him on television and thinking his performance brilliant, fell asleep again when the programme ended, and awoke at ten o'clock to find herself stiff, cold and alone. Struggling out of bed, she put on an old sweater of Danny's and decided to go down to the kitchen to make herself a cup of instant coffee. The house was quiet. Those who worked were out and those who didn't slept, mostly from hangovers incurred by taking various substances the previous night. A sweetish smell lingered on the landing outside Danny's room. Mark, in the room next door, was growing his own dope in a cardboard box lined with silver foil, with the aid of a naked electric bulb suspended through a hole in the lid. Sometimes Poppy worried that the heat would make the box catch fire, but Danny said knowledgeably there was no chance of that. The box was too big.

Down in the kitchen, a whirlwind of activity had been and gone since she'd made Danny's tea at dawn, leaving in its wake stacks of dirty dishes, pans, and an overflowing dustbin full of unmentionable garbage. Wrinkling her nose, and for a split second wishing she was in the kitchen at home, which Mrs Maitland kept so clean you'd think it was going to be photographed for *House & Garden*, she decided to slip home for a bath and a change of clothes. Maitland thought she'd been spending the weekend with friends in Gloucestershire; at least that's what she'd told him, and whether he believed her or not was his problem as far as she was concerned. She was sixteen and could do as she liked.

Leaving a note on Danny's bed to say she'd be back later, Poppy caught the underground at Whitechapel, and, changing trains at King's Cross, arrived at Hyde Park Corner shortly after noon. Conspicuous in a strange assortment of clothes, including an Indian top and the droopy hat she'd worn to Malcolm's funeral, she cut an eccentric figure as she walked through the staid streets of Knightsbridge. Elderly ladies turned and stared and passing shopgirls tittered. A bus conductor nearly lost his balance as the 74 bus swung past on its way to Fulham and he spotted Poppy striding along on her thin legging-covered legs. But Poppy didn't notice, so wrapped up was she in her own thoughts.

When she arrived in Wilton Crescent, her pace quickened until she reached the house. Then she ran up the marble front steps and let herself in.

'Maitland?' Her voice floated across the hall. He emerged from the dining-room where he was polishing the long table.

'Good morning, Miss Poppy.'

'I'm back . . . from Gloucestershire.' There was a defiant tilt to her chin, an arrogant this-is-my-house-I'll-do-as-I-like air about her, but all Maitland saw was a ludicrous-looking waif-like girl clutching her army surplus holdall, daring him to challenge her.

'I hope you had a pleasant time, Miss Poppy,' he enquired smoothly.

'Yes, thank you.'

His grave expression told her he knew she was lying. Poppy turned away and started to climb the stairs.

'Will you be in for luncheon, Miss Poppy?' Maitland asked with exquisite politeness.

She paused, her hand on the banister, her nose raised delicately, sniffing the air like a cat who suddenly notices a whiff of fish. Maitland's mouth gave the tiniest twitch. Mrs Maitland was baking a steak and kidney pie and there was the most delicious aroma of meat and thick gravy emanating from the basement kitchen.

Poppy shrugged. 'As I'm here I might as well stay for lunch, I suppose,' she said with exaggerated nonchalance. Suddenly her mouth was watering and she realised she hadn't eaten properly for three days. Vegetarian food didn't count. 'Perhaps I'll have a bath after lunch,' she added grandly. Danny need never know she'd eaten meat, she reflected. And she hadn't actually promised not to . . .

'Very well. I'll serve lunch on a tray in the study, in five minutes.'

'Don't bother, Maitland,' she called down as she hurried on up the stairs. 'I'd rather have it in the kitchen with you and Mrs Maitland.'

Since the death of her grandfather, the Maitlands had felt increasingly sorry for Poppy, seeing her more as a victim of neglect than anything else. With Malcolm Elliott's death she'd lost the last of her male relatives. There were not even any uncles or cousins to lend their support and act as a protective guiding force. There was only Camilla, and in Mrs Maitland's view she'd become so wrapped up in her own life and career since the death of Poppy's father that it seemed she had little time for her daughter.

Two hours later, well fed, bathed, and changed into another no less incredible collection of clothes, Poppy was about to leave the house to go back to Whitechapel where surely Danny would be waiting for her now, when the phone rang. Maitland answered it, and she heard him talking to her mother.

'Yes, madam,' she heard him say. 'A little while ago, just in time for luncheon in fact. Yes, madam. I'll get her for you.'

Poppy, realising they were talking about her, signalled to the butler that she did not wish to speak.

'I've already told Mrs Eaton you're here,' he said with such firmness that Poppy wilted. Maitland could be very determined at times.

'Okay,' she said sullenly, 'but I've got to rush.'

'How's everything, darling?' Camilla was asking over the phone. 'Did you have a nice weekend at the Foresters'?'

'Yup.'

'And you're well?'

'Yup.'

There was an awkward pause but Poppy had no intention of being communicative.

'We're staying near Grandpa's house. I've left the phone number with Jean, and Maitland has it. Shall I give it to you in case you need to get hold of me?' Camilla asked.

'I can get it from Maitland,' Poppy replied coolly.

'Very well. Lucy sends you her love.'

'Right.'

'I'm not sure when I'll be home, Poppy. Edith isn't here and everything's a bit complicated, but I'll talk to you in a few day's time again.'

'Okay.'

'All right, darling?'

'Yup.'

'Take care of yourself.'

'Okay.'

Then Camilla added the phrase she'd always used at the end of a phone conversation when Poppy had been a child.

'Love you lots.'

'Okay. 'Bye.' Poppy's tone was more uninterested than ever.

''Bye, sweetheart.'

Mother and daughter hung up, divided by a great deal more than geographical separation, and Poppy had no intention of bridging the gap.

'I'm off now,' she shouted down to the basement a moment later.

Maitland came trotting up the stairs, straightening his tie. 'Will you be in for dinner this evening, Miss Poppy?'

For a split second a vision of the lamb cutlets she'd seen in the larder, grilled with tomatoes and served with creamed potatoes, followed by one of Mrs Maitland's special apricot flans, caused Poppy to hesitate, but then a deep stirring like the plucking of the strings of a musical instrument caught at her groin as she thought of Danny, and she knew she had to be with him.

'No, thanks. I'm dining with friends,' she replied with unusual politeness. She saw the disappointment in Maitland's eyes, but all she could really think about was Danny and the way he looked when he was aroused. She glanced at her watch. She'd been away from Wyvel Street for nearly four hours. Now she could hardly wait to get back.

But Danny wasn't there waiting for her as she'd hoped, and he didn't come back until the following morning. Lonely, scared at being on her own in a houseful of sometimes violent people, and consumed with jealousy and worry as to where he might be, Poppy spent a sleepless night in his bed.

It was dawn the following morning when he reappeared, striding into the room still in the leather gear he'd worn for his television appearance. For a moment he seemed surprised to

142

see her, lying exactly where he'd left her twenty-four hours before. Then he scowled.

'For fuck's sake, Pops, why are you wasting your time, staying in bed when there's work to do? Don't you realise you ought to be getting in more money for our funds? You should be selling T-shirts, and handing out leaflets, not bleeding well staying in bed all the time!'

Poppy, who was keyed up to fever pitch by anxiety and lack of sleep, burst into tears.

'I . . . I was waiting for you,' she sobbed.

'Well, you needn't wait any longer, because I'm going out again,' he snapped.

'Can't I come with you?' She wiped her eyes with the back of her hand, smudging the makeup she'd failed to remove the previous night.

'No, you fucking can't! I've got people to see.' He was rummaging around in a cardboard box as he spoke, looking for something.

'Why can't I come with you?' She'd got out of the bed and was straightening her clothes, running her fingers through her long wispy hair, trying to make herself presentable.

'Because I don't want you to. Get it? Go and do something useful, for Christ's sake, instead of always hanging around me like a bitch on heat.'

After Camilla had spoken to Poppy on the phone, she put through her daily call to Jean to pick up any messages and to give any necessary instructions. It was a quiet time of year at Eaton & Eaton and it did not take them long to attend to the business.

'I do have some mail from your home,' Jean added. It was one of Maitland's jobs when Camilla was out of town, to collect any letters from Wilton Crescent and take them to the office, where Jean had instructions to open everything, even of a personal nature.

'Anything interesting?' Camilla asked.

'The insurance company are refusing to meet your claim in full for the silver that was stolen.'

'How much are they giving me?'

'A third of the total value of the missing items. There is an accompanying letter, saying the police report of a break-in is inconclusive and therefore they don't feel able to meet the claim in full.'

'God! I wonder what happened? I must say, even I have no idea how it was stolen. Not that money is ever going to replace David's beautiful family silver.' She sighed.

'There's also a letter from your stepmother,' Jean continued.

'From Edith? What does she say?' Camilla asked eagerly. 'Thank goodness we've heard from her. Where is she?'

With prim efficiency, Jean read the letter over the phone. When she'd finished, Camilla thanked her and hung up, anxious to relay the news to Lucy and Philip. As usual they'd arranged to meet in the lobby of the Ballageich Hotel after breakfast, and dressing swiftly in a warm skirt and jacket, for the weather had broken and the summer warmth had gone from the atmosphere, she hurried down to find them already ensconced and Lucy well into her second cup of coffee.

'One of our problems has been solved anyway,' she announced, as she sat on the sofa beside Philip, who was attempting to read a newspaper in spite of his mother's persistent talking. He put down the *Daily Mail* instantly and turned his attention to Camilla.

'You mean you've had the result of the post-mortems?' he asked. The previous afternoon he'd driven over to Oban and left the carcasses of a young bitch and a three-month-old puppy with the large veterinary practice in the town.

'No. You're phoning them later, aren't you?'

'Yes, so what's happened?'

'You look excited. What is it?' Lucy observed.

'I've had a letter from Edith.'

'Well? What does she say?'

'She explains she decided to shut up the house and go abroad

144

for a spell to try and get over Daddy's death. Of course when it was written she'd no idea I planned to visit Creagnach. She speaks of visiting Venice and then going to Florence, but she doesn't say when she'll be back, merely that she hopes I'll understand her need to get away and how everything is a painful reminder of Malcolm at the moment. She is missing him terribly, I'm afraid.'

Lucy's voice was soft. 'Poor woman. How sad. I can quite understand how she feels.'

'So can I. It's what I longed to do myself when David died, but with Poppy to look after, and the company to see to, I never had the chance.'

'But what does she say about the dogs?' Philip queried.

'She doesn't refer to them at all.'

'Isn't that rather strange? Weren't they her *raison d'être*? Wasn't it because of them she and your father came up here to live in the first place?'

Camilla nodded. 'Yes, it was.'

'Then I think I know what's happened,' said Lucy. 'She's left someone in charge of the dogs, and they've either neglected them so they died of distemper or even starvation, or they've poisoned the lot of them in order to be rid of the responsibility.'

Philip looked at his mother doubtfully. 'But what happens when Edith gets back?' Then he turned to Camilla. 'That's a thought! She won't know anything's happened to them, will she? Did she leave an address where she could be contacted?'

'No. Jean said she wrote on plain paper because she's touring around. There's no way I can contact her.'

'My God, she'll get a terrible shock when she returns. Now that the carcasses have been removed, would you like me to clean up the kennels and thoroughly disinfect them?' Philip asked.

'I wouldn't dream of letting you do anything so awful,' Camilla exclaimed. 'I'll get one of Daddy's ex-gardeners to do it. Meanwhile, though, could you ring the vet in Oban?'

Philip glanced at his watch. 'Yes. The results should be

through by now.' Rising, he strode over to the phone booth, a strong muscular figure, fit and agile and eager to be doing something useful. Full of energy, he hated sitting around.

Lucy looked at Camilla and smiled. 'Do you get the feeling,' she asked gently, 'that we've been making mountains out of molehills? I honestly believe, having come up here, that you're going to have to face the fact your father *was* suffering from paranoia, you know.'

Camilla looked at her oldest and dearest friend, a person who would always be straight and whom she could trust, and yet she felt deeply hurt.

'Do you really think so, Lucy?' she asked wretchedly.

'I do.' Lucy nodded vigorously. 'Think about it. Think about what Geoffrey told you and what Hector Ross said. You may not like the vet, but that's beside the point. Why should he lie? Think about the letter you've just had from Edith. Everything points to the fact that people who were fond of your father covered up the fact he was ill, because they didn't want to upset him, or you either!'

Camilla hesitated. 'I suppose so,' she said doubtfully, 'but I just can't accept it.'

'It's no disgrace you know, my dear.' Lucy reached across and put her gold-ringed hand on Camilla's arm. 'Mental illness is no longer regarded with the horror it used to be.'

Camilla shook her head as if to rid herself of binding threads that were imprisoning her thought process. 'Oh, I know, Lucy. I know. It's not that. I can't explain . . . but Daddy and I were so close and the fact that I may not have realised he was mentally ill upsets me. Then, contrarily, I feel dreadful about doubting his word. Supposing everything he said *is* true? How awful if we brush it all aside as paranoia on his part when in fact he was trying to warn me about something!'

Lucy looked sympathetic. 'I can understand how you feel.'

At that moment Philip came back. The two women looked up at him inquiringly.

'It's as you thought,' he said enigmatically to Camilla.

'What? They died of natural causes?' Lucy asked.
'No. They were poisoned by massive doses of strychnine!'

Chapter Nine

The heart of Ardachie lies in its small but busy harbour where the fishing boats put out to sea before there is even a pale flush in the east and the chill moon has slipped away behind the surrounding mountains, to return much later with their precious haul of mackerel, cod and haddock. All lanes and paths lead down to the old quayside, including the one meandering narrow road that runs through the village as it follows the coastline from Oban down to Minard Point. Because they are off the main road, few tourists ever discover the tight little clutch of granite stone cottages, the one post office-cum-general store, the bakery or the inn, which has a dusty sign in one window advertising Bed and Breakfast. Surrounded by small farm holdings, which supply most of the produce needed, Ardachie is a self-contained village, isolated, introverted, self-sufficient.

Driving through it now on their way from the Ballageich Hotel, Camilla could understand the resentment her father's arrival might have caused. Creagnach, situated on the far side of Ardachie and set in its own grounds, had belonged to the previous owner's family for three hundred years; no doubt the late laird's ancestors had originally owned the entire village and fishing port as well. McVean was a distinguished Scottish clan, and Hamish McVean would no doubt have been highly respected by the locals. And then along came Malcolm Elliott, successful retired London banker, with an English wife and a kennel full of Alsatian dogs whose barking no doubt disturbed the peaceful atmosphere.

'Isn't that the place where your father's mail was supposedly confiscated?' Philip asked, as they passed the post office and general store, selling everything from newspapers and potatoes to shampoo and paraffin.

'Yes. Looks so innocent too, doesn't it? As if the most exciting thing that could possibly happen is that they'd run out of picture postcards! Geoffrey said they were all very friendly and helpful,' she added, in a strained voice. It was so difficult to reconcile herself to the conflicting reports she was getting. One minute she found herself trying to get used to the idea that her father had imagined the whole business, and then the next minute something happened that proved without doubt that he'd been telling the truth. Something *was* going on in Ardachie. The question now was, what?

'Do you think Edith is involved?' Lucy asked, from the back seat of the Mercedes where she was sitting. 'After all, wasn't she the one who wanted to come up here to live? Didn't you say that the minute she saw Creagnach she insisted your father buy it?'

'That's true,' Camilla replied thoughtfully, 'but what would her motives have been? Why should she get Daddy to live here, in order to get the village to persecute him and then poison her dogs? It doesn't make sense.'

They were all still trying to come to terms with the chilling results of the post-mortem. Whoever had poisoned the dogs meant business.

'You've got to face the fact, though, that Edith is now a very rich widow,' Philip pointed out. 'Presumably Malcolm left Creagnach to her and he'll have made sure she's well provided for, won't he?'

'He's left the house to her for life, and then it comes to Poppy and me,' Camilla explained. 'He also left a trust fund which provides her with an income, but is dissolved on her death, the capital then to be shared between Poppy and me. He worked it all out very carefully when he remarried, and it's a very fair will.'

They were nearing the entrance to Creagnach and Philip slowed down. 'What do we do now?' he asked.

'I'd like to stay up here a bit longer and try and find out what the hell's going on,' Camilla admitted.

'So would I,' Lucy rejoined stoutly. 'It would be too maddening to leave now with so many questions unanswered. You don't have to rush back to London, do you, Philip?'

His tanned face broke into an attractive grin. 'And deprive myself of your company, Mum? No, of course I can stay.' Then his eye caught Camilla's, making him realise how much he'd like to prolong this trip. He'd never before met anyone as fascinating as she was and he longed to know what made her tick. She seemed tough and yet vulnerable, warm and at the same time aloof. And always, always her sharp intelligence challenged him to keep up with her. It seemed to him as if underneath her strong exterior there was someone longing to be conquered.

In silence he turned in at the drive of Creagnach and, parking the car in front of the right-hand pavilion, switched off the engine. Then he turned and looked directly at Camilla in the seat beside him. Her hair was windblown and whipped like dark honey around her shoulders, and her apricot-coloured sweater reflected warmly in the sun, making her face glow.

'Where do we start?' he asked quietly.

'Let's go inside and work out a plan of action,' she replied, looking back at him, her lips slightly parted in the hint of a smile.

The front door opened easily, swinging back to reveal the flagstoned hall which was now filled with brilliant sunshine. Burnished copper bowls and the polished panelling and furniture gave it a sparkling air and Lucy looked around exclaiming: 'How different it feels today! There's quite a happy atmosphere about the place, isn't there?'

'It feels warmer, much better,' Camilla agreed. 'It's probably because we've had the dogs taken away. That ghastly sight in the kennels was enough to cast a blight over the most perfect place.' She walked round the square hall, opening wide the doors to the library and dining-room and drawing-room, so that more light from the rooms flooded the hall. 'Philip, could you open a few windows, please?' she asked. 'It would be nice to get some fresh air flowing through the rooms.' She could see now why her father and Edith had loved Creagnach so much. There was a feeling of tradition about the place, a sense of history, of timelessness, and the knowledge that whilst this building might have stood here for three hundred years, the spectacular view from the main windows, of majestic mountains towering above the waters of the Firth of Lorne had been there for thousands of years. I, too, could be happy here, she thought, with sudden understanding, and at that moment felt her father's presence and knew she had never been closer to him.

'Camilla?'

She turned to Philip who had spoken her name. He was holding something in his hand, looking at it strangely, his brow furrowed.

'What is it?'

'A . . . a note . . . it's addressed to you . . . I just spotted it in the letterbox.' He held it out to her, a sheet of white paper on which someone had scrawled a message. The handwriting was uneducated, immature. A scratchy pencil had been used and the paper was the cheap variety used for memo pads.

Slowly, disbelievingly, Camilla read it aloud to the others.

Get you away and go home as fast as you can. No good will come if you stay. You'll not be wanting to end up like your father and the others. This is from a well-wisher.

There was a moment's silence, and then Lucy spoke.

'Well! What do you make of that?'

'It's a warning all right,' said Philip. 'I wonder who the hell sent it?'

Camilla remained silent, her mind racing.

'Who knows we're here?' she asked at last. 'Only Hector Ross and his son, Alastair!'

'And Jock, the vet's assistant,' Philip reminded her. 'He was a strange young man, I thought. Hardly spoke. When I offered to give him a hand he merely said, in his broad Scots accent: "If ye want." I tried, but I couldn't get anything out of him.'

'I think we should do three things,' Camilla said decisively, leading the way into the library and going to sit at Malcolm's desk. Lucy followed, seeing a glimpse for the first time of the hard-hitting chairman of Eaton & Eaton; a woman who was capable of running a multi-million pound company, of hiring and firing a large staff; a woman who appeared unafraid of anything.

'What should we do?' Lucy asked.

'Firstly, we must go to the police and report the findings of the post-mortem, and also show them this letter. Secondly, we must tell Hector Ross that the dogs *were* poisoned, and thirdly, it may be an awful thing to do in Edith's absence, but I intend to go through all the papers in this desk and anywhere else Daddy kept his stuff. Maybe he got anonymous letters, too, or perhaps he kept a diary? Something that will give us a clue.'

'That's a good idea,' Philip agreed. 'Shall I go to the police for you? I discovered the other evening that the nearest police station is in the next village . . . Caoldair. There isn't one in Ardachie. I could drive over now if you like, and show them that letter.'

'Thank you, Philip.' She turned to Lucy. 'Would you like to have the doubtful pleasure of phoning Hector Ross and telling him the dogs did *not* die of distemper?'

'My dear, I can hardly wait!' She threw back her head and laughed. 'I must hear what he says.'

Philip jumped to his feet. 'Let's get going then. I should be back within the hour, Camilla.'

She handed him the scrawled note. 'If you can find a place that has a photocopier it would be a good idea to make a few copies of this before you hand over the original to the police. I've got to the stage when I don't trust anyone.'

'Surely the police are straight?' Lucy remarked, in a shocked voice.

'Mum, you forget how long you've been in Hong Kong,' Philip protested laughingly. 'This is no longer the little old country you used to know. Things have changed.'

'What would you know about it? With your head stuck in Renaissance architecture at university?' she demanded.

He grinned in a way that made young women's hearts flutter, the skin crinkling into deep laughter lines, the eyes dancing with amusement. 'Ah, but I'm streetwise!' he teased. Then, with a wave of his hand, he was gone, striding across the hall and leaping down the front steps two at a time. A moment later they heard the car start and the swish of gravel as he drove off.

Lucy sighed as she looked across at Camilla. 'Do you ever feel the generation gap between yourself and Poppy?' she asked wearily. 'Sometimes Philip makes me feel so outdated, so old!'

Camilla laughed. 'Poppy and I are on different planets! We don't even talk the same language!'

'That's just a phase, as I've told you before. She's going through a beatnik phase, or is it punk? You see? Philip would laugh himself to death if he heard me talking now.' She shook her head with woeful good humour.

'I don't believe there's really a generation gap between you two,' Camilla observed. 'I feel he's our equal, perhaps because he's so mature.'

'My dear, he's an absolute child at times. He only seems mature because he puts on a grownup manner,' Lucy assured her. 'Now, where's the vet's telephone number?'

An hour later Camilla was still going through the drawers of Malcolm's desk, and whilst she discovered meticulously kept files for everything from insurance policies to receipts for dog food, there was nothing that gave a clue to the strange happenings at Creagnach during the past few months. There were no personal diaries, no memos, no records of the unpaid stud fees that had got 'lost' in the post; no letters of complaint from people whose enquiries about puppies had been 'confiscated'. No

154

copies of replies either from her father or Edith, apologising for their seeming laxity in dealing with enquiries. And yet there were detailed copies of all transactions carried out in connection with the dogs.

When she got to the folder marked 'Veterinary Accounts' she opened it eagerly. Surely this would show if Hector Ross's fees for professional services had risen at the time Malcolm claimed eighteen of his puppies had been poisoned? Her eyes scanned the invoices eagerly but nothing had been itemised so there was no way of knowing what the fees were actually for. They could have been for anything from attending a difficult whelping to de-worming, and they didn't seem to increase around the dates on which the puppies had died.

Camilla looked up from the papers she was examining to where Lucy was looking at some of the beautiful leatherbound books that lined the library shelves. Some of them Malcolm had bought with the house, others he had collected over the years.

'What time did you say Hector Ross was going to be home?' she asked.

'His son, at least I suppose it was the son who answered the phone, said he thought about three o'clock,' Lucy replied.

'If Philip gets back soon, why don't we drop in on the surgery on our way back to the hotel? I don't think there's much more we can do here. Let's see how Philip got on before we do anything else.'

'Good idea.'

At that moment they heard the car coming up the drive, and Camilla went into the hall to meet Philip.

'Well?'

He looked dispirited. 'It's a bloody farce, Camilla,' he replied, and his tone was full of anger and frustration. 'They just weren't interested in what I had to say,' he continued as they walked back into the library. 'The police at Caoldair said the letter was probably a practical joke!'

His mother's mouth fell open and she looked at Camilla with round eyes. 'A *joke*? They said it must be a joke?'

'That's right. The policeman said some of the lads in the village are real pranksters, though that wasn't the term he used, and that they enjoyed playing silly tricks on people.'

'Then why doesn't he put a stop to it?' Camilla demanded crisply. 'Honestly, some of these country policemen . . . they've no idea what the real world is like. What did he say about the strychnine? Was that supposed to be a joke too?'

Philip looked at her squarely. 'He said that as the vet had had all the dogs incinerated by now, we have no evidence . . .'

'Which vet did he mean? Hector Ross?' she cut in.

'Yes. He's the only vet around here and . . .'

'Let's get this straight.' Camilla resumed her seat at Malcolm's desk. Somehow after working for three years in an office she was unable to think clearly and logically unless she was seated at a desk. 'How does he know Hector Ross has had the dogs incinerated? Was he just presuming . . . or has he been in touch with Hector?'

'I don't know,' Philip replied. He thought for a moment. 'Actually, he spoke as if he already knew the dogs had been destroyed.'

'Except for the two you took to the other vet in Oban?'

'Yes.'

'Was he shocked that we'd taken two of the bodies to have a post-mortem performed on them?'

'He seemed very surprised,' Philip admitted. 'And then he grew angry. Asked what we were trying to prove? I said none of us was satisfied with the theory that they'd died from distemper.'

'What did he say then?' Lucy interjected.

'He growled something about townsfolk having no idea about country matters.' Philip recalled the thin, sharp-featured constable with his unsmiling face and beady eyes and sanctimonious way of talking.

'What did he mean by that?' Camilla asked.

'He went into lengthy descriptions of a certain paint that contains poison, and that if anyone is stupid enough to use this paint on stables, or kennels, or even rabbit hutches, and the animal

156

in question then licks or chews the painted surface, it could poison them and they could die,' he said grimly.

'Is that possible? Could that be true?' gasped Lucy. 'What a dreadful thing! Why does the government allow this stuff to be marketed?' Her hands flew up to her face in horror as a thought struck her. 'My God, supposing one painted a nursery with it or a child's cot? Oh, that's dreadful!'

'It's also an absurd yarn if ever I heard one,' Camilla commented drily. 'I'll ring Jean this afternoon and get her to make some inquiries to see if such a paint even exists, but I think it's a lot of baloney.'

'But I've heard of cows dying because they licked paintwork in their barns,' Lucy pointed out, while Philip remained silent, deep in thought.

'That's lead, Lucy,' Camilla retorted. 'Anyway, paint manufacturers were forbidden to put lead in paint years ago. I think someone is trying to pull the wool over our eyes.'

There was a pause and then Philip spoke. 'So do I, Camilla,' he said quietly, looking directly at her. 'I think this constable, Robert MacKay, did everything he could to put me off the scent.' He turned to his mother. 'Camilla's right, you know. This whole business stinks!'

Hector Ross was still out on his rounds when they stopped at his house on the far side of Ardachie, on their way back to the Ballageich Hotel.

'Och, he'll no be back for a wee while yet,' said the pretty dark-haired young woman who answered the door.

Camilla had been told some time before, by Malcolm, that Hector Ross was a widower, but somehow she hadn't expected his housekeeper to be so young or so attractive. They were just about to leave when Camilla had a sudden thought.

'Is Alastair at home by any chance?'

The woman's manner changed, and her face seemed to fold into itself, the eyes becoming impenetrable slits, the mouth tight and unrelenting.

'What would ye be wanting with him?' she demanded coldly. 'He's not a vet, you know.'

Camilla was taken aback. 'I'm well aware of that, but we spoke on the phone a few days ago and I'd . . . well, I'd like to meet him.'

'He's no at home, either.' The accent had become thicker and now the woman seemed agitated, glancing over her shoulder as if she feared someone was coming up behind her from the darkened and gloomy rooms of the old shooting lodge that had become the vet's home and surgery.

'Very well,' Camilla replied calmly. 'But tell him I called, will you? And tell Mr Ross that I'll phone him later.'

For a split second the face seemed to open up again, the eyes widen and the mouth soften, as if with relief; but the voice remained tight.

'I'll tell them.'

'Thank you.' Camilla climbed back into the car, and without a backward glance drove off.

'She was strange wasn't she?' Lucy observed, who'd been watching through the open car window. 'As if she was scared of something.'

'She certainly didn't want me to see Alastair Ross and that's for sure!'

There were two messages waiting for them when they got back to their hotel. One for Camilla and one for Lucy.

'Mine's probably from Jean,' Camilla commented. 'We're waiting to hear if we've landed the Brooksby Buildings account. This might be it.' Eagerly she unfolded the sheet of paper the receptionist had given her. Then she drew in her breath sharply.

'What's the matter?' Philip asked.

'Look at this!' She was pale as she handed him the note.

Lucy, absorbed in reading her own message, looked up with a preoccupied expression. 'Oh dear, I've got to ring up Charlotte's headmistress. I hope to goodness there's nothing wrong!' Distracted, she hurried off to the phone booth across the lobby, not noticing the tense way Philip was looking at Camilla.

'Will you do as they ask?' he said. Camilla was standing still, a frown puckering her brow. She seemed to be in a reverie, not hearing him, not even noticing that Lucy had left them.

'What?' she asked absently.

'Will you do what they say?'

Her head shot up and her eyes were defiant. 'Certainly not! Of course I won't do as they say. Nothing, not even this,' she pointed to the message, 'is going to make me pack my bags and go home. Not now.'

'It could be dangerous to stay,' he pointed out. His eyes scanned her, to see if he could detect fear, but there was none.

'I owe it to my father.' She spoke undramatically and unemotionally. Just as she had taken over the running of Eaton & Eaton when David had been killed, because that had seemed the right thing to do, so it seemed to her to be her duty to uncover and expose whatever activities had caused her father such misery.

At that moment Lucy came hurrying back, unaware anything was wrong and fussed by her own bad news.

'Would you believe it? Charlotte's fallen over playing tennis and broken her arm. The headmistress says she's got to be sent home because it's her right arm and she can hardly do anything for herself.' Flushed and brimming over with maternal anxiety, she ran her hand nervously through her hair. 'I'm going to have to go back to London, Camilla. I'm terribly sorry, my dear, but there's nothing else for it! Anthony's away fishing, and Henrietta's in Paris, and she'd be useless with Charlotte anyway. I'll have to leave right away.'

'Of course you must go,' Camilla agreed. 'I'm so sorry. What a worry for you. I hope Charlotte's not in too much pain?'

'I didn't speak to her myself, but they want me to collect her first thing in the morning.' Lucy turned to her son. 'Philip, you can drive me down to Stuart Hall, can't you, to pick her up? It's only in Surrey, so it shouldn't take long.'

He looked apologetic but there was a determined set to his

jaw. 'I'm sorry, Mum, I can't. Camilla's had another anonymous message and . . . well . . . I must stay and help her find out what it's all about.'

Lucy looked completely astonished and Camilla, taken by surprise but touched by his offer, cut in quickly.

'No, Philip, you must go and help your mother bring Charlotte home from school.'

'You can't be left here on your own. You don't know what sort of danger you might be in!' He handed the note Camilla had received to Lucy. 'Read this, Mum. It's a much stronger warning than the one we found at the house.'

Lucy scanned the note briefly.

You have been warned before. Mind your own business and stop meddling in what doesn't concern you. Leave now and no harm will befall you but I can't say what will happen if you stay.

'My God, who sent this?' she asked aghast.

'I don't know. The receptionist who took the message over the phone, gave me a very funny look when she handed it to me,' Camilla replied. 'She said a woman had called to speak to me, and I thought it must be Jean, but obviously it wasn't.'

'You can see, Mum, that Camilla can't stay here on her own,' Philip reasoned.

'Of course she can't,' Lucy said briskly. 'She can't stay here at all! It's courting disaster to pursue this any more, Camilla. You must come away with us, tonight.'

'No, I can't. I have to stay. I have to find out what's going on. But Philip doesn't have to stay with me. I'm quite prepared to go it alone, at least until the end of next week when I have to return to work. By that time I should have got to the bottom of this whole affair.'

'Oh God, you're being stubborn, just like you were when you were a girl,' Lucy groaned. 'For goodness' sake, come back to London, Camilla. You're mad to stay!'

'Look,' Philip intervened, 'we'll be here all night if we go on like this. If Camilla wants to stay, then I'll stay with her. But if we're all going back to London, then we'd better get a move on.'

'That makes sense,' Lucy said in a resigned voice. 'What's it going to be?'

'I'm staying,' said Camilla firmly.

'Then so am I,' said Philip.

'All right then,' Lucy conceded. 'You stay on, but be careful. Don't do anything silly.'

Camilla and Philip looked at each other and then burst out laughing. Suddenly Camilla felt ridiculously young again. Lucy's motherly admonitions had reminded her of when she'd been a girl setting off on some adventure, while her mother cautioned her.

'I think we can look after ourselves, Lucy.'

'But it could be dangerous. You don't know what you're dealing with.'

'We'll be fine, Mum,' Philip reassured her. 'I'll go and find out about flights this evening. Why don't you both sit down and order tea and I'll make the arrangements for you?'

'Very well, darling.' Lucy still sounded reluctant, but Camilla sat down on the sofa in front of the fireplace and with a big smile on her face signalled for the waiter to take their order.

'Come on, Lucy,' she said cheerfully, 'it's my one chance of being a sleuth! I'm just so sorry you can't stay on too.'

'You will be careful, won't you?' Lucy pleaded. 'If these people are capable of poisoning all those dogs, they're capable of anything.'

'I know,' Camilla nodded. 'Philip needn't stay with me if you'd rather he didn't,' she added.

'Of course he must stay. You certainly can't be on your own.'

When Philip came back a few minutes later, he looked pleased with himself. 'All fixed,' he said breezily, dropping into one of the armchairs. 'I've booked you on the last flight to

Heathrow tonight. It leaves Glasgow at eight-fifteen, so if we leave here at five it should allow plenty of time for you to check in.'

'Thank you, darling. That's fine.' Lucy glanced at her watch. 'I'll go and pack as soon as we've had tea.'

Camilla leaned forward and spoke conspiratorially, in a low voice. 'We'll *all* go and pack when we've had tea, and we'll all check out of the hotel together!'

Lucy and Philip looked at her blankly. 'Why?'

'You and I aren't going anywhere, are we?' Philip asked.

'Yes, we are. We're going to pretend to obey the note I received. We'll leave here, drive to Glasgow, and as far as the locals are concerned we'll all be back in London by tonight.'

'But in reality?' Philip asked.

'I'll tell you my plan on the way to the airport.'

The darkness was so black, so solid, they could barely see what they were doing. Philip had turned off all the car lights as they approached Creagnach, and now, as he turned in at the gates, driving very slowly with only a mist-covered moon to guide him, he let the car roll soundlessly forward. They had taken the long way round so as to avoid going through Ardachie and alerting the village people of their presence. As soon as Philip stopped the car, Camilla jumped out and hurried over to the right-hand pavilion. Then she eased open the garage doors that were set into one of the ornamental arches and Philip drove the Mercedes forward, inch by inch, until it was swallowed up in the shadows. A moment later she had closed the doors again and was helping him unload the boot.

'We've got enough food here to feed an army!' he commented, heaving out a large cardboard box containing an assortment of groceries. She lifted out a second box.

'I don't intend we should starve, and this has to last us for as long as we're in hiding here. There can be no slipping out for a pound of butter now.'

Stealthily, feeling like intruders, they carried the boxes, and then half a dozen bulging plastic carrier bags, round to the back entrance of the house, which could not be seen from the road. When they'd finished Philip murmured, 'I'll get our cases now,' while Camilla fished in her handbag for the keys. When she'd unlocked the back door she crept into the kitchen and made sure the wooden shutters were firmly closed before she turned on the light. If they were to remain secretly at Creagnach, there must be no sign of the house being occupied. They were going to have to stay indoors during the day, and only venture out at night after it was dark to carry out their surveillance on the village, in the hopes of stumbling on something that would tell them what had been going on.

When Philip came back, dumping their cases on the floor, he looked flushed and excited.

'I must say this is all rather a laugh, isn't it!' he exclaimed with enthusiasm. Now that they were safely installed and no one had seen their arrival, Camilla felt herself relaxing.

'I feel as if we were doing something really wicked,' she smiled. 'Would you like some coffee?'

'Yes, please. Shall I start putting all this stuff away?' He indicated the supplies of food. They'd spent half an hour in one of Glasgow's largest supermarkets on their way to taking Lucy to the airport and Camilla had thoroughly enjoyed choosing what to buy. She'd scurried up and down the aisles, pushing a trolley, and grabbing whatever she thought would come in handy.

'Maitland usually does all the shopping,' she explained to an amazed Lucy. 'This is a novelty for me.'

'It will be even more of a novelty when you see how much you're spending,' her friend responded.

Camilla put on the kettle and then helped Philip fill the cold slate shelves in the old-fashioned larder that led off the kitchen.

As they sat drinking coffee, a companionable silence fell upon them. It was one o'clock in the morning and Camilla suddenly realised how tired she was.

'We'd better use a couple of the spare rooms,' she remarked, yawning. 'I hope the beds are made up, but we mustn't turn on any lights until I check the curtains tomorrow to see how thick they are.'

'Is that why you brought candles and matches as well as a couple of torches?' he asked.

Camilla nodded. 'You do think we're doing the right thing, don't you?'

'If we're to find out anything I think we've done the *only* thing,' he replied, 'and if they think we've all gone back to London, so much the better. They'll be off their guard. You'll also have time to search through your father's papers more thoroughly.'

She rose, stretching her arms above her head, a slim shapely woman in beige slacks and a thick navy-blue sweater, with her hair caught back in a ponytail held in place by a silk scarf. Philip, looking at her, marvelled at the difference from the Camilla he'd first met in London. She'd been an elegant-looking woman, a touch hard, slightly brittle. He'd liked her but had been rather scared by her formidable self-assurance. Now, as she stood before him, she seemed humanised by familiarity and shared interests, and secretly, he was glad that his mother had gone back to London. Now, he felt, he had more chance to get to know the real Camilla, the woman who hid behind the façade of super-efficiency. The person his mother had known and been fond of all her life. There were depths to her character, he felt sure, that no one had plumbed for years.

'I wish I'd been able to get hold of Edith to tell her I was going to be staying here,' she was saying with a troubled look. 'After all, it is her house and I feel rather dreadful to be snooping around. She may be furious when she finds out.'

'She'll only be angry if you discover she was lying and your father really was suffering from senile dementia – but that isn't at all likely now, is it?'

Camilla shook her head. 'I think we can rule that out. These threatening notes I've had have been real enough. It's not shadows we're chasing here but something very substantial. Daddy was as sane as you or I, and I believe he uncovered something and that is why the locals did everything they could to get him to leave.'

'I still don't understand why anyone would want to get rid of all the dogs, though. What harm were they doing?'

'With their acute hearing, I think they were disturbing whatever is going on. Although this house is on the edge of Ardachie, its grounds lead down to the Firth of Lorne and the inlet at the mouth of the harbour. Sound travels over water. One of the reasons I particularly wanted to stay on here is to keep a watch at night. I don't expect anything unusual to happen during the day.'

Philip raised his eyebrows, acknowledging her theory. 'Maybe smuggling, do you think? Drugs brought in by fishing boats?' He was silent, thinking about this for a moment, and then he gave a little snort. 'To Ardachie? Cocaine and heroin and that sort of thing, smuggled into Ardachie?' he added incredulously. 'It's a bit unlikely, isn't it?'

Camilla shrugged. 'I don't know. It would explain a lot, though.'

He fell silent again. Then he looked at his watch. 'D'you want to keep watch tonight?'

Camilla groaned. 'God, no! I don't know about you but I'm knackered. Let's go to bed, it's nearly two. We can talk about it in the morning.'

'Right.' He jumped to his feet, still full of energy. 'If I hear strange noises in the night, I'll let you know.'

'Thanks, and, Philip . . . thanks for staying with me. I was quite prepared to be here on my own, but I think I might have lost my nerve at the last minute.' She smiled self-deprecatingly. 'I'm very grateful to you for giving up your time like this.'

His smile was suddenly shy and a flush showed through the tan on his cheeks. Looking at him, Camilla was not only struck afresh by his good looks but also by his proximity. Standing only two feet away from her, he exuded a powerful sexuality. For a fleeting moment she was reminded of David when she'd first known him; that same easy masculine grace, the broad shoulders relaxed, the strong legs. Philip looked just as virile as David had done and for a moment she felt her own body stir with longing. It had been such a long time and David had been such a wonderful lover.

Philip spoke. 'I wouldn't have missed this trip for the world, Camilla.'

Chapter Ten

Danny's words had cut Poppy to the quick. It was love, over-whelming passion and devotion, that made her hang around waiting for him and not, as he'd so crudely put it, because she was like a 'bitch on heat'. She'd thought he loved her too, that their coming together had been a magical fusing of bodies and minds and spirits. Now it seemed she was mistaken.

Gathering her things together disconsolately, she then thought that perhaps Danny was only testing her! Perhaps he was pushing her as far as he could in order to prove to himself that she was the right girl for him! If that was the case, and she began to cheer up as the thought took root, then she must show him just how much she really loved him. She would go and do something useful. She would get more money out of her bank to give him. She would hand out leaflets and sell T-shirts and go and visit the homeless who slept in doorways in the Strand. She would tell them about Danny Fox, and give them hope by telling them help was on the way: Danny had a plan to rid the country of the Establishment, so that everyone would be equal and no one would suffer deprivation any more. Surely that would prove to him her feelings were genuine, her love sincere?

Poppy left a little note on his pillow, written with a cheap biro that left blobs of ink in its wake and smudged when she touched it. In it she said she'd gone to 'raise some more money for the cause' and would return later.

Within an hour she was back in Wilton Crescent to the delight of Maitland, who immediately suggested she might like to have lunch as Mrs Maitland had just made a shepherd's pie. Poppy heard herself accepting as she hurried up to her room to get her cheque book, kept hidden in one of her shoe boxes in case her mother were to see the large amounts she'd withdrawn in recent weeks. She daren't carry it about with her either, because if Danny were to find out she came from a rich background and the money she'd been giving him hadn't been stolen, but was hers, he'd certainly want to finish with her. When she thought about his attitude to rich people she wished she'd been born into a deprived family where they had to struggle for existence. If only that had been the case Poppy was sure Danny would have more respect for her. Not that he didn't respect her now, she reflected quickly. She'd told him her mother was an alcoholic, who abused her and knocked her about, and he'd felt quite sorry for her at the time. The fact that he translated his sympathy in a more carnal than emotional way nevertheless made her feel she 'belonged'.

'I'll be back in time for lunch,' she sang out, running down the stairs again a few minutes later. Maitland looked up at her, startled. Then he smiled. Miss Poppy without all that dreadful makeup, and in the simple black dress she'd worn to her grandfather's funeral, looked just like her old self, a sweet clean young girl from a good home – not a drop-out tart.

'Very well, Miss Poppy,' he beamed. 'Mrs Maitland is also running up an apple charlotte for your lunch. You can have it served with either clotted cream or custard.'

Poppy closed her eyes for a moment and experienced a wave of faintness. God, she'd had no idea she was so hungry. Eating was not a priority in Danny's list of pleasurable activities. A bit of salad, a few pulses, some bran and the odd piece of fruit was all he considered necessary in the way of nourishment.

'Oh! Oh, I think both,' she replied, and then felt guilty. How awful of her to be here in this opulent setting, about to enjoy a delicious lunch, when there were others who were lucky if they had a hot cup of tea and a borrowed fag. It made her resolve to take more out of the bank to give Danny than she'd originally intended. Five thousand pounds, perhaps? Better make it an odd figure or he'd ask too many questions. Maybe four thousand seven hundred and thirty pounds. She could tell him she'd stolen a handbag on the Underground, and that it contained a cheque book and bank card. Danny already knew she had quite a knack for forging other people's signatures because she'd told him that was how she'd done it before.

Poppy hurried up Wilton Crescent into Knightsbridge, feeling naked without her usual gear but aware that was how the bank clerks expected the daughter of Mrs Camilla Eaton to look. That first time, when she'd gone dressed in her usual garb, she had drawn suspicious looks that might have been her undoing. Now she was more careful. Of course, after lunch . . . and again her mind lingered longingly on the exquisite meal she was about to have . . . she'd change back into her usual leggings and floppy T-shirt and collection of waistcoats and shawls, because to visit Cardboard City looking like some flighty débutante would be enough to get herself lynched.

Poppy had heard the inhabitants of Cardboard City had been removed from the precincts of Waterloo Station, ousted from setting up nightly squats in shop doorways in the Strand and heavily discouraged by the police from dossing down in the main area of Victoria Station. Nowadays, she'd been told, they resided in boxes of all shapes and sizes, much to the embarrassment of the government and the local council, under the arches, near the Embankment, by the Festival Hall. Danny had expounded at large on the plight of these young people who were homeless, jobless, and did not qualify for social security. It was time, she decided, to find out for herself. Besides, her visit would really show Danny she was serious about the cause.

Stuffing nearly five thousand pounds in cash into a plastic shopping bag, she set off from Wilton Crescent. She didn't intend to hand it out willy-nilly, but a fiver here and a tenner there might make the difference between starvation and a hot meal. She'd have to say she'd stolen it, of course, and wanted to 'share her luck' with a few fellow vagrants. As she travelled on the tube she elaborated on her invented background. Danny had never asked her anything in detail, but some of the young men and women she was about to meet would surely want to swap experiences.

The thing that struck her first when she arrived was the stench. The gloomy arches, fifty feet wide and fifteen to twenty feet high in the centre, stank with the rancid smell of urine, decay and damp, overladen as one got closer to the collection of people, boxes and rags, by the acrid whiff of cigarettes. Although it was only half-past three in the afternoon, men and women already lay, as if to sleep, on their filthy pallets made of newspapers, huddled on this summer's day as if it was the middle of winter. White faces and blank expressions peered out of the shelter of cardboard boxes which had originally held ovens and dishwashers and fridge-freezers for the rich. Brand names were printed on the side in bold lettering, Hoover and Zanussi replacing what would have normally been Mons Repos or Dunroamin'. Despair hung heavy in the atmosphere. A baby cried in the arms of its young mother. Distant strains of music coming from a transistor rose and fell on a sudden sharp breeze coming up from the river.

Poppy stood uncertainly, aghast at the spectacle, not knowing what to say or do, embarrassed by her own wealthy background. She decided to go and talk to the mother first, who looked as if she needed a square meal.

'Hi!' Poppy squatted on the ground beside her. 'How old is your baby?'

Pale apathetic eyes met hers and the girl, who was about the same age as Poppy, spoke with unexpected sharpness.

'What's it to you?'

Taken aback, Poppy blinked, and then looked around trying to make up her mind about something.

As if she read her thoughts the girl snapped: 'You can't stay here. All the places are taken.'

'Oh! Really? It's all booked up?' Too late she realised she

sounded exactly like her mother when all the tables in her favourite restaurant had been taken. Blushing, she tried to retrieve the situation.

'I'm not staying, I'm just passing through. How long have you been living here?'

The eyes became less apathetic, turning to cunning slits, and Poppy realised the girl hadn't believed a word she'd said. Poppy knew it was because she was too clean, too well fed and too glossy-looking. Even her clothes didn't give her the necessary street-cred.

The young mother held her baby, who had fallen asleep, closer to her bony body as if protecting it from the likes of Poppy.

'Mind your own business,' she said tartly.

'Isn't there anything I can get you? I managed to pinch some money from a woman on the tube so I'm a bit flush for once.' Suddenly Poppy felt very shy and awkward, wishing she hadn't come.

'Don't you try your lady bountiful act with me! I don't want no bloody charity! It's the government who ought to be housing the likes of us! I'm not taking no bloody hand-outs! I'd rather survive on the streets than take charity!' The voice was harsh, the face harsher.

Retreating hurriedly, Poppy walked on, passing a dozen or so recumbent figures without a glance, so scared did she suddenly feel. Far from begging pathetically as she'd been led to believe, one look at all the hostile faces who now watched her progress made her realise that it could be here, under the damp arches by the Embankment, that the seeds of a revolution could be sown. Was this what Danny was planning? An uprising of the people, demanding their rights? It's what he'd always *said* was his aim, but hearing it from his lips in the warm confines of friendly pubs, when he inspired those around him with brave rhetoric, was very different from seeing what the stark reality of deprivation could lead to. This was ugly. The coarse brutal face of humanity, under these circumstances, became deprived of heroic glamour. Any uprising such as

Danny had talked about would be brutal.

Walking ever more quickly to the far end of the arches, out of the semi-darkness and into the light, Poppy suddenly felt a tap on the shoulder. Gasping, she turned round and found herself face to face with a very tall thin young man whose skin seemed stretched tightly over the bones of his face; his glittering eyes were red-rimmed, sunk deep into two hollows.

'Want some work?' he asked, without preamble.

'W-what kind of work?' Poppy stammered. It occurred to her at that moment that she'd been exceedingly foolish to come to this place with nearly five thousand pounds in a plastic bag.

He ignored her question. 'I bet I can get you more business than you can get for yourself, lovey.' He eyed her up and down from her blond wispy hair, bundled up into a tangle on top of her head, down to her thin legs and heavy Doc Martin shoes. 'I only take a small percentage, and I'd see you all right. No messing around, though. If I found you doing business on your own account, that pretty little face wouldn't be pretty no longer. Geddit? How much are you making at the moment?'

Poppy hadn't the foggiest idea what to say. She'd no idea how much a prostitute made in a night, far less in a week. She didn't even know what they charged. Suddenly she had a brainwave.

'I already have someone looking after me . . . er . . . my business,' she replied boldly.

'Not round here, you haven't,' he said suspiciously. 'What are you doing round here, anyway. This is my territory!'

Poppy quickly recovered herself, smiling in a friendly way but involuntarily clutching her plastic bag tighter. 'No, I'm from Ealing. I've been visiting a friend. I never work round here.'

The bloodshot eyes peered into her face and his breath had an unpleasantly sweetish smell. 'Mind you don't. What's in that bag?'

She hesitated, wondering what to answer. Should she say sandwiches? But he might be hungry and demand one. Perhaps she should say it was medicine for a sick friend! But then he might think she was referring to drugs and that would be worse. Clothes? It was a comparatively small bag, which would only have held a sweater. Maybe she should say it was kinky underwear for her job? No, that wasn't a good idea. He might want to see it.

'It's twenty thousand pounds from a bank raid I just did!' she retorted with a cheeky toss of her head.

For a second the skeletal face looked searchingly into hers, and then he opened his mouth, exposing yellowing teeth, and gave a roar of laughter.

'I like your style, lovey,' he said, nodding approvingly and still laughing. 'I bet you turn a good few tricks. Sure you don't want to move from Ealing so's I can look after you?'

'Leave Ealing! It would break my heart,' said Poppy, with mock solemnity.

'Be seeing you then!' With a wave of his hand he was off, thin legs striding away in flapping blue jeans, bomber jacket hunched up under his chin.

Poppy didn't hang around. Walking as quickly as she could, because running would have looked suspicious, she reached the main road just as an empty taxi was approaching.

'The Whitechapel Road,' she told the driver when she'd seated herself in the back.

He looked doubtfully at her shabby clothes. He'd also seen her emerging from the arches.

'Sure you've got enough for the fare?' he grunted.

'Yes.' Poppy grinned, clutching the five thousand pounds to her chest. 'I've got enough money, thanks.'

Philip was up early their first morning at Creagnach, creeping around the house so as not to disturb Camilla, but also aware that if their presence was to remain undetected, it would mean keeping quiet most of the time. Radio and television would have to be listened to with the volume turned down; there must be no chopping of wood or slamming of doors. Even though the road was several hundred yards away at the end of the drive, and the mouth of the estuary which led to the harbour only at the bottom of the meadow, it was possible villagers had cause to cross the land. He and Camilla were going to have to lie low.

Feeling like a fugitive, he slipped into the kitchen and eased open one of the wooden shutters. Immediately sunlight flooded in, almost blinding him. Then he peered out, getting his bearings now that it was daylight. From the kitchen windows, which were down the right-hand side of the house, he could see the woody area where pine, spruce and birch grew in profusion. From the village the house could not be seen because the trees grew on a gently rising hillock. The main rooms, which ran along the back of Creagnach, looked straight out to the Firth of Lorne and were more exposed to passing fishing boats, commanding as they did a clear view of the still waters. In the distance were the mountains of Mull. Lawns, sweeping down to the water, glistening with dew on this sunny morning, lay invitingly green, but on the left the now deserted kennels stood bleakly. If this was my house, Philip thought as he moved silently about the kitchen, I'd have those kennels torn down, burnt, all traces removed so that in time wild flowers and heather could mend the wound that must forever mark that patch of soil.

Putting on the kettle, he got a mug from the dresser and made coffee, deciding to let Camilla sleep on. The past few days had been so stressful for her he knew she must be exhausted although she wouldn't admit it. In fact he felt very sorry for her because she'd had such a tough time for the past few years, and wondered vaguely as he made his way into the library why she hadn't remarried. It was a waste of a beautiful woman, he reflected, to live as she lived, just for her work. Lucy had told him Camilla didn't even have a boyfriend and although he believed her, he wondered at the reason. Surely men must pursue her? Or hadn't she time for them? And it suddenly struck him, as he stood in the library window, looking at the sun-bathed landscape, that she looked as if she was capable of great passion. There was something in her eyes and the husky warmth of her voice . . . I wonder when she last had sex? he asked himself.

Camilla awoke with a start, wondering where she was for a moment, not recognising the pretty pale blue bedroom with its blue and white patterned chintz curtains. Sitting up with a jerk, she couldn't remember ever seeing this room in her life before . . . and then it all came back to her; leaving the Ballageich Hotel the previous day, and creeping into Creagnach late last night. She glanced at her slim gold wristwatch. Ten o'clock! She'd no idea it was so late. Slipping out of bed, she took the large shoulder bag she'd left on the dressing table back to bed with her, and then, arranging herself comfortably, withdrew the one thing she'd sworn she'd never possess but which Philip had persuaded her to buy in a shop in Glasgow airport the previous evening. It was a mobile phone. She could see the sense in having it now, of course, but there was something about a mobile phone that made her feel she would never have a moment's peace again. She dialled the offices of Eaton & Eaton, as she did every morning, and a moment later was talking to Jean.

'There's nothing much to report, Mrs Eaton. The contract for Pretty Primrose lingerie has been renewed for another year, as you'd predicted, and Logan's Garden Furniture want to set up a meeting with you as soon as you return as they're thinking of increasing their advertising budget. That's about it. There are no problems. Are you having a good rest?'

'Jean, I'm no longer at the Ballageich Hotel. It's a long story but I've moved into my father's house, with Philip Hamilton to keep me company. His mother had to return home yesterday.'

'Is everything all right?'

'So far we're fine. I'll give you my phone number . . .'

'I already have the number of your father's house.'

'Ah, but you don't know what I've done,' Camilla said in a teasing voice. 'I have another number to give you.'

'You mean . . .?'

Camilla laughed outright. 'Yes, I've actually, at last, bought myself a mobile phone.'

'After all this time!' Jean was laughing too. 'That's fantastic. Now I can contact you at any time.'

'That's what I've always been afraid of,' Camilla said, wryly. 'This is my number.' She gave her secretary the ten digits. 'I'll talk to you again tomorrow.'

Then she got out of bed again, and went to shower in the adjoining bathroom. On the one occasion she'd stayed with her father and Edith she'd occupied another room, further along the corridor, and at the time she'd admired the flower theme her stepmother had chosen for the guest rooms. This one was Bluebell, the room Philip was in she'd called Sunflower, and the others were Camellia, Rose and Wistaria. Each was decorated in the colour of the flowers, and each had appropriately patterned fabrics. At the time her father had planned to do a lot of entertaining, hoping Poppy would be a regular visitor and encouraging her to bring her friends to stay, as well. Camilla had planned to stay more often, too, but somehow the weeks had grown into months, and the time had passed, and she was always too busy. Now Camilla regretted it. If only . . . the words pulsed through her head as she stood in the shower. If only things had worked out differently, what fun they could all have had at Creagnach. Lucy and Anthony could have come to stay with their children, and she and Poppy might have shared the Camellia room, which had twin beds, and they'd have gone on picnics with her father . . . Suddenly she pressed the face flannel to her face to stem the flow of imminent tears. It could all have been so wonderful, they could all have had such a good time together, and at that moment she realised the depth of her desolation at Malcolm's death. She missed him so much she wondered for a moment how she was going to manage without him. She missed his rich golden voice and the merry understanding twinkle of his eyes. She missed his bear-like hugs, and the fact he was always there.

Forcing herself to stay calm, she reminded herself why she was here. This was no time for tears and regrets. She must be positive. She'd come to Creagnach to find out what had happened and that's what she would do.

Ten minutes later, in white linen skirt and a navy blue top, she hurried downstairs and met Philip in the hall as she was coming out of the library.

'Hi!' she greeted him gaily. No one looking at her would realise that fifteen minutes before she'd been crying like a little girl longing for her daddy. 'God, I never meant to sleep so late. Have you had breakfast?'

Philip smiled at her, thinking how fresh and rested she looked compared to the previous night.

'I made myself some coffee. Shall I get you some?'

She looked impish. 'I fancy eggs and bacon and tons of toast, actually,' she admitted.

'Great! Shall I cook some for us both?'

'Supposing we share the cooking?'

He nodded in agreement, and laughing companionably they went to the kitchen. While he grilled the bacon, she lightly fried some eggs. Philip sliced a crusty loaf and got out the butter and marmalade.

'This is much more fun than Maitland's breakfasts,' Camilla observed. 'Then I have just a chilled grapefruit, while Poppy wrecks one of his beautiful pyramids of fruit.'

'Why do you only have a grapefruit?'

She patted her hips. 'Anything to keep from getting fat! Never mind, this is a bit of a holiday for me. I'll fast when I get back to London to make up for it.'

'I don't like women to be too thin,' Philip remarked, eyeing her with appreciation. Suddenly Camilla found herself blushing under his scrutiny.

'Not much chance of that!' she said lightly, pouring out the coffee into two large cups.

In silence, he turned over the bacon to grill it on the other side. Tension crackled in the air between them. They were both embarrassed by the intimacy of the way he'd looked at her and neither knew quite what to say to restore the atmosphere to one of camaraderie. It was as if they'd stepped over a boundary line, but having stepped back again, could not forget what they'd seen.

'So what are the plans for today?' Philip asked at last, not looking at her.

'I'm going to go through everything of Daddy's again, even his collection of books in case he's stuck something between them. I'm determined to find some evidence.'

'What about Edith's things? Has she got a desk?' Philip flipped the bacon on to two plates as he spoke, then he added the fried eggs. 'You might find something of hers that would be interesting.'

'Philip, I don't really think I can. I feel bad enough about going through Daddy's stuff when she's not here, but I really don't think I can start riffling through Edith's papers in her absence.' Relieved that the moment of awkwardness between them seemed to have passed, she continued: 'If we could only get a lead, find out who is behind this whole thing!'

'I think I'll go up to the top of the house after we've had breakfast, to get my bearings. I might even be able to see the village from one of those loft windows.'

'That's a good idea, as long as you're not seen.'

'I wish we'd brought a pair of binoculars with us,' he observed.

'Daddy had some for bird watching. I think they're on the table in the window in the library. More coffee?' she held up the pot.

'Oh, great. Thanks.'

In companionable silence once again, they finished breakfast and then Camilla cleared away while Philip went in search of the binoculars. That moment, when he had appraised her with obviously approving eyes, lingered in her mind, making her feel strangely jumpy. Only Geoffrey had looked at her like that in recent times. Then she shrugged and gave a little self-deprecating grimace. It was nice to know, even though it meant nothing, that she hadn't lost all her sex appeal.

An hour later, having gone through all Malcolm's desk drawers again, she had still found nothing of interest. Then she began going along the rows of books that filled the shelves from ceiling to floor, along two walls. Her father had a wonderful collection of old leatherbound and gold-tooled volumes, nearly two thousand in all, and it struck her she'd never be able to do more than a superficial search unless she was going to be here for weeks. It was a hopeless task. She went back to the desk and sat down behind it again feeling disheartened. What was she going to do now? Wait until nightfall so they could get out of the house and see what was going on down by the quayside? Whilst idly wondering how she and Philip were going to pass the day, her eyes strayed to a newspaper cutting propped up on her father's desk. It looked as if it were from a local newspaper . . . but why had Malcolm pasted it to a piece of stiff card and propped it up behind the card on which he'd written his list of useful telephone numbers?

Camilla picked it up, and it was only then that she realised it was a timetable of the local tides. Certain times were underlined, and beside them Malcolm had written something in his small neat handwriting. It was barely decipherable, but grabbing the silver-handled magnifying glass that lay by his inkwell, she took the clipping to the window where the light was better. Being careful to keep out of sight, in case a fishing boat passed the bottom of the meadow on its way out to sea, she peered at the writing. Suddenly her heart quickened its pace! This was the first piece of evidence she'd discovered that might prove her theory. There were only a few words she could make out, but they were 'cargo', 'activity', and, more clearly, 'fourth time this week'.

What had Malcolm referred to? Smuggling? At times when the tide was right? That's what it looked like. Elated, she rushed out of the library, up the two long flights of stairs to the attic, where she arrived panting. Philip was crouched by one of the small dormer windows, looking out through the binoculars.

'This is fantastic,' he announced as soon as he heard her. 'I can see the port from here and a part of the village. There's very little activity, though.'

'Perhaps that's because the tide's not right.' Camilla dropped breathlessly on to a trunk that stood with a lot of luggage she recognised as having belonged to her father. 'Take a look at this.'

Philip examined it carefully. 'That's it!' he exclaimed. 'The times when the boats smuggle in drugs!' He looked at it more closely. 'I wonder if we can work out when it's likely to happen again?'

'It looks like an old cutting to me,' Camilla observed. 'These times of high or low tides may not apply at the moment.'

'I wish we could get hold of a local newspaper today, with the current tides. D'you suppose I could slip down to the village and buy one from the general store-cum-post office?'

Camilla stared at him as if he'd gone mad. 'What are you talking about? What's the point of our hiding here if you then go into Ardachie and give the whole game away?'

Philip grinned at her, not at all put out. 'As far as the people in the village are concerned, you and my mother and I left the Ballageich Hotel yesterday, and we're all in London by now. I doubt if they know what I look like. Anyway, I've never set foot in the village and have only passed through it sitting in the back of a car.'

'Even so . . .' she protested hotly.

'Look, only Hector Ross and his assistant Jock would recognise me. I think it's worth taking a risk and having a quick look round while I buy a newspaper. You can't go, they probably all know what you look like, but I could be a tourist passing through. No one knows me around here.'

Camilla remained doubtful. 'Where would you be staying if you were a tourist, though? And you can't take the car because they know what that looks like. Suppose you bump into Hector's housekeeper, too?' She shook her head and looked worried. 'I think it's too big a chance to take.'

'The housekeeper never even looked into the car yesterday.

She was too busy trying to stop you from entering the vet's house,' Philip declared. 'I promise you, Camilla, it'll be all right. If necessary, if anyone asks me anything – and why should they? – I'll say I'm staying in the next village. I'll be careful, don't worry.'

'I *am* worried, Philip.' Her eyes were troubled as she looked at him. 'If you want to get a newspaper, why don't you go to the next village? If I remember rightly it's bigger than Ardachie.' She could tell he was itching to get out of the house to do something active.

'But I won't learn anything, will I? Honestly, Camilla, it will be all right. I promise I won't take any risks. I'll just potter around keeping my ears and eyes open. After all, didn't you say they were a friendly bunch? Didn't your friend Geoffrey get on with everyone very well? Why should they suspect me of having anything to do with you or this house if they've never seen us together?'

'I suppose so.' With misgiving, a reluctance so strong she hardly understood it herself, she watched him bound down the stairs, his strong legs taking them two at a time. He reminded her of a young colt suddenly released from confinement, exhilarated by his freedom.

'I won't be long,' he called out gaily. 'Is there anything I can get you?'

Hurrying down the stairs behind him as he bounded to the bottom, Camilla was suddenly aware that he had turned to look up at her and that his eyes were sweeping the length of her legs. Again there was that appreciative look. Pausing, she pretended not to notice his appraisal.

'No thanks,' she said brightly.

When she returned to the library she was glowing. Then she chided herself for being so foolish. Fancy taking the idle flattery of a young man so seriously! Lucy had said he'd had lots of girlfriends and no doubt he was a bit of a Lothario, although she hadn't thought that before. Anyway, he was twenty-four and she was forty-four, she reminded herself, so she'd better not get like those awful women of a 'certain age' who suddenly took on a new lease of life, skittering around town in skirts that were too short and hair that was too long, just because a young man had looked at them. But then . . . but then, she paused in the doorway to the library, and it was as if her body were made of harp strings, and someone had trailed their fingers across them from side to side, so that they reverberated, zinging, echoing and re-echoing, and she felt weak. The memory of Philip's eyes, penetrating, stripping away in their intensity, came back to her, and her heart started thumping like a drum. What was this? she asked herself, on the verge of panic. When had she last experienced this inner trembling – this sharp, probing sensation? She hardly dared answer the question even in the silence of her mind. She tried to suppress the words that were forming, taking shape, speaking of forbidden pleasures and feelings she must deny, even to herself. But she couldn't. What she felt was both thrilling and disturbing. And utterly, utterly impossible.

'You're a bleedin' marvel, aren't you?'

Poppy opened her eyes languidly, a smile parting her lips as Danny ran his hands over her slim body. They'd been making love all evening but still she wanted him again and gave a little wriggle of pleasure as with easy familiarity his large fingers once more searched out the intimate creases and folds and smooth planes of her skin, while his breath, hot and faintly smelling of peppermint chewing gum, fanned her face, the eyes narrowed and glittering.

She looked up at him, adoration softening her features, and then she stroked his spiky blond hair, liking the feel of it, like a soft brush, loving the colour as it glinted by the light of the one electric bulb that hung from the whitewashed ceiling of his room.

'I love you, Danny,' she whispered. 'I love you more than anything else on earth.'

There was silence. He didn't respond and then she heard him laugh, not with the gentle laughter of embarrassment at someone revealing their feelings with such honest abandon but with the scorn of an adult who laughs with cruel mirth at the sayings of a child.

Poppy looked earnest. 'I *do*, Danny. I really do love you.'

'And you're a great fuck yourself !'

'No. No, I mean it.'

'Love? What's love? Who needs it anyway? Life is about surviving and fucking, sweetheart, in that order. Surviving. And fucking.' He buried his face in the softness of her neck while she lay there, cold and empty. She would have given her life for him, she thought. She would do anything, anything on earth, for this man with his rough manners and gentle hands and the power to drive her into a frenzy. For a moment she felt so hurt she couldn't speak, but then she remembered that coming from different backgrounds.they used different words to mean the same thing. That was it! He just didn't use the word 'love'. It was sissy, too soft and feminine. Strong men like Danny never talked of love. She'd heard the men in the pub discussing their women. They were 'fixed up', or they 'had a nice bit', but they never spoke of love.

'You're right, Danny,' she said, suddenly feeling happy again. 'It *is* all about surviving and fucking.' But a little voice in her head denied it even as she spoke.

The walk from Creagnach to Ardachie took about eight minutes and Philip, striding out on this glorious gold and purple morning, breathed in the fresh air as if he'd been confined indoors for weeks. By nature he was an outdoors man, enjoying sport in the countryside when he'd been sent from Hong Kong to boarding school in England at the age of nine. He loved cricket and swimming in summer, and rugger and riding in winter, but all his holidays had been spent in the exotic surroundings of the East, which at times had made him feel his existence was that of a rarefied orchid in a humid greenhouse, rather than an active schoolboy eager for adventure.

The road was rough underfoot, bordered on either side by

tufts of pale coarse grass and heather in full bloom. Up on the hill, grazing peacefully, a herd of deer moved slowly across the landscape, their coats blending in perfect natural disguise with the surrounding countryside. At the sound of Philip's footsteps on the road below, they looked up sharply, ears pricked, gentle gaze watchful. Seeing him pass by they soon lost interest and resumed their rhythmic chewing.

It was a perfect morning for a walk and Philip's pace was brisk until he drew level with the first cluster of cottages that marked the outskirts of the village. Then he slowed down to a leisurely saunter, all the better to observe as much as he could, to try and commit to memory every detail, no matter how trivial, in case it came in useful later.

The activity in Ardachie was typical of mid-morning life in any village in the British Isles. Women shopped and hung out lines of washing, children ran about playing their own invented games, men went about their work, the younger ones down by the quayside while the older ones pottered in small front gardens. The houses, he observed, looked well cared for if not prosperous, and the few shops well stocked with goods.

Determined to take advantage of this visit, in case for some reason it could not be repeated, Philip paused to look into the window of as many shops as he could without drawing attention to himself. In the bakery a mouth-watering display of oatcakes and griddle scones, shortbread and cream cakes caught his attention. Passing the local fishmonger next, whose produce was advertised as having been caught that morning, he saw lobsters, salmon and scallops set out on a marble slab in the window, the whole arrangement garnished with sprigs of livid green plastic parsley. Further up the street the butcher decorated his display of mutton, hare and rabbit with the same type of fake greenery.

At last, on the opposite side of the main road that ran through the centre of Ardachie, he came to the post office-cum-general store where Malcolm Elliott's post was supposed to have been confiscated. A general store it certainly was, Philip noticed, taking in the wide range of stock they carried, ranging from woollen socks to sweets, buttons to toys. The actual section that could be called a post office consisted of a battered wooden counter and tarnished metal grille, with some out-of-date leaflets about National Savings pinned to the wall behind. An elderly woman in an overall was counting out postage stamps for her one customer, a youngish woman with a child in a push-chair.

'And how's the wee bairn today?' she was asking, peering over the counter at the child whose face was sticky and pink from the lollipop he'd been sucking.

'Ach, he'll be doin' fine,' replied the mother in a lilting Scottish accent. 'But I'll be glad when he gangs to school. He's a right little bletherer!'

'Noisy, is he?'

The mother cast her eyes to heaven while her plump gold-ringed finger stroked her child's head. 'He's gae the devil in him!'

Philip picked up a copy of the local newspaper and took it to the main counter to pay for it, but he did not hurry because he wanted to eavesdrop on the conversation of the locals. Not that he learned anything. Five minutes later he emerged from the shop, having heard that 'old Mrs Hunter was worse', 'Eileen was expecting her baby any day now' and 'there's going to be a mighty wind tonight'. Disappointed, he left and walked to the far end of the village, passing the quay, which was quiet except for a couple of old fishermen mending nets. The whole scene, as Camilla had said, was totally uneventful.

In this tranquil bywater village life was being conducted with quiet serenity, and so with nothing exciting to report Philip made his way back to Creagnach.

They crouched by the attic window, sharing the binoculars, strain-ing to see what was happening on the quayside. In the dark-ness the surrounding mountains brooded like slumbering monsters under a sky sprinkled with stars, and to the west the

Firth of Lorne shimmered like black silk in a landscape of shadows.

'There's not much going on,' Philip observed, squinting through the powerful lenses.

'Let me have a look.' Camilla took the glasses from him. 'I don't know much about deep sea fishing. Will they be getting ready to set sail at dawn?' She could just make out through gaps in the trees that grew on the hillock between Creagnach and the village, people moving around. Some were getting into boats and climbing out of them again; others were talking to each other in groups of two or three; some wandering back into the village and becoming lost among the darkened cottages, others staying by the quayside. She looked at her watch.

'It's nearly two in the morning,' she observed. 'Would they be getting ready to go out fishing at this hour?' She was aware of Philip beside her, dressed in slacks and a thick sweater. She could even feel the heat of his skin, his cheek glowing next to hers, his breath warm and sweet as they leaned forward together watching intently, their heads almost touching.

'There's such a thing as night fishing,' Philip replied, 'but if that's what they're supposed to be doing, why the hell don't they get on with it?'

At that moment they heard the rumbling sound of a heavy vehicle that drew nearer, seemed to pass the end of the drive, and then grew fainter again. Through the bushes and trees that lined the main road down to the village, they could see the glow of the tail-lights. It was heading for the quay.

'That'll be the lorry to collect the fish and take it back to Glasgow, I suppose.' Philip's voice sounded flat. The day had produced nothing out of the ordinary, and it didn't look as if the night was going to reveal anything of importance either.

'God, I wish we could see more from here,' commented Camilla fretfully. There seemed to be renewed activity on the quayside now, with an occasional flash of torchlight and people huddled round the back of the lorry. Then, just as suddenly as the activity had started, it stopped again. Headlights were snapped off, torches put away; even the lights in the dockside cottages went out one by one, and after a few minutes everything was in darkness.

'Well, that's that! They've obviously all gone to bed,' she remarked. It was such an anti-climax she felt quite deflated. 'I'm not sure what I was expecting, but something a bit more dramatic than that, I suppose.'

In the darkness of the attic Philip was moving cautiously about. 'We might as well go to bed ourselves.' He trod carefully, avoiding bumping into the trunks and suitcases and general clutter that filled the space under the eaves. 'Shall I make us some coffee first?'

Camilla followed, just able to make out his outline. 'All we seem to be doing is eating and drinking,' she observed, 'but, yes, let's have some coffee.'

In silence they made their way down to the kitchen, the only room where it was safe to have the lights on. Swiftly and efficiently she plugged in the kettle while Philip got out the cups.

'Damn!' she exclaimed suddenly. 'I left the sugar bowl in the library.' They'd had tea there that afternoon, sitting by Malcolm's desk whilst looking at some of his books.

'Shall I get it?' he offered.

'No, it's all right.' Slipping out of the kitchen, she closed the door carefully behind her before hurrying across the darkened hall to the library. Entering the room, she moved swiftly and surely to the far side in a silence that was as enclosing and as absolute as a tomb. The darkness was solid too, like a wall, a barrier that could not be penetrated, and seemed to hold her in its binding grip for a moment. Pausing, she allowed her eyes to become accustomed to the total lack of light after the comparative brightness of the kitchen, and as the desk and chairs became slowly visible so too did the wide stone fireplace, the outline of books along the walls and the two high uncurtained windows that overlooked the meadow leading down to the Firth of Lorne. Like two grey panels the windows seemed to hover in mid-air, reminding Camilla for a moment of a conjuring trick when items float about in the darkness without any obvious means of support. Then the greyness gave way to a paler shade and the glass panes became more defined, and as her eyes grew better adjusted, a shadow outside the window took on a definite shape, getting clearer all the time. She watched as the shape came closer, pressing itself against the glass, materialising into features, first a nose and then eyes, until a face was revealed, pale and with hollow cheeks. It was looking straight at her.

Chapter Eleven

'Would you recognise the face again if you saw it?' Philip asked.

Camilla, seated at the kitchen table, a cup of steaming coffee clasped as if for warmth between her hands, was still trembling.

'I don't know. It was dark, and after a moment he stepped away from the window and vanished. I just had this fleeting impression of a pale bony face with deep sunken eyes.' She shook her head. 'He was there one minute and gone the next.' Her heart was still pounding uncomfortably and she was thankful for Philip's reassuring presence.

'You think he saw you?'

'That's another thing I can't be sure of. The library was in darkness . . . I was groping my way across to the desk when I suddenly saw this figure, peering in. He seemed to be looking at me but I can't be sure.'

Philip frowned. 'Perhaps someone was just doing a recce around the house,' he observed doubtfully.

'You don't think going into Ardachie this morning aroused suspicion?'

'Why should it? I didn't talk to anyone, and no one seemed to even notice me.'

'But in a small community like this a stranger in their midst is bound to be spotted. Because they didn't say anything to you, it doesn't mean your presence wasn't noticed.'

'It is a bit frustrating, though, sitting here doing nothing, isn't it?' he said mildly.

'I know.' She sipped the coffee thoughtfully.

Swinging his leg over the seat of a kitchen chair so that he sat astride, he looked at her eagerly.

'Tomorrow night I think we should go down to the quayside and find a hiding-place from where we can really see what's going on,' he suggested.

'That's a bit daring, isn't it?' she asked, but there was that look of admiration in her eyes.

'Maybe, but I don't know what else we can do. It's obvious that during the day this is a normal rather dull little fishing village, but by night something sinister happens. We're not going to find out what that is by sitting in an attic window with a pair of binoculars, are we?'

'You're right,' she agreed. 'I'd be happy to snoop around and see what's going on, but it could turn nasty if we're caught! It's not as if we even know what we're up against, except to suspect they're smuggling drugs into the country via the fishing boats.'

'Are you sure you ought to come?'

'Of course I'm coming!' Camilla exclaimed. 'D'you think I'd risk letting you go on your own? My God, supposing something happened to you? What would I do then?' As she spoke, she knew she had unwittingly exposed her feelings for him, these strange tender feelings that were rippling through her every time she looked at him. Her cheeks flushed scarlet and she looked hurriedly away, but not before she'd caught him staring curiously at her. She forced a light laugh. 'I mean, what would your mother say if anything happened to you? She's my oldest friend and the least I can do is to make sure her eldest offspring is returned home safe and sound.' She was in safe waters again, putting herself on the same level as Lucy, reminding him she was old enough to be his mother.

'But you could be in danger.'

'Nonsense. I wasn't suggesting we stroll up to the first fisherman we see and ask him what sort of dope he's landing tonight!'

They both laughed, the tension broken.

190

'Let's get some sleep now,' Camilla suggested, rising from the table and going over to the sink with her cup which she rinsed under the tap.

'I've a good mind to go into the garden and have a look around before we turn in,' said Philip. 'Just to make sure the prowler has gone.'

Camilla turned to look at him. 'Please don't,' she said in a small voice. 'No one can get into the house, as we've locked up for the night. Let's leave it at that.'

He hesitated. 'I'm not sure . . .'

'Yes, leave it, Philip,' she insisted. 'I'd rather you did.' Was it her imagination or was he suddenly looking at her strangely again? Camilla didn't stop to find out. Grabbing a torch from the dresser, she headed for the hall and up the stairs to the spare room she was occupying. They'd decided not to turn on any lights after nightfall, and so they found their way to bed by torch-light. Only in the mornings did they have leisurely baths, taking their time to dress, before coming down to breakfast.

In darkness she undressed, hearing Philip moving around in the next room, imagining him getting into bed, laying his head on the pillows, pulling up the duvet against the chill of the night.

Climbing into bed herself, Camilla stayed awake a long time, trying to force her mind to think about practicalities, like had they enough bread to last out the week, and what should she cook for lunch tomorrow? Housekeeping was a novelty these days, and something she hadn't done for over twenty years. David had always insisted she be a lady of leisure and so Maitland had looked after all the arrangements. Mrs Maitland was such a superb cook too. Camilla had no need even to boil an egg. Now, with Philip to look after . . . her mind strayed back to him with obsessive persistence. What would he like for breakfast . . . for lunch . . . for dinner? How best to make him happy? How best to keep him amused during the long hours of the day when they must remain hidden in the house? Over and over again her mind lingered on the way his eyes crinkled up at the corners when he smiled, the humorous tilt to the corners of his mouth, the way the hair grew at the nape of his neck, and his hands . . . strong and capable-looking. Then she would start recalling every remark he'd made during the day, analysing every inflection of his voice, always analysing until she thought she would go crazy. What was happening to her?

Turning on to her side, wishing she could switch on the bedside light so that the substance of the room could help banish her fantasies, Camilla resolved that whatever happened she must resist these feelings that were overcoming all her normal good sense. What did she think she was doing? Why was she behaving in this crazy manner? How could she possibly be falling in love with a twenty-four-year-old man . . . make that boy, she thought fiercely, the son of her best friend. For one thing, he no doubt had a dozen girlfriends in London who were pitying him for having to go up to Scotland on some wild goose chase with his mother and her old schoolfriend. Of course she hadn't heard him mention anyone in particular, there'd been no references to a Jenny or a Mary or a Kate, but nevertheless the fact remained he was twenty-four and she was forty-four and the difference in years between them was a black ravine, a gap of such magnitude it could never be bridged. Must never be bridged. Tossing and turning, so hot that she felt almost feverish, Camilla remembered how Lucy had said Philip would be a perfect match for Poppy. Her daughter. Lucy's son and her daughter. A perfect match.

'Christ, I can't bear this,' Camilla muttered aloud, throwing back the duvet and reaching for the torch. She was going out of her mind and didn't know how to stop herself. She was at the top of a dangerously slippery slope, a downward path strewn with agonising pitfalls, and at the bottom of it was Philip's face looking up at her with admiration. At that moment she resolved that they must return to London at the soonest possible moment, before she became dangerously lost in her own obsession. If she suggested they leave first thing in the morning, he'd wonder what the hell was up. She'd have to go through with her plan to go down to the quayside the next night; but after that, whether they found out anything or not, she'd say they must go home. And once back in the normal busy routine of her life, working at Eaton & Eaton during the day, and perhaps entertaining in Wilton Crescent at night, she would surely forget the effect he was having on her?

Jean's remark on the phone early the next morning temporarily sent everything else out of Camilla's mind.

'The bank want to know if you're going to authorise the sale of some of Poppy's shares from her trust fund, as her current account is overdrawn.'

'It's what?' Camilla couldn't believe what she was hearing. 'Jean, there must be some mistake. Her bank account can't possibly be overdrawn. The interest from the capital is paid into it every month. The last statement I saw showed a balance of eighteen thousand pounds! I've countersigned only one cheque for her since, for a hundred and fifty pounds!' Poppy had little need for large amounts of cash. Living at home, her expenses only amounted to enough for fares, books and magazines, and as far as her clothes were concerned, she insisted on buying them for next to nothing at Oxfam shops.

'Shall I read you their letter, Mrs Eaton?' Jean's motherly voice sounded rather anxious.

'Please do, Jean.'

In her clear voice, she read the letter out aloud. As Camilla listened she thought the bank would be unlikely to have made a mistake of such magnitude. So what the hell was going on!

'For God's sake!' she burst out involuntarily when Jean got to the part that said Poppy was overdrawn to the tune of seventeen thousand, six hundred and forty-five pounds, which had been withdrawn during the past four weeks, and that funds should be made available for 'Miss Eaton's future needs'.

'Christ! There *has* to be a mistake, Jean!' There was an edge of panic in her voice. 'It's just not possible. Even Poppy couldn't get through that sort of money in a month . . . besides, I haven't countersigned any cheques since the last one, and they aren't allowed to cash cheques without both our signatures. Look, leave it to me. I'll ring them now and sort it out.'

'Very well, Mrs Eaton.'

Ten minutes later Camilla walked into the kitchen where Philip had come down to start cooking breakfast, looking stunned.

'What's the matter?'

'I don't believe this,' she said, almost to herself, sitting down heavily at the scrubbed wooden table in the middle of the room on which he'd already put out crockery, bread and marmalade. She dropped her head into her hands. 'How could she have done this? And why? Why?'

Philip laid down the spatula with which he'd been turning the bacon, and came over to her.

'Who?' he asked gently. 'What's happened?'

Briefly she told him what the manager of the Knightsbridge branch of the Capitol Bank had said.

'Poppy's been cashing huge amounts of money. Three, four, five thousand pounds a time; the worst part of it all is she must have forged my signature to get it.'

'What has she been doing with it?' Philip asked, astonished.

'God only knows. I could kill the bank for letting her have it, though. I don't understand why they didn't check with me. How could they have let her have all that money? Don't they realise she's only sixteen?'

'Have you spoken to her?'

'Not yet. I rang home but Maitland says she's out. The trouble is, she's never in. I don't know what to do, Philip. I'm worried to death about her.'

'She's very tied up with this revolutionary movement, isn't she?'

'Did she tell you that?' Camilla shook her head. 'You see, she never tells me anything. She won't talk about her friends, or where she goes or what she does!'

'It's a phase, I'm sure.'

Camilla sighed in exasperation. 'Philip, everyone says "it's a phase", or "she'll get over it soon", but meanwhile what do

I do? There are times when I feel like locking her up . . . if only for her own good! David was right to insist her money was put in trust, and that I should be a co-signatory; not that it's done any good. What else did she tell you about this revolutionary organisation?'

'Not much really, we only talked for a few minutes that first evening we met. But it's run by her boyfriend, and the aim is total equality for everyone.'

'Oh, for God's sake! As if we hadn't heard that one before!' Camilla shook her head. 'Poppy and I have argued this out over and over again, and she won't even listen to sense.'

Philip's mouth twitched. 'There are some people who do believe in equality, you know. Poppy hasn't exactly invented the idea.'

'I know that, but she's so pigheaded.' Camilla sighed heavily. 'The trouble is that since David died I've lost all control over her. She won't do a thing I say, and now that Malcolm has died too there isn't anyone to talk sense to her.'

'I'm sure she'll grow out of it,' Philip said confidently. 'At sixteen I'm not sure I didn't have Trotskyite tendencies myself.'

They both laughed, but Camilla still looked troubled. 'What really distresses me is her deceit, going behind my back like this, forging my signature as if she were a common criminal . . . Oh, my God, I've just thought of something else!' Her hand flew to her mouth, and her eyes were aghast as she looked across the table at Philip.

'What on earth is it?' he asked.

'Do you suppose it was Poppy who took the silver?'

Philip looked appalled. 'Surely not, Camilla.'

'But that would explain everything.' She felt terribly disloyal talking about her own daughter like this, but she needed to confide in someone and her feelings for Philip somehow eased her conscience. Besides, she knew she could trust him.

'Why not ask her?' he suggested.

'It will make our relationship even worse if I'm wrong. It won't help if I'm right, either,' she added drily.

'Maybe it's not her fault. I mean, maybe she is under the influence of this boyfriend of hers. Isn't it possible that he's urging her to get money, especially if he knows she comes from a wealthy background?'

'One thing is for sure,' she declared, 'I'm not going to sanction any more money going into her bank account. David left her a considerable fortune and she's not going to get her hands on it until she's sensible enough to handle it.'

'I think that's wise,' Philip agreed. 'Now have some breakfast. We've got a long day and a long night ahead of us.'

Camilla remembered her resolve of the previous night. 'I think we should go back to London tomorrow,' she announced firmly.

'Why? I thought the plan was to stay at least a week? Or until we find out what is going on?'

'This business with Poppy changes everything,' she said brusquely, thinking what a perfect excuse it was to get away.

'Yes. I see.' Philip sounded disappointed.

'I can't let her go running around giving away thousands to some crank, can I?'

'No, of course not, but if her bank account is empty, she's got nothing more to give, has she? So why do you need to hurry back? Another few days isn't going to make any difference, is it?'

Camilla suddenly felt both frightened and angry. It was imperative she get away from this situation in which she and Philip were closeted together in such an intimate way, and it was also true that Poppy had to be firmly dealt with. The fault lay not with Philip but within herself, and yet it was with him she now felt angry.

'There's plenty more family silver she can pinch,' she pointed out, 'and when she's done that, there are always lots of objets d'art and paintings around the house she could start on.'

In silence, they finished eating the eggs and bacon he'd cooked; they were delicious but she'd lost her appetite. Then she rose to go back to the library.

'I'm going to try and get on to Poppy again,' she said shortly as she closed the door behind her.

An hour later, Camilla was still in the library, making phone calls. By keeping in touch with the normal world of Eaton & Eaton and Leslie Forbes, she could feel the stress of her present situation fading and diminishing, so that she was more able to get her emotions into perspective. Having spent some time discussing the campaign for a new combined shampoo and conditioner called One-Step, which they were to launch on the market in three months' time, she became so absorbed that she actually forgot about Philip for a little while; stopped thinking about his eyes and full young mouth, and the way his broad shoulders hunched forward when he was talking earnestly; stopped dwelling on his capable hands, and the way he twisted the gold signet ring on his little finger when he was thinking; stopped remembering, and going over again and again every word he had said and the way he said it . . .

'Can I speak to Geoffrey Hennessy, please?' she asked firmly when the operator on the switchboard of the *Globe* answered.

'Think-yew,' said the girl in a mock-refined voice. 'Ai'm putting yew through.' The next moment he was on the line, exuding his usual good-humoured warmth.

'Camilla! How wonderful to hear from you.' Suddenly she felt grateful for his kindly voice and reassuring manner. Geoffrey was the sort of person who was always there, unchanged and rock-like, no matter what.

'I'm fine. How are you?' she replied.

'Great. Can you talk?'

'Yes. I've actually bought myself a portable phone.' She laughed, feeling warm and reassured again. That was the effect Geoffrey had on people. 'No doubt they'll find a way of bugging it too, before long,' she continued gaily, 'but meanwhile I'm conducting my business from here and it's great. I might actually get to like it.'

'By the time you've learned to juggle a glass of champagne, a notepad and pencil and your mobile phone, while lying in a bubble-bath, you're going to love it!' he joked. 'Just give it time, my dear.'

Camilla burst out laughing. 'Why don't I install a jacuzzi at the office, and all the directors and myself can plunge in and have our meetings there?'

'A Think Tank,' said Geoffrey swiftly.

'Oh, very witty!'

'Now tell me what's happening?'

As she outlined the past few days, she knew she was right in wanting to get back to London as quickly as possible. Even to think of Philip in terms of anything more than her best friend's son was madness. Talking to Geoffrey made her realise that if she wanted to get into a serious relationship, it had to be with someone who was a more equal partner, someone nearer her own age. What sort of madness is it, she asked herself, that makes me dream of someone young enough to be my son? Someone who is still a student living off a small private income given him by his parents? It was laughable. Crazy. Didn't she realise she was a mature woman, chairman of a large public company worth several millions, and with a position in society? The trouble was, she reflected almost morosely, she didn't feel it. When she was with Philip she felt deliciously young again, as if her life was just beginning, so that anything seemed possible.

'... Then how about dinner on Wednesday night?' Geoffrey was asking. 'I won't be able to get away from the *Globe* until seven but we could meet at Scalini's at eight o'clock? Would that suit you?'

Camilla thought of the glittering sophistication of Scalini's in fashionable Walton Street, where the rich and famous dined in a setting of jungle plants and mirrors, concealed lighting and snowy smooth damask tablecloths, and immediately accepted his invitation. She needed the culture of trendy modernity to jolt her out of her present frame of mind; a taste of reality, instead of the Gothic drama that she had been surrounding herself with during the past week.

'I'll look forward to that,' she said aloud.

'And be careful tonight,' he cautioned. 'You could end up

in trouble, you know. I don't understand why you don't let Lucy's son go down to the harbour on his own, if he's that keen!'

Did she detect a certain dryness in Geoffrey's voice? An indifference towards a very young man who was obviously out for adventure but whose safety didn't concern him?

'But I want to go,' Camilla replied. 'I started this whole business and I want to finish it. Then I can go to the police in Glasgow where they're sure to take me a lot more seriously than the local cops here.'

There was a pause and then Geoffrey said heavily: 'That's because the local police have no doubt been corrupted, my dear Camilla. I think it's madness on your part to get involved like this.'

Oh yes, madness, she suddenly thought, but a different sort of madness to the kind you're referring to, dear Geoffrey. This is a madness of the mind that must, at all costs, be quenched, doused, put out, so that not even a glimmering ember remains . . .

'I'll see you when I get to London,' she said brightly, 'and I'll tell you all the news then.'

'There was a call for you, Miss Poppy, from Mrs Eaton,' Maitland informed her as she stomped into the hall, banging the front door behind her as usual and flinging her baggage down on the floor. She could see Maitland wince as she cluttered up his exquisitely tidy hall; he was even peering at the floor to make sure her heavy shoes hadn't left muddy marks on the mirror-like surface. Not that she cared. There were more urgent matters on her mind than worrying about what Maitland thought.

'Yeah?'

Maitland raised his chin, so that for a moment he reminded her of a penguin just about to go down a slide.

'Mrs Eaton will be phoning back in approximately twenty minutes, Miss Poppy,' he said with heavy importance. 'She particularly asked me to make sure you were here to take her call.'

'Oh, shit! And what would you have said if I hadn't come back this morning?'

Maitland would never have done anything as vulgar as shrugging his shoulders. A mere upward raising of the eyebrows was all he allowed himself as he spoke with flat coldness.

'I would have dealt with that eventuality when and if it had arisen,' he said with dignity. 'Would you care for a bath before breakfast?' he added pointedly. 'Or after?'

Poppy looked dreadful: her black eyeliner was smeared around her eyes, making her resemble a panda, and her hair hung in greasy wisps. As usual, he reflected, her clothes looked like layers of rags.

'Before,' she said vacantly. 'What's for breakfast?'

'Mrs Maitland was proposing to cook some pork and herb sausages with grilled tomatoes and crispy bacon, Miss Poppy.'

She seemed to brighten. 'Okay.' Then she paused, halfway up the stairs. 'Do I really have to talk to my mother, Maitland?'

For a moment he was reminded of the little girl she'd once been, sweet, coaxing, quite obedient really, although she'd always try and wind the grown-ups around her little finger.

'Yes, you really do, Miss Poppy.'

She frowned. 'D'you know what it's about?'

'I'm afraid I don't.'

'Did it really sound that important?'

He nodded, almost vehemently. 'Yes. Yes, it sounded as if she was most anxious to speak to you.'

'Oh, shit!' she said again as she went up to her room.

Lying in the scented bubbles of her en suite bath, ten minutes later, Poppy reflected that life was a bitch. Life at home in Wilton Crescent was bad enough, but sometimes, like now, life with Danny was worse. At least she knew how to get the better of her mother. Danny, on the other hand, was implacable. They'd spent most of the night quarrelling, because he was still refusing to tell her what his plans were for July. The fact that something was happening then was definite because she'd overheard him referring to it again with one of his mates. In fact, 'See you in July' had recently become a standard remark when saying goodbye to any of the members of Class Warriors. And yet he refused to elaborate.

'But *why* can't you tell me?' Poppy asked for the umpteenth time, as dawn crept with chilly fingers over the slums of Whitechapel. 'Haven't I shown you I'm a committed member of the organisation? Why are you keeping me in the dark?'

'Oh, for fuck's sake, Pops, you're becoming a nagger! And I can't stand women who nag.' He rolled over in bed, away from her, reaching for a copy of the previous day's *Morning Star* as he did so.

'I'm not nagging,' Poppy expostulated, 'but I have a right to know.'

He rolled back to look at her. 'Listen, babe, you've got no fucking rights where I'm concerned.'

Poppy wasn't through, though. 'Who's "Big Marge" then?'

Danny lay silent for a moment, and then he said cautiously: 'Who?'

'Big Marge. I hear she's running the women's division of Class Warriors. Who is she? Why have I never come across her?'

'There's no reason why you should,' Danny replied shortly.

'Does she lead the women's movement?'

'Sort of.'

'What do you mean "sort of"? Are you rivals?' Poppy added, with sudden insight.

Danny suddenly burst out laughing, a deep-bellied roar of amusement.

'What's so funny?' she asked crossly.

'The thought of Big Marge and me being rivals.' He was shaking his head in amused disbelief.

'Well, how should I know? I wish you wouldn't have secrets from me, Danny. I am your girlfriend, after all, and I've a right to know what's going on.'

Suddenly he turned on her, grabbing her hair with his hand and twisting her head so that she was forced to face him.

'You have no rights!' he stormed. 'No rights at all. I never

201

asked you to join Class Warriors and just you remember it! You were brought along by a girl you'd met at a bus stop, and that, lady, doesn't give you the right to tag yourself on to me for the rest of bleeding time! I don't have to tell you *anything*, and if you don't like it you know what you can do, don't you?'

'But Danny . . .'

'There are no buts! Get that? Mind your own business, or get lost. The ins-and-outs of Class Warriors have nothing to do with you.'

'Why not?' She felt desperate now, as if he was slipping away from her, excluding her from the thing he cared for most, rejecting the thought of her being a part of his life.

'I have my reasons,' he said shortly, picking up the newspaper again.

Poppy snorted. 'What sort of reasons can you have? Look at all the money I've given you! If it hadn't been for me . . .'

'Oh, here we go. The Great-I-Am. Grow up, Poppy, and stop trying to use emotional blackmail, because it won't work. You've never really belonged to the organisation and you don't belong now. Handing over great lumps of money isn't what it's all about. It's your soul that counts . . . and you haven't the conviction to be an inspirational force in the cause we're working towards.'

'What's Big Marge got that I haven't?' Poppy demanded indignantly.

Danny sounded scathing. 'Guts, that's what, guts. And total dedication to the cause. She's not afraid of anyone or anything. She'll fight like a man and she's inspiring women all over the country to follow her example and become powers to be reckoned with, in industry and in the consumer trade. When the time is right, Big Marge will be right up in the forefront of action, with me, making sure the changes we demand are put into action, getting results so that there will be equal rights for everyone in this country for the first time in history.'

'She sounds like a paragon of virtue,' Poppy scoffed pettishly. 'I don't know what makes you think I'm not as committed as she is! You've never given me the chance to show what I can do. I can help rally other women . . .'

'No you can't because you don't belong. If you can't see that you're a bigger fool than I thought!' Danny got out of the bed and started struggling into his clothes with impatient jerky movements, so angry did he seem to be.

'I do belong,' Poppy wailed.

'No you don't! You're nothing but a spoilt brat from a middle-class background, playing at slumming it, and probably dipping into your dress allowance from Mummy so you can act the Lady Bountiful,' he said savagely.

Poppy's jaw dropped open. How had he found out? How long had he known? Seeing her discomfort, he continued: 'Did you think I didn't guess you weren't really one of us? With your la-di-da accent? Disappearing off to have scented baths? You couldn't fool me, kid. And all that crap about stealing silver . . . I've known all along what you were really about. And you want to compare yourself to Big Marge!' Danny threw back his head and gave a mirthless laugh. 'That's a joke, that is!'

'I feel I belong with you more than anyone else.' For a moment Poppy couldn't remember whether she'd said her parents were dead or alive.

'Forget it,' he said. By now he was fully clothed and zipping up his leather jacket, ready to go out. 'You'll never belong.' As he got to the door, he turned and made a final remark. 'But you're a great little fuck.' A moment later he was gone, and once again Poppy was alone in his room, surrounded by the clutter of his life. Only she wasn't going to wait all day for him to return this time. She was going to go home, have something decent to eat for a change instead of all that vegetarian muck, and then she'd work out a plan to win him back. It didn't matter what he might say, she belonged to him and would for the rest of her life. Danny *was* her life and he wouldn't be able to deny it by the time she'd finished.

Poppy got out of the bath refreshed and full of determination.

Wafting up the stairs from the kitchen was the heady aroma of coffee and frying sausages. At that moment there was a knock on her bedroom door and she heard Maitland speak.

'Mrs Eaton is on the phone for you, Miss Poppy.'

'Shit,' she muttered under her breath as she put on the blue terry towelling robe her grandfather had given her last Christmas. 'Tell her I'll be there in a minute,' she shouted, winding a towel round her wet hair. Then, as there was no phone in her room, she went downstairs to the floor below and entered her mother's bedroom. Although she'd never have admitted it, Poppy loved the rose-patterned fabric Camilla had chosen for the curtains and the drapes on the eighteenth-century four-poster bed. It was an old-fashioned room, furnished with antiques, several delicately painted pictures framed in gilt, and a lavish abundance of all the little luxuries Camilla loved so much. Bowls of sweet-scented pot-pourri stood on sidetables, crystal perfume bottles were reflected in the dressing-table mirror, a dozen lace pillows and a cream cashmere wrap were arranged on a chaise longue at the foot of the bed, and books, magazines and family snapshots, framed in silver, were arranged on the low round table in the middle of the room.

Sniffing the perfumed atmosphere appreciatively and thinking how nice and peaceful the house was when her mother was away, Poppy sat on the edge of the bed and picked up the phone.

Chapter Twelve

The quarrel had left both of them exhausted. Accusations had been exchanged, in escalating anger and bitterness, and the counter-accusations had been cruel and taunting.

'You only care about yourself,' Poppy had flared. 'When Daddy was alive we were a real family. Now all you think about is business and who you're going to invite to your next dinner party!'

'That's not true,' Camilla exclaimed. 'That's a very unfair thing to say, Poppy. And nothing excuses the fact that you've behaved like a common criminal, stealing the silver and forging my signature in order to get money from the bank.'

'*My* money! And the silver will belong to me one day anyway. Daddy would have wanted me to have it. And all I did was help myself to an advance on my inheritance,' she added haughtily.

On and on the argument went, with recriminations, and taunts, and Poppy refusing to offer any explanations. Stubbornly she kept repeating that the money was hers to do with as she liked, and the silver would have belonged to her eventually anyway.

When Camilla finally put down the phone, she sat looking out of the window and wondering what she was going to do next. She and Poppy had never been more estranged. David would have known how to handle her. Malcolm, even, could usually get her to see sense. Now there was no one. She could no more reach Poppy than she could fly to the moon. The bonding of childhood seemed to have been fatally severed and she no longer knew how to bridge the gap and heal the wound. And yet she desperately wanted to. Poppy was her only child and she loved her dearly. Where had she gone wrong as a mother? And what could she do to put it right now?

'Is there anything I can get you?' Philip asked. He'd come into the room towards the end of her conversation with Poppy, and although he'd immediately apologised as he turned to leave, Camilla waved to him to stay.

'Nothing, thanks,' she replied. 'Tell me, Philip, do you and your brother and sisters have fights with your parents? Do you rage at each other and find it impossible to communicate?'

Philip looked thoughtful. 'On the whole we get on very well. Our parents are very easy-going, you know.'

'I don't think I'm being exactly harsh on Poppy,' Camilla said reasonably. 'I worry about her and what's going to happen to her. I still don't know what she did with all that money.'

'She didn't mention her boyfriend and the revolutionary movement he's involved in?'

Camilla shook her head. 'I asked her about that but she said it was none of my business.'

'As Mum's in London, why don't you get her to call Poppy?' Philip suggested. 'The only time she had a problem with Henrietta, and that was when she refused to keep up her studies, Mum got Aunt Helen to have a chat with her, and it worked wonders. Hetty opened up as she'd never have done to Mum, and it turned out she had some notion of becoming a model and didn't think academic qualifications mattered.'

'Ummm. I suppose I could,' Camilla replied, but she sounded doubtful. It was galling, she realised, not to be able to cope with one child when Lucy had brought up four with the minimum of fuss. And it really was admitting defeat if she had to go to her friend to seek help now.

'If I had a problem I'd probably rather talk it through with you than with Mum,' Philip continued. 'One can be too close to one's family at times to see the wood for the trees.'

'Ummm,' said Camilla again. His remark, placing her in the

same category as his mother, was a reminder of their age difference, bringing her back sharply to the present. Unaccountably she felt hurt by it. There had been, she supposed, a tiny fragment of her mind that secretly hoped Philip felt the same way about her as she felt about him, but being reminded that he would turn to her as a surrogate mother if the need arose, stuck in her throat like a bitter pill. It seemed only yesterday that she'd been the same age as Philip, and had thought of someone over forty as old, past it, practically waiting for death. Was that how Philip saw her now? Alongside his grey-haired mother? Someone who would 'understand' the problems of the young, being no longer personally troubled by them?

'Yes,' she said in a positive manner. 'I will phone Lucy and ask her to talk to Poppy.' She hoped she sounded mature and sensible, a woman who had reached a certain plateau in life and left all silliness behind. Someone who took her adult responsibilities seriously. But then why could she feel a young woman, trembling with a new love that could never be returned, inhabiting her body?

'Come and have some lunch,' Philip suggested, breaking into her thoughts. 'There's nothing like food to cheer you up, and you look as if you need cheering!' Companionably he took her arm and led her to the door.

'What shall we have? Are there any sausages left?'

'Better than that.' He looked mysterious. 'I've been busy while you were on the phone.'

Camilla raised her eyebrows. As they crossed the hall, a delicious smell emanated from the kitchen, and she suddenly felt hungry.

Triumphantly, he opened the oven, and there, keeping warm, was a dish of grilled lamb chops, surrounded by mashed potatoes and green beans. He'd even made some gravy.

'Philip!' A delighted grin spread across her face.

'I'm not just a pretty face!' he joked. 'Wait until you have my roast beef and Yorkshire pudding, one day. That's my speciality!'

Laughing, they settled themselves at the kitchen table, but as she ate the delicious lunch he'd prepared, she found her mind drifting, partly worrying about Poppy's behaviour, and partly about her own emotions.

'You're very quiet,' Philip observed at last.

'I've a lot on my mind,' she replied vaguely.

'You should rest this afternoon. We've got a long night ahead of us. You don't want to be exhausted before we start.'

Camilla felt herself bristling. 'I'm not tired. I'm fine. Just worried.'

'At least Mum is going to talk to Poppy so that's one load off your mind.' She'd spoken to Lucy earlier on the phone and she'd been very sympathetic and understanding.

'I'm very grateful to her. I shall be glad to get back to London though,' she added fervently.

Philip looked at her curiously. 'Haven't you enjoyed our stay here at all? I mean, I know it was ghastly at first, when you found all the dogs and everything, but in the last couple of days we've had quite a good time, haven't we?'

She had to turn away and busy herself getting yoghurt out of the fridge because the wistfulness in his voice was breaking her heart. Of course we've had a good time, she longed to say; of course I've enjoyed myself. In fact I haven't had such a good time for years, just doing all the simple things I don't usually do, like shopping and cooking and talking late into the night – and not about business, either. Having someone to share my thoughts with and feel close to. And it's because it's been so good, too good, that it has to stop.

Aloud she said briskly: 'Of course it's been fun. I'm sorry Lucy couldn't stay on but we'll have a lot to tell her, won't we?' Philip didn't reply, and thinking she'd perhaps offended him by showing insufficient gratitude, she added: 'I don't know what I'd have done without you. Thank you for staying on, Philip.'

'You've thanked me already. There's no need.'

Camilla glanced quickly in his direction and saw him fiddling unhappily with his spoon.

'I wish we didn't have to leave,' he said suddenly.

She came back to the table and took her seat opposite him again.

'But we do, Philip,' she said gently. 'Sooner or later we have to go back, and I think it's better if it's sooner.'

He levelled his gaze directly at her and she wished she knew what he was thinking. Of one thing she was sure, and that was he had no idea why she wanted to get away so urgently.

'Are you longing for the bright lights again?' he asked. 'Are you bored being stuck in the countryside?'

Camilla was taken aback. 'Not at all,' she replied honestly. 'I don't lead all that social a life, you know. It's mostly to do with the business. If it wasn't for the company I'd be happy to spend my evenings quietly at home, in spite of what Poppy says. I don't want to get back to London just to resume a hectic social life!' Then she thought of Geoffrey and how she was dining with him in two days' time. Thank God for dear old Geoffrey. He seemed to be the one constant thing in her life at the moment, and she was depending on him to pull her back from the brink of insanity.

'Why do you want to go back then?'

Camilla gave a start, hauled out of her reverie by Philip.

'What did you say?'

'Why do you want to go back? I very much doubt if we'll find out much tonight, and then in a way the whole trip will have been a waste of time,' he pointed out.

'We could stay here a month and still not find out what's going on.'

'That's true, but I do think we should stick at it longer.'

He was right of course, she knew that, and under different circumstances nothing would have dragged her away, but by staying she faced a danger of a different kind and she couldn't afford to let that happen.

Later, she took his advice and went up to her bedroom. She'd planned to lie on the bed and finish the novel she was reading, but instead found herself gazing up at the expanse of blank white

209

ceiling, going over in her mind what Philip had said. She did that all the time now, recalling to mind every word, every sentence, analysing obsessively not only the meaning of his words but the nuances too. And what had his expression been when he'd said this . . . and that? As unhealthy as she knew it to be, it was impossible to get him out of her mind. In some utterly mad way she knew she was hoping for a sign that might tell her he found her attractive too, and yet as she lay there day-dreaming, she also cursed herself for even thinking such a thing might be possible.

Camilla picked up her book and tried to read but the words danced meaninglessly in front of her eyes and the page was filled with Philip's face; sometimes laughing, the way he did when his eyes crinkled at the corners; sometimes whimsical, with eyebrows raised and mouth twitching with humour; sometimes serious, the gaze direct, the jawline firm. In some ways, of course, she had to admit he reminded her of David when he'd been young, but then didn't they say one was always attracted to the same type? It wasn't because there was a faint resemblance to David that she felt this way, though. Philip was very much a person in his own right, with a less abrasive personality than David but much more sensitivity. She smiled to herself as she lay there. Lucy had said something about the younger genera-tion of men being much gentler and more unselfish than their fathers because they'd had to recognise women's rights and there was no room for male chauvinism in the New World. Was Philip this new breed of man? Thoughtful and sympathetic? Supportive and generous? David had been all those things up to a point, but it was he who had ruled the roost in their marriage and expected her to provide all his domestic comforts. Somehow Camilla didn't think Philip would expect a wife to spend her life catering to his whims. Perhaps that was what Lucy meant when she talked about the younger generation.

At last, unable to sleep and too distracted to concentrate on her novel, she rose and went downstairs to make tea. Philip was not, as she expected, in any of the ground-floor rooms. The drawing-room was empty, the library deserted. In the kitchen, the afternoon sunshine shone in through the partly shuttered windows, revealing the absence of human life, and suddenly Camilla felt intolerably lonely. In this great silent house nothing stirred. Even the fridge in the corner seemed mute when usually it hummed with secret internal activity, and as she stood there feeling desolate without Philip's presence, she wondered if this moment was symbolic of the rest of her life.

Was she destined to roam the large rooms of elegant mansions, all by herself, listening to the sound of her own footfalls and the sad pounding of her own heart? How am I going to manage? she thought, in momentary panic. I'm still young. I've still got all my faculties – I'm as active as I was at twenty-four, still as sexually aware as I was at eighteen . . . and I don't want to spend the rest of my life alone. Camilla clenched her fists and stood there in the centre of a sudden whirlpool of despair. I want to live again, she thought. I want to laugh, and do crazy things, and go dancing, and take a boat on the river as the sun is rising. I want to start my life again, and feel the heat of a lover's skin next to mine, and the touch of his hands in the night, and the sound of his voice all around me. But fatally she knew that the fantasy hands and voice had a substance in her mind, and it was Philip she was thinking about all the time. And what would he be doing while she indulged herself in these impossible daydreams? The answer came to her with agonising clarity; spending time with his family, going to lots of parties for young people, taking out pretty twenty-year-old girls . . . I've got to stop this, Camilla told herself fiercely. This way lies madness.

She was putting on the kettle when Philip came in through the kitchen door, looking flushed and windblown. He was carrying one of Malcolm's walking sticks and there was mud on his thick shoes and pieces of dried bracken clinging to his trousers and sweater.

'Good timing,' she observed, managing to sound normal and matter-of-fact although a great weakness had come over her at the sight of him. 'I'm just about to make tea.'

'Great.' He was smiling and looking pleased with himself. 'I've been working out our route for tonight, and I think if we go into those woods,' he indicated through the window the direction he meant, 'until we get to the top of that hillock, and then we veer to the left instead of going towards the village on the right, we can get down to the harbour wall, and some fishermen's huts, without being seen. We can get a really good view from there of what's going on, and if we want to we can always follow the wall along to the village to get nearer the quayside, though that's riskier.'

Camilla set out cups and plates and a tin of biscuits on the table. 'Did anyone spot you now?'

'Not a soul. At this time of day it's really quiet in the village, and at the port.'

'What time shall we start?'

Philip looked thoughtful. 'It doesn't get dark until nearly ten o'clock, does it? I think if we set off at about eleven, we can get ourselves into a good position before the night's activities begin.'

She gave a little shudder. 'I wish Edith was here to tell us what we're getting into.'

'Perhaps that's why she went away in the first place.'

'Because she knew what was going on? I can't think why she didn't go to the police! They would have offered her protection, wouldn't they?'

'I'm not so sure. Look at their reaction to us. They weren't even interested in the dead Alsatians. Whatever is going on in Ardachie, I'm convinced the local police are in on it too.'

'Geoffrey suggested as much,' Camilla said. 'So what are we going to do, even if we do find out what's going on? Go to the police in Oban?'

'We could, but I think we would do better to go to Glasgow. That is the headquarters for this region, so don't let's mess about with some local constabulary.'

A strong wind from the north had whipped its way across the

western coast earlier in the evening, and as Camilla and Philip, dressed in dark slacks and sweaters, crested the hillock that rose from the grounds of Creagnach, it tugged at the branches above their heads and agitated the fronds of bracken at their feet. Keeping close to the trees they walked swiftly and as silently as they could, until they reached the top, and then stood looking down on the harbour below.

'Nothing much happening yet,' Camilla observed in a low voice.

'It's still early. The last time we watched from the attic window things didn't start hotting up until nearly one in the morning, did they?'

'That's true.'

Philip dropped to his haunches, indicating she should do the same: 'Just in case anyone looks up,' he explained.

'I doubt if anyone can see us, it's so dark,' Camilla said. She was acutely conscious of Philip beside her, his broad shoulders and muscular arms making him look quite sturdy in the thick sweater he wore, his hair ruffled by the wind, which was gathering in strength.

They stayed like that for nearly an hour while all around them the northerly gale blustered in icy blasts, belying the fact it was July and that earlier the temperature had been consistent with a summer's day. Now the whole countryside seemed to be in perpetual motion, whipped and tossed by an importunate wind, so that the muscles and skin in her face felt tired as if she was being buffeted by a heavy feather pillow.

'Look!' Philip whispered suddenly. Below a flurry of activity had started among the shops and houses that overlooked the quay. The post office too backed on to the little port. A moment later they heard the now familiar rumble of a lorry coming along the main road that passed the gates of Creagnach. As it passed them, below and on their right, they could just make out the outline in the darkness. Then the headlights dipped as it swept up to the back entrance of the post office.

'Let's go,' Philip whispered, moving off down the hill towards the fishing huts. He crouched as he half ran, half walked, and Camilla followed, hoping she wouldn't trip or put her foot into a rabbit hole.

It didn't take long to reach the flat ground at the bottom and Philip, swift and sure-footed, led the way to the nearest hut.

'We can stay in the shadows and watch from here,' he whispered. The buildings, three of them in all, were more like large barns, the wooden slats of which they were built painted with a black tar-like substance to protect them from the ravages of salt air and rough weather. A strong repugnant smell of fish emanated from the very structure of the buildings which were reached by a narrow road that ran along the quayside from the village.

'What do they keep in these sheds?' Camilla asked as they stood between the narrow gap that divided the two huts furthest from the village.

'All sorts of things, I imagine. Fishing nets, crates for packing the fish in . . . they probably carry out engine repairs as well in them.'

From where they stood in the blackness of the night they waited and watched, while the sting of salt in the air made Camilla's eyes smart, and the wind, stronger now they were nearer the water's edge, came hurtling down from the surrounding mountains and off the sea.

'We're not going to see much from here,' said Camilla. 'Can't we get closer?'

'Let's wait a bit. Look, the lorry has pulled up by the edge of the quay now. See? And lots of people are doing something around the back of it.'

'It looks as if they are unloading packing cases.' Camilla stood on tiptoe, leaning against the hut to keep her balance so that she could get a better view.

As they strained to see what was happening, with only the side lights of the lorry and a dim light showing through the open back door of the post office, they could just discern groups of people milling around. They did not seem to be hurrying. It was as if, methodically and almost choreographed, they each had their allotted task and were quietly getting on with it, with the silent dedication of a small colony of ants.

'It looks like a highly organised operation whatever they're doing,' said Philip. 'It's a pity about the wind. I'd like to be able to hear what they're saying.'

'Can't we get closer?' Camilla suggested.

'It wouldn't make any difference. In this howling gale you'd have to be right beside them to hear anything.'

As he spoke, they noticed another group of men by the two largest fishing boats moored by the dockside. With torches to guide them, they were working on deck and it was obvious to Camilla and Philip that they were getting ready to set sail.

'What the hell is going on?' Camilla said, frustrated that she couldn't see more or hear anything. 'Are they going out night fishing or not?'

'They could be,' Philip sounded doubtful, 'but I don't understand what that has to do with that lorry unloading all those packing cases. Of course there may be no connection between the two, but I wonder how we're going to find out.'

At that moment, one of the group from outside the post office walked over to the quay. He was waving his arms as if signalling to the fishermen.

Camilla grabbed Philip's arm with a sharp intake of breath.

'My God,' she gasped, 'I know what's happening.'

'What?' He looked perplexed, eyes narrowed against the wind, trying to see what the man was doing. One of the fishermen had climbed off the largest of the boats on to the dockside now and was deep in conversation with the man from the post office.

'What's going on?' Philip repeated.

Camilla looked at him with a triumphant expression. 'They're not smuggling stuff into the country like we thought, but *out*. Whatever is in those crates the lorry brought to Ardachie is about to be loaded on to a fishing boat and smuggled out! Don't you see?' Excitedly she squeezed his arm. 'I wonder what they're smuggling?'

'What has Scotland got that someone else would want?'

Camilla started to giggle, on the edge of nervous hysteria.

'Haggis,' she gurgled, biting her lip to stop the rolling waves of laughter that were about to engulf her. 'Black pudding, porridge.' They had withdrawn between the huts again, to shelter for a moment from the gale.

Philip smiled, but he was not on her wavelength at this moment. Then he spoke, and his voice was tense. 'What about mink? There are mink farms up here, you know, and they're terrified that the animal activists will find out and release all the mink into the wild.'

'How do you know that?'

'I was out walking early one morning, when we were all staying at the Ballageich Hotel, and I came upon a high fenced-in area with a sign saying "Strictly Private". I was so curious, of course, I went through a gate which wasn't locked. I thought I must have come across a nuclear power station! Then I met the man who owned the mink farm. He swore me to secrecy. Apparently twelve families in the area depend on mink for their living. They're terrified of being forced out of business.'

'Could it be skins they're smuggling out of the country?' Camilla asked doubtfully. 'Surely they'd send the skins to London, wouldn't they? To furriers there?'

'God knows.'

They crept out from between the huts again. People were still going to and fro between the lorry and the fishing boats under an icy moon. The scene was so unreal and somehow remote she was reminded of a production of *Peer Gynt* she'd seen some months previously. The quayside, barely lit, and the dark figures methodically carrying crates from the lorry to the two moored boats, only required a grand overture to be staged at Covent Garden.

'I wonder when they'll put to sea?'

Philip shrugged. 'Your guess is as good as mine.'

In silence they watched while the wind continued to sweep down, causing the Firth of Lorne to swell and ruffle turbulently, sending up a deluge of spray along the harbour wall – and all the time the loading of the boats continued, sinister in its orderliness. Yet what innocent activity could take place under such circumstances, in the middle of the night, on the quayside of a silent village? Because of the wind they didn't at first hear footsteps coming along the road towards the huts. Suddenly Philip froze.

'This way, quick!' he whispered urgently, grabbing Camilla's arm.

Slow to realise what was happening, she turned to ask him what was wrong when she saw a figure walking briskly towards them. It was a stockily built man, dressed in oilskins and wearing a sou'wester. He was walking purposefully and coming closer every second. Philip groped frantically for the handle of the small doorway which was set into the large double doors of the hut. At last his hand came into contact with the rusty metal catch and, pressing it with hands that were now shaking, he felt it give, but only a fraction.

'Watch out,' he breathed frantically, pushing Camilla to one side while he put his shoulder to the door. She clung close to the side of the building, the pounding of her heart in her ears rivalling the roar of the wind so that they seemed one and the same. She felt as if she were being battered both without and within.

With a creaking, wrenching sound the door flew open and Philip nearly fell forward as it gave under his weight. Then Camilla felt his arm round her waist and he was dragging her bodily through the doorway and into the pitch darkness of the shed. A moment later, he'd shut the door behind them and was leaning against it to prevent it being opened from the outside.

'God, that was close,' he panted. Standing near to him she could feel his breath on her cheek and smell the sweet musky scent of his body. For a moment a wave of weakness nearly caused her legs to buckle under her, and as if he sensed something she felt his hand under her elbow, steadying her.

'Are you all right?' he whispered.

'I'm fine,' she said firmly, recovering herself. 'What do we do now?' she whispered, in what she hoped was a strong resolute tone.

'Stay here until the coast is clear.'

'Do you think that man saw us?'

'I don't think he did. He was bent against the wind and it looked, from what I could see, as if the brim of his sou'wester was pulled down.'

'If he had seen us he'd have barged in here by now, anyway,' she said hopefully.

'I'd be happier if we could find something to wedge this door with, though. With this gale I can't hear what the hell's going on outside. Maybe he did see us and he's gone to fetch the others!'

'I'll try and find something.' Camilla reached in her pocket for the pencil slim torch she'd brought.

'Don't point it anywhere near this door,' Philip warned, 'in case they're watching from outside.'

'Christ, what a place to be stuck! Supposing we have to stay here until it's daylight?'

'We might have to,' he conceded.

Camilla switched on the torch and it gave out a sharp narrow beam of light, straight as a knife's edge in the darkness, piercing as an arrow as it fell on something large and metal with shining parts that occupied almost the whole of the floor area. She swung the torch wildly to and fro, etching the outline in a stunned and shocked silence. The implications of this find were shatteringly apparent as the beam of light finally came to rest on a three-inch high silver replica of an Alsatian dog. She knew the emblem well.

'What is it?' Philip asked her urgently.

Camilla leaned against him, hardly able to speak. 'This is my father's car,' she whispered at last. 'The one he was killed in.'

Chapter Thirteen

Philip peered through the open crack in the door, screwing up his eyes against the wind, edging forward inch by inch in case the fisherman still lurked outside. An hour had passed since they'd entered the hut. The moon had long been obliterated by clouds so dense they seemed to form an impenetrable blanket over the bay, and large spots of rain were splashing into the fast-growing puddles on the quayside and dropping heavily on the roof.

'Can you see anything?' Camilla breathed. Cold and sick with misery, she wanted only to get away. These people were killers. What lay behind the sinister activities of Ardachie was the work of a highly organised group who were quite ruthless, and who, she was now sure, would stop at nothing. Whatever they were smuggling out of the Highlands in fishing boats was obviously of such a secret nature that anyone who discovered the contents of the cargo was in jeopardy.

In the pitch blackness she heard Philip whisper: 'I think he's gone. Hang on, I'm going outside now to get a better look.'

'Do be careful,' she urged, straining to see what lay beyond the now open door of the shed.

Silently, Philip stepped forward and paused, looking to left and right. Visibility was down to twenty yards as the rain came lashing down like a beaded curtain and the wind swept gustily across the harbour.

'I think it's okay,' he said, having to raise his voice above a whisper in order to be heard. 'Let's go.'

They'd planned to get back to Creagnach and then phone the police in Glasgow. As long as they had not been seen, no one would think of removing Malcolm's car, a vital link in the evidence they needed. And if they were quick there might even be time for the fishing boats to be halted and searched before they set sail.

Philip grabbed hold of Camilla's wrist to lead her back the way they had come and, acutely conscious of the warmth and strength of his fingers, she clasped his hand and followed. In a matter of seconds they were soaked, the rain running down their faces and necks, squelching in their shoes, making the ground treacherously slippery in the dark.

'Not so fast,' she called out, but the words were whipped away from her lips by a gust of wind that nearly made her lose her balance.

Making their way round to the back of the sheds, they moved with cautious stealth, bent forward, eyes stinging from the rain, hardly able to see in the wet blackness. They wanted to make for the wooded hillock again which rose between Creagnach and the quayside. Once at the top they knew the worst danger would be over and with any luck they would be back at the house in less than ten minutes. She gripped Philip's hand, and he squeezed hers reassuringly.

Then it happened. Springing out of the blanketing darkness, two burly figures leapt upon them, plummeting as if out of the sky with such force that Camilla was flung to the ground, her hand torn from Philip's. A mattress of thick heather broke her fall and she rolled in the wetness, aware of Philip falling away from her, of their attackers' glistening oilskins and rough voices raised against the wind that howled across the harbour. The thing that Camilla feared most at that moment was her own panic; the type of panic that blots out all senses, leaving its victim paralysed in its icy clutches.

'Run!' she heard Philip yell. His voice rose from the moving huddle of black shapes that writhed beside her on the ground. She could hear the grunts of throats seeking air, and the thud of fists against resisting bodies. 'Run!' Another gust of wind came roaring up the coast now, so that feet squelching and staggering in the mud was added to the sickening sounds of the three men as they struggled in combat.

There was nothing she could do but go to try and get help. If she stayed what use would she be? Her strength was less than puny beside theirs. She had no weapons, not even a stick. Apart from which, she could not see. In the darkness her eyes were sockets of watering pain, the wind pricking her eyeballs like tiny needles.

'For Christ's sake, *run!*' she heard Philip roar. She wanted to stay with him, to help him. If she left and these men killed him . . .

'GO!'

Camilla turned her head and, with a sob of fear, started running. If she could fetch help quickly, it would be better than standing by helplessly. Deciding to keep to the flat ground that lay parallel to the quayside for as much of the way as she could, she bent her head against the wind and struggled forward. Her clothes were waterlogged, though, and her feet, in trainers, seemed heavy as lead. Already she was gasping for breath, her chest tight and hurting, her heart pounding as if it would explode. In a moment she'd have to start veering to the right, climbing up the hill, but for just a few more yards she could keep going straight. Then her skin started to prickle with horror. She was being followed. One of the men must have broken away from the fight and he was coming after her. She could hear the sound of his legs and feet thrashing through the wet heather and bracken . . . and then she heard his breath, hoarse and rasping. He was coming closer all the time.

She knew she had to make up her mind what to do, and quickly. She could either start climbing the hill immediately, and hope to be able to hide among the trees when she got to the top, or she could continue to run alongside the quay and into the village, where the buildings would provide greater protection and places to hide. There was the risk she would run straight into the others, of course, if they were still loading up the boats, but it was a chance she had to take. At least, in a whole village full of people, there was a chance there would be someone who was on the side of law and order and who would help her.

Once decided, she abandoned the rough ground and started along the narrow road that ran like a shiny black ribbon straight into the village. There was a stumbling sound behind her, a muttered oath, and although she did not pause to look round she felt she was gaining on her pursuer. If she could only keep up the pace she had set herself until she reached the safety of the buildings, she was sure she'd be all right, but her breath was coming in burning, tearing gasps now, so out of condition was she from having spent the last four years behind a desk. With aching muscles and calves that threatened to seize up with cramp if she went much further, she pounded along the road, and in her ears the heavy tread of boots still followed and it seemed they were very close behind now. A scream rose to her throat and terror made her dizzy. But then, out of the darkness, there rose a shape . . . and another, and then the looming outlines of cottages and windows, doorways and garden walls. She had arrived at the outskirts of Ardachie. Ahead of her a dark alley-way divided two of the houses, disappearing into a tunnel of blackness. Without pausing to consider, she shot up it and found herself in a yard, dimly lit by the light of a curtained window. She wouldn't be able to stay here for long. If her pursuer followed her up the alleyway she'd be cornered, but for the moment she sank on to her haunches, crouching behind a water-butt, half fainting from breathlessness and exhaustion.

Leaning back against the stone wall of the cottage, which formed part of the small quadrangle, she felt the sweat freezing on her back and running in icy rivulets between her breasts. With one hand she wiped her forehead, pushing back the soaking hair, fighting to steady her nerves. Fearfully she listened and looked around and then jumped as something flew across the yard a foot above the ground. What the hell . . .? Was it an animal?

A bat perhaps? Maybe a large leaf carried by the wind?

Struggling to keep calm she strained to hear if the footsteps were coming nearer, but there were no sounds from the road. Had she given her pursuer the slip? And what was happening to Philip? The thought of him being beaten up by the thugs who had attacked them galvanised her into action. She must get help. For all she knew Philip might be lying behind the shed with his head kicked in.

Desperation made her brave. Rising slowly from her hiding place, aching all over, she knew she must nevertheless act fast. There was no time to go back to Creagnach now. If she went by the road it might take her as long as fifteen minutes, and there was no way she could go back the way she had come and risk being caught going up the hill and through the woods. There was nothing for it but to go to Hector Ross's house and seek his help. Her father had trusted him and so must she. Maybe he had told her the dogs had died of distemper because he, too, had been threatened. Maybe he hadn't dared tell her the truth.

Keeping close to the buildings, she edged her way to the entrance of the yard, making out in the dim light the narrow alleyway that wound its way back to the main street. All was silent except for the buffeting sound of the wind and the splatter of rain.

The vet's house was several minutes' walk away but she knew she could reach it by taking the next right-hand turn and then going along the road that ran parallel with the quayside. In spite of having been there only once before she remembered it as a square house, larger than the others and set back from the road by a small front garden. She'd have to wake him up, of course, but the need to get help was desperate enough to make her feel anything was possible. Having come so far her confidence was returning. She'd succeeded in getting away from her attacker and now, as she scurried along the deserted street, her relief was so great she felt almost bold. It was the same sensation she'd experienced when, after David's helicopter crash, she'd had to go to his office and take control of the business. Fear, apprehension, and the seriousness of the situation had psyched her up to a fever pitch of endeavour so that she had succeeded. Now she must do the same. Saving Philip was all she cared about. She would not even allow herself to think that help might come too late for him.

Still it rained, falling in great swathes across the road, carried inland by the wind, but above it, muffled and intermittent, she could hear voices and an engine starting up. The lorry must be departing from the dockside, its load removed, its mission over. Camilla was level with the post office now, and from the other side of the two-storey building she could hear shouts on the quayside as an engine was revved up. A door slammed somewhere near, and although there were no light on she knew people occupied the post office, going about their secret activities.

She hurried past, sprinting though it seemed her heart would burst and her lungs split wide. Who was the mastermind behind this operation? It could hardly be the little old lady who ran the post office, or the doughy-faced youths who worked in the shop. And then the answer flashed through her mind. It had to be a mariner, someone from the fishing fleet who set out at dawn to trawl the treacherous waters.

Hector Ross's house was in sight now, looming through the torrents of rain like a great grey box set among trees and bushes. There were no lights on anywhere and the place looked deserted. There was nothing for it but to bang on the front door if she wanted to rouse the household.

At that moment a car, headlights cutting brilliant twin beams of light through the rain, appeared from the opposite direction. The road was bathed in dazzling brightness, as if from a searchlight, and Camilla instantly cowered back into the shadows of a doorway. As the car drew nearer the luminosity grew, increasing until the whole street and all the buildings glowed and the road was like burnished silver, the air alive with a million dancing droplets. Then, as it drew level with Camilla, it braked, and she stood rigid, knowing all was lost. She'd been followed all along and now they'd come by car to seize her and there was nowhere else to run. An enormous sense of defeat and desolation swept over her and she was consumed by guilt. It was only because of her that Philip had come to Scotland, and for all she knew he was now lying battered to death on the far shore. Feeling herself grow weak with misery she was startled to hear a voice speaking to her in gentle surprise.

'Mrs Eaton? Why, what in the world are you doing out on a night like this?'

Wide-eyed, she peered into the car and saw the genial crumpled face of the vet.

'Mr Ross!' she burst out, overwhelmed. 'Thank God it's you. I was coming to see you. I've got to go to the police.'

He looked startled. 'The police? Is that so, dear lady? Then you'd best be coming into ma wee house. I've just got back from delivering a calf that didna want to be born.' He smiled. 'I'll just put the car awa', and then we'll go into the house and you can phone from here.'

'Oh, thank you,' she said gratefully. 'It's urgent. We must ring them at once. Have you got a car phone?'

He raised bushy eyebrows and the lines on his forehead deepened. 'I dinna hold with expensive gimmicks like that,' he retorted disdainfully.

Camilla leaned forward. 'This is a matter of life or death. My friend has been attacked . . . over there by the fishermen's sheds. I was attacked too but I got away . . . we've got to get help quickly. I think they're smuggling something on to two of the fishing boats. We should tell the police to search them before they set sail.' The words tumbled out and she was gesticulating frantically. 'We've no time to lose,' she added desperately.

Ross gave a decisive nod, put his foot down on the accelerator and swung the car up the drive that ran alongside his front garden. Camilla followed, praying they wouldn't be too late in getting help to Philip. A moment later Hector had jumped out of his car with great alacrity for a man his age, and was making his way swiftly across his squelching front lawn. Then he unlocked the front door and hurried into the hall, followed by Camilla. He turned on a light, revealing the shabby cream and brown paintwork. The place smelled of disinfectant.

'There's a phone in the surgery,' he announced, opening a brown varnished door on his right. The smell of disinfectant was even stronger in here and involuntarily Camilla wrinkled her nose. 'I'll just turn on the light,' he muttered, and then strode over to a desk in the corner on which stood an old-fashioned-looking black phone. He grabbed the receiver and started dialling. A moment later Camilla heard him say succinctly: 'Police. This is an emergency.'

Relief washed over her.

'This is Hector Ross of Ballimore Road, Ardachie,' she heard him say. Then with surprising precision and fluency she heard him outline what she'd told him about Philip, and the fishing boats being loaded up with a strange cargo. 'Can you send someone? Quickly?' she heard him add. Then he turned to Camilla. 'Would you like to explain where your friend is, exactly? It'll be quickest that way.'

She nodded, taking the phone from him. Briefly she repeated what had happened. 'Hurry . . . for God's sake.' She was unable to continue. Exhausted, cold, and soaked to the skin, she felt hot tears spring to her eyes. It was no good trying to deny her feelings for Philip now. She was in love with him.

'We'll get you a warm drink and some dry clothes,' she heard Hector say as she hung up. Then he went into the hall, and although it was the middle of the night he shouted up the stairs: 'Morag!'

'Please don't wake up your housekeeper for my sake,' Camilla protested.

'Och, she always gets up in the night if I've been called out,' he replied easily. 'There'll be a robe or something you can put on while we dry your things.'

'No, really. I have to get back.'

'You'll no go out in this rain again without a wee dram inside you first. What were you doing down by those auld

sheds in the first place? It's a terrible night to be out, so it is.'
Hector opened a locked cupboard which Camilla expected to
hold stocks of animal medicines but which appeared to be full
of brandy and whisky. 'You'll join me, won't you?' he added
conversationally, holding up a bottle.

'Thank you.'

'Why were you attacked? Who would want to do a thing like
that?' he asked.

Camilla turned to face him, knowing she ought to be able to
trust him because her father had yet for some reason as uncertain as she'd been the first time they'd met.

'We went into one of the huts,' she explained cautiously. 'The
door wasn't locked or anything. It began to rain and we were
sheltering.'

'Yes?' He smiled encouragingly, the folds and hollows and
creases of his face crumpling into an expression that was wholly
charming.

She bit her lip, unable to continue for a moment, and then
blurted out: 'We found my father's car. The one he was in when
he was killed.'

A look of understanding crossed Hector's face and he nodded
knowingly. 'Och aye! You would find it there, waiting to be
repaired, I've no doubt. Young McTavish bought it from your
stepmother when your father died. As she doesn't drive it was
no use to her, so she let him have it for three thousand pounds.'
Hector chuckled. 'All his savings it took but he reckons it will
give him a head start over the other lads when it comes to
impressing the girls. "Pulling the birds" I believe it's known
as amongst the youngsters these days, isn't it?'

'Edith sold it?' Camilla asked, stunned.

'That's right, dear lady. You didn't think it had been stolen,
did you? If you like I'll introduce you to young McTavish
tomorrow and you can ask him for yourself. He'll be back
from fishing about noon.'

'No, that will not be necessary.' Camilla sipped the whisky
and a trail of fire scorched her throat and went down to her

227

stomach. She looked covertly at the vet out of the corner of her eye and wondered how much he really knew. Philip had examined Malcolm's car very carefully by the light of her torch. It was probably true, as Hector had said, that Edith had sold it to a fisherman; the question to be asked was, who had drained off the brake fluid which would have caused her father to lose control of the car and crash? Who was it who had wanted Malcolm dead?

'Will you be making us a hot drink, Morag? And find something warm for Mrs Eaton to change into. She's a wee mite wet from the storm.' Hector spoke to his housekeeper in a kindly but commanding fashion.

'I haven't time, I must go to Philip,' Camilla cut in desperately. 'The police must have arrived at the quayside by now.' She didn't dare let herself think that the last time Philip had had contact with the nearest police station in Caoldair they hadn't seemed interested in anything he'd had to say. Maybe they would pay more attention to someone as important in the community as the local vet!

Morag, wrapped up in a woollen dressing-gown tightly belted over her nightdress, looked even prettier than Camilla had remembered. It was because her hair was flowing loose tonight, long dark tresses that curled round her shoulders and hung in heavy waves down her back. The last time she'd seen Hector's housekeeper she'd been primly clad in a dark dress with her hair wound round her head in thick plaits.

'Will it be tea you're wanting?' she asked.

'No . . . really, I must go,' Camilla protested.

'To do what?' Hector asked, astonished. 'Dear lady, what would be the point of you going out, back into that dreadful storm, and running the risk of meeting the attackers from whom you've just escaped? I expect the police will be dealing with everything this vurry minute!'

'Can we phone them and ask what's happening then?' she fretted. 'Could you, or your son, though I hate to ask this, drive me to the quayside so I can see if my friend is all right?'

Hector's expression changed. 'My son?' he asked curiously. 'Do you mean Alastair?'

'Yes. I spoke to him on the phone when I first came up here. Of course if he's asleep . . .'

Hector shook his head. 'You have'na met him, then?'

Camilla looked perplexed. 'No.'

'I thought not. Ma son's a cripple, Mrs Eaton. He canna go out.' Hector's accent had grown broader and his voice was gruff. Morag, Camilla noticed, was standing tensely just inside the door, watching her employer in a strange way, almost as if she was afraid of something.

'I'm so sorry. I had no idea,' Camilla said in a small voice.

'Dear lady,' Hector seemed cheered by the sympathy in her tone, 'God sends us these tragedies to try us. Ma son's affliction is something we have to bear.' He turned to Morag. 'Get on with the tea, girl, and dry clothes for Mrs Eaton.'

As Morag slipped silently from the room Camilla wondered at the relationships in this household. Something was going on, of that she was sure. There were undercurrents she couldn't fathom and they concerned Morag. There was no time to think about that now, however. Her main concern was Philip.

'Can I use your phone?' she asked. 'What's the number of the police station? I must find out what's happening.'

'Allow me, dear lady,' Hector replied. He reached for the phone again. 'I'll find out what's happening.'

While she finished her drink and felt, surprisingly, the warmth spread to her outer extremities, she heard Hector questioning whoever was on duty at the Caoldair police station. He grunted and nodded and said 'Aye' several times, before hanging up.

'Well?' Camilla demanded anxiously. 'What's happening?'

'No cause for alarm,' he said reassuringly. 'They went straight to the fishing sheds but there was no sign of your friend or anyone there. The area was deserted. They think your friend must have got away and the attackers run off.'

'What about the fishing boats? Have they found out what's been loaded on to them?'

'I don't think there's been a report back to the police station about that yet. We must give them time, dear lady. They may not be able to search the boats without a warrant either. Anyway, it looks as if your friend is safe, and probably back at Creagnach by now. Shall I run you home if you're anxious? There's nothing we can do about the mysterious cargo you mentioned. That's in the hands of the authorities now. The main thing is *you're* all right after your terrible experience, and it looks as if your friend is all right, too.'

'I would like to get home,' Camilla admitted.

'Vurry well. You'll no have a cup of tea first?'

'If you don't mind . . .'

'Vurry well. We'll gang away. I'll just get my raincoat. It was a fine night when I first set out to deliver that calf over at Garfarren, and listen to it now! Still coming down cats and dogs by the sound of it.' He smiled as if he found the raging storm something to be amused about, then he left the room to get his coat.

Morag came in a moment later with a tray, set with a brown teapot, two cups and a jug of milk. She seemed to crash it down on a table in the window with unnecessary violence before turning to Camilla and glaring balefully at her. Neither woman spoke. Morag held her fixed stare for several long seconds, not uttering a word, while Camilla tried to fathom what was going on. There was something in the girl's amber-coloured eyes that was strange and angry, as if she hated Camilla with undisguised loathing, as if she deeply resented her presence in the house. And then, just as swiftly as she'd entered the room, she turned and left it again on silent slippered feet. Hector Ross came back, shrugging on a massive oilskin coat of the type worn by fishermen.

'Shall we be off then?' he asked conversationally.

It was only when he dropped her off, five minutes later, that it struck her he'd not queried her still being in Ardachie when she'd taken pains to appear to have left Scotland for London three days previously. Had he known all along she was staying in Malcolm's house?

Creagnach was as dark and deserted as when they'd left it two hours before, and the moment Camilla entered by the kitchen door which they'd left unlocked, she knew instinctively that Philip hadn't come back. Switching on the light, she saw the kitchen was exactly as they'd left it, with their dirty coffee cups still on the table.

'Oh, my God!' she said aloud, running her hands through her dripping hair. He must still be out there, in the storm, perhaps lying injured and unable to get back on his own. Why hadn't the police checked properly? Why had they merely assumed, because they didn't find him by the sheds, that he'd escaped the attacker and was all right?

Running to the library, turning on all the lights as she went, for there was no need for secrecy now, she went to Malcolm's desk and grabbed the list of emergency numbers he'd compiled. Then, with shaking hands, she dialled the number of the Caoldair police. In London, she reflected, an emergency call would have brought out a fleet of cars ages ago, with sirens wailing in the night air. And then, as she heard the number ring, a dreadful thought occurred to her. Why hadn't she heard sirens tonight? Surely, in an emergency, consideration for sleeping citizens would be outweighed by the need to get to the trouble spot in time!

Five minutes later Camilla replaced the phone, filled with numbed disbelief and shock. And yet all along something hadn't been quite right. She'd wanted to trust Hector Ross, yet nothing he had said or done had rung true. Her father had been mistaken, and so had she. It was a bitter pill to swallow. The police sergeant on night duty at Caoldair, to whom she had just spoken, had just informed her that neither they, nor any of the other local police stations, including Oban, had been contacted by anyone in the Ardachie area that night. No one had reported a fight down by the fishing sheds; and no one had phoned and asked for their help.

* * *

Camilla stripped off her clothes, throwing the sodden garments into the bath before towelling herself briskly. Then she put on a pair of warm trousers and a sweater, and hurried down to the kitchen again. Feeling sick with anxiety, she put on the kettle to give herself something to do, but visions of Philip, lying in the heather too injured to move, haunted her. Supposing he'd been beaten unconscious and his body thrown into the sea! A low moan broke from her lips as she tried to fight the clamouring fears that were crowding out all reason.

It was over an hour since she'd left him by the huts. How long would the police take to reach him now? They'd asked for her address, but she presumed they'd go looking for him before coming to visit her. 'Philip, Philip . . .' she said his name aloud, not caring now what happened as long as he was all right. Suddenly she slumped into a chair at the kitchen table, her head in her hands, hot tears smarting in her eyes. That her father had been murdered because he knew too much was terrible enough, but the thought that something might have happened to Philip . . . that she couldn't take.

And why had she, against her better judgment, trusted Hector Ross, for God's sake? Why had Malcolm trusted him? She did not believe for a moment that Edith had sold Malcolm's car to one of the fishermen either; and if she had, why was it being kept hidden, rusting where it stood, in a shed down by the quay? Camilla shook her head, cursing herself for having gone back to the vet's house. She'd wasted valuable time in getting on to the police, and now it might be too late.

Wiping her eyes she jumped to her feet again, unable to endure being alone with her thoughts any longer. The silence of the house was appalling, the emptiness without Philip intolerable. She started to pace around the kitchen, tormented with fear, straining to hear a distant police siren, the sound of a car coming up the drive, the front doorbell ringing and the police coming to tell her . . . Oh, God, what had happened to Philip?

Suddenly she froze, watching with wide eyes and breath held in check as the kitchen door opened slowly and cautiously.

A cold blast of damp air came whirling through the widening gap as the door was pushed further open, and then out of the darkness of the wild night a figure stepped forward and stood for a moment, looking at her.

Chapter Fourteen

'Camilla, are you all right?' Philip stood there, soaked to the skin, hair dripping, every line of his body tense.

She looked back at him, relief at seeing him standing in the kitchen doorway sweeping her along in a rush of emotion.

'I'm fine.'

'Thank Christ!' he burst out. 'I thought . . .'

'What about *you*? I was so frightened . . . Oh, Philip!' Her voice caught. She was unable to describe the dark images that had been torturing her mind.

Suddenly he looked haggard, his expression strained. 'I tried to stop them following you, but one of them ran off after you. Are you sure you're okay?'

'Yes.'

They stood facing each other and the atmosphere between them seemed to crackle with tension. Their eyes locked and she felt as if all the breath were being sucked out of her body. Then she dropped her gaze, unable to go on looking at him as she realised there was no point in pretending any longer. Not to him. Not to herself. Useless to keep up a charade of mere friendship and camaraderie when what she felt was overwhelming love. What was the point of hiding feelings that could no longer be ignored?

Camilla raised her eyes again and there was no mistaking in her expression the yearning and longing of a woman who has been denied love for a very long time.

As if in response Philip, with a gesture of helplessness, of having been overcome by something he could no longer control either, stepped towards her. Then, with all the intensity of newfound passion, he flung his arms around her and pulled her close. His cheek was chill against hers and when, after a moment, his lips sought hers, it felt as if they were carved from ice. Camilla held him close against the warmth of her body, stroking his hair, his neck, and gradually as they kissed he seemed to melt, grow hot, become feverish in her arms.

'Camilla,' he murmured brokenly, between kisses, 'I didn't dare hope you felt the same.'

She felt no surprise at his words now, whereas before she would have been astonished. A strange sense that this was meant filled her, as if all along their coming together had been predestined and was therefore inevitable.

'I love you,' she said simply. 'I feel as if I've loved you for a long time.'

Philip kissed her again, sweetly, wildly, murmuring her name again and again as she clung to him, her heart beating with joy.

At that moment a great pounding on the door of Creagnach made them break apart, startled.

'What the hell!' Philip exclaimed.

Briefly she told him that in the end it was she who had called the police. 'Didn't you see them just now, down by the quayside? They were supposed to come to your rescue!'

He shook his head. 'Don't let's tell them more than we have to,' he said quickly as the loud knocking started again and the peal of the front doorbell echoed through the empty house.

She stared at him blankly. 'Why not?'

He spoke urgently. 'I believe they're part of what's going on here. Can't you say you called because we accidentally got involved with a couple of drunks down by the quayside and there was a scuffle?'

'What? At two o'clock in the morning?' Camilla shook her head. 'They'll never swallow that.'

'How much did you tell them?'

'I said . . . Oh God, I can't remember! I was in such a state when I found the call Hector Ross made wasn't to the police at all. And who was I talking to . . . from his house?' She clapped her hand over her mouth. 'Whoever it was, I told them where they could find you . . . I said we'd been attacked . . . Christ, Philip, I can't remember how much I said.' Now that she knew he was safe, all the other nightmares were crowding back, filling her with fresh anguish. Finding her father's car hidden in the fishing hut with its brake fluid drained, the death of over forty dogs . . . the warning notes . . . Something horrifying was happening, and the only thing that seemed clear to her at this moment was that they were in danger.

'We'll have to answer the door,' Philip was saying, taking her hand and leading her out of the kitchen into the hall. 'Remember, tell them as little as possible. Try and pretend everything's fine,' he added.

Camilla nodded, squeezing his hand for comfort. Then she straightened her shoulders and raised her chin. It reminded her of the time shortly after David's death when she'd had to face her first board meeting as the new chairman.

There were two of them, looming out of the darkness at the top of the front steps. They regarded Philip and Camilla for a long moment, and then one of them spoke directly to her, ignoring Philip.

'Are you all right, Miss?' He was a shifty-looking man with foxy features and Camilla wondered if he was the one Philip had seen at the Caoldair Police Station when he'd reported the murder by strychnine of Edith's dogs.

Camilla summoned up her most gracious smile. 'I'm sorry to have called you out on a dreadful night like this,' she said, apologetically. 'We're both fine, as you can see.'

They seemed to eye her suspiciously, she thought.

'You're the lady with the dogs, aren't you?'

'My stepmother has . . . er, had a lot of dogs.'

'There's nothing to worry about,' Philip cut in with an attempt at breeziness. 'Everything's fine, really. Mrs Eaton got worried when we were separated in the darkness and there were a few rather drunk fishermen around at the time. But as you can see, we're quite okay.'

At that moment the policeman with the foxy face seemed to recognise Philip. 'We've met before, haven't we – sir?' The fractional delay before calling Philip 'sir' was almost insulting.

'I think we probably have,' he said smoothly, then put his arm round Camilla's shoulders in a protective gesture. His smile gave nothing away. 'I'm sorry you've been troubled.'

Foxy Face turned back to Camilla. 'We understand that you were under the impression someone had phoned us earlier, asking for help?'

'Yes . . . well, when I lost my friend in the dark, I asked someone to phone the police for me . . . and I presumed that's what they'd done.'

'And who might it be that you asked, Miss?'

Camilla felt Philip's grip on her shoulder tighten as if in warning.

'I don't know. I'm not sure,' she floundered. 'It was just someone in the village. It was so dark I couldn't see properly.'

'Anyway, all's well that ends well,' Philip remarked with another reassuring smile. 'I'm sorry you've been troubled.'

Almost reluctantly, the two policemen went back to their car which they'd parked in the drive. Then, with a last curious look at Camilla and Philip, standing framed in the doorway, they climbed in and drove off.

'Thank God,' she said in relief. 'I'm sure they didn't believe a word we said.'

Philip shivered, and she realised he was still in his soaking clothes.

'You must get those things off,' she told him, leading him by the hand. Together they climbed the stairs as he began to pull off his drenched sweater.

'Go into my bathroom and put your things in the tub with mine. There are lots of towels in there too. I'll get some dry clothes for you from your room,' said Camilla.

While he showered in the adjoining bathroom, she sat on her

bed, talking to him through the open door, recounting the conversation she'd had with Hector Ross in his house, and how he'd claimed a young fisherman had bought Malcolm's car because Edith had no further use for it.

'Is it true that she can't drive a car?' Philip asked through the gentle roar of a steaming shower.

'I don't know,' Camilla replied. 'It seems unlikely, though. She's lived in the country all her life and she must have been able to drive.'

'One would think so,' he agreed, turning off the shower and wrapping himself in a large towelling sheet. 'What do you know about her?' he asked, coming back into the bedroom. 'How did your father meet her?' As he spoke he came and sat on the bed beside Camilla, his skin glowing. He reached for her hand again and this time his fingers were warm.

Camilla thought back. 'Daddy met her through mutual friends at a houseparty in Gloucestershire, where she used to live. She was a widow, with no children, and dogs seem to have been her life.'

'It is possible, you know,' Philip observed, 'that she's involved in all this.'

'But what would be her motive, Philip? What has she gained by what's happened? She's lost her husband, her dogs . . .'

'Maybe something went wrong,' he pointed out.

Camilla looked thoughtful. 'I think we should stay on here a few more days, after all, you know. We can't leave things up in the air like this. We need proof. We need to know what's being smuggled out of Ardachie!'

Philip heaved a great sigh of relief. 'I hoped you'd say that.'

She looked at him. 'Why?'

'All along I've wanted to stay on for a while,' he reminded her.

'Yes, I know you have.' She smiled, catching his eye. He was looking at her intently now, and her heart skipped a beat. Then he leaned closer and kissed her on the lips, lightly and sweetly this time.

'I was afraid that if we went back to London you wouldn't want to see so much of me. I was afraid I'd lose you, before . . .' He faltered and his cheeks flamed. 'Before . . .'

'Before you'd even had me?' she asked softly. 'Oh, Philip, I only wanted to go back because I was afraid.'

'Afraid of what?'

'Loving you; being rejected; getting hurt; making a complete fool of myself . . .'

He silenced her with another kiss. 'Do you think the same thoughts didn't go through my mind, night and day?' He sat up straight on the bed and looked at her squarely. 'I think I fell in love with you that first evening, when we all came to dinner at your house. Mum was trying to pair me off with Poppy and you looked so distressed by the way she was dressed.' He paused, chuckling. 'I thought you were the most fascinating woman I'd ever set eyes on.'

Camilla took his hand in both of hers, stroking the strong tanned fingers. 'And now?'

'And now I think you're the most fascinating *and* lovable woman I've ever met.' This time his kiss was ardent, hungrily demanding, and folding her arms around his neck she pulled him close, the scent of his hair and skin making her momentarily dizzy, the quick upsurge of desire taking her breath away. Now there was no need for words. The doubts of the past few days were banished.

The first fiercely hot flame between them was kindled and set alight. Slowly, gently, he pulled Camilla down beside him on the bed as she gave herself to him with all the ardour of her love.

The lull that usually precedes a storm came the morning after when the wind had abated to a strange stillness, bringing with it the tangy scent of seaweed and salt, a purifying air that was both bracing and cleansing. Camilla and Philip had hardly slept, and now as the first pale streaks of dawn blossomed on a grey horizon, they rose to bathe and dress and have breakfast, no longer needing to hide their presence at Creagnach.

'I've made up my mind,' she announced, 'to go through Edith's desk. I know it's an awful thing to do, and I wish we could get hold of her to ask her permission, but I don't know what else to do.'

Philip nodded in agreement. 'While you're doing that I'm going to walk into the village to see what's going on. We need bread and milk anyway.'

'You'll be careful, won't you?' she said anxiously.

He grinned. 'I think I'm safe in broad daylight. I'm going to go into the pub for a pint when it opens. I might pick up something of interest if I can get chatting to the fishermen. At least if I'm asked I needn't pretend to be staying in some hotel in the next village.'

As she watched him go, it seemed as if every nerve in her body quivered and strained to follow him, as if he were bound to her with invisible threads that stretched between them, plucking painfully at her heart-strings. This new love that had come to her, when she thought that part of her life was over, was terrifying and sublime, exalting and fearful. She knew she trod a path that could be flower-filled one moment and a minefield the next – but then she also knew something else.

If Philip was twenty years younger, so what? It happened all the time these days. Nobody thought anything of it. If people jibed that she had a toy boy, or accused her of cradle snatching, so be it. She loved Philip with all her heart and soul, and felt transported back to the days of her youth in a way she'd never have believed possible. Who but a fool would turn away from the chance of such happiness now?

When she'd cleared away the breakfast things, she went up to Edith's bedroom and, pulling up a chair to the pretty antique escritoire, set about going through her papers.

Philip's pace was brisk as he walked the short distance into Ardachie, and he felt happier and more light-hearted than he could ever recall having felt before. He was still unable to believe that someone as wonderful as Camilla could return his love. It made him feel ten feet tall! She'd actually said she loved him too, many times during the night, whispering the words with deep emotion as she responded to his kisses. It was the most amazing thing that had ever happened to him and it seemed as if all his previous romances with girls like Fiona, and even the exotic Lai-Lai from China, paled to nothing by comparison. They had all been a dress rehearsal for the real thing, and Camilla was definitely the real thing. Looking about him, he decided he loved the world today. Everything – the mountains and the cloudless sky, the sparkling waters of the Firth and the small neat houses of the village – looked new and special and more beautiful than on previous days. Camilla cared for him which was all that mattered. Last night she had given herself to him, trustingly and generously, and he had lain within her, held fast in the tight warmth of her love, and felt he had never known such ecstasy.

He decided that what he'd really like to do was buy her a present. Something to remind her of their time up here together. If he could only find a shop in Ardachie that sold something suitable, something small but precious, then he'd take it back to her and give it to her as a tiny token of his love.

Almost immediately, he spotted a small antique shop, set off the main road, and the word 'junk' sprang to his mind rather than the painted word 'antiques' on the small dusty window. Nevertheless, on closer inspection, and seeing a tray on which were laid out some trinkets, he pushed open the door and went in. An old man in wilting tweeds and with a drooping moustache came from the shadows at the back of the shop.

'Will it be help you're wanting?' he enquired politely.

Philip had stopped by the tray, attracted by something that lay in a little white box. 'This is pretty,' he remarked, picking it up. On a pad of cotton wool lay a brooch of typical Highland design. It was a circlet of engraved silver, classically and simply shaped, but what made it special was that in the centre, quivering from a pendant fitting, a clear yellow stone shimmered and glittered in the light.

'Och aye, that's a nice wee piece. It came originally from the laird's family, up at the big house,' the old man replied, polishing his gold-rimmed glasses on the elbow of his jacket as he spoke.

'What . . . Creagnach?' Philip asked in surprise.

'Aye. The laird's mother gave it to one of the servants as a wedding present. It must have been going on sixty years ago. It was a wee maid called Flora. She died a couple of years ago, aged eighty, and it was sold to me with several other things from her cottage.' He nodded brightly. 'She used to say it had belonged to the laird's great-grandmother. That it was a wee family heirloom. I dinna ken about that, but it's vurry old, and it's real silver all right.'

'What's the stone?' Philip held it up to the light, seeing it change according to the angle from palest primrose yellow to the deep rich gold of honey.

'That'll be a cairngorm. It's a yellow quartz from the Blue Cairn mountain. They're a very popular gem stone in these parts,' the shopkeeper added knowledgeably.

'Do you only find them in Scotland?'

'Och aye. Only on the Cairn.'

Philip made up his mind instantly. It was exactly what he was looking for, something local and special and very beautiful too.

The old man put the box in a little brown paper bag and was quite happy to accept Philip's cheque. Tucking the brooch into his pocket, Philip then proceeded to do the rest of the shopping before going on to the post office to buy the morning newspapers.

Edith was a meticulous person, Camilla discovered, as she went through the drawers of her desk. All her papers were carefully filed in neatly headed folders. Some were devoted to various charge accounts, such as Harrods or John Lewis, others referred to American Express, Access or Barclaycard. Then there were headings for insurance, tax, pension scheme and trust

243

fund. On closer inspection, though, it was all routine stuff and of little interest. Most of it dated to a time before she'd married Malcolm anyway, and seemed to be of a domestic nature.

Trying to be careful not to disturb anything, and still feeling embarrassed to be snooping on her stepmother, Camilla nevertheless continued her search.

The first jolt of surprise came when she opened one of the small side drawers and discovered Edith's driving licence. A quick glance confirmed it was up to date and there were no endorsements, so Hector had definitely lied when he'd said Edith had sold Malcolm's car because she couldn't drive.

The second shock, sharper and sending a frisson of fear down Camilla's spine, was a handwritten letter dated the previous year. It began 'My dear Edith' and continued: 'It is delightful that you will be coming to live in Ardachie. I can hardly wait...' And then further on were written the words, 'I'm sure, between us, we can get some very satisfactory results.' It was signed 'Hector'.

Leafing through the rest of the papers in the drawer, Camilla came across an out-of-date diary, barely written in, some blank postcards, and then, tucked inside a travel brochure, some sheets of writing-paper in Edith's familiar scrawl – a letter to her sister Harriet. It was unfinished, broken off in mid-sentence, but it told Camilla all she needed to know.

Philip laid the bunch of flowers on the kitchen table. Camilla, who was peeling some potatoes for their lunch, turned to look and, seeing them, dried her hands and went to pick them up.

'They're beautiful,' she said wonderingly while he stood quietly watching her, a secret smile on his face. 'Did you really pick them yourself?'

'No, I got Ken Turner to fly up from London to select them for me,' he teased.

'Fool!' She burst out laughing. Giving her a bouquet of wild flowers was the nicest thing he could have done. She went over to him and, reaching up, kissed him gently on the mouth.

'Thank you, darling,' she whispered.

'Do you want a jug or something to put them in?' he asked, arms round her waist, pulling her close.

'Yes, I'll get that . . . Oh!' She gave a startled little cry, and then looked at the flowers as if she couldn't believe her eyes. 'Philip! Oh, sweetheart . . .' Carefully she unpinned from a stem of wild gillyflower the brooch.

'Do you like it?' His voice was husky.

'It's exquisite!' she exclaimed. 'Oh, Philip, how sweet of you.' Touched, she pinned it to the lapel of the denim jacket she was wearing. Although it was an antique piece of jewellery it looked great worn with her modern clothes, and she was thrilled. Flinging her arms round his neck she looked up at him with shining eyes, knowing that this token of his love was more precious to her than all the fine jewels she possessed.

'That was a lovely thing to do,' she said softly. 'And a lovely present to give me.'

For answer he kissed her long and deeply, holding her close, feeling the supple slimness of her body against his, smelling the fragrance of her skin and hair, aware that his body had become aroused again, so that he wanted her with a passion that could not be stemmed. There, in the kitchen, they sank to the floor, becoming one again, united in a renewal of mutual desire that swept them away and could not be denied. And after it was over they lay breathless in each other's arms, and she traced the lines of his mouth and his cheeks and his brow, with her fingers.

'I love you so much,' she whispered, and sounded surprised at the discovery.

'Not as much as I love you,' he replied, dazed by the strength of his own feelings. 'Oh, God, Camilla, I love you more than life itself.'

Later, as they prepared lunch, she told him she'd found a letter from Edith, written to her sister but unfinished.

'What does she say?' he asked, cutting some tomatoes in half

245

and putting them under the grill, to go with the lamb chops he'd bought.

Camilla stopped her task of laying the kitchen table and looked at him. 'It's much more serious than we thought.'

'What is? The smuggling? Is it drugs?'

She shook her head. 'They're gun-running for the IRA.'

'*What*?' He spun round, his dark eyes wide with astonishment and concern.

'Yes. Someone in the village, Edith doesn't say who, is behind the whole organisation, supplying arms which come from Czechoslovakia. They are hidden in shipments of domestic appliances apparently, then brought to Ardachie and smuggled over to Northern Ireland in fishing boats.'

'So that's what the lorries were carrying?'

'Yes.' Camilla glanced at Edith's letter again. 'She says there's a secret radio station in the vicinity as well.'

Philip let out a long low whistle. 'This is much more serious than I thought.'

'I know.'

'There's only one thing that puzzles me.' He was frowning thoughtfully. 'We know now why your father was murdered, because he knew too much, and why the dogs were killed.'

'Because their barking would disturb all the nocturnal activities?'

'Exactly. But what I don't understand is why a village of Scottish people are helping Sinn Fein? It doesn't make sense.'

'Yes it does, because Edith says in her letter that this man, the leader, whoever he is, belongs to an extremist branch of the Scottish Nationalists who sympathise with the IRA.'

'Ah!' Philip nodded knowingly. 'Minority political groups do operate a worldwide network. They all help each other and support each other's terrorist activities.'

'Quite.'

'We've got to get out of here you know, and fast.'

Camilla looked anxious. 'Do you think they realise we know what's going on? I wonder why Edith never finished this letter?

Something disturbed her, I think, because it was stuffed inside a travel brochure as if she'd put it away hurriedly.' She folded the letter and put it in her pocket. 'I wonder where she is now! I wish she'd get in touch again but I suspect, you know, that she's too scared to come back.'

'Meanwhile, I suggest we pack, lock up the house, and go,' Philip said tersely. 'This is no time for us to be hanging around either.'

All at once he was the more mature of the two, telling her to parcel up what was left of the food, which he then stowed away in the boot of the car with their luggage. Then he went around the whole house checking every window, locking doors and switching off the hot water system.

Grateful to have someone take charge for a change, Camilla phoned Jean to tell her they were leaving Creagnach, before taking a final look around.

'Okay, let's go,' Philip said at last. 'The sooner we're out of here, the better.'

The police station, situated off Sauchiehall Street, was a brand new addition to Glasgow's skyline, a large solid building designed along the lines of a child's Lego construction, with a flat roof, neat rows of windows symmetrically set into the red brickwork, and double-fronted white doors at the top of a short flight of stone steps. Its very solidity was as reassuring to law-abiding citizens who depended on its protection as its enforcement of law and order was forbidding to potential criminals.

Camilla and Philip, having parked the Mercedes in the forecourt, hurried inside. Fifteen minutes later they were in the office of the chief superintendent making a joint statement.

247

Chapter Fifteen

Geoffrey arrived at Scalini's just before eight o'clock and was immediately shown to the table he'd reserved. This was his favourite restaurant. The discreet lighting, smoked mirrors and general air of expensive lushness was soothing after a day in a large noisy open-plan office staring at a word processor, and he immediately ordered himself a dry martini. He glanced at his watch. It was just eight. Camilla would be here any minute.

He'd been looking forward to this evening ever since he'd arranged it with her. Thoughts of Camilla had been filling his mind more and more in recent days, and he realised with a start that while she'd been away in Scotland he'd actually been missing her. It was a long time since he'd missed anyone, and even longer since he'd been in love. His brief marriage to a fellow journalist some years before had left him at first bitter, when she ran off with the editor of a rival newspaper, and then cautious. He'd often asked himself in the ten years since his divorce if he really wanted to go through all the hassle of a heavy relationship again, and always before the answer had been no. But with Camilla it was different. She was a warm and loyal woman who had been a loving and faithful wife; when her world had blown apart she'd shown incredible courage. Now, all he wanted to do was to bring some happiness into her life. He wanted to see her face glow with love once again, and to hear the sound of her laughter. Most of all he wanted to bring passion into her life once more.

As he sat there sipping his drink, he indulged himself in a

little day-dreaming. Camilla was far more sexy than she realised, and far more desirable, too. He would love to reawaken those dormant feelings; love to see her in loose romantic clothes with her hair flowing, instead of square-shouldered designer suits and a chic chignon; love to talk with her late into the night, and make love at dawn; love to . . . Geoffrey looked at his watch again and saw it was eight-twenty. Ordering himself another drink he wondered if she'd been delayed by heavy traffic, coming down from Scotland. She'd be here any minute, though. Camilla was so punctilious she'd have phoned the restaurant if she was going to be seriously delayed.

Unperturbed, but a little disappointed, he continued to wait, starting every time someone came into the restaurant, his heart missing a beat with each new arrival; but still no Camilla.

By nine o'clock, he was worried. She was never this late. Something must have happened. Terrible visions of her in a pile-up on the motorway flashed through his mind. Then he was struck by another thought, equally horrifying. Supposing something had happened in Ardachie last night? Supposing . . .? He couldn't bear it any longer. Reaching for the mobile phone in the pocket of his suit, he dialled her new mobile phone, which he presumed she would have in the car with her. After a few clicks and bleeps the recorded voice of the operator informed him that the number was at present unobtainable. Was that a good sign or a bad? he asked himself with growing apprehension. At that moment he would have given anything to have seen her step into Scalini's, with her warm smile and bright eyes, wearing one of the elegant little black dresses she always wore in the evenings, with ropes of gleaming pearls cascading from her neck.

By now he was certain something had happened to her. Cursing himself for ever having let her go to Scotland, he dialled the number of Wilton Crescent. Perhaps Poppy or one of the servants had heard something. When he got through, the line gave the busy signal. There again, was that a good sign or a bad? he thought distractedly, ordering himself a third drink.

'Jesus,' he muttered to himself, feeling sick. 'If anything's happened to her . . .' He dialled her number again, but the phone still gave the busy signal. Perhaps he should go round there? Maybe the phone was in use because they were talking to hospitals, or the police?

'Can I have my bill, please?' he asked a passing waiter.

'Your bill, sir?' The young Italian looked perplexed. 'Do you not want dinner, sir?'

'Something's happened,' Geoffrey replied. 'I have to go. I'd like my bill for the drinks.'

'Certainly, sir.' With elaborately polite body language, the waiter bowed and then skimmed off, leaving Geoffrey dialling Camilla's number one more time.

His heart nearly stopped when he heard the phone give the ringing sound. Someone was in! Someone could tell him . . .

'Hello?' said a young female voice.

'Poppy, is that you?'

'Who's that?'

'Geoffrey Hennessy.'

'Oh. Hi!' Poppy sounded bored.

'Hello, Poppy. Is your mother there?'

'Nope.'

'She hasn't returned from Scotland today?'

'Nope. Is there a message?' She sounded preoccupied, as if she wanted to get rid of him.

'Well, yes. I'm very worried about her, Poppy. We were supposed to be meeting for dinner tonight and she hasn't turned up. I know she was supposed to be driving down from your grandfather's place today. Have you any idea where she is?' Geoffrey tried to keep his voice calm. There was no point in alarming the girl too much.

'Oh, I know where she is,' he heard Poppy say, and felt an intense wave of relief wash over him.

'Where is she? Is she on her way?' he asked eagerly.

'Nope. She's staying at one of those stately homes that have been turned into a hotel, somewhere in Scotland.'

'What?'

'Yup. She spoke to Maitland earlier today. I don't know when she'll be back.' Poppy sounded as if she didn't much care either.

He felt stunned and hurt. 'I thought she was returning today.'

'No. I don't think she's coming back yet. I haven't spoken to her myself, but Maitland said something about her having a few days' holiday before she comes back.'

'I see.' Disappointment dug deep into his heart, and another realisation came to him. 'She's with Lucy Hamilton's son, isn't she?' Instantly, too late, he regretted saying it. For one thing he shouldn't be discussing Camilla's private life with her daughter; for another, he was revealing the sudden jealousy he felt.

'Could be,' Poppy was saying nonchalantly.

'Will you tell her I called, please?'

'Okay.'

There wasn't much more to say, so he thanked her and hung up. At that moment the waiter brought his bill. Geoffrey paid it and left the restaurant. He hadn't had anything to eat since a grabbed sandwich at lunchtime, but somehow he'd lost his appetite.

Poppy gazed at Danny with wide-eyed astonishment. 'A riot?' she said in a low voice.

'Yup, that's right.' He looked pleased with himself as he moved restlessly around his room. 'But you're not to tell anyone, understand? I'll kill you if you let on.'

'Oh, I won't tell a soul,' she breathed. 'Have I told anyone you and your friends kept whispering about "July"? So what's so special about this month?'

Danny looked mysterious. 'Something big is happening next week.'

'What?'

'The American President is coming to this country on a state visit on the nineteenth.'

'So?' Poppy was intrigued. She couldn't see what the President of the USA had to do with the underprivileged in Britain.

252

'The Queen's giving a banquet for him at Buckingham Palace, isn't she.' It wasn't a question but a statement of fact.

'Is she? I still don't see . . .'

'Dumb bitch!' he suddenly thundered, losing his temper. 'Where will the eyes of the world's media be focused that day?'

Poppy looked at him with dawning understanding. 'On Buckingham Palace?'

'Exactly.'

She gave a little gasp. 'You mean you're going to . . .?'

'We're going to storm the palace! Thousands of us from all over the country. Big Marge is leading the women while I concentrate on the men. We'll be armed, of course, with fire bombs, and then there's our secret weapon!'

'What secret weapon?'

Danny tapped the side of his nose and looked at her askance. 'That's one secret I'm not telling you.'

'Oh, Danny, please. You can trust me. You've told me so much already, you might as well tell me everything.'

'No way.' He flung himself down on the bed and lay inert, staring up at the ceiling.

'Please?' Poppy wheedled, going over to the bed and sitting down beside him.

'I've told you too much already,' he said shortly.

She stroked his thigh and let her hand trail up to his hip.

'It's no good trying to get round me that way,' he said.

'I'm not trying to get round you.' Poppy sounded earnest. 'I want you to trust me. I'm not going to tell anyone of your plans.'

'You'd fucking better not!'

There was silence in the room and she shifted uneasily. 'What sort of secret weapon is it? Not guns?'

Danny snorted. 'Stop going on about it. I wish I hadn't told you anything now.'

'I bet Big Marge knows what it is,' Poppy said crossly, moving away from him. She'd become obsessed by the thought of the large raucous woman being in Danny's confidence. She knew they'd even had meetings to which she had not been invited in that house in Chalk Farm where Danny had told her to take the silver she'd stolen. So why was Big Marge being singled out? Why didn't he take Poppy into his confidence? After all, they were practically living together. She had a right to know. What was so special about Big Marge?

'You're like a bleeding gramophone record, aren't you?' Danny grumbled. 'You keep your trap shut. Another word about our plans or Big Marge and you can forget the whole thing.'

Poppy knew she'd almost pushed her luck too far. She didn't dare risk losing Danny. Without him she knew she'd never survive. He was all she cared about. He was her life.

'I'm sorry,' she whispered contritely.

He didn't reply but continued to stare at the cracked ceiling.

She moved closer again. ' I don't care about anything, so long as we can be together. You're the boss. You don't have to tell me anything if you don't want to,' she added desperately, her eyes brimming. If he said he didn't want to see her any more . . . If he told her to fuck off and not come back . . . She slid her small hand across his groin, averting her face so he would not see the desperation in her eyes.

After a moment he grabbed the hair at the nape of her neck and, twisting its fine strands round his fist, pulled her head backwards so that she was facing him.

'Remember who's boss, then,' he said, glaring into her eyes with that hypnotic stare that had at first fascinated her.

Poppy nodded. 'Oh, I will,' she promised.

'Right then.' Winding her hair still tighter so that she almost flinched with the pain in her scalp, he brought his mouth down on hers with swift and sudden passion. Poppy didn't struggle. Submitting herself to him, she lay passively as he undressed her, his large rough hands for once gentle, his kisses tender.

'Sexy little bitch,' he said fondly, and Poppy knew she was back in favour. She flung her arms around his neck and pressed herself close to him.

'I love you,' she cried out passionately. 'Oh Danny . . . Danny . . .'

'Come here,' he muttered. Then, eyes glazed, he pulled her on top so that she sat astride him. As if blinded by his own desire he thrust himself inside her, groaning aloud with delight as he did so. With his gaze on some secret lascivious horizon, somewhere past her left shoulder, he proceeded to pump away while Poppy arched her back and stroked his chest and rode him triumphantly, revelling in the power she held over him at that moment.

Then the strangest thing happened. Just as she was about to climax, just as she was reaching a peak of almost unbearable pleasure so that her cries filled the room, echoing each bellow that Danny uttered, she suddenly thought of her mother, of Camilla, chic and cool in one of her executive suits with her hair in a smart chignon and her makeup immaculate. Camilla, stepping into the chauffeur-driven company car, carrying her briefcase; Camilla, always in command of the situation; chairman of a successful advertising agency, hostess of glittering dinner parties, disdainful of people who didn't conduct their lives with the same efficiency with which she managed her own existence. She'll never experience this passion, Poppy thought with a jolt, this sense of total abandonment, this wondrous thing called love, because she'll always be in control of her feelings.

Suddenly she felt quite sorry for her mother.

'Take me, Philip, my darling, my love, take me . . . ' gasped Camilla, her eyes closed, her lips parted. 'I want to belong to you.'

Gathering her closer, Philip kissed her neck and sucked the lobes of her ears, while he stroked her breasts, teasing the nipples, smoothing the soft creamy skin of her stomach, setting her on fire so that she cried out his name again, driven crazy with longing.

'Give yourself to me,' she moaned. 'Oh, God, Philip, give yourself to me. I want to feel you inside me.'

Never had she felt like this before. David had been a gentle and considerate lover, but he'd never aroused her to this frenzied state when she felt her heart would stop. This is the forbidden fruit, she thought. This is everything I've ever wanted. He kissed her again, and then they came together in a rush, clinging to each other, swept along as if by a strong current, a rolling swell that bore them to dizzy heights so that only on the ebb tide of their climax did they subside, drenched and spent, and crying out in each other's arms.

Earlier that evening they had booked into Glencaple Castle, a stately home some miles outside Glasgow, near Dumfries, which its impoverished owners had turned into a hotel a few years before.

'Do we have to go back to London yet?' Camilla had asked as they left the police station in Glasgow where they had been answering questions for several hours.

Philip grabbed her hand. 'Not yet, if you don't want to. We could find somewhere to stay up here if you like.'

'Somewhere quiet and remote?' She looked up at him with an intimate smile. 'We deserve a break, don't you think?'

He grinned back. 'Anywhere except Creagnach, of course!'

The police had warned them not to go back to Ardachie on any account. 'As soon as we put our Anti-terrorist Intelligence department on to this, they'll know it was you who tipped us off,' the chief inspector told them. 'At that point you'll be on their hit list, I'm afraid.'

The police had also promised to put out a call to Interpol to find Edith. 'We've got to get hold of her to help us with our enquiries,' the inspector continued. 'It's a pity she didn't report what she knew before she went abroad.'

'I think she was probably too frightened,' Camilla suggested. 'Not only had her husband died, but her dogs had been killed too. At that point I believe she fled in terror.'

'Do you know if her sister has heard from her recently?'

'Apparently not.'

It was with a sense of relief that Camilla and Philip finally got into their car and drove south, out of the busy city of Glasgow and into the rich surrounding countryside. They had no idea where they were heading, but then Camilla saw the crenellated battlements of a castle in the distance, set like a jewel among the purple mountains, and felt intrigued.

'I wonder who lives there,' she remarked as Philip drove with swift assurance along the silver ribbon-like winding roads. After another few minutes, her question was answered. An elegantly painted sign pointed to the Glencaple Castle Hotel.

Close up, it was even more attractive.

'Doesn't it look marvellous!' said Camilla as they drew level with the imposing entrance to the drive.

'Let's see if they have a room,' Philip suggested.

As it happened they had several vacant rooms, including what the charming receptionist referred to as the State Room.

'That sounds rather grand,' Philip remarked.

Camilla dissolved into giggles. 'It certainly does.'

'It's a lovely room on the first floor, overlooking the Solway Firth,' the receptionist explained. 'I think you'll find it very comfortable.'

They were also to find it had a massive four-poster bed draped and festooned in crimson velvet.

'My God, it's positively medieval! I feel I should come to bed in a suit of armour!' Philip exclaimed laughingly when he saw it.

'As long as I'm not supposed to wear a chastity belt,' Camilla giggled, starting to unpack.

He came up behind her, wrapping his arms round her and hugging her close.

'I've never slept in a four-poster before.'

'The first time I slept in one was when I was six,' she told him. 'I was staying with a great-aunt, and I remember being terrified in case there was a bogeyman hiding in the curtains.'

Philip was nuzzling her neck, pressing himself against her. 'You have nothing to fear tonight.'

Camilla turned to him, her eyes widening. 'Do you know something?'

'What?'

'This will be the first night for over a week when I haven't felt scared . . . or lonely.'

He looked back into her eyes. 'You need never feel lonely again. You know that, don't you?'

Camilla wanted to believe it, more than anything in the world. It was wonderful to be in love again, wonderful to be loved in return. She hadn't felt as vibrantly alive as this for years, and yet did she dare hope it could last?

'You do believe me, don't you?' Philip persisted, seeing the fleeting look of doubt in her eyes. 'I love you, Camilla. I love you more than I thought it possible to love anyone.' He spoke with such sincerity she could not doubt what he said any more.

'I love you too,' she replied with equal honesty. For her this was a moment of grave commitment. Not since David had died had she felt able to give her heart and her soul and her body to anyone with such complete abandonment. For the first time in four years, she wanted to feel she belonged to a man, utterly and totally, and that man was Philip.

'Let's take a shower together,' he was saying softly now, as he reached forward and started undoing the buttons of her shirt. Slowly, never dropping their gaze from each other's eyes, they undressed each other, lingeringly removing the layers of clothes until they stood naked. Then they drew closer together, until their bodies were touching, eyes still locked, arms hanging at their sides, relishing the excitement of proximity. Camilla was the first to break the heightening tension. Gently she took Philip's manhood in her hands, as she reached up to kiss him. For a second he stood rigidly before her, his eyes closed so that his other senses became more acute, then he swept her up in his arms, and carried her into the adjoining bathroom. Her perfume filled his nostrils as he breathed deeply. The silky smoothness of her skin made his own flesh tingle, as he lifted her into the shower and closed the glass door behind them. Within moments a jet of warm water cascaded down on them and, as they kissed, it rained on their faces, splashing in bright droplets off their shoulders, coursing down their entwined limbs until it surged around their feet.

Camilla raised her leg and, placing it around his hip, strained to get as close to him as she could. With strong hands that stroked and smoothed, and finally touched the swelling nub of her being, he aroused her so that she gasped with longing, wanting to be a part of him, wanting him to become a part of her, wanting more than anything for this moment to last forever. Then she felt him inside her, thrusting so hard she cried out again, her head thrown back, her eyes closed. His face was buried in her neck, gently biting her skin, loving the taste of her . . . the smell of her . . . the slippery wetness of her . . . there was a roaring sound in his ears as his excitement increased and then she was squeezing him, milking him, draining the life out of him, and her cries were mingling with his, and it seemed as if his soul had soared up to heaven and he was being touched by the angels.

Lucy hung up impatiently. 'I've been trying to get through to Camilla and Philip all morning. There's no answer on her mobile phone.'

Charlotte, who was reclining on the drawing-room sofa surrounded by glossy magazines, her arm in a sling, looked up from *Vogue*.

'They've probably gone for a walk.'

'But they didn't want anyone to know they were staying in the house. They're supposed to be in hiding while they find out what's going on,' her mother pointed out.

'It all sounds rather farfetched to me.' Matter-of-fact, like her mother, Charlotte was not given to flights of fancy.

'I'd have said the same if I hadn't seen those dogs for myself,' Lucy admitted, 'and Camilla did get a couple of nasty letters warning her not to meddle!'

'At least I bet Philip's having a good time,' Charlotte smiled slyly.

'What do you mean?'

'Well, you know! I bet he quite fancies Camilla.'

'Don't be absurd.' Lucy was bristling now. 'She's my age.'

'So?'

'So how could he possibly be attracted to someone old enough to be his mother, for goodness' sake? You are ridiculous, Charlotte. You've been reading too many silly novels.'

Charlotte sat upright and looked indignant. 'I have not. Masses of women have lovers years younger than themselves these days. It's quite the done thing.'

Lucy frowned. 'Maybe, but not Camilla, and certainly not with Philip. The idea's absurd! Anyway, you're far too young to know about that sort of thing.'

'I'm not! She's a fun go-ahead woman, interesting to talk to and probably still quite sexy.' She put her head on one side reflectively. 'Philip could do a lot worse.'

Suddenly, Lucy found herself feeling grey and dumpy beside her daughter's description of Camilla. Charlotte was right, of course; Camilla had kept herself in remarkable shape, in every sense of the word. Even so . . .

'You don't really think there's anything going on between them, do you?' she asked distractedly.

Amused, Charlotte shrugged. 'Who knows?'

There was silence in the room and then Lucy remarked, in what she intended to be a casual tone but which sounded rather strained, 'I think I'll try the number again.'

By four o'clock in the afternoon she still hadn't been able to get a reply from either Creagnach or Camilla's mobile phone. Then she remembered Jean. Dialling the offices of Eaton & Eaton, she was swiftly put through to Camilla's secretary.

'Ah, Mrs Hamilton,' Jean exclaimed, recognising her voice, 'they've left Ardachie and are spending a few days at Glencaple Castle Hotel, near Dumfries. Shall I give you the number?'

When Jean hung up a few minutes later, she added Lucy Hamilton's name to the list of people who had phoned for Camilla that day. It amused her to note that it came next to a message from Geoffrey Hennessy. Camilla, in her opinion, was going to have quite a lot of explaining to do at this rate.

Camilla suddenly found herself awake at four o'clock the next morning, alert and with her heart pounding. Instantly she sat up in the large bed, her hand stifling a gasp.

'How *could* I have done such a thing!' she said to herself, appalled. 'What on earth can I say to him?'

Camilla had remembered she'd forgotten all about her dinner date with Geoffrey. She lay down again, quietly so as not to disturb Philip, but feeling perturbed. She'd never done anything like that in her life. Forget dinner with a close friend? It was unthinkable. And then she realised that during the past few days she hadn't even glanced at her engagement book, had barely talked to Jean, had forgotten about everything except how much she wanted to be with Philip.

He stirred beside her as if aware of her disquiet.

'Are you all right, sweetheart?' he murmured, reaching out for her. Camilla sank into his welcoming arms, glad of the warmth of his body.

Briefly she explained what had awakened her. 'I'm slipping,' she confessed. 'That's the effect you're having on me, Mr Hamilton! The next thing is I'll be forgetting to turn up for board meetings.'

'Good!' His voice in the darkness was smug.

Camilla pretended to scold. 'It's not good at all! I'll go bust if I don't earn an honest crust!'

'A likely story,' he mocked, nuzzling her. 'Anyway, give me a couple of years to get my finals, and then I'll be able to keep you in the style to which you're accustomed.'

Camilla cuddled closer to him. 'How blissful. You mean I'll be able to give up work?'

'Of course.' He was kissing her now. 'Let's stay here until the weekend at least. Neither of us need start thinking about work until Monday.'

'Nothing would suit me better,' she agreed, kissing him back.

'There's been another postcard from your stepmother,' Jean informed her the next morning when she phoned the office.

'Where from?' Camilla asked eagerly. She'd promised the police in Glasgow that she'd let them know if she heard from Edith again.

'Portugal. There's no address, just a view of Lisbon. Shall I read it to you?'

'Yes, please.' As Camilla listened, she realised with a sinking heart that it was a wish-you-were-here type of card, giving no details. Edith added she planned to go to Venice in a few days.

'Damn! That doesn't tell us anything much,' Camilla commented, 'but I'd still better tell the police.' They talked for a few more minutes and Jean assured her that everything was under control and there were no problems . . . apart from several calls from Geoffrey Hennessy, and one from Lucy Hamilton.

'In that case, I won't be in the office until Monday, but you can always get me here if anything urgent comes up. And I'll get on to Geoffrey now and apologise for standing him up.'

There was hidden laughter in Jean's voice. 'Very well. Have a good rest, Mrs Eaton.'

Camilla looked at Philip askance when she hung up. 'The tongues will soon be wagging, I fear.'

'About us?' he looked amused.

'Certainly about us! It may not all be pleasant either!'

'I don't mind, if you don't, and there's nothing wrong with our relationship. We're both free to do as we like.'

'Yes, I know.'

'It's the age difference that's worrying you isn't it?' he said intuitively.

She nodded briefly, not looking at him. 'Yes,' she replied quietly.

'Age doesn't matter these days. Nobody cares a damn.'

'I'm not worried about it myself,' she assured him, 'but not everyone will see it that way. A lot of people will disapprove.'

'Let them! Who the hell cares?'

'What about your mother?'

He looked startled. 'What about her?'

Camilla went over to him then and, sitting down beside him on the edge of the giant bed, reached for his hand.

'Lucy had you earmarked for Poppy, you know,' she told him.

'Poppy!' Philip looked aghast. 'But she's only a child!'

'She's sixteen.'

'Maybe, but . . .' He looked genuinely bewildered. 'I'm sure she's a sweet girl,' he said hurriedly, 'but she's not remotely my type.'

'Nevertheless,' Camilla said, smiling, 'I think Lucy's going to be terribly shocked.' She thought of her friend who had only ever been to bed with one man in her life and whose view on morals dated back to the 'fifties.

'Mum? Shocked? I'm sure she won't be.' Philip threw back his head and laughed. 'I've always thought of her and Dad as being pretty broad-minded. Of course they're protective towards Henrietta and Charlotte, but they're girls.'

'And that's different?' Camilla asked, amused.

He blushed, and grinned sheepishly. 'I suppose they think so.'

She didn't pursue the subject. This new relationship was too new, too tender, to be dissected and discussed as if it were a business deal. There was time enough to face Lucy when they returned to London, but Camilla felt fairly certain she knew what her friend's reaction was going to be.

'Geoffrey, can you ever forgive me?' Camilla spoke with sincerity. 'I've been so distracted by what's been happening up here that I have to confess I completely forgot our dinner date. Isn't that terrible?'

'At least you're being honest about it,' Geoffrey replied, although he felt a cold despair at her words. It wasn't the discoveries she'd made in Ardachie that had distracted her, he was sure, but the presence of young Philip Hamilton. 'We can make another date, can't we?'

Camilla seemed to hesitate, as if not wanting to commit herself. 'Why don't I give you a ring when I return to London?' she said at last. 'Perhaps you can come to dinner one night?'

It was a brush-off if ever he'd heard one. A very charming rejection but a rejection nevertheless. You only had to translate 'dinner one night', he thought, into 'I'd like to see you but I want lots of other people there too', to realise what she was getting at.

'Thanks,' he replied, trying to keep the disappointment out of his voice.

'Good. Then we'll be in touch, Geoffrey.'

It broke his heart to hear her sound so happy, so carefree. Not since before David's death could he remember her sounding so full of joie de vivre.

'Fine,' he replied, but it wasn't fine at all. It was the end, he was sure, of his wonderful plans for the future.

Chapter Sixteen

They drove down to London on the Sunday, leaving Glencaple Castle shrouded in the pink mist of a Highland dawn.

'We must come back here again,' Camilla said, as she took a last look at the ramparts and battlements receding into the distance. 'We've had such a wonderful time, haven't we?'

Philip negotiated the car through the entrance gates with care. 'We certainly have. The most wonderful time ever. We should come back every year, to celebrate.'

Camilla said nothing but smiled, touched by his belief in their future together. A week ago she'd have thought it impossible, but now she really believed that their relationship was going to last. No two people, she told herself, could be as close as this only for it to end. It was as if they had always been together, destined to be a part of each other, made for each other.

By the early evening they were entering the outskirts of London, and the smog and the dirt and the noise of the city hit them like a barrage, overwhelming and claustrophobic.

'God, I wonder why we live in a place like this!' Camilla remarked, winding up the car window.

'It really hits you after you've been in the countryside, doesn't it?' Philip agreed as he joined the long queues of cars in Park Lane. He was going to drop Camilla off at her house first before going on to his own flat in Pimlico. They'd planned, though, that he would be spending his nights at Wilton Crescent in future.

'I'll be back at eight-thirty,' he promised when they drew up outside the house.

Maitland, who was expecting her, opened the front door as soon as the Mercedes came to a halt. Then he hurried forward to help Philip with her luggage.

'Welcome back, madam, sir. I trust you had a good journey?'

'Yes, it was fine, thank you,' Camilla replied. Pleasantries exchanged, she whispered to Philip: 'I'll see you later, sweetheart.'

Once inside she decided to take the bull by the horns and inform Maitland of the new arrangements. After all, she reasoned, she was a mature woman who could do as she liked, and it was her house. If he and Mrs Maitland disapproved, then that was just too damn bad. But first she wanted to know if Poppy was home.

'I'm afraid not, madam. She hasn't been in all day.'

'Do you know if she'll be back for dinner tonight?'

He shook his head. 'Miss Poppy's rarely in for dinner these days, madam.' The lips were prim, the bulging eyes chilly.

Suddenly she spotted several very large cardboard boxes at the far end of the hall. They all had THIS WAY UP printed in large lettering on the side.

'What are those?' she asked. 'We haven't ordered half a dozen dishwashers, have we?' she added jokingly.

His face remained serious. 'They were delivered late yesterday afternoon, madam. I was told not to open them but that you would do it yourself.'

'Where did they come from?' she asked.

'This card came with them.' He handed her a tiny white envelope. Incredulously, she opened it and took out the card, recognising the quote from Jean Anouilh.

Love is, above all, the gift of oneself.
Forever, Philip

'They're flowers!' she gasped. 'My God, however many flowers has he sent?'

'I'll get a knife, madam.' Maitland was all smiles now, bustling around, slitting open the thick cartons.

Gazing at them Camilla felt overwhelmed. She had never seen so many white lilies in her life. There were hundreds of them, held upright by the sides of the boxes, their stems immersed in buckets of water wedged at the bottom.

'How fantastic!' she said, breathing in the heady perfume. 'We're going to need every vase in the house.'

Maitland laid a sheet on the drawing-room carpet and then carefully carried the boxes through. 'I'll go and get the vases now,' he announced, obviously enjoying himself.

When he returned, she said casually: 'Oh, by the way, Maitland, Mr Hamilton will be staying here in future. He's keeping on his own flat, but you can expect him for dinner every night.'

Maitland didn't so much as flicker an eyelid. 'Certainly, madam,' he said smoothly.

'You might check that everything in the dressing-room is in order, though I don't expect Mr Hamilton will be leaving many clothes here,' she continued. After David had been killed she'd ruthlessly given away all his suits and shoes, their presence being too painful a reminder, and so she knew that closets and drawers were empty if Philip did want to use them.

'Very well, madam.'

'Right!' Camilla commented brightly. 'Now I think we're going to need some more vases! And maybe a few jugs, too. What a pity we're not giving a party. I've never had so many flowers at one time.'

An hour later, Maitland was still trotting up from the kitchen with every type of container he could find, and so far Camilla had emptied only four of the six boxes.

'This is madness!' she laughed. Huge vases of glistening silky blooms stood on every available surface in all the main rooms and in the hall. He had also carried up vases to her bedroom and bathroom and the dressing-room beyond.

'I think you'd better bring up some buckets,' she continued, 'they'll look all right in the fireplaces when they're full of flowers.'

'Yes, madam, and how about that spaghetti jar? That would hold a few, and look nice.'

'Anything you can find,' she replied, laughing with happiness, 'and anything Mrs Maitland can spare in the way of deep bowls or jars.'

She pushed the hair out of her eyes and sank back on to her heels to rest for a moment. As she'd said, this was madness, a wonderful, extravagant, crazy orgy of lilies and Philip's gesture was wildly over the top, but nevertheless the most joyous celebration of love she'd ever experienced. She wished these exquisitely scented blooms would last forever, filling the whole house with their sweet heady fragrance, lending their graceful beauty to every room.

When Maitland returned with two buckets, she submerged the pale green slender stems into the water, no longer being careful or artful in her arrangements, no longer placing the blooms one at a time, but stuffing in great handfuls, pushing the fleshy shanks into the cold water in a wild profusion of blossoms. Maitland placed a silver wine cooler in front of her. 'This is the only other receptacle I can find, madam, but it should do all right.'

Camilla looked at the remaining dozen or so blooms that lay on the sheet by her side. 'That'll just do it. Well done, Maitland!' She looked around the room at all the magnificent displays, her face radiant with pleasure. 'It's an incredible sight, isn't it? Lilies, lilies, everywhere,' she said softly.

Maitland left the room, smiling to himself. It was a very long time since he'd seen madam look so happy.

Immersed in her task, cutting the stems shorter so they fitted into the wine cooler, she suddenly looked up, startled, to find Philip standing in the drawing-room doorway, smiling at her.

'Darling!' she exclaimed. 'I didn't hear you arrive . . . Oh, and thank you so much for all these flowers. They're unbelievable!' She held out her arms to him, a delightfully dishevelled figure sitting on the floor with her hair falling into her eyes and her face alight with happiness.

Philip went over to her then dropped to his knees and took her in his arms.

'I've never seen you look so . . . so young and beautiful,' he said in wonderment. With one hand he pushed back her hair and gazed into her eyes with tenderness.

'Oh, Philip.' She reached up and her lips brushed his. Then she wound her arms slowly round his neck. All around them the redolent perfume of the lilies filled the air with intoxicating scent so that they felt quite drunk.

'I love you,' he gasped.

For an answer she kissed him again, lingeringly, sweetly, kissing the corners of his mouth with light butterfly kisses.

'Oh, I love you . . . I love you . . . I love you . . . ' she exclaimed impulsively. 'You've brought me back to life! You've made me so happy when I thought I would never be happy again.'

For a moment he was unable to speak, so moved was he by her words, but then with a wave of longing he drew her closer, kissing her now with an urgency she couldn't resist. Together, clinging to each other, they sank on to the floor, crushing the remaining lilies as Philip rolled her on to her back so that there was an explosion of perfume. Consumed by a strange madness, they became oblivious of their surroundings. Camilla's world had become an ambrosial cocoon in which she and Philip were embedded, and all that mattered was that they belonged to each other.

Feverishly, she returned his kisses while he, in a frenzy of passion, forgetful of everything else, held her close, pressing his hardness against her, lifting her so that she lay on top of him, and then turning her over so that she was once more on her back. Over and over they went, squashing the lilies so that their clothing, their hair, their skin became impregnated with the heady fragrance, and all the time he was kissing her and whispering his love for her.

Abandoning herself to the glorious moment, Camilla was unaware of Maitland quietly pulling the drawing-room door shut before creeping away. Her world was filled with only Philip

269

and the lilies now, and she was oblivious of everything else. She wanted him and she must have him. He and the flowers were a part of nature, of which she was a part too now, and so she urged him on with cries of ecstasy, taking him, holding him inside her, matching his rhythm, writhing with him among the fragrant blooms.

So unaware of her surroundings had she become, so carried away, that she did not notice the drawing-room door being opened, and Poppy standing there, aghast, as she watched them.

'What do you mean, Philip, you spent the night at Camilla's house?' Lucy demanded. 'What's wrong with your own flat?'

'There's nothing wrong with it. I'm here now, getting everything sorted out before I start my studies at the AA,' he explained, suddenly finding it more difficult than he'd imagined to tell his mother what was happening.

'Then why did you stay at Wilton Crescent? Surely it would have been more sensible to have gone home when you got back from Scotland?'

He took a deep breath. 'I shall be staying at Camilla's house every night in future, Mum . . . with Camilla.'

His remark was greeted with a stunned silence.

'I don't understand,' Lucy said slowly. 'Charlotte said something . . . but surely you're not having an affair with Camilla, are you?'

'Yes, I am.'

'Philip!' She sounded horrified.

'What's wrong with it?' he asked, his hackles rising. Too late, he knew it was a stupid thing to say because it gave Lucy the perfect opportunity to reply, predictably.

'Because she's old enough to be your mother.'

'Age doesn't come into it, Mum. We love each other. You've no idea how happy we are. Anyway, what does age matter? It's only the number of years you've been alive. People aren't any different because they've lived longer than others.'

'You know perfectly well what I mean, Philip. This could

ruin your life,' she added dramatically.

'Don't be ridiculous,' he snapped. 'Camilla is the most wonderful woman I've ever met. There's no one like her!'

'I know what she's like. I've known her all my life.'

'Yes. Well, quite! Why are you making such a fuss then?' Philip protested.

'Because she's too old for you. Surely you can see that?'

'As I've said, age is unimportant.'

Lucy tried another tack. 'Philip, it's your happiness I'm worried about. Camilla is a strong woman, and a very courageous one too, but she is rather dominating. She'll have you running around in circles in no time, especially as she's so rich. "He who pays the piper calls the tune." You've heard that saying, haven't you? I'm afraid she'll manipulate you, and then you'll get hurt.'

'Of course I won't.' Exasperated, Philip felt tempted to crash down the receiver. He felt so disappointed in his mother. He'd really expected her to be happy for his sake.

'I'm surprised at Camilla allowing this to happen,' Lucy was saying, as if she felt falling in love was in some way preventable. 'I should never have left you alone in Scotland with her.'

'For God's sake! I'm not a child!' he stormed, losing his temper. 'I'm in love with Camilla and she's in love with me. End of story.'

'No, it's not the end of the story,' Lucy said hotly. 'I won't allow you to ruin your life like this. Your father bought you a flat and you must live in it. I don't know what you think you're doing, having an affair with a woman who is much older than yourself when there are so many pretty young girls . . . what about Fiona? She was nice, wasn't she?'

But Philip wasn't listening any more. His mother was going on like a stuck gramophone record but no matter what she said, nothing would change his mind. He and Camilla were meant for each other and nothing, and no one, was going to stop him loving her.

Poppy had slipped out at dawn before anyone was awake, having locked herself in her room all evening. It was bad enough finding her mother sprawled all over the floor in utter abandonment, but to find her sprawled with Philip, who was not much older than Poppy herself, was disgusting. Sick with shock, Poppy crept into bed and lay there trembling. Was her mother drunk? she wondered. Or had she taken drugs? Of one thing Poppy was certain – Camilla had been neither seduced nor raped. Judging by her whimpers of delight as she rolled around the floor, she was a more than willing partner in what was going on, and Poppy thought it was the most degrading thing she had ever seen. Sex was for the young. It was not something one's mother did. At least not with a boy young enough to be her son.

Mixed up with Poppy's feelings of bitter distaste was a deep sense of jealousy, too. She wasn't sure whether it was because she quite fancied Philip herself, though she'd never admit it, or because he might squeeze her out of her mother's affections. Either way, she lay in bed shivering and shaking, wishing she'd stayed at Danny's place overnight although he wasn't there himself because he'd said he had important things to see to in connection with his 'secret weapon'.

'Things are hotting up, Pops,' he'd told her that morning. 'It won't be long now before we swing into action.' He rubbed his hands in satisfaction. 'Not long at all now.'

'Why can't I come with you?' she asked.

Danny shook his head.

'Where are you going?'

'The Bristol area.'

'Bristol! What's in Bristol? It's miles away.'

'Got to check up on things. Don't you worry about it. I'll be back tomorrow.' His tone was breezy and she could feel the excited tension in him, which had been getting stronger for days now, as if he were approaching some critical event.

'Is Big Marge going with you?' she asked sulkily.

'No, Big Marge has other things to do,' he said, with a sly smile. 'You've got it in for her, haven't you?'

Poppy raised her chin haughtily. 'No, I haven't. I couldn't care less about Big Marge. I just want to know what you're up to in Bristol?'

Danny patted her playfully on the bottom. 'You'll know soon enough, and it'll blow your mind.'

He'd refused to say any more and so she'd decided to go home, get something decent to eat, and then go to bed after a lovely hot bath.

Now, as she hurried along Wilton Crescent, having helped herself to some bread and fruit from the larder before the Maitlands were awake, she decided that she'd never go home again. She'd leave school, move in permanently with Danny and get some sort of a job. She wouldn't see her mother again, either. Not ever. The scene in the drawing-room she'd witnessed last night would be imprinted on her brain forever. And the smell of lilies would make her feel sick for as long as she lived.

'Why is the traffic so bad this morning?' Camilla asked Ferris as he drove her to the offices of Eaton & Eaton. The congestion around Hyde Park Corner was so bad they'd been sitting in a traffic jam for ten minutes already, and nothing seemed to be moving.

'It's the State Visit, madam,' Ferris replied. 'Several streets have been blocked off and traffic is being diverted all over the place.'

'I'd forgotten. It's the American President, isn't it?'

'Yes, he and his wife are arriving this morning to stay with the Queen. Traffic is being diverted because they'll be driving in open carriages from Victoria Station to the Palace.' Ferris and the Maitlands took a great interest in the Royal Family, and everything they were doing.

'Thank goodness it's a fine day,' Ferris continued, 'they're in for a busy time. The Queen is holding a State Banquet at the Palace on Thursday night.'

'Well, we can expect London traffic to be disrupted for at least a couple of days, can't we? Luckily I don't think I'll need the car except to take me to and from work,' Camillà observed.

'Very well, madam.'

As soon as Camilla entered her office, Jean greeted her with warmth.

'We really have missed you, Mrs Eaton,' she said.

Camilla laughed. 'I've had a good break, and in spite of all the dramas I'm feeling more rested.'

'You look wonderful,' Jean said with a searching look. 'You must be glad to have got to the bottom of all the troubles at your father's place.'

'Yes, I am . . . in a way.' A shadow fell over Camilla's face for a moment. 'It's been dreadful finding out that my father was undoubtedly murdered because he knew too much, but with all the information we've given the police I sincerely hope they will be able to arrest the suspects very soon.'

'Have you any idea who they are?'

'So many people seem to be involved that one can't be sure. It's obviously a highly organised gun-running operation, and I think the local vet is at the head of it.'

'And he was supposed to be a friend of your father's, wasn't he?' Jean asked.

Camilla nodded and said wryly: 'Some friend! Now let's get on with some work, Jean.' She settled herself behind her desk. 'Bring me up to date on what's happening, will you?'

For the next three hours Camilla worked steadily through a stack of correspondence, art work, presentations for promoting new products, and a briefing on the financial state of the company which she liked the Accounts Department to prepare for her each week. At noon there was a light tap on her office door.

'See who it is, will you, Jean?' she asked.

It was Annabel, Jean's assistant, standing there looking rather scared.

'What is it?' Jean asked.

Camilla, from her desk, noticed the strained look on the girl's face. 'Come in,' she called out.

Annabel spoke in a hoarse whisper. 'The second post has just arrived, and the post room has phoned the police. We've been told to evacuate the building right away.' Her hands shook as she spoke and she was obviously highly agitated.

'What's happened?' Camilla asked, springing to her feet.

'They think there's a bomb in a package addressed to you, Mrs Eaton!'

Philip and Camilla watched the six o'clock news on television as they sat in her study. She'd been home all afternoon, frantically trying to get hold of Poppy to tell her what had happened and to warn her to be careful, but to no avail. None of Poppy's school friends had seen her in ages, they said, and none knew where she was. In the end Camilla reluctantly had to give up, and hope Poppy would come home during the evening. Meanwhile the police had carried out a thorough search of the offices of Eaton & Eaton in case there were more explosive devices, but so far nothing further had been discovered.

But in just one morning her life had been changed. Scotland Yard, whose job it was to gather Intelligence on IRA activities, told Camilla that she was now on the organisation's Wanted List for her part in reporting what was going on in Ardachie. From now on, and until the police gathered sufficient evidence to make arrests, she would be provided with a police bodyguard. Meanwhile she'd been told she must be on her guard night and day. Even then, there could be members of the IRA who would be out for vengeance.

'I don't believe it!' Philip had exclaimed when she told him what had happened. 'That's scary, sweetheart.'

'I know. It's a really nasty feeling, realising that somebody . . . or several people in this case . . . wish me dead. As they wished my father dead,' she added in a quiet voice.

Philip put his arms around her and held her close, not knowing what to say, terrified something would happen to her, cursing the day she'd ever got involved in this terrible business.

'Do you think it'll be reported on TV?' he asked, stroking her hair.

'There were plenty of press around after the bomb was discovered. I can never understand how they get to the scene of an incident so quickly. Television cameras were there too.'

They settled themselves on the sofa in front of the TV set, watching as the news began with the main event of the day, the American President and his wife stepping off the train on to a crimson-carpeted platform, and then their arrival at Buckingham Palace, to be welcomed by the Queen and various other members of the Royal Family. Camilla watched with unseeing eyes, and ears that did not hear the fanfare of silver trumpets, or the drums of a military band, or the jingle of brass as the horses pulled the open landau taking the state guests to the Palace. Her thoughts were miles away, in a little fishing village in Scotland where her father had perished at the hands of evil men.

Philip looked at her tenderly. 'Try not to think about it,' he said, guessing what was on her mind.

Camilla turned to him with a faint smile. 'I'll try, darling, but I suppose that bomb arriving at the office today made me realise what pressure Daddy was under. I wonder if he sensed they were going to kill him?'

'That's something you'll have to ask Edith. I wonder if she's on their Wanted List, too?'

'I don't know, but no doubt I can ask Scotland Yard. You will be careful, won't you Philip? I asked in particular about you and Poppy, but it seems it's me they're out to get. Poor Ferris has been warned to examine the Mercedes every morning before he takes me to the office, and they told Maitland to report any mail that looks suspicious.'

'What a terrible business this is!' he exclaimed, shaking his head. Then he gripped her hand and pointed to the screen. 'Look! There's your office!'

There was a shot of Upper Grosvenor Street with the offices of Eaton & Eaton cordoned off while police vans with flashing blue lights blocked the road preventing anyone getting too close.

'A small explosive device was discovered in the mail room of the Advertising Agency, Eaton & Eaton, at noon today,' the newscaster was saying. 'The anti-terrorist bomb squad were able to dispose of the device in a controlled explosion and there were no casualties. The Metropolitan Police has issued warnings . . . '

'At least they didn't give my name,' Camilla said with relief. 'It's bad enough being a wanted woman without the whole world knowing it's me,' she added, trying to make light of it. 'What worries me,' she continued, 'is that it'll be bad for business. Who's going to want to see me at the office with this sort of thing happening?'

'But there'll be security guards watching the premises, night and day, won't there?'

Camilla nodded. 'I'm not sure that won't make matters worse. It'll be a constant reminder to our clients that the situation could be dangerous.'

When the phone rang a moment later, she started nervously.

'I wonder if that's Poppy,' she said. 'I've left messages with all her friends to get in touch with me.'

Philip jumped to his feet 'Shall I get it?'

At that moment they heard Maitland pick it up in the hall, saying he would see if Mrs Eaton was at home and who was calling, please? Then he came into the study. 'It's Mrs Hamilton for you, madam.'

Camilla's face fell. 'Oh, I had so hoped it was Poppy. Thank you, Maitland, I'll take it in here.'

Philip, who had suddenly become tense, shot her a warning glance. 'She knows about us,' he whispered. 'I told her this morning.'

'And?'

He made a grimace. 'She wasn't too thrilled.'

Camilla sighed. 'I was afraid of that.'

'Good luck.'

Camilla seized the phone and, although her heart was unaccountably ploughing around in her chest, decided to sound bright and breezy.

'Lucy! How lovely to hear from you. I was just going to ring you, anyway. Philip's told you all about our adventures at Creagnach, has he? And did you know someone sent a bomb in a package to the office today? It's just been on the television news.' Camilla knew she was gabbling but she'd become instantly aware of silent waves of hostility coming from Lucy and, although she remained silent, Camilla could sense her anger.

'Yes, I did hear something,' Lucy said at last. 'Camilla, can we meet for lunch?'

'Oh God, Lucy, I've got business luncheons *every* day, for the next ten days, but how about dinner? Is Anthony back from his fishing trip? Why don't you both come and dine? Is tomorrow any good? Or Wednesday?'

'I'd prefer to see you on your own,' Lucy replied stiffly. 'Surely you can manage a quick lunch somewhere? Or tea?'

There was regret and sadness in Camilla's voice. 'You're angry about Philip and me, aren't you?' she asked directly. 'And you're determined to have a showdown?' she sighed. 'Why don't you come for a drink tomorrow evening, then? I'll be back from the office by six.'

'And you'll be on your own?' Lucy asked pointedly.

'Yes.'

'Good. This is really serious, you know. I can't let you ruin Philip's life like this. We have to talk . . . '

'That's a bit strong, isn't it?' Camilla said. Philip was watching her as she spoke, guessing what his mother was saying. 'I promise you,' she continued, 'it isn't anything to get upset about, Lucy.' Although she'd expected it, she felt deeply hurt that her oldest friend wasn't sharing her new found happiness. Worse, that she was urgently opposing it.

When she'd hung up, she turned to Philip sadly. 'As you said, your mother hasn't taken too kindly to the idea of our being together.'

'Pay no attention to her. You know what mothers are like, especially with sons. I bet if Henrietta was having an affair with someone in their forties, she'd think it was terribly glamorous.'

Poppy had arrived back at Danny's place that morning and was surprised to find him in bed, nursing a hangover. It was eight-thirty and he was still fully dressed from the night before.

'I thought you were going to Bristol yesterday,' she said, flinging herself on top of him as he lay under the grey blankets.

'Steady on, for Christ's sake,' he admonished crossly. 'My head's killing me.'

She snuggled down by his side, her face buried in his neck. 'When are you going, then?'

'Later on today, I expect.'

'Can't I come with you? Oh, please, Danny, let me come with you?' she begged. 'If it's something secret you know I won't tell a soul. I've no one to tell anyway,' she added, her voice tinged with sadness.

Danny sighed, loudly in resignation. 'I suppose so,' he said grudgingly. 'But, mind, you're to keep your trap shut.'

'I will,' she promised. 'You know you can trust me, Danny.'

They set off for Bristol two hours later, with Danny at the wheel of a white Ford van he'd borrowed from a friend. When they arrived, he drove through the city to the far side and then took a turning to the right.

'Where are we going?' Poppy asked curiously. The journey had been a silent one with Danny still saying his head was bad.

'Just someplace,' he replied laconically. He was careering along winding country lanes at high speed now, the van was swaying from side to side, and although she was wearing a safety belt, Poppy was having to clutch on to the sides of her seat to keep upright. Then he turned sharply to the left and they went through a dense forest, oppressively dark, before coming out into the open again. Ahead of them, and set back from the road, stood a disused factory, an ugly conglomeration of grey buildings with corrugated-iron roofs. There were no windows or visible doors that Poppy could see, and the whole property was surrounded by a fence topped with loops of barbed wire.

Danny drew up at the metal entrance gates, on which a sign had been hung saying: 'No Entry. Strictly Private Property'. He put his hand on the van's horn and tooted loudly.

'What is this place?' she asked.

Danny didn't answer but leaned forward to get a better view of the building through the windscreen. 'Where are the buggers?' he muttered, tooting the horn again.

At that moment a man in a pair of tattered jeans and a dirty sweatshirt, under a brown nylon anorak, emerged from behind the building. As soon as he saw Danny he hurried forward and opened the gates.

'About time too,' Danny yelled at him. Then he swung the van into the compound and drove it round to the back. The man followed sullenly.

'Where are the others?' Danny demanded harshly. 'What are you all doing?'

'They're inside.' The man cocked his head towards the building.

'Okay, let's go.' Danny jumped down from the driver's seat. 'Pops, you wait here,' he commanded.

'No, I'm coming with you,' she replied with equal determination. She followed Danny and the man to a sliding metal door. Danny tugged it open. At that moment, as they entered the building, an explosion of barking rent the air in a feverish maddening cacophony of sound, so that she drew back for a moment, alarmed.

'It's okay, they're tied up,' Danny shouted over his shoulder.

Cautiously she followed him into what seemed like an aircraft hangar, but as the only illumination came from two skylights high in the roof, it was a couple of minutes before her eyes adjusted to the dimness. The sight that met her eyes terrified her even more.

Chained down one side were forty or fifty savage-looking

dogs, half starved and filthy as they stood in their own excrement and pools of urine. A few crusts of bread lay just beyond their reach. They strained at their short chain leads, their eyes glinting dangerously.

Keeping her distance, Poppy yelled: 'What are they?'

'A cross between Rottweilers and Pit Bull terriers.' There was pride in Danny's voice. 'We've been breeding them up here for ages now. Meet Tom.' He indicated the man who had come out to meet them. 'He looks after them most of the time.'

Tom looked Poppy over as she stood there in her layers of strange clothes and vivid makeup, and seemed to find her fascinating.

'Where are the others?' Danny asked him.

'Out the back.' He led the way through a door at the far end and Poppy found herself in what had obviously been offices when the property had been used as a factory. Dingy cubicles, where small windows let in a minimum of light, led off a narrow corridor, and through the glass partitions that divided the top half of the small rooms, Poppy could see several men lounging around on camp beds, playing cards or watching television on a small portable set.

'How y'doing?' Danny yelled cheerfully to the assembled company. A few came forward to see him, others waved, and there were shouts of 'Okay'.

'Want a cuppa?' Tom asked Poppy.

'Yes, please,' she replied. He'd shut the door behind him and the dogs seemed to have stopped barking, making normal speech possible. A steaming, chipped mug was handed to her and she sipped at it gratefully.

'So we're ready to go, are we?' Tom asked Danny.

'Yup. Tomorrow night.'

'What about transport?'

'All arranged. You'll leave here at five.'

'Five in the morning?'

'Five in the afternoon, you sodding idiot!' Danny sounded angry. 'Get your head in gear. We're not striking until nine o'clock at night. What would you sodding do all day if you left here at five in the morning?'

Tom's cheeks flamed and he shrugged.

'Now, you know what you've got to do!' Danny took a swig of tea, swallowing noisily. 'I'll have a word with the others, but you're in charge. Geddit?'

'Yes. Everything will be all right. They're ready to go.'

'The men or the dogs?'

'Both.'

Satisfied, Danny turned to Poppy. 'You stay here. I'm going to have a word with the others,' he commanded.

Obediently, Poppy sat on a hard metal-framed chair, her curiosity aroused. Something was going on but she couldn't make out what it was. What had all those vicious dogs to do with the riot that was imminent? And who were these men, sitting around passing the time, as if this disused factory was some kind of prison?

Danny was going from cubicle to cubicle, like a soldier rounding up the troops, and she wished she could hear what he was saying.

At last he came back, saying brusquely: 'Come on, Pops. We're finished here.'

Thankfully she jumped to her feet. 'Okay. I'm ready.'

'Let's go then.'

Tom led them back past the long row of dogs. Once again the air was filled with deafening barking as they leapt forward, straining to reach them with bared teeth, held back by chains. Tom had a whip in his hand this time and he lashed at their heads as he went past, infuriating them even more so that globules of saliva dripped from their gaping mouths.

Danny laughed. 'You got them well trained, Tom.'

Poppy shrunk back, knowing they would be torn to pieces if a chain snapped or a metal ring broke free of the wall.

Tom looked gratified. 'Starving and beating does wonders,' he admitted, shouting above the din.

At last they were out in the open again, leaving the noise and the stink behind. Poppy climbed back into the van feeling sick and shaken. Danny got in beside her and started the engine. Tom unlocked the iron gates again and a moment later they were out on the road once more, travelling at high speed.

'What on earth was that all about?' Poppy asked.

'I've just been employing a few guys who would otherwise have had nowhere to go,' he said shortly.

'Why not?'

'They're all ex-convicts. It's bleeding disgraceful that the government don't look after them when they come out.' Danny looked at her speculatively, as if wondering if he could trust her. Intuitively she knew what was going through his mind.

'I won't tell anyone,' she said in a small voice. 'I promise, Danny.'

'After tomorrow it won't matter.'

'Why not?'

'They're coming to London on Thursday as part of the riot we're staging. They've had their final instructions from me today, and they all know what they're to do.'

'And those dreadful dogs?'

A smile spread across Danny's face. 'They're our secret weapon. Them and about a hundred others that have been bred in disused factories and warehouses all over the country for the past couple of years.'

Poppy looked confused. 'I don't understand! What have they got to do with the riot?'

He chuckled. 'You'll see soon enough.'

Chapter Seventeen

Lucy arrived at exactly six-thirty, looking grim-faced and full of self-righteousness.

'Good evening, Maitland,' she said stiffly as the butler let her in. Then she raised her head, sniffing. 'What a strong smell of perfume.' Her tone was critical.

Maitland smiled politely. 'It's the lilies, madam. Their scent becomes particularly pronounced in the evening.'

'Lilies?' He showed her into the drawing-room, and as soon as she saw the many massive arrangements, she exclaimed: 'Goodness! What a lot of flowers! Is Mrs Eaton giving a party?'

'Not that I know of, madam,' the butler replied with equanimity. 'Mrs Eaton will be down in a minute. Can I get you a drink, madam?'

'Thank you. I'd like a glass of sherry.' Lucy seated herself on the sofa, looking around the room, seeing it with different eyes, imagining how it must have struck Philip the first time he saw it. Wealth, great wealth, was the first impression one received, she thought. The paintings, the silk Chinese carpet, the French antiques, not to mention the hundreds of lilies, gave the impression that Camilla was a very rich woman who indulged herself on a whim. How could she have bought so many lilies! What a vulgar display of ostentation! Lucy pursed her lips and felt quite put out.

At that moment Camilla came gliding into the room, startling Lucy even further. Her hair was loose and flowing and her makeup light, making her look years younger. She'd obviously changed since coming back from the office for she wore a becomingly draped cream cashmere dress, with long ropes of pearls and pearl drop earrings.

'Lucy, my dear.' She kissed her friend on both cheeks. 'I'm sorry I wasn't down when you arrived. Have you got a drink? It's been such a hellish day at the office after yesterday's disruptions that I'm behind with everything.' Going to the drinks tray, which Maitland had placed on a sidetable, she poured a gin and tonic for herself.

Lucy watched her resentfully, wondering how she managed to look so young and slim. 'I hope we're going to be on our own, Camilla,' she said stiffly. 'We have to talk.'

'Philip will be here in due course, but we're on our own now,' Camilla replied gently. She sat down on the other end of the sofa, regarding Lucy with candid eyes. 'You needn't look at me as if I was going to harm Philip,' she continued more gently, 'if anyone is going to get hurt it will probably be me. Meanwhile, we're very happy, Lucy. You've no idea how much I love him.'

Lucy looked painfully embarrassed. 'I think it's indecent, you and Philip. What can you be thinking of? For God's sake, Camilla, how can you do this? He's not much older than Poppy! You remember when he was born? We were living in Surrey then, before Anthony got posted abroad, and you came to visit me in hospital!' Her voice rose. 'I never thought you'd do anything like this. What will people say?'

'Ah!' Camilla drew out the exclamation. 'Is that what's worrying you? People saying Philip's been seduced by a cradle-snatcher? Or perhaps they'll think he has a mother complex?'

Lucy flushed with annoyance. 'Don't be so ridiculous.'

'Honestly, Lucy, I'm not being ridiculous. I had no intention of falling in love again, and I certainly had no designs on Philip. It's as amazing to me as it must be to you that he cares for me in a way I never dreamed possible.' She waved her hand, pointing to the lilies. 'Look at these flowers!'

'Philip gave them to you?'

Camilla nodded. 'When we got back from Scotland I found them waiting for me. It's the most wonderfully romantic gesture. Believe me, Lucy, we're ecstatically happy. I wish you could understand what he means to me. Can't you even be a little bit happy for us?' Her tone was wistful.

'What you don't seem to understand is that it could ruin his life,' Lucy replied flatly. 'Oh, I can see why he's attracted to you, all right. Three years at university, without much money, and then a year in Florence, and back-packing trips around the world during the vacations . . . he's in no way prepared for all this now.' Her voice took on a carping edge. 'Here's this rich widow, with a lovely house and the money to buy anything she wants, and he's bowled over. Can you blame him? No doubt you paid for everything in Scotland, including staying at that castle on the way back! He's never had such a good time in his whole life. And now he's going to be living here, with servants to wait on him and all the trimmings . . . *of course* he's infatuated!'

Camilla's face hardened and her eyes glinted dangerously. 'If that's your attitude, Lucy, I think you'd better leave. I think you're doing Philip a great disservice by suggesting he's a gold-digger, and you're certainly insulting me by suggesting that I'm buying his favours.'

Lucy wrung her hands in obvious distress. 'Oh, don't talk like that! That's not what I mean. I'm trying to tell you how the situation must look to a young man. He's not as sophisticated as he makes out, you know. I'm not saying it's all your fault that he seems to have lost his head, but I'm frightened for him. This . . . this affair will spoil him for girls his own age. Don't you see that? You're obviously a woman of the world, and probably more interesting and amusing than a girl of twenty, but you *are* forty-four! And he's twenty-four! It can only lead to trouble.'

'It doesn't have to,' Camilla said quietly. 'Apart from which, we had no choice. We fell in love while we were up in Ardachie. It really was something beyond our control.'

'Rubbish!' Lucy replied angrily. 'You're old enough to control your feelings even if he isn't! And what on earth is this doing to Poppy? How does she feel about it?'

'She doesn't know yet.'

'She doesn't know? How can she *not* know when Philip's been here for the last two nights?'

'She's been away, staying with friends,' Camilla said hurriedly. 'Listen, Lucy. Philip and I love each other, and no matter what you say, that's the way it is. We are two adults who can do as we like, and I think it's time you untied Philip from your apron strings, as I've done with Poppy, and let him lead his own life.'

'The trouble is you've lost control of Poppy, and you resent my still being close to Philip,' Lucy responded sharply. 'You don't even know where she is, do you? Be honest, Camilla, you've got problems with Poppy, and it's because you've been so wrapped up in your own life that you don't know what she's doing half the time.'

Tears stung her eyes at the hurtfulness of Lucy's words, and she felt a deep sense of anger too. It was easy for Lucy, with a husband to support her, to be self-righteous. Camilla rose, her face averted so that Lucy couldn't see her expression.

'That's enough,' she said, trying to keep her voice steady. 'I'd like you to leave now before we both say things we're going to regret.'

Lucy gathered up her handbag and gloves and stormed out of the room without another word. A moment later Camilla heard the front door slam and, covering her face with her hands, sank down on to the sofa. Lucy's lack of understanding had wounded her and she suddenly felt terribly alone. Poppy had no use for her, and David and her father had gone. Thank God for Philip, she thought gratefully. He was all she had left in the world who really mattered.

They'd finished dinner and were sitting in the garden by the light of concealed floodlighting, drinking coffee. All around them, honeysuckle, roses and lilies bloomed and filled the air with their fragrance. The small garden that led off the back of Camilla's house was like a tiny oasis of countryside, set amid the tall grey stone buildings, whilst in the distance the roar of traffic from Hyde Park Corner sounded like surf pounding on a far shore.

'What's wrong, sweetheart? You've been very quiet all evening,' Philip observed, refilling their Sèvres coffee cups from the silver coffee pot that Maitland had placed on the white wrought-iron garden table.

'I saw your mother this evening,' Camilla admitted with a wry smile. 'To say she doesn't approve of our relationship is an understatement.'

'I told you not to pay any attention to her. You know what Mum's like! She's very possessive with us all, and I'm not sure that any woman would meet with her approval when it comes to me. She'll be the same with Reggie when he's older.'

'Even so . . . ' Camilla's voice drifted off as she remembered Lucy's remarks. The ones about Poppy, which she did not intend repeating to Philip, hurt the most. Was she really such a bad mother? Was Poppy's waywardness really her fault?

Seeing she was troubled, Philip put his arms around her. 'Don't worry about it, my love. All that really matters is that we have each other. We'll show them that age doesn't matter.'

Camilla leaned her head on his shoulder. Everything had seemed so straightforward when they'd been in Scotland, and she wished they could have stayed away forever. Now, their love for each other seemed to be on display for all and sundry to comment on, and it made her feel very exposed and vulnerable.

'Have you spoken to your father?' she asked thoughtfully. Anthony, she was sure, would be an ally.

'Not yet,' he replied, 'but Dad won't be a problem, and neither will Mum in time. I'm sure of that, Camilla. It's probably just been a shock to them, but once they get used to the idea of our being together I'm sure they'll back us all the way.'

Gradually, as he talked, Camilla found herself being lulled into a state of well-being and happiness. Of course Lucy would accept the situation in time. And of course the problems with Poppy had little to do with her, but were caused by the difficult age and phase her daughter was going through.

Philip was kissing her gently and lovingly. 'Let's forget about everyone and go to bed,' he whispered.

'I think that's the best idea I've heard today,' she murmured, kissing him back. Together they went up to her bedroom, their arms around each other, talking quietly and laughing as they went.

Maitland, hovering in readiness to shut up the house for the night and turn off all the lights, heard Camilla's bedroom door shut. He knew Poppy had crept in earlier while her mother and Philip had been listening to music after dinner, and he knew she was still in her room. For that reason he did not lock the front door or set the alarm, because he was sure she wouldn't be staying for long.

Poppy left the house an hour later, tiptoeing down the wide carpeted stairs with a large holdall stuffed with clothes. She hesitated at the bottom, wondering if it would be safe to slip down to the larder to steal some food, but then decided against it. The last thing she wanted was to see anyone and there was always the chance that the Maitlands were still in their sitting-room which adjoined the kitchen, where they watched television in the evenings.

Opening the front door cautiously, she crept out of the house, making sure there was no one about. Their neighbours were quite nosy at times and the last thing she wanted was to run into them returning from a dinner party or something. But Wilton Crescent was deserted, its elegant grey stone curved façade dimly lit by the street lamps. Poppy glanced up at their own house and saw her mother's bedroom lights were already turned off. Sick with disgust, she turned away and hurried up the street. The sooner she put some distance between her mother and herself the better, she thought, and her mind was filled with memories of her father. Darling Daddy, she reflected, her eyes stinging with tears. If only he'd still been alive none of this would have happened.

The next morning dawned grey and dismal; a typical English summer's day, with the air so damp it might have been drizzling.

In the offices of Eaton & Eaton, Camilla had meetings at hourly intervals before having lunch at the Savoy with a client. For her it was a fairly routine day taken up with planning and discussing various advertising projects. That evening she and Philip planned to meet some clients of hers at Harry's Bar for dinner.

Lucy spent the day shopping, an occupation dear to her heart. Although it was still only mid-July, she'd already drawn up a list of Christmas presents and as she made her way from Harrods to Peter Jones, she decided she might as well get some kitchen equipment for their new house as well.

Geoffrey Hennessy, in his office at the *Globe*, tried to settle down to write a feature about privatisation in industry, but somehow found his mind straying to thoughts of Camilla. He hadn't talked to her on the phone recently and he missed her lively company and intelligent conversation. She was no longer interested in him, though, and the thought depressed him deeply. At noon his editor sent for him.

'Something's up,' he announced briefly.

'What sort of thing?'

'There's wind of trouble tonight. The police are mounting extra security around Buckingham Palace and along the Mall. The Queen's giving a banquet to honour the US President, but they don't usually go to these lengths. Check it out, will you? Try and find out what sort of trouble they're expecting.'

'Okay,' Geoffrey replied, glad of any excuse to get out of the office.

Inside Buckingham Palace, preparations were being made for

the banquet to which a hundred and seventy guests had been invited. Thirty-four dozen gold plates and hundreds of gold knives, forks and spoons were being polished, crystal glasses were being arranged on the horseshoe-shaped table, and gilt salt cellars, one for each person, were being set in place. At regular intervals down the centre of the table, gilt étagères were filled with breathtaking arrangements of pink flowers. In the vast kitchens chefs were preparing a menu which would include fresh salmon, rack of lamb, home-grown vegetables, and the Queen's favourite champagne sorbet with raspberries. The House of Windsor was about to show the White House how things should be done.

For Poppy, unaware that she was in the eye of the coming storm, it was a day when she felt in limbo. Danny hadn't come back and so she'd spent a miserable night alone in his bed imagining him with Big Marge. She told herself she was being stupid because Big Marge was at least forty and weighed fifteen stone, and Danny wouldn't be interested in a woman like that. Nevertheless she felt lonely and worried.

At dawn, she scurried down to the communal kitchen before anyone was up to make herself a cup of instant coffee. The only milk she could find was sour and so she had it black. Not daring to go out in case Danny returned and she missed him, she sat on the bed watching television. At noon someone banged loudly on the door, startling her.

'Who is it?' Poppy called out.

'Message from Danny.'

She flew to the door and opened it. The young black man who had the room below stood there, hands on hips.

'That was Danny on the phone just now.'

'What did he say?' she asked eagerly.

'You're to meet him on the east side of Trafalgar Square at nine o'clock tonight,' he informed her, 'and you're not to be late.'

At five o'clock, the first of the vans drove into central London from the provinces and parked for the time being near Marble Arch. By six o'clock another hundred vans had converged on the city, each of them disgorging a dozen or more young men and women, their emblazoned T-shirts hidden under anoraks or sweaters. Then came the lorries, more than a dozen of them, rumbling into town from all directions before parking in quiet back streets.

Geoffrey Hennessy, talking to the police outside Buckingham Palace, could sense something was about to happen, although the chief constable assured him that the presence of dozens of extra policemen, drafted from other areas, was no more than 'routine security' in view of the importance of the Queen's guests, who would include the Prime Minister, members of the Cabinet, the House of Lords, the Judiciary, and several foreign ambassadors.

Geoffrey wasn't convinced. There was a definite atmosphere of trouble brewing and a strange sense of excitement in the air. He'd experienced it before, when he'd been reporting uprisings in various parts of the world. Something was going to happen tonight. He could feel it in his bones. Even the TV crews who'd arrived to cover the State Banquet, seemed more alert than usual. The BBC TV Film Unit were already set up inside the Palace, positioned to relay to millions of viewers the historic sight of the Queen and the American President leading the procession into dinner, to be followed by speeches which would be flashed around the world by satellite to mark the recent trade treaty signed by both countries that morning.

The world's media were poised to record events as they happened but Geoffrey had a gut feeling that they'd end up reporting a great deal more than a mere banquet. His intuition had never failed him in the past. He was certain he'd be proved right tonight.

Lucy and Anthony decided to have supper on a tray in front of the television, as they'd be on their own. Charlotte, in spite of her arm being in plaster, had gone to the cinema with some friends and was staying over with one of them for the night.

'There's a good play on BBC Two,' Lucy remarked, 'with Maggie Smith.'

'Fine,' Anthony replied, settling himself in his favourite armchair with a bottle of whisky by his side. 'I could do with a quiet evening.' He loved his children dearly but there were times when he longed to be alone with Lucy.

Camilla and Philip arrived at Harry's Bar just before eight o'clock. As usual it was packed with the rich and famous, and the bar area was so crowded she suggested they go straight to their table.

'We're expecting another couple,' she told the Maître d' as he ushered them to a table at the far end, reserved for VIPs.

'Can I get you something to drink while you're waiting, Mrs Eaton?' he asked. Camilla had been a member of Harry's Bar from the beginning, taking the wives of David's clients to lunch there when he'd been alive. Now she used it for entertaining her own clients as an alternative to inviting them to Wilton Crescent.

'Shall we have some champagne?' she asked Philip. He nodded in agreement, looking round at the celebrities who were dining at adjacent tables.

'This is some place, isn't it?' he whispered when they were alone again.

Camilla smiled, pleased at the impression the elegant restaurant was making.

At that moment more people arrived and, as they were shown to their table, one of the women and Camilla recognised each other. She was the wife of a client and Camilla hadn't seen her for some time.

'How are you?' Camilla greeted her. Her husband was the managing director of one of the largest soap and detergent manufacturers and their advertising budget ran into six figures.

'My dear Camilla, how nice to see you again. You're looking so well.' The smartly dressed and quite pretty middle-aged woman turned with a charming smile to Philip. 'And this must be your son?'

Camilla froze and for a moment Philip looked aghast.

'No, this is a friend, Philip Hamilton,' Camilla said as smoothly as she could. 'Philip, this is Mary Alexander.'

Polite greetings were exchanged, but when Mary had gone to her own table, Camilla looked shaken.

Embarrassed, Philip tried to make a joke of it. 'The trouble with her,' he said succinctly, 'is that she's jealous of you because you look twenty years younger than her. Don't let her get to you, sweetheart.'

Camilla tried to smile, but she was appalled. Did people really think they looked like mother and son? ·

A few minutes later they were joined by Charles Laing, chairman of Empress Cars whose advertising campaign Eaton & Eaton had just undertaken. He was accompanied by his wife Sandra.

This time, swiftly, and before anyone could jump to the wrong conclusion, Camilla said: 'May I introduce my friend, Philip Hamilton? And this is Charles and Sandra Laing.'

At the same time as Camilla and her guests were ordering *oeuf en cocotte*, with white truffles, Lobster Thermidor, a green salad, and finally crème brûlée, plus more Veuve Clicquot followed by a bottle of Gewurztraminer, Poppy stood waiting for Danny in Trafalgar Square. Her feet and hands were frozen and she was hungry, having had only a slice of bread and jam and another black coffee, because that was all she could find in Danny's house. She hadn't been able to buy anything either, having spent her last few pence on her underground ticket.

There were a lot of people milling around, some of whom she recognised from pub meetings. It seemed, though, as if they had just turned up at random, without a plan of campaign, without any idea of what they were supposed to be doing.

The young man she'd met, who had admitted to reading the *Tatler* in order to psych himself up, was sitting on the wall that enclosed Trafalgar Square. When he saw Poppy, he grinned.

'How y'doing?' he called out.

She went over to him. 'I'm wondering what's happening,' she replied. 'Danny just sent me a message to meet him here at nine o'clock.'

The young man, who said his name was Dick, glanced at his watch. 'It's not even eight-thirty yet. Plenty of time for things to get going. Not everyone's here yet.'

'Do you know exactly what's happening?' she asked.

'We've all been told to converge on Trafalgar Square.'

'Then what?'

Dick grinned. 'Then it's a case of Follow-my-Leader.'

'Who? Danny, you mean?'

Dick nodded. 'Danny and Big Marge.'

Poppy felt her heart plunge. 'Why Big Marge?'

'Because she's the leader of the women's movement.'

'I know that,' Poppy said impatiently. 'But I'm Danny's girlfriend. If anyone is going to be leading the rally with Danny, it's going to be me.'

'I wouldn't be too sure of that,' Dick replied. 'Anyway, this is hardly going to be a rally,' he chuckled.

'Whatever it is, my place is by Danny's side.'

Dick gave her a strange look. 'You're not afraid of Big Marge, then?'

'Why should I be?' Poppy asked, frowning.

'Well, she's only his wife, isn't she?'

At Buckingham Palace the guests had already arrived in a steady stream of black shining limousines. Each one was then met by an equerry or a lady-in-waiting and conducted to the state apartments where drinks were being served. In a few minutes they would be joined in this magnificent cream and gold and crimson setting by the Queen and the American President, Prince Philip and the First Lady, and several other members of the royal family. Tonight was the grandest of all grand occasions and the dazzling display of the women's jewels would be matched only by the ten million pounds' worth of gold plate on the dining table.

Dukes and duchesses, ambassadors and members of the government were mingling in this unrivalled setting, the TV crew sweating under the blaze of lights waiting to televise the royal procession which would be led by the Lord Chamberlain and the Lord Steward, walking backwards all the way from the State Drawing-room to the State Ballroom so as not to turn their backs on the Monarch.

Outside the gates of the Palace Geoffrey still hung around, watching the arrivals and wondering why the hell he was there at all. It didn't look as if anything particular was going to happen now, and he was just about to get in touch with the editor on his mobile phone to say he was packing it in for the night when he heard one of the policemen on duty say something about a 'rally' to one of his colleagues.

'What rally?' Geoffrey asked.

'There's something going on in Trafalgar Square,' he was told. 'It's a bunch of students protesting about something. I don't think it'll amount to much, though.' The middle-aged constable sounded sanguine. He'd seen it all before. Nothing fazed him these days.

'Let's watch the nine o'clock news,' Lucy suggested. The drama she'd been looking forward to had turned out to be a disappointment, and using the remote control she was switching from channel to channel to find something interesting to watch.

'Good idea,' said Anthony, yawning. Television always made him sleepy and he was looking forward to going to bed.

It wasn't until nine-fifteen that there was a Newsflash and the newsreader announced a 'disturbance' that was happening in Trafalgar Square. His voice was tense and held a note of suppressed excitement.

'We're going over to John Abbott, our reporter in the Mall, to find out what's happening,' he told the viewers.

Lucy leaned forward, alert now. 'I wonder what it's all about?'

Poppy felt sick with misery and a sense of betrayal. How could Danny be married to Big Marge? Why had he never told her? She clenched her fists and felt icy and shaky inside. Why hadn't *anyone* told her? All these months she'd been thinking she was his girlfriend and all the time he'd been married to Big Marge, who lived in the house at Chalk Farm where Poppy had taken the family silver. Dick had also offered the information that they'd been married for nine years!

Tears filled her eyes, multiplying the street lights around Trafalgar Square, before she dashed them angrily away. Members of Danny's movement were gathering thickly around her but she didn't even notice them. Her whole being was concentrated on watching for Danny's arrival. He'd sent a message for her to meet him here so surely he'd come looking for her? Perhaps he was finished with Big Marge? Clinging wildly to what was left of her dreams, Poppy tried to control her emotions and keep a grip on herself. Whatever happened, she would stay by Danny's side tonight. That much he had promised her. Together they would march through the streets, proclaiming the injustice of the class system. Tonight they would let the people know they were going to do something about it. Danny's words, heard at so many of his meetings, repeated themselves in her mind. They would change the world! There would be equality for everyone!

At that moment she saw him, striding up from Northumberland Avenue, his fair cropped hair standing out among the jostling supporters who surrounded him, his black leather clothes gleaming sexily in the semi-darkness.

Poppy ran up to him. 'Danny!' she exclaimed breathlessly. 'I'm here.'

He gave her a curt nod, and as he strode on past her she caught a glimpse of Big Marge coming from the opposite direction. Poppy trotted after him, trying to keep up, but the men grouped around him seemed to close ranks and form a tight circle around Danny and Big Marge, as they met and stood close together talking in urgent tones.

Poppy tried to squeeze her way through the men, but they ignored her as they stood shoulder to shoulder, listening to Danny's instructions. She strained to hear what he was saying, but the noise of passing traffic and the hubbub around them drowned most of his words.

'. . . straight up the Mall . . . keep close together . . . don't release the dogs until . . . attack anyone who . . . Once inside . . .'

She decided to stay as close to him as possible and follow him wherever he went. Danny had his back to her, but over the shoulders of his gang of supporters she got a closer look at Big Marge. The woman had strong features and her hair was cut short like a man's. By the street lights her un-madeup face looked puffy, like uncooked dough, and she was dressed in trousers and a khaki bomber jacket, that did not meet across her vast chest. She seemed to be nodding in agreement at what Danny was saying, and for a dreadful moment Poppy thought they were going to embrace. Big Marge laid a hand, the nails black with dirt, on Danny's arm, but then they moved apart and with a gesture that was almost a salute she walked away to join a group of other women who were waiting at the corner of the Square.

'Danny,' Poppy called out desperately. He *had* to see her and acknowledge her presence. She loved him and belonged to him, even if he did have a wife, and she must be by his side tonight whatever happened. He didn't seem to hear her so she shouted his name again, waving her hand frantically to attract his attention.

''Ere, who are you shoving?' demanded one of the men, turning angrily.

'I must get to Danny,' Poppy cried out. 'He told me to meet him here. He's expecting me.'

'He told us *all* to meet him here,' the man retorted in a surly voice, 'so don't go thinking there's anything special about you.'

At that moment Danny turned and she caught his eye through the throng that was building up around him by the minute.

'I'm here, Danny!' she yelled.

He ignored her. 'Let's go!' he shouted over his shoulder to the people around him. They surged forward, and suddenly Poppy found herself being swept along as if by a human wave. The torrent of people turned and rushed forward, heading for Admiralty Arch and the Mall, and then Buckingham Palace beyond.

The air was filled with cries of 'Let's go!', echoing and re-echoing as people who a few minutes before had resembled tourists or ordinary citizens suddenly turned and joined in the tide of humanity that was swarming inexorably forward. They'd stripped off their outer garments so that suddenly they were a sea, a turbulent mass of white T-shirts emblazoned with the words 'Class Warriors'.

Petrified for a moment, Poppy looked around wildly for Danny but somehow he was ahead of her now, striding forward amid a mass of supporters who had produced from under their coats and anoraks an assortment of weapons, including steel bars, axes, and machetes.

Suddenly it seemed as if the whole of Trafalgar Square had erupted as the angry rabble surged forward, while genuine passers-by who had been going about their business peacefully, screamed and tried to escape by running up side streets. There was no escape though. With sick horror, Poppy realised that this was no rally; Class Warriors intended to destroy everything in their path that symbolised law, order, and the Establishment. Every word Danny had said, when he'd held those meetings in pubs, came back to her now with fearful clarity. She'd imagined he'd been talking symbolically about attacking the Establishment and ridding the country of the rich and privileged but now she knew he had meant it literally. He had said the streets would run with blood. He had promised his followers urban anarchy, and now he was about to deliver. The floodgates had been opened, and as the multitudes squeezed their way under the high stone archway that straddled one end of The Mall, she knew the police would stand no chance. They would be outnumbered, outranked, and they were without weapons.

'Danny!' she screamed piteously as she found herself jostled along so that her feet hardly touched the ground. Any moment now she was sure she would slip and be trampled underfoot. Ahead of her she heard the smashing of glass and saw that several groups were smashing the pavement flagstones with a pick and then hurling the lumps of stone through nearby windows. They were baying like animals now, and she had lost all sight of Danny.

Then she smelt petrol. Something skimmed over her head and a moment later there was an explosion and a burst of fire ahead as a petrol bomb exploded. More followed, aimed at the lines of police who had materialised in an effort to halt the flood of violence. Poppy tried to go sideways in an effort to escape the forward-thrusting mainstream that filled the roadway but she was held by the sheer mass of advancing bodies. There was only one way she could keep going and that was forward.

Just beyond Admiralty Arch dozens of policemen, arms linked, had formed a line across the width of the Mall, while behind them more police were rushing forward to lend their support. Missiles and more fire bombs rained down, injuring some of the police, and the line broke and the rioters gained a few yards. Then, from St James's Park on the left and Carlton House Terrace and Marlborough Road on the right, hundreds more Class Warriors emerged, cutting off the police who were suddenly surrounded by the screaming mob. The lorries which had quietly moved into the area during the past half hour unloaded their occupants, and at that moment Poppy realised the significance of Danny's 'secret weapon'.

Nearly a hundred savage dogs on leads were being used by several dozen handlers to head the procession towards Buckingham Palace. Slavering and wild-eyed, the Rottweiler crosses looked ready to rip to pieces anyone who challenged their progress.

Sirens were screaming through the night now, bringing with them white police vans filled with riot squads. Helmeted, padded and with shields, they formed a secondary barrier across the Mall to prevent the Class Warriors reaching the Palace. Overhead a helicopter clattered, whilst by the Palace gates police horses pranced nervously as the sound of the fighting grew nearer.

Caught up amongst the surging maelstrom of violence, Poppy had only one wish now – to get away. As she was pushed to the front of the stampede she saw the policemen try to rush the dogs, wielding truncheons while they protected themselves with their shields that glinted glassily under the street lights as the night closed in. One of the dogs leapt high, snarling, and then with deadly accuracy knocked one of the riot squad sideways. He fell, and a moment later the Rottweiler was at his throat, tearing the flesh with fangs as sharp as knives.

The air was glowing orange all about her now from fires that had been started, and to the pandemonium of yelling and screaming and the barking of dogs was added the loud ringing of fire-engine bells. Hysterical with fear, Poppy found herself propelled to the front of the charging mob. Before them, only a few hundred yards away, lay Buckingham Palace in all its stately grandeur. Windows were ablaze with light from the crystal chandeliers that had been lit for the banquet, and above from the flag post fluttered the Royal Standard.

Suddenly Poppy saw a gap in the crowd. Charging through it, she saw amidst the smouldering fire bombs that burned, melting the tar on the roadway, a crowbar that someone had thrown down. Bending to grab it, more for self-defence than anything else, she ran towards Birdcage Walk. Maybe she could escape, get away from the scene of fearful ugliness. As she straightened up, crowbar in hand, she saw a police horse charging the crowds. Too late, she realised she was standing directly in its path.

'Shall we go back to Wilton Crescent for coffee?' Camilla

asked Philip and the Laings. She always thought it was a nice way to round off an evening, apart from which she hated to stay in a restaurant once dinner had been served.

Sandra Laing, who was dying to see what sort of house Camilla lived in, nodded vigorously. 'Yes, let's,' she said, looking pointedly at her husband.

Charles Laing smiled pleasantly in his usual good-tempered way, and said: 'That would be very nice.' Even if he hadn't wanted to, he'd still have said yes because he did everything he could to please his pretty second wife. They'd been married for only ten months and he was besotted with her. The age difference between them was similar to the age difference between Camilla and Philip, except it was the other way round. The more acceptable way round, he thought, guessing Camilla and Philip were lovers. His friends had congratulated him on marrying a woman in her early twenties, but he couldn't help wondering what Camilla's friends were saying behind her back at her having an affair with a much younger man.

Ferris was waiting in the car in Charles Street as they came out of Harry's Bar. He jumped out as soon as he saw them and opened the doors. The car radio was on, Camilla noticed, which was unusual for Ferris who preferred to read if he was waiting.

'. . . Casualties have been reported, and several fires started . . .'

'What's happening, Ferris?' she asked from where she was sitting in the back of the car with Charles and Sandra Laing. Philip, in the front seat, was straining to hear the commentary.

'. . . Extra police have been drafted in to try and quell the riot. Many have been badly injured by the dozens of Rottweilers . . .'

'What on earth is going on? Where is this happening?' They were all looking questioningly at each other, alarm in their eyes.

'Buckingham Palace has been stormed by hundreds of people who call themselves "Class Warriors", madam,' Ferris explained as he turned on the ignition. 'They're throwing fire bombs over the gates of the Palace, and they've got dozens of killer dogs with them.'

There was stunned silence in the car until Camilla exclaimed: 'I don't believe it! My God, this is anarchy!'

'Can we watch television when we get to your house?' Sandra Laing asked. Her tone was ghoulish.

'I wonder if it's an anti-American protest prompted by the President's visit?' Philip observed.

'I don't think so, sir,' said Ferris. 'From what I can gather, it's an anti-Establishment protest. I think Buckingham Palace was chosen as the main target because the world's media are focusing on it, in view of the State Banquet tonight. They're ensuring themselves maximum publicity.'

Camilla looked grave. 'What sort of people would do such a thing? As if there wasn't enough trouble around the world already.'

Ferris tried to take a short cut through Mayfair because of the congested traffic. The police had closed off all roads leading to the Palace and cars were creeping along, bumper to bumper, tail-lights gleaming red in the darkness. In the distance they could hear the constant wail of police cars, ambulances and fire engines, and overhead the loud clattering roar of a helicopter, circling round and round, was at times deafening.

'If you don't mind, madam, I think I'll go the long way, otherwise we'll be stuck at Hyde Park Corner for hours,' Ferris observed.

'It's quite exciting, isn't it!' Sandra squeaked. 'Like a war!'

'Don't be silly, darling,' said Charles indulgently. 'It sounds like a serious situation to me.'

'It probably is a substitute for war,' Camilla observed with sudden insight. 'This country hasn't had a war for a very long time, and this sort of thing is pent-up, misdirected energy.'

When they got back to Wilton Crescent, Maitland was there to greet them. He'd turned on all the drawing-room lights and there was even a delicious aroma of coffee coming from the kitchen.

'Have you heard what's happening, Maitland?' Camilla asked as he took their coats.

'Yes, madam. It seems like a very nasty business. Some of the rioters have even scaled the gates and got inside the Palace!'

'Let's see what's happening on TV,' Philip said, striding ahead of them into the drawing-room. He turned on the large set and immediately the screen blossomed into a picture of hordes of people clashing with police in a headlong battle by the main entrance gates to the Palace. It was difficult in the dark to make out exactly what was happening in detail, but sudden bursts of light as a fire bomb exploded in the foreground were enough to show that the police were outnumbered by about five to one.

'. . . Earlier in the evening,' the commentator was saying, 'a supposedly friendly rally in Trafalgar Square quickly escalated into an ugly scene of street fighting. An angry mob, armed with fire bombs and other weapons, surged up the Mall towards the Palace. Stones and pieces of broken masonry were hurled at windows and there were several casualties. It was then the rioters released dozens of dogs, which have been identified as a cross-breed between Rottweilers and Pit Bull Terriers. They forced the police to retreat, and until reinforcements could be rushed to the scene the dogs attacked anyone who approached them.'

Camilla watched in horror as they showed a clip of film taken earlier. Suddenly she gripped Philip's arm. 'There's Poppy!' she cried out. 'Look! There! Oh, my God!' She let out a little scream as a mounted policeman charged the crowd, and a blond girl, running forward, collided with the horse. She seemed to be almost lifted off the ground by the impact and then flung down in the roadway. A moment later she disappeared under the feet of the rioters as they surged forward again.

Camilla sat, speechless with horror, her hand clasped over her mouth.

'Who's Poppy?' asked Sandra Laing, but Camilla wasn't listening. Stricken, she turned to Philip.

'What shall we do?' she asked frantically. 'Oh, my God, what was Poppy *doing* there? How shall we get to her?'

Philip looked grim as he took her hand. 'The only thing we can do is to ring all the hospitals until we find where she's been taken.'

'Who's Poppy?' Sandra repeated.

Camilla glanced at her absently. 'My daughter.'

Charles Laing raised his eyebrows in surprise. 'Your daughter?' There was disapproval in his tone. 'What's she doing, caught up with a mob like that?'

'I wish I knew.' Camilla leaned back in her chair, watching with dazed eyes as the TV continued to show scenes that resembled a battlefield. People with blood pouring down their faces filled the screen one minute, then there was a general shot the next with scattered fire bombs blazing like bonfires, police horses rearing and prancing and the rebels charging with their weapons. At one point the camera zoomed in to a close-up of a man clinging to the tops of the railings that surrounded the courtyard of the Palace, kicking with heavily booted feet at anyone who tried to reach him. The scene was chaotic. Confusion was rife as people fought with the police in isolated skirmishes away from the main body of the onslaught. And it seemed as if three out of four people were wearing white T-shirts with 'Class Warriors' printed on the front.

'What does it mean?' Sandra asked.

Camilla stared at her, wondering how anyone could be so stupid.

'It's a sort of revolution, my pet,' Charles explained, as if he were talking to a child.

'Don't be silly, darling,' she giggled. 'We don't have revolutions here! They happen in places like France and Russia.'

Charles caught Camilla's eye and turned a dull red. 'I hope your daughter is all right,' he said in an apologetic tone. Then he turned to his wife. 'I think we'd better be going, Sandra. It's getting late and I'm sure Camilla has a lot on her mind.'

'Oh, there's no need for you to go just yet,' she said, remembering that Charles was a very important client. 'Maitland is bringing in some coffee in a minute. Do stay for a cup before you go.' Her smile was strained but her charming veneer was as good as ever.

'Thank you very much,' Sandra piped up before Charles had a chance to say anything.

Ten minutes later, Philip came back into the room. 'I've phoned round the casualty departments of all the London hospitals and they're in a pretty chaotic state. So far, though, no one answering to Poppy's description has been admitted.'

'I'm sure that was Poppy being knocked down by a horse,' Lucy protested as she got ready for bed.

'I don't see how you could tell,' Anthony argued. 'The picture was so blurred. What would Poppy be doing there, anyway? Camilla would never allow it.'

'Most of the time,' Lucy said succinctly, 'Camilla has no idea what Poppy's doing, or even where she is! I *know* it was her, Anthony.'

'Well, what are you going to do about it? Phone Camilla and ask her what's happening?'

'I don't think I can. We haven't spoken since I told her I disapproved of her having an affair with Philip.'

'You should have stayed out of it, you know,' Anthony observed with a touch of severity. 'All you achieved is bad feeling on all sides. Philip is twenty-four, for heaven's sake, and must be allowed to lead his own life. He told me he was furious with you for interfering.'

Lucy looked aggrieved. 'How could I stand by and see him get hurt?'

'What makes you so sure he's the one who's going to get hurt?' Anthony smiled at his wife indulgently. She was displaying all the characteristics of a lioness protecting her favourite cub. God help anyone who in any way caused harm to any of her children. He went over and put his arms round her. 'Don't let's worry about other people, darling,' he said softly. 'Philip can look after himself and so can Camilla. We've got each other and that's what really matters.'

Geoffrey, known as a bona fide and respectable journalist, sat in the Press Office of Buckingham Palace, glad to be away from the raging mêlée of rioters. He felt bruised and battered and his head ached where a missile had hit him above his left ear, but he had the best scoop of any journalist in the country. He'd been the only one at the scene of the action, before it even started. By the time the mob was in full flood, charging up the Mall like a bunch of lunatics, the police had sealed off all the surrounding roads so no one who wasn't already in front of the Palace could get near to report what was happening.

The television crews of course, there to cover the State Banquet, had been in a prime position. According to one of them, they were just about to film the President making his speech when things really started hotting up.

'Fuck the speeches, let's get out on to the balcony!' the director had yelled, and the whole crew had charged past the footmen and all the Palace officials, and running at full speed had reached the long room from which the Royal Family always stepped out on to the balcony to wave to the crowds below. It was a perfect vantage point for covering the attack and they lost no time in transmitting the riot, live, to the watching world.

Geoffrey, seeking protection inside the Palace gates, thanks to a co-operative policeman who let him in before locking them, managed to watch what was happening by climbing on to the top of one of the sentry boxes. It did mean he was in the firing line for a few well-directed missiles, though far enough back from the railings not to be badly injured.

As he wrote his copy, he could see the whole thing again in his mind's eye, and it was something he'd never imagined could happen in England. The sheer venom of the rioters was awesome. They were hell-bent on destruction as they stormed forward, wielding weapons, throwing fire bombs, and yelling obscenities. They seemed blinded with rage. Geoffrey had heard of their leader before, Danny Fox, but had never seen him and had no idea what he looked like. Now as he saw a towering man with spiky blond hair and fanatical blue eyes, leading his warriors down the Mall, Geoffrey was suddenly reminded of old film clips he'd seen of Hitler. There was a thin borderline between genius and insanity in both men, and both had the uncanny ability to inspire people to believe in them. It would make a great story. Only one thing nagged at him as he read through what he'd written. He could have sworn, for just a fleeting second, that he'd seen Camilla's daughter in that ugly mêlée, her wispy fair hair hanging to her shoulders, her mouth wide open as if she was screaming 'Danny'. But then she vanished, swamped by the crowds, and he never saw her again. Geoffrey shrugged. He was probably mistaken. After all, Poppy was hardly likely to be caught up in that mob.

The pain in her head was so acute Poppy felt quite sick and dizzy. It seemed as if she'd been lying on the hard roadway, being trodden on and kicked, for hours although she knew it had only been a few minutes. Bruised and grazed, she ached all over and there was a ringing sound in her ears. The fighting was still going on all around her and the noise was deafening. Men were yelling, women were screaming, bombs were crashing in sheets of flame, and beyond it all the sirens and fire-bells still filled the night with their shrill sounds.

Crawling forward on her hands and knees, which were bleeding, she managed to stumble to her feet. Slowly, she stood up, swaying, feeling she was going to faint any minute. Nobody paid any attention to her. She could have been dying and no one would have noticed. People were too busy throwing missiles and tussling with the police even to be aware of a small frail girl who was too frightened to call out for help.

Poppy looked round. The madness was escalating. She'd never meant to be a part of this . . . this nightmare. All along she'd thought Danny was going to change the country by persuasion; by peaceful rallies and the promotional leaflets she'd been handing out by underground stations. She'd thought 'Class Warriors' was just the name for an organisation that planned to declare war on the class system . . . not on the people themselves. Not a real bloody war. Yet so besotted had she been by Danny that she'd never questioned what was going on, not even when she'd been taken to see the Rottweilers in Bristol. She'd been fool enough, she reflected, to accept everything up to now because of her love for him. Then another fearful thought struck her. Her father's legacy had probably gone toward funding tonight's riot. She'd given Danny thousands of pounds for . . . what? Vans to bring the dogs to London in? Weapons? Printed T-shirts? Fire bombs?

Suddenly, through a gap, she saw Danny. He had a long iron bar in his hand and was beating a policeman about the face and head, laughing as the blood spurted from the wounds he was inflicting, laughing even louder as the man slumped unconscious to the ground.

I've got to get away, she thought, panic taking her to the edge of hysteria. Oh God, I've got to get out of here . . .

Running now, in spite of the pain, tripping and stumbling, zig-zagging crazily through the debris, dodging around the fighting groups, she headed almost instinctively for St James's Park. Her mother had taken her to feed the ducks and swans here, down by the lake, when she'd been a little girl. Tears, mingled with blood from her head, trickled down her cheeks. Away . . . I've got to get away. Then she suddenly felt in the darkness the soft cool grass beneath her feet. Tall trees and dark shrubs surrounded her, offering her shelter and safety. Poppy ran a few more yards but pain and exhaustion overcame her, so that she dropped to her knees by a large flowerbed in which grew high lilac and camellia bushes, rhododendron and azalea. Creeping under their protective branches, she lay on her side. Tears trickled down her cheeks unchecked. Never before in her life had she been quite so unhappy, and never before had she found herself with nowhere to go. To return to Danny was impossible. He didn't love her. He'd shown tonight he didn't even care for her as another human being. Tonight she'd seen a side of him she hadn't known existed. A cruel side; a savagely unmerciful side; he was someone who enjoyed having the power to inflict pain and trample on anyone who got in his way. Danny had behaved like an animal, and whatever she'd found exciting about him in the past now filled her with profound disgust.

She couldn't go home either. Not with Philip there, screwing her mother silly every night. Why, oh why, did Daddy have to die? she thought, wiping the tears with the arm of her sweater so that the heavy black eyeliner smeared across her face. And Grandpa, too. The people she had loved the most had gone.

Curling herself up tighter as she lay on her side, hurting all over, she finally sobbed herself to sleep in her quiet little corner of St James's Park. The only lullaby that filled the air that night was the sound of troops, urgently seconded from nearby Wellington Barracks, who were now fighting it out with the rioters.

Chapter Eighteen

Geoffrey left the front courtyard of Buckingham Palace just as the first faint light of dawn stole over the trees of St James's Park, where the chorus of awakening birds was drowned by the sound of emergency forces clearing the wreckage of the previous night. He had to get back to the offices of the *Globe* in Kensington High Street to file his story and hardly knew what words to choose to describe what had happened. It defied belief. Today would be a watershed for the people of the United Kingdom when they awoke to realise the extent of the damage. Not just the physical damage to the Palace and surrounding buildings, but the harm done to the very heart of the Kingdom.

Phrases to express his abhorrence of what had amounted to anarchy swept through his mind as he walked across Green Park towards the main road that ran down from Piccadilly, where he hoped to pick up a taxi. But what a story he had to tell! What a scoop he'd managed to get! With his eye-witness account of the night, he'd be able to write a first-class piece, describing the violence in detail. As far as he knew, he'd got an exclusive, and the thought filled him with excitement. In his opinion there was nothing to equal the thrill of finding oneself in the right place at the right time. Pictures of the night's carnage flashed through his mind, vivid and clear. Firebombs hurtling through the air, the nervous stampede of police horses, the cries of vengeance, the screams of terror as people were trampled underfoot, the crash of breaking glass, the barking of those fearsome slavering dogs . . . Geoffrey closed his eyes for a moment as if to obliterate the horror, but the images stayed; brutal, ugly, savage.

More than anything, at this moment, he wished he had someone close he could talk to. Someone with whom he could share his thoughts, and at that moment he longed to see Camilla. There was nothing he wanted more than to be with her, and his heart ached because he feared it would never be so. The word around town was that she was a definite item with Philip and that there was even talk of marriage. Feeling pessimistic about the future, he grabbed a passing cab and gave the driver the address of the *Globe*.

Camilla dialled Westminster Hospital for the third time. It was now six o'clock in the morning, and no one had seen or heard anything of Poppy.

'What name did you say?' she was asked each time she got through to the Casualty Department.

'Poppy Eaton,' Camilla repeated. 'She's sixteen, blond, very slim.'

Each time she was asked to hold, and then each time they came back to say that no one of that name had been admitted. It was the same at all the other London hospitals.

'What shall we do, Philip?' she asked frantically. 'She must be hurt. No one could have been knocked down by a horse like that and not be hurt.'

'Listen, sweetheart,' he said urgently, 'according to the latest news the rioters have dispersed. Why don't I go to Buckingham Palace and look for her? I can ask around. Someone's bound to have seen the accident. Maybe I can find out something.'

Camilla jumped to her feet from where she'd been sitting at her study desk. 'I'll come with you.'

'No, Camilla, you mustn't,' he said firmly. 'It may not be safe.'

'You just said the fighting's over. Of course I'll go with you.'

'But it may be awful. They may not even let us near the Palace or the Mall. You'd be far better waiting here while I find out what's happening.'

'I'm coming with you,' she said firmly.

Philip took her hand as they hurried along Wilton Crescent. With the other he held the mobile phone, so they could keep in touch with the hospitals.

'I don't know what I'd do without you,' Camilla said, looking up at him gratefully. 'I'm scared, Philip, really scared. Supposing Poppy is lying somewhere and no one has found her? Suppose . . .'

He squeezed her hand tightly. 'Don't think about it. Remember, if anything dreadful *had* happened you'd have been informed by now. We've been sitting by that damned phone all night so there's no way they couldn't have got hold of you.'

'Even so . . . God, I thought what happened to us in Ardachie was frightening enough, but this is something else.' Already her eyes were searching the streets for Poppy as they hurried along. At any moment she prayed she'd spot her walking along, a funny little waif-like figure in strange clothes, her pretty face spoiled by too much makeup.

'Maybe things are more scary when they're happening to someone else,' he pointed out. 'I nearly went out of my mind with worry about you, when we were attacked. I imagined every sort of horror.' He shook his head at the memory.

'I felt the same about you,' she reminded him. 'Your imagination runs away when someone you love is in danger.' For a moment Camilla looked into his eyes and felt as if they were two souls who had found each other and become one. It was like finding the other half of herself, the perfect reflection, and she knew that without Philip she'd only be a shadow of herself now.

When they got to Hyde Park Corner, they found all the roads leading to Buckingham Palace had been cordoned off. No traffic had been allowed through for several hours and police vans, cars and motorbikes were parked in groups to prevent anyone slipping past the barriers.

'Let's talk to that cop,' Philip said, leading her to a large burly policeman who sat straddled on his gleaming black bike. He was wearing a crash helmet, with the goggles pushed up on top, and black leather boots up to the knee.

'I'm looking for my daughter,' Camilla said. 'Can we get through to the Mall? I last saw her on television in front of the Palace, but we don't know what's happened to her since.'

'Sorry, lady.' He shook his head, his face weary. 'No one's allowed this way.'

'But I've got to find her,' Camilla insisted.

'We saw her being knocked down by a police horse,' Philip cut in. 'We've phoned round the hospitals but she hasn't been admitted. We're very worried that she may be wandering around injured.'

'Sorry, but no one goes this way.' The policeman's eyes were steely, and Camilla and Philip knew they were wasting their time arguing with him. As they turned to walk away, he said: 'You can try round the other side of the Palace, by Birdcage Walk. That'll bring you a bit nearer the front of the Palace. But I think all the casualties have been picked up by now,' he added heavily.

'Thanks,' said Philip briefly.

For a moment Camilla paused to look along the straight length of Constitution Hill. The road was littered with the aftermath of battle. Lumps of broken masonry and bricks lay scattered across the road, and the iron benches from the adjacent Green Park looked as if they'd been hurled through the air, to land in a tangled mass of metal.

Philip tugged at her hand. 'Let's go round the other way.'

'Okay,' she said, her eyes lingering on the flashing lights of police cars in the distance, by the Palace gates. 'Suppose she's lying injured in Green Park?' she said suddenly.

'Let's go to where we saw it happen on the TV,' Philip suggested, 'then we can work from there, but I'm sure there are enough people on the spot who would have taken care of her.'

'Maybe the . . . the rioters have taken her with them?' she said with sudden alarm. The same thought had crossed Philip's mind, ever since he'd seen the footage of Poppy with a weapon in her hand, before the horse had charged into her. Nothing would surprise him about Poppy.

'If that's the case,' he said carefully, 'she's probably being looked after.'

'You think she belongs to this Class Warriors movement, don't you?' Camilla asked intuitively.'

'Yes,' he said with honesty. 'I do. It would explain an awful lot, you know.'

She nodded thoughtfully. 'I blame myself, Philip. I should have paid more attention to what she was doing. Poppy used to be such an easy child, and now . . . Oh, I don't know, we're like strangers. We can't communicate on any level. I shall never forgive myself,' she added suddenly, 'if anything's happened to her.'

Philip put his arm round her shoulders and hugged her close to his side. 'Don't even think like that, sweetheart,' he said firmly.

'I can't help it. I'm responsible for her. Oh, my God, let's hope she's all right.'

'Knowing Poppy, she's probably sitting with a bunch of her friends, or comrades, or whatever she calls them, talking her head off over last night's adventures,' Philip said, to cheer her up, although he didn't really believe it himself.

As they neared the front of Buckingham Palace, the full extent of the uprising became apparent. An enormous amount of damage had been caused. Some of the Palace windows were broken, a truck had tried to ram the magnificent central gates, debris including fire bombs, had been thrown over the high railings into the courtyard, and the road in front was ankle deep in masonry broken off from the Queen Victoria Memorial which stood opposite the palace.

'Christ,' gasped Philip, looking up at the mutilated statue.

White marble hands and arms lay grotesquely scattered on the ground with abandoned weapons and branches of trees from St James's Park. A khaki-coloured van, with Ministry of Defence painted on its side, was slowly making its way round the streets outside the palace, picking up the carcasses of the Rottweilers shot dead during the fracas.

Camilla turned her head abruptly away. 'This reminds me of the scene in the kennels at Creagnach,' she said as a wave of nausea swept through her. 'I seem to be haunted by dead dogs these days.'

Philip looked around at the terrible damage. Fires were still smouldering in the buildings down one side of the Mall. Pavements had been dug up and smashed. Parked cars had been overturned and set alight. Everywhere he looked, the aftermath of last night's fighting had scarred the immediate landscape with a blackened ugliness.

'It's like a war zone,' he said at last, almost to himself. 'I wonder where they've all gone?'

'You mean the rioters?'

'Yes. It said on the radio that hundreds of arrests had been made, but last night we saw thousands of people storming the Palace, didn't we? Do you suppose they've gone home? I wonder where they all live? I wonder what sort of lives they normally lead?'

Camilla wasn't listening. She'd spotted an ambulance parked by the palace gates on the far side. 'Let's go and ask them if they've seen Poppy,' she said.

Late that afternoon, Camilla curled up on the drawing room sofa, filled with despair and exhaustion. They'd walked for miles, made dozens of phone calls, asked hundreds of people and gone to the Casualty Departments of all the likely London hospitals, but no one had seen or heard anything of Poppy; dead or alive. She seemed to have vanished and Camilla could only suppose that she'd gone off with the rioters who had escaped arrest. But where had they taken her? Was she all right?

Camilla drank some more tea Maitland had made them on their return half an hour before, and wondered what they should do next.

At that moment Philip came bounding into the room from the study. 'She's been found!' he announced without preamble. 'She's . . .'

Camilla sat bolt upright, feeling the blood drain from her face and her heart almost stop with fear. Please God, give me the strength to get through this, she prayed inwardly.

'How is she?' she asked fearfully.

Philip sat down on the edge of the sofa beside her, and took her icy hands in his.

'She's been admitted to the Casualty Department of Westminster, half an hour ago. They couldn't tell me anything, because I'm not a relative but she's alive and is being examined. They did mention something about waiting for the result of X-rays,' he added.

'We must go to her,' Camilla said urgently. 'Is Ferris still here?' The chauffeur had been waiting all day with the Maitlands in the kitchen in case he was needed.

'Yes.'

'We'll need him to drop us off, because there won't be anywhere to park at the hospital,' she pointed out.

When they arrived at the entrance to Casualty, Camilla told Ferris to go home. 'I don't know how long we'll be,' she explained, 'but we can get a taxi.'

Ferris touched his peaked cap, 'Thank you, Madam. I hope you have good news about Miss Poppy.'

Camilla smiled briefly and wanly. 'At least we know where she is now.'

Philip gripped her elbow as they entered the doorway marked 'Casualty'. The first thing she noticed was the sickening smell of disinfectant. Then she took in the scene of patients on stretchers, nurses rushing to and fro, white-coated doctors dashing in and out of cubicles, and rows of tubular chairs on which sat an assortment of injured men and women

319

waiting for their turn to be examined. It was hot, noisy and unnerving.

Her eyes flew over the assembled company, searching for Poppy. Philip tightened his grip on her arm.

'Let's ask at the reception desk,' he said, raising his voice to be heard above the clamour.

Camilla nodded, and he saw the agony of apprehension in her eyes.

The secretary in charge of reception looked harassed.

'Yes?' she barked, barely looking up from the papers she was sorting out.

'I believe . . .' Camilla croaked. 'I believe you've admitted my daughter, Poppy Eaton, within the last hour. Can you tell me how she is?'

'Just a minute.' The middle-aged woman started going through a stack of files on an adjacent table. Halfway through, she looked up again. 'Eaton, did you say?'

'Yes, Poppy Eaton. She's sixteen . . . and has fair hair . . .'

'Wait there a moment.' The woman turned away and disappeared into an office at the back.

Camilla looked at Philip in desperation. 'This is the right department, isn't it? There couldn't be another.'

'This is the right place, sweetheart,' he reassured her quietly.

Five minutes passed and the receptionist had not reappeared. 'Oh God, what are they doing now?' she fretted.

At that moment the swing doors opened again, letting in a blast of cold air from the street, and a young man hobbled in, a makeshift bandage round his head. Just discernible under his open jacket was a T-shirt. The words 'Class Warriors' had almost been obliterated by blood.

I think I'm going to faint, Camilla thought, as sweat broke out all over her body and she felt sick. Such unmitigated ugliness! Taking a deep breath, determined not to give way, she looked around again. There was no dignity here. The scene was mankind at its most basic. Dirt, gore and poverty mingled in the atmosphere, with man's hatred of man evident in the wounds

320

she witnessed. Turning away, she wondered what had led Poppy into this unsavoury world.

'She's just down from X-ray,' she heard the receptionist say. 'Will you wait over there? I'll send the doctor to see you presently.'

'Thank you,' Camilla said. Resignedly, she went over to the bench that had been indicated.

'Shall I get you some tea or coffee?' Philip asked. 'I expect there's a vending machine somewhere.'

She shook her head. 'I don't want anything, darling. All I want to know is what's happening to Poppy.'

He nodded understandingly. 'I wish there was something I could do.'

Reaching out, she took his hand. 'Just having you here is enough,' she whispered gratefully.

He looked into her eyes and saw the pain. In the short time they'd known each other, so much had happened. So much that was frightening, dangerous and tragic. Some couples didn't go through such a wide range of experiences in a lifetime together. But it had made them close, so close he felt nothing could come between them now. He squeezed her hand and smiled at her.

'Everything's going to be all right,' he promised. 'You'll see.'

'Philip hasn't been home all day,' Lucy complained to Anthony that evening. 'He usually gets back to his flat by the late afternoon before he goes to Wilton Crescent, but I've been phoning them and there's been no reply.'

'Then he's out, isn't he?' Anthony said, stating the obvious.

'Yes, but shall I go round?'

'What! To his flat?'

'Yes. I want to find out if that was Poppy we saw on television last night, and he's bound to know.'

'But if he isn't answering his phone, it's hardly likely he'll be there. I don't know why you don't give Camilla a ring? Why don't you phone Philip at Camilla's?'

Lucy looked shocked. 'I refuse to do that. It would be condoning him staying there, which I don't intend to do.'

Anthony shook his head. 'You're mad, woman. At this rate you're going to lose both your son and your best friend.'

'Nonsense! He'll soon get over his infatuation,' Lucy replied stoutly.

'So why not try and be friendly with them both meanwhile? You'll only make them keener on each other if you go on opposing their affair like this.'

Lucy covered her eyes with her hands for a moment. 'Oh, I can't bear to think of them having an affair! It really is too awful. I'm not sure I'll ever forgive Camilla for putting us through all this.'

Anthony looked at her with mild astonishment. 'I'm not going through anything,' he pointed out. 'I say good luck to them.'

Lucy looked at him balefully. 'Well, I'm going through hell! Just thinking about it! I wish we'd never bought him a flat of his own. This wouldn't have happened if he'd been living at home.'

Anthony decided to change the topic of conversation. When Lucy was in one of these moods nothing would appease her.

'We might ring up a few hospitals to see if Poppy has been admitted,' he suggested, 'although of course we don't know that she was actually injured.'

'She must have been injured!' Lucy protested. 'She ran headlong into that police horse, and then a moment later the crowds trampled all over her.' Suddenly she brightened. 'I could speak to Maitland, of course. He always answers the phone. All I need to do is ask if Poppy is all right and then I'd know.'

'Just as you like, my dear,' Anthony said peaceably.

'She is my goddaughter, after all,' Lucy added. 'I'll ring up Maitland now.'

Camilla watched as the white-coated doctor walked slowly towards her. He looked weary, and she guessed he'd been on duty all night. She tried to gauge by his expression what he was going to say, but all she could see was how tired he looked, with deep circles under his eyes.

Half rising from her chair, she felt Philip's hand grip her arm, as if he were trying to stop her going forward to meet the doctor. She sank back, glad of a few extra seconds' respite from what might be bad news, yet at the same time desperate to know what was happening.

'Mrs Eaton?' she heard him ask, as he came to stand before her.

Camilla nodded silently, suddenly unable to speak.

'I've examined your daughter,' he continued in an even voice. 'As you know, she was found in St James's Park earlier this afternoon.'

'No, I didn't know,' Camilla managed to say. She shot a quick questioning glance at Philip. 'How is she? Is she badly hurt?'

'She's been up to X-ray, but there are no bones broken. She has got concussion, though, and she's quite badly bruised and has a few nasty abrasions but they'll clear up in time. However, she is suffering from exposure and malnutrition so I'm afraid we're keeping her in for a couple of days, just to keep an eye on her.'

Camilla's jaw dropped. 'Malnutrition?' she gasped. 'How can she have malnutrition?'

The doctor looked at her levelly. 'It's usually caused by not eating enough.' There was a hint of sarcasm in his voice.

She flushed. She felt his tone implied he was critical of the care she had taken of her daughter. Yet there was always plenty of good food on the table at Wilton Crescent. Poppy could eat as much as she liked and always had been able to.

'These young girls have such dieting fads,' she said lightly but inside she felt shame. She should have made sure Poppy was eating properly, and yet how could she? Poppy was never there.

'I'll talk to her about that when she's a bit stronger,' the doctor said. 'More young girls ruin their health by dieting than anything else,' he added severely.

'Can I see her now?'

He raised his eyebrows and gave a slight grimace. 'Ask Sister to take you to the cubicle.' He indicated a middle-aged nurse who was coming down the corridor. Then, with a nod he hurried away in the opposite direction.

'Why did he look like that?' Camilla murmured, watching his receding back view.

'What do you mean?' Philip asked.

'He was . . . well, he made a funny face when I asked if I could see Poppy . . . like, I don't know . . . like why should I want to?'

'Let's ask anyway,' Philip said hurriedly.

The Casualty Sister also looked strange when they asked to be taken to Poppy.

'You wouldn't rather wait until she's up in the ward?' she asked pointedly.

Camilla frowned. 'No. I want to see her now.' Then an awful thought occurred to her. Supposing Poppy's face was such a mess with grazing and bruising that they were scared to let them see her before she'd been cleaned up? 'I do want to see her,' she repeated, feeling quite angry now. First the doctor had made her feel like a neglectful mother because she hadn't ensured Poppy ate enough, and now this Sister was implying she might be too squeamish to see her daughter's injuries.

The Sister's eyes were candid. 'The trouble is,' she said slowly and with obvious reluctance, 'she's told everyone she doesn't want to see *you*.'

It was like a slap in the face. Camilla blinked and drew back, almost reeling. Tears of hurt sprang to her eyes.

'What do you mean, she doesn't want to see me? I'm her mother.'

The Sister looked sympathetic for a moment. 'That's what she said, Mrs Eaton. She didn't want to see you . . . or anyone else.' Her eyes darted to Philip and then back again. 'As she's got concussion and isn't in very good shape because of lying on the damp ground most of the night, I do think it might be better to leave it for the moment, don't you? We'll be taking her up to the ward in a moment and settling her in a nice warm bed, so that she can get a good night's sleep.' She smiled fleetingly, and not very convincingly. 'I'm sure she'll feel differently tomorrow. Why don't you come back then? I'm sure she'd love to see you in the morning.'

Camilla hesitated, torn between making a scene and slipping quietly away in humiliation. She looked up at Philip who was watching her anxiously. She was ready to crack and he knew it. Slipping an arm round her waist, he spoke to her gently.

'It might be a good idea to come back tomorrow, sweetheart. You're worn out and Poppy's in the best hands here. You don't want an argument with her at this time, do you?'

The Sister looked from one of them to the other. 'I should take your son's advice, Mrs Eaton.'

It was the final straw, more than Camilla could bear. Twice in twenty-four hours Philip had been mistaken for her son.

'He's *not* my son,' she blurted, tears streaming down her cheeks. 'He's . . . he's . . . .'

'I'm a family friend,' Philip cut in hurriedly. 'I think we'd better come back tomorrow. Thank you for your help.'

Then he led Camilla out of the Casualty Department. She was racked by sobbing, her head bent, her hands covering her face. By a lucky chance an empty taxi came up the street at that moment. Philip hailed it and then helped Camilla into the back. She sank on to the bench seat, her face the picture of woe.

'Poor darling,' he said, handing her one of his large handkerchiefs. 'You're exhausted. You must go straight to bed when we get back.'

He didn't say 'home', she noticed, and unreasonably her misery increased. What's happening to me? she wondered. I've always been so in control, so brave, always able to cope and be strong. And now . . . She felt as if her whole world was collapsing. Everything awful that had happened came to her in a blinding rush. David's death. Her father's. The horrors they'd experienced in Scotland. And this dreadful twenty-four hours of wondering whether Poppy was dead or alive. Then her rejection . . . 'She doesn't want to see you,' the Sister had said. And finally Philip being taken for her son! Where had she gone wrong? And why, now, when she needed to hold herself together, was she falling apart? The most frightening thing of all was the feeling of being out of control, she thought, as she wiped her eyes and gazed unseeingly out of the taxi window. She was *never* out of control. Nothing in her life was allowed to be out of control. All her security came from knowing that she was in control of her life, from the moment Maitland served her breakfast in the dining-room at eight-thirty right through the day at the office until she got home at night where everything was the way she had ordered it to be. Poppy was the only wayward element, who didn't respond to being controlled, but then, as she'd always told herself, it wasn't a perfect world. One day Poppy would see the sense in an orderly existence. She'd outgrow the vagaries of youth and learn to be organised. Like her mother.

Camilla wiped her eyes again and blew her nose. The servants mustn't see her like this when she got back to Wilton Crescent. That much she could still control.

'You'll find my keys in my handbag,' she said to Philip. 'Could you go ahead and open the front door so I can go straight up to my room without anyone seeing me?' There was a pitiful catch in her voice and Philip nodded sympathetically.

'You get into bed, darling. Would you like me to go back to my flat tonight, so you can be undisturbed?' he asked tenderly.

Camilla looked at him, not knowing what she wanted. Ever since Philip had unlocked the key to her emotions with his passion and devotion, she'd felt as if she'd lost several layers of skin. She was vulnerable to everything these days. Everything touched her emotionally, so that she hardly knew herself any longer. Even sad music moved her to tears. She was no longer in control. She hated the feeling.

'Perhaps I'd better be on my own,' she whispered. 'I'm not going to be brilliant company tonight, that's for sure.'

He kissed her still-damp cheek, and gave her a hug. 'I'll let you in and then I'll get on home.'

Camilla made a determined effort not to wince this time. Of course his flat was 'home' to him, and she was just being touchy. But there lingered at the back of her mind a wish that her house could be his home. Perhaps one day it could be. Not that she had any thoughts of their getting married. In her mind she saw their relationship as something that would last . . . forever? Forever is a long time, she reminded herself. Ten years. Maybe fifteen. She couldn't think further ahead than that.

As she entered the doorway of her beautiful house, she turned to Philip. 'Could you do me a favour, darling? Before you go, could you tell Maitland that I've gone straight to bed and don't want to be disturbed?'

'Of course my love.' He kissed her again, lightly and gently. 'Sleep well, and I'll see you in the morning.'

She ought to have felt comforted, but somehow she didn't.

'So *there* you are!' Lucy cried triumphantly down the phone. 'Where have you been, Philip? I've been trying to get you for days!'

'Don't exaggerate, Mum,' he replied easily. The phone had been ringing as he let himself into his two-room flat, and even before he'd answered it, he guessed it was one of his parents.

'How's Poppy?' she asked. 'I spoke to Maitland earlier and he said she was in Westminster Hospital.'

'She's going to be all right.'

'Has she been badly injured?'

'Concussion and bruising. That sort of thing.' He didn't mention the malnutrition.

'How did she seem? Did she tell Camilla what she was doing with that dreadful bunch of hooligans?'

'We didn't actually get to see her . . .'

'Why not?' Lucy demanded.

'Er . . . well, she was being transferred from Casualty to a ward, because they're keeping her in for a couple of days, and . . . well, they thought it would be better if we waited until tomorrow,' he added lamely.

'I see,' said Lucy, in the sort of voice that indicated she didn't see at all. 'I might go and take her some flowers myself tomorrow. Poor little Poppy.'

'Why d'you say that?'

'Because I feel dreadfully sorry for the child, that's why. Camilla doesn't give a damn what happens to her . . .'

'That's not true!' Philip exclaimed. 'She was very upset about Poppy tonight.'

'Oh, I expect she was, but in my opinion it's a bit too late in the day. She's let Poppy run wild. No wonder she's been keeping company with unsavoury people, like these . . . what are they? . . . Class Warriors! God, I think it's disgraceful that she was ever allowed to have so much freedom. Look where it's got her.'

Philip was having difficulty in keeping his temper. To his way of thinking, Poppy was a spoilt brat. An ungrateful, rude and wayward girl who was horrid to her mother. He dreaded to think how she'd react when she was told about their affair, too.

'Are you still there, Philip?' he heard Lucy ask, almost querulously.

'Yes, Mum. I'm still here. But I've got to go now.' He didn't add to get himself some supper, because such a remark would prompt Lucy to insist he go over to their house to eat, and tonight he wanted to be on his own.

'All right, darling,' she replied reluctantly. 'Take care of yourself. Daddy sends his love.'

Camilla awoke the next morning and decided not to go to the office. Jean could take care of any immediate problems that might arise. And anyway, why pay enormous salaries to twelve Account Directors unless they were capable of acting for themselves? They took care of the clients when she was in Scotland; let them do it again.

Bathing leisurely in her mirror-panelled bathroom, she buzzed down to Maitland on the intercom to say she'd like tea and toast in her bedroom at nine o'clock, and could he ask Ferris to bring the car round at nine-thirty? Then she phoned Jean.

'Is there anything urgent I should know about?' she asked, when she'd announced she was taking the day off.

'There's another card from your stepmother.'

'Where from?'

'This one's from Lausanne.'

'I wonder what she's doing in Switzerland? Does she say where she's staying? Interpol are desperate to get hold of her so that they can question her.'

'No, Mrs Eaton, there's nothing to indicate which hotel she's at. Shall I inform the head of Special Branch at Scotland Yard that you've heard from her again?'

'Yes, get on to them right away. Providing she hasn't already moved on, they should be able to trace her in Lausanne. I'm going to the hospital to see Poppy, but I'll be back home this afternoon if you need me.'

By nine-forty-five Camilla had arrived at Westminster Hospital, having stopped on the way to buy a large bouquet of roses and lilies. Poppy, she was informed, was in Herriot Ward on the second floor.

Going up in the large metal lift, which rattled and rumbled before shuddering to an uncertain halt, she made up her mind that this was no place for Poppy to be. She must get her into a private clinic right away. No doubt the treatment here was good, but the environment was wretched. Cold bare floors, tiled walls, dim lighting and the overpowering smell of disinfectant. Her only experience of being in hospital, apart from when Poppy was born, was when she'd had her appendix out, and how different that had been! She'd felt as if she were being cosseted in a five-star hotel, for David had insisted on her going to the smartest private clinic in Harley Street. She must have Poppy transferred to a similar establishment at the earliest possible opportunity.

Herriot Ward contained thirty-six beds, ranging down both sides of a long narrow room. Camilla started walking slowly down the centre, looking to left and right, searching for Poppy. Most of the women patients were much older, some in their seventies. She caught sight, before turning hurriedly away, of amputated limbs, drains and drips attached by tubes to various parts of the body, and chests bruised purple and black from heart surgery. Shuddering, Camilla continued her search, feeling increasingly conspicuous in her cream Giorgio Armani suit and gold jewellery.

'Can I help you?' a brisk voice demanded. Swinging round, Camilla found herself face to face with a young nurse in a cap and apron rigid with starch.

'I'm . . . I'm looking for my daughter, Poppy Eaton,' she said, suddenly feeling uncomfortable. The nurse was eyeing her with disapproval, and curtly she nodded to a bed at the far end of the ward.

'You'll find her over there, but she's sleeping. I'd rather she wasn't disturbed.'

'Oh!' Camilla felt taken aback for a moment, then she smiled. 'I've brought her these flowers. Could you be so kind as to put them in a vase, please?' Her tone was polite and not without charm, but she was unaware the cost of the flowers represented almost a week's salary to the nurse. The scrubbed face looked pinched.

'There are vases in the sluice room,' she replied tartly. 'Help yourself.' Then she turned on her heel and marched off, her heavy lace-up black shoes squeaking on the polished linoleum.

Blushing, Camilla continued down the ward until she saw a very small figure with wispy blond hair, lying curled up on her side. Her face was deathly pale and there were blue hollows under her closed eyes. For a moment Camilla felt like crying. Poppy looked as if she was about ten again, her fair skin scrubbed clean, her soft little mouth slightly open.

Camilla stood by the bed for a long time, looking at her daughter and wishing she was still ten. Poppy had been so easy then, so sweet and good-tempered. Was it really her fault, as Lucy had said, that Poppy had changed?

'There's a seat under the bed,' she heard the woman in the next bed say. 'It'll save you standing, luv.'

Thanking the elderly patient, Camilla felt under the high iron bed and found a long narrow wooden bench which she pulled out.

An hour passed. Poppy remained in such a deep sleep she was impervious to the noisy activity that filled the ward. But Camilla was in no hurry. To pass the time she went in search of a vase and, as they were small, brought back two. Then she arranged the flowers on Poppy's bedside cabinet where she would see them when she awoke.

At last Poppy's eyelids flickered, and leaning forward Camilla spoke to her gently.

'Darling, how are you feeling?'

Poppy's eyes flew open, and with a jerk of alarm she half sat up, before slumping down again with a groan.

'Sweetheart, don't move,' Camilla urged. 'You've got to take it easy. Shall I call a doctor to give you something for the pain?'

'I don't want anything,' Poppy muttered, her eyes closed again.

'Never mind, darling. I'll have you out of this dreadful place by this afternoon. I'm going to get you into the Cromwell Road Clinic where you'll be beautifully looked after.' Camilla put out her hand and stroked Poppy's pitifully thin arm.

'Go away.'

'What, darling?'

Poppy opened her eyes again. 'I want to be left alone,' she said more clearly. 'I don't want to go to some damned clinic, and I don't want to see you again either!'

* * *

'What shall I do about Poppy?' Camilla asked Philip that evening. She didn't tell him that the Ward Sister had finally asked her to leave because Poppy was getting upset and it was bad for her condition. 'I'm at my wits' end! Why won't she have anything to do with me? What have I done wrong?' Genuine bewilderment filled her eyes.

Philip shook his head, equally confused. 'Have you seen her since we got back from Scotland?' he asked. 'She was all right before that, wasn't she, except that she refused to come with us because she said it would be boring?'

'Something's happened while I've been away,' Camilla said worriedly. 'It can't be because of us. I haven't had a chance to tell her yet.'

He smiled at her wistfully, and put his arm around her. 'You look tired, my love. Why don't we have an early night? That is . . .' He paused, and looked into her eyes. 'I can stay tonight, can't I? I felt lonely without you last night.'

Camilla put her arms round his neck and pulled him close. 'Of course I want you to stay tonight, and every night,' she added. 'I need you more than ever now.'

He nuzzled her neck. 'You've no idea how much I love you.'

'Shall I tell you something?' She ran her fingers through his hair, pressing him closer. 'I love you too.'

When he kissed her, everything else seemed to slide from her mind: her troubles with Poppy; the workload at Eaton & Eaton; her grief at Malcolm's death. Everything. Her mind became suffused with Philip's mouth and strong hands, with the feel of his body against hers and the sound of his voice in her ears. When she was with him it was if she had found the perfect reflection of herself, so that he provided the missing gaps in her life. With him she felt she was rising high above the world, above the universe, so high that no one could touch her. Young, strong and re-vitalised, she felt reborn and as if the whole of life lay once more before her.

'Let's go upstairs,' he whispered. She smiled. It was only half-past nine. What on earth would the Maitlands think? Then she laughed. To hell with what they thought . . . or anyone else for that matter!

Chapter Nineteen

Lucy spoke carefully, wondering how much Poppy already knew. 'Why don't you want to go home or see your mother?'

Poppy, propped up by pillows, fiddled with the fruit her godmother had given her.

'I just can't,' she replied evasively.

In spite of her own misgivings, Lucy knew she shouldn't say or do anything to alienate Camilla and Poppy further, but at the same time she was anxious about the young girl. This was Poppy's third day in hospital and Lucy was shocked by her appearance. Not just the grazes and bruises, but her thinness. She looked painfully frail and it crossed Lucy's mind that Poppy might be anorectic.

'Are you eating enough?' she asked bluntly.

'Yes. The food's quite good in here.'

'Where were you staying before all this happened?'

Poppy looked vaguely around the ward as if searching for words. 'With friends,' she said at last.

'And you don't want to go back home?' Lucy repeated.

'I can't go back.' Sadly Poppy shook her head, and two large tears rolled down her cheeks.

'What's wrong, darling?' Lucy asked gently. 'Is there anything I can do?'

'There's nothing anyone can do. I wish I was dead.' Poppy started sobbing bitterly.

'You musn't talk like that!' Lucy was shocked. 'You've got the rest of your life before you. Is it boyfriend trouble?'

Poppy nodded. 'Partly,' she admitted.

'A romance that's come to an end?' Lucy suggested.

'In a way.'

'Is there a chance of your getting together again?'

'He's married.'

'Oh! In that case you certainly can't go back to him. Did you know he was married?' Lucy continued to probe, anxious to get to the bottom of the matter.

'No. Not until the night of the . . .'

'He's one of them, isn't he? One of those Class Warrior hooligans?'

There was a quiet pride in Poppy's face and voice as she replied: 'He was their leader.'

'Oh, my God!' Lucy eyed her with something like horror. 'My dear child, how did you get mixed up with a man like that?'

'I loved him. I thought he was wonderful.' Poppy spoke so low Lucy had to strain to hear her.

'Well, you'll have to get over that, won't you?' she said briskly. 'At your age, the heart soon mends, my dear.' Then she thought of Philip, and how she'd hoped he and Poppy would fall for each other. That was before Camilla got her claws into him. Lucy's mouth tightened.

The tears were streaming down Poppy's cheeks now, plopping on to her cheap hospital nightgown, wetting her hands. 'I'll always love Danny,' she wept. 'I thought he loved me, too. I thought we were going to be together forever, but then when I heard about Big Marge . . .' She was sobbing loudly now, and several of the other patients turned to look at her.

'Hush, darling.' Lucy put her arms around the thin shoulders and hugged her. 'You'll feel better when you're up and about again. How long do you think they'll keep you in here?'

'I don't know.' Poppy reached for a tissue and blew her nose loudly. 'I'm not even sure where I'm going now.'

'This is absurd, darling. You must go home. Shall I talk to your mother for you?' Lucy had no idea what she would say to Camilla under the circumstances, but something had to be done. Poppy needed to be properly looked after. If she wasn't, there was a grave risk of her going back to the undesirable life she'd been leading.

'I'm surprised you're even talking to my mother,' Poppy remarked with a touch of her old acerbity.

'What do you mean?' Lucy asked cautiously.

'Well . . . you know . . . she and Philip.'

Lucy's eyes widened. 'You *know*?'

'Know?' Poppy repeated. 'Christ, I walked in on them . . . they were at it . . . on the drawing-room floor. Even Maitland knew what was going on.'

Lucy drew in a long breath. 'Oh, my God!'

Poppy seemed better now, as if by mentioning her mother and Philip she'd got a load off her chest. 'How can I possibly go back now? It's gross! He's young enough to be her son. It's the most disgusting thing I've ever heard of.' She plucked a grape from the bunch in front of her. Popping it into her mouth, she chewed it with satisfaction.

Lucy looked stunned, choosing her words with care. 'I don't want to say anything bad about your mother because she is my oldest friend. I'm sure she wouldn't have wanted you to find out in that way, though.'

Poppy shrugged. 'Oh, I can handle it. It's typical of her! She was screwing around when Daddy was alive, so what's new? Of course she was more discreet then, in case he found out, but she's had masses of lovers.'

Lucy's jaw dropped and she looked at Poppy with startled eyes. 'Oh, no, Poppy, I'm sure that's not true. Your mother was devoted to your father. She'd never have been unfaithful to him.'

'I don't care whether you believe it or not, it's true,' Poppy replied defiantly. 'I bet she seduced Philip.'

Lucy continued to stare at her, not knowing what to say. She didn't believe for a moment, knowing Camilla as she did, that she'd been promiscuous when she'd been married, but she was disturbed by the fact that Poppy thought so. Or was she just being malicious? Girls could be strange when they became aware of their mother's sexuality, and perhaps seeing Camilla and Philip together had traumatised Poppy.

'I bet Philip's impressed by all her money,' Poppy was saying knowledgeably. 'I bet she's bought him Giorgio Armani suits and taken him to Harry's Bar and . . .'

Lucy flushed. 'He's not a gigolo,' she protested. 'I know Camilla's a very generous woman but Philip's not the type of person who can be bought.'

'I'm not saying he is, but Mummy's very manipulative. Very controlling.' Poppy was tucking into the fruit now, as if she hadn't eaten for days.

'Ummm,' murmured the older woman thoughtfully. 'Poppy, I have an idea.'

'What is it?'

'Would you like to come and stay with us . . . in Kensington? Henrietta's staying on in Paris to do a language course so you could have her room. What do you say? The summer holidays are nearly over, and your school term must be starting soon, isn't it? It would be easy to get from Scarsdale Villas to Sloane House by bus, so that would be good, wouldn't it?'

Poppy considered the situation and realised she didn't have much choice. She couldn't go back to Danny's, not now she realised he didn't care a damn for her. And she couldn't bear to be in the same house as her mother and Philip. She gave the faintest shrug and then smiled politely.

'Thank you. That would be lovely.'

'It'll be very different from living at Wilton Crescent,' Lucy warned. 'I'll expect you to help around the house, and be on time for meals, and to keep your room tidy. And to be back by a reasonable time at night. I must also insist you give up all this Class Warriors stuff.' Seeing Poppy's increasingly hostile expression, Lucy laid a kindly hand on her shoulder. 'I know you think I'm being hard, darling, but frankly, if your mother had been a bit firmer, I don't think you'd be in the mess you're in today. You look ill, undernourished . . .'

'The doctor said I'm suffering from malnutrition.'

'There! You see! You need proper looking after. I'll fetch you and take you home tomorrow if they'll let me.' Lucy beamed with delight, loving nothing more that to have a reason to exercise her maternal instincts.

'What do you think Mummy will say?'

'There's nothing much she can say. If she didn't object to you living with the married leader of an anarchist group, she can hardly object to you staying with us.'

Poppy looked down at her scrawny hands and suddenly felt quite relieved that someone had taken charge of her life. It would be like being a child again. Lucy was a person who would stand no nonsense, either. She'd have to toe the line and do as she was told. She leaned back against the pillows and contemplated her godmother, feeling more secure than she had in a long time.

'Thanks,' she said with a wan smile, and coming from Poppy that was an enormous admission that she felt grateful.

'Then that's all settled. I'll tell your mother, shall I, rather than leaving it to you?' Lucy offered.

'Yes, please.'

Lucy patted her hand. 'We'll soon fatten you up,' she said cheerfully. 'We'll have a lovely time together. You'll be company for me, too. The house is so quiet with Hetty away.'

A few minutes later she left Herriot Ward, waving goodbye and promising to return the next day. She didn't notice the young man in an anorak and jeans entering at the same time, his arm in a sling, a sticking plaster covering a wound on his temple. Nor did she hear him go up to a nurse and ask for Poppy.

Incensed, Camilla gripped the phone. Lucy had announced that Poppy would be staying with them when she came out of hospital.

'How dare you interfere like this?' Camilla stormed. Jean, who was sitting on the other side of the desk taking dictation, looked up, surprised at the outburst. 'You're just trying to turn her against me,' she added accusingly. 'I suppose you've told

339

her about Philip and me, before I had the chance?'

'She already knew,' Lucy said shortly.

'How could she know? She hasn't been home since we returned from Scotland.'

'She came back and caught you and Philip red-handed . . . on the drawing-room floor!'

'On the . . .?' There was a stunned pause, and then Camilla said: 'Oh, my God.'

'Exactly.'

'I'd no idea. How absolutely awful.'

'Apparently Maitland saw you as well.'

'What! Oh, Christ!'

'Poppy said something else, something really nasty, and I think you should know about it, too.'

'What did she say?'

'That you'd had lovers, lots of them, even while you were married to David.'

There was a long silence and then Camilla said brokenly: 'I don't believe it! How could she say a thing like that? Oh, Lucy, you didn't believe her, did you? It's the most awful thing to have said about me . . . and so untrue.'

'No, I didn't believe her, Camilla, because I know you too well, but I do think Poppy must be terribly unhappy to have said a thing like that. You're going to have to talk to her, you know.'

'I've tried, God knows I've tried, but you're not helping, Lucy,' Camilla retorted. 'Having her live with you is driving the wedge between us deeper and deeper.' She felt so wounded by Poppy's accusations that her mind reeled. Surely her daughter didn't seriously believe that she'd ever even looked at another man while David had been alive?

'You're going to have to give up Philip if you want to get Poppy back,' Lucy was saying. 'While you two are together Poppy doesn't want to know. And it's not fair on Philip either, you know. He's got his life before him and this could mess up his studies and everything.'

Camilla, weary of all the criticism, sprang to her own defence.

'I don't think you realise how much we love each other, Lucy. You've no idea how wonderful it is, just when you think all that joy is behind you, to realise you've been given another chance! I never thought I'd be this happy again. It's like turning the clock back and suddenly finding you're eighteen again, and the world is your oyster! With Philip, I feel young again. Age doesn't matter between us.'

'Like when he's forty-four, you'll be drawing your old age pension?'

'Don't be ridiculous! If you knew how much we love each other you wouldn't even think like that. You'd be glad for us.'

'My God, now I do know what's wrong with you!'

Camilla bridled. 'What do you mean? What's wrong with me?'

'You're showing all the classic signs of the onset of the menopause, my dear. Anything for a final fling! A chance to prove to yourself, for the last time, that you're still attractive . . .'

Camilla crashed the phone down and Jean gave a startled jump. She'd seen her boss in many moods over the years but never in one like this.

'Is there anything I can do?' she asked nervously.

Camilla slumped back in her chair, suddenly spent. 'No, nothing, thank you, Jean,' she said wearily. 'Let's get on with answering these letters. I want to leave early this afternoon.'

Poppy eyed the young man suspiciously. 'Danny sent you?' she queried.

He nodded, helping himself to one of her grapes. 'He heard you were in here. He asked me to come and see you as he couldn't. My name's Ben. I've seen you at meetings and I saw you the other night.'

'Why didn't Danny come himself?'

''Coz he's in jail, that's what! He got arrested outside the Palace. Bleedin' bad luck!'

Poppy steeled herself to ask the question. 'Is he all right? He wasn't hurt?'

Ben shook his head. 'Not Danny!' Then he sighed, 'But I guess he'll be put away for a long time now.'

'Why?'

'He killed a policeman. Beat him senseless, then got one of the dogs to finish him off.' Ben spoke with relish at the memory. Poppy covered her face with her hands, feeling nauseated. She remembered seeing Danny wielding an iron bar. There had been murder in his eyes, and evil in his heart that night.

'What about . . .?' she asked tentatively, and then paused.

'What?'

'Er . . . Big Marge?'

'Oh, her! Got arrested too.' Ben chuckled. 'They deserve each other, those two. Sad about the kid, though.'

Poppy felt herself go cold, as if an icy hand had clutched her heart. 'What kid?'

'Their son, of course. Didn't you know Danny had a son? He must be going on for eight. I suppose he'll go and live with his gran.'

Poppy was silent. Danny still loved her enough to send Ben to see her in hospital. Yet he was married with a son. In a way one cancelled the other out, and yet if Danny were to be released she didn't know if she'd be able to resist him. He'd been her life for so long now, her every waking moment, her reason for being happy. Without him she was going to be very much alone.

'Can I see him? Can I visit him in prison?' she asked, in a small voice.

Ben shrugged. 'I dunno.'

'Can you find out for me? I really want to see him again, even if . . .' Her eyes suddenly brimmed with tears. No more nights when Danny held her in his arms, his muscular legs wrapped around hers, so she felt pinioned to him for ever, a part of his heartbeat, a part of his soul. No more waking up to find him making love to her, exciting her with his fantasies. No more rushing back to his room after she'd been to Wilton Crescent, to find him lying on the bed watching television, ready, always ready, to start making love again. How was she going to exist without him?

'I doubt if you'll be able to see him,' Ben was saying.

'Why?'

'Why should you want to?' Ben smiled suggestively. 'You don't have to be on your own. That's why Danny sent me to see you.'

Poppy frowned, dashing away the tears. 'What do you mean?'

'Danny knows he's going to be banged up for years. That's why he sent me here today. To take his place, like.' He was leering at her now and his tone was insolent. 'Danny said I might like to have you. You're a good fuck from what he said. We could live in . . .'

'Get out!' Poppy shrieked.

The ward was suddenly silent. Nurses stopped in their tracks to turn and stare, and patients craned forward in their beds to see what the commotion was about.

'Get out, you bastard!'

'Here, who are you calling a bastard?' Ben shouted. 'You should be bloody grateful that I'm . . .' He ducked as a glass, filled with water, came flying through the air, skimming past his left ear and landing on the floor with a splintering crash.

'How dare you talk to me like that!' Poppy was hysterical now, and sobbing loudly. 'I loved Danny! I belonged to him, no one else. Get the hell out of here.' Two pillows, one after the other, hurtled towards him.

'You stupid slag!' Ben exclaimed angrily, backing away. 'I don't know what Danny ever saw in you!'

'He loved me. We loved each other. We'd still be together if he hadn't been arrested.' She rocked herself backwards and forwards in the bed in an agony of desolation.

'Danny never loved no one except himself,' Ben retorted. 'He used to tell us how you fancied him. Proper little raver, he said you were.' Ben turned to go, his cheeks flushed. 'You can go fuck yourself now, for all I care!'

The starchy Ward Sister hurried over to Poppy's bed. 'What's going on?' she asked severely. Her eyes flashed as she looked

343

at Ben. 'Kindly leave this minute. There are sick people in this ward and you're causing a disturbance.'

'I'm going,' he snapped.

Poppy still sobbed loudly.

'Now stop that nonsense,' the Sister told her briskly as she smoothed the coverlet. Ben stalked off down the ward, his hands in his pockets, a look of defiance on his face. When he reached the doorway he turned once more to look at Poppy.

'Stinking little bitch!' he roared, his voice echoing the length of the ward. 'Danny's better off in the nick than he is with you.' Then he was gone, with the swing doors rattling behind him.

'What shall I do?' Poppy moaned. 'I'll never see Danny again.'

'It seems to me,' said the Sister bluntly, 'that if that young man is anything like your boyfriend, you're better off without him. Now dry your eyes and I'll get you a fresh glass of water.'

Poppy heard the crackle of a starched apron and the sensible tone of voice, and suddenly she felt comforted, reminded of her childhood when she had a nanny who was not unlike this Sister. Nanny had used those firm tones too when Poppy had been small. Meekly she wiped away the tears as her pillows were rearranged for her.

'Men aren't worth all the grief they give you,' the Sister remarked with a touch of acid.

Tomorrow, Poppy thought, I'll be staying with Lucy and her family, and life will be so different from living with Danny. There'll be no excitement, no heart-stopping thrill, no moments of magic. On the other hand, she reflected, for the first time in a long time she'd know where she stood. Lucy wasn't unlike a kindly but firm nanny. And anything would be better than going home to her mother.

Camilla arrived at Westminster Hospital the next afternoon, determined to talk to Poppy. Things couldn't go on like this, with them not communicating as they sank deeper and deeper into a quagmire of misunderstanding. Somehow, she had to get

Poppy to understand that no matter how much she loved Philip, she didn't love Poppy any less. And she had to persuade her to come home. Kind though it may have been of Lucy to invite Poppy to stay, it was nevertheless harmful to their family relationship, a misguided gesture which had to be stopped. Anyway, she longed for Poppy's return, hoping that now she'd escaped the clutches of Class Warriors they might get back to normal. Apart from that, there was her education. They'd know the results of her GCSE exams in August, and Camilla worried that Poppy might have done badly because of all the distractions whilst she was involved with Danny Fox.

Carrying a box containing a beautiful white lawn and lace nightdress, and a white woollen wrap so finely crocheted it looked like a delicate cobweb, she walked briskly along the corridor to Herriot Ward. Before she saw Poppy she wanted to find the Ward Sister to ask her when they were going to release her daughter. At home her room was all ready for her, with fresh flowers on the dressing table and new magazines by the bed. Camilla had also bought her a few presents which she'd had gaily gift wrapped, fun things like a makeup box, a pair of hooped gold earrings, and an amusing wrist-watch and a knitted sweater covered in little white daisies on a navy blue background.

Glancing round quickly, she spotted the Ward Sister sitting at her desk. She hurried over to her.

'Good afternoon, Sister. I was wondering when I could take Poppy home? Will she be well enough to leave tomorrow?'

The Sister eyed her curiously. 'You're her mother, aren't you?'

'Yes. I don't want to raise her hopes by saying anything until I checked with you. Will tomorrow be all right? Or even today?'

The Sister rose, looking embarrassed. 'But she's already left. She went earlier this afternoon.'

'Left?' Camilla drew in her breath sharply. 'What, on her own?'

'No, someone came to collect her. The doctor passed her fit enough to go and so . . .'

'Who collected her? Camilla asked urgently. She had a terrible vision of Poppy being taken off by one of those rough-looking hooligans she'd seen taking part in the riot. 'Why did you let her go? I'm her mother. I should have been consulted before she left. You should *never* have let her go,' she said furiously.

The Ward Sister drew herself up to her full height of five feet four inches, and regarded Camilla coldly. Her starched white cap and apron didn't seem to have a single crease. On her chest, Camilla noticed, the second-hand of her fob watch was ticking away relentlessly.

'Mrs Eaton, I'll thank you not to talk to me like that. Your daughter was collected by her godmother this afternoon, and they left together, very happily. I resent the fact that you seem to think I would be irresponsible enough to allow one of my patients to leave with just anyone.'

'Her godmother?' Camilla flushed with anger and humiliation. She knew what had happened. Lucy had taken Poppy under her wing, to protect her no doubt from her and Philip together. 'I s-see,' she stammered. 'Yes, of course. I forgot Mrs Hamilton was coming to pick her up.' Then she turned away and hurried out of the ward.

'I'd like to go back to Wilton Crescent,' she told Ferris as she climbed into the back of the Mercedes, still clutching Poppy's present.

'Very well, madam,' he replied, trying to hide his surprise at how quick she'd been.

In silence they drove home and once inside Camilla hurried up to her room. Her mind was in turmoil. Philip wasn't due for another hour and she desperately needed someone to talk to. Normally she would have called her father. For a moment she contemplated ringing Geoffrey, but then she remembered how badly she'd treated him. She couldn't just ring him up now, out of the blue, to ask his advice about her daughter.

Feeling desperately alone, she wandered into Poppy's bedroom, which looked warm and inviting with its floral chintz and bowls of fresh flowers. Everything had been prepared for her homecoming. So why in hell had she chosen to go and stay with Lucy? The answer was crystal clear and very disquieting. And yet, in spite of everything, she knew she couldn't give up Philip. In time Poppy would get over her objections. The young always did. In time.

'Poppy is staying here with us,' Lucy said firmly when Camilla got through. 'She was traumatised by seeing you and Philip . . . well, you know.' Her voice dropped to a whisper in case she could be overheard.

'I'd still like to talk to her,' Camilla replied with equal determination. 'I agree that it was the most dreadful thing for her to see Philip and me like that, but I didn't mean it to happen.'

'That isn't any sort of an excuse,' Lucy pointed out. 'Poppy really is upset, Camilla, and for that matter so am I. I don't understand how you can be behaving like this. Philip is my son. Both Anthony and I are horrified by the whole thing. Poppy won't even think of going home until you put an end to it.'

Camilla sighed heavily, frustrated by Lucy's attitude and yet still determined to put over her point of view, even if it did mean another argument.

'Why should we stop loving each other, even if we wanted to?' she demanded. 'Why don't you talk to Philip? I'm not being conceited when I say he's every bit as much in love with me as I am with him, and now that we've found each other there is no way we're going to part. It's unthinkable, Lucy. Would you have given up Anthony all those years ago, when you first fell in love, because someone told you to?'

Lucy's tone was frosty. 'That's totally different, and you know it. We were both in our twenties and we had the rest of our lives before us. This is ridiculous. You won't have a friend left, you know, if you go on like this. It's obscene! Especially as we've been almost like sisters. If Philip doesn't want to end this affair then you must, for his sake. It can't go on, Camilla. You'll ruin his life.'

'How can you say that?' she said heatedly. 'I love him.'

'More than your own daughter?'

'That's unfair!' Camilla's voice rose to a quaver. 'Of course I adore Poppy, but this is different.'

'It certainly is.' Lucy's tone was dry. 'Let me tell you something. You're about to screw up two young people's lives and I think it's more than selfish! I think it's downright wrong. The girl's miserably unhappy, Camilla. Can't you see that? You're out all day. You don't know what she's doing with her life, and you don't even know who her friends are. On top of that you have an affair, right under her nose, with a boy of her own generation. And you don't even seem to care!'

Guilt bored a dark hole into Camilla's mind for a moment, but then she remembered it was Poppy who had been difficult long before Philip had come on the scene, and it was Poppy who had accused her of being unfaithful to David.

'Poppy is not always as easy as she appears to be,' she said carefully. 'If you knew how she refuses to tell me anything, you wouldn't accuse me of not caring for her. I do care for her, but she won't listen to a word I say. She's been totally rebellious for a long time now, and I admit, at times, I've been at my wits' end! But other people with daughters have told me it's a phase, something she'll grow out of. I just hope to God, for all our sakes, it's soon.'

There was silence on the line for a moment, and then Lucy spoke with a sigh: 'I did get her to admit she was lying when she said you'd been having affairs behind David's back, but the point is, why did she feel she had to lie in the first place? Anyway, none of this solves the problem of you and Philip.'

'There's no problem with me and Philip! Except in your head, Lucy! I have no intention of breaking it off with Philip. I can't break it off with him. I love him too much. For the first time in years, I'm happy. Really happy.'

'And what about Philip?'

'What do you mean?'

'For how long is he going to be happy? If you refuse to give him up, then he's . . . he's trapped! He's not the sort of man who would hurt anybody, either. He'll stay with you rather than hurt you, even when he falls out of love with you,' Lucy insisted.

Camilla's heart lurched painfully as she heard the words 'when he falls out of love with you'. The very thought of Philip not loving her any more was like a final severance she couldn't bear to contemplate. Life without Philip wouldn't be worth living. Surely Lucy could understand that? He was her son. Didn't she love him too, although in a different way?

'Poppy will understand, in time,' she said in desperation. 'I want her to come home, Lucy. You'd no right to take her back to your place. This is where she belongs.'

There was another painful pause, and then Lucy spoke bluntly. 'I'll be honest with you, Camilla, Poppy doesn't want to go home. Don't think I brought her here against her will. I didn't. She hates what's happening between you and Philip, and I can't honestly say I blame her.'

'No doubt you encouraged her,' Camilla replied bitterly. 'I just wish you'd try and understand.'

'How can I understand when it's so wrong?' Lucy retorted.

Suddenly Camilla lost her temper. 'You're not even trying, Lucy! You're so damned possessive with your precious son, you're never going to approve of any woman in his life. I want Poppy home, and I want her to return now.' Trembling with anger, she slammed down the phone. At that moment Philip came slowly into the drawing-room. From the strained look on his face she could tell he'd heard every word.

Poppy awoke the next morning feeling relaxed and contented. Henrietta's bedroom, in which she'd slept, wasn't nearly as lavishly decorated as her own at home, but it did exude a certain comfortable charm with its patchwork quilted coverlet, blue and white Laura Ashley curtains, and a collection of china and wood animals on the windowsill.

'Good morning, darling,' said Lucy brightly, coming into the room with a mug of steaming tea. 'It's going to be a wonderful day. Did you sleep well?' She placed the tea on the small bedside table and then crossed the room to open the curtains.

'Yes, very well,' Poppy replied, surprising herself. It was true, though. She'd slept deeply and dreamlessly and now she felt rested.

'Breakfast in the kitchen in half an hour,' Lucy continued, drawing back the curtains. 'I thought we'd go to the Chelsea Garden Centre this morning and buy some plants. The people who used to live here have let the garden go to rack and ruin. Have you seen what a mess it is?'

Poppy lay still for a moment, trying to gauge her reaction to Lucy's words. She'd never had the slightest interest in gardens and the idea of all that digging and weeding appalled her; but as she began to think about it, she was struck by the thought that it was at least something to do. For so long now her days had been unstructured. Drifting hours of boredom, waiting for Danny to reappear. Well, he wasn't going to appear any longer and she wasn't going to wait for him any more either.

'Perhaps we could redesign it?' Lucy was saying as she gazed out of the window. Like with most London houses, the garden was oblong-shaped. The lawn was patchy and moth-eaten looking and half-dead foliage straggled in the stony flowerbeds. 'Anthony thought of putting a path down the centre and having a gazebo under the trees at the end, but I'm not sure. I'd prefer to have a pond with some goldfish.'

Intrigued, in spite of herself, Poppy slid out of bed and joined Lucy at the window.

'It is rather a mess,' she agreed after a moment. 'What sort of things would we buy?'

'Rose bushes, maybe a small lilac tree, some camellias. I'd like to get a honeysuckle, too. When I was in Hong Kong I used to dream of having an English garden. Will you help me?' Lucy had been observing Poppy out of the corner of her eye as she spoke, and was rewarded to see an expression of growing interest in the girl's eyes.

'Yeah. Okay.'

Lucy beamed. 'Good.' As she turned to go, she added:

'Would you like porridge, and eggs and bacon?'

Poppy grinned. 'Yes, please. Sounds great.'

'It'll be ready in thirty minutes.'

Poppy put on the jeans and red and blue checked shirt Lucy had given her the night before, together with several other garments that Henrietta had outgrown. Then she brushed her hair and tied it back with a scarf. Without her makeup, most of which was still at Danny's, she looked fresh and clean, and extremely pretty in spite of being so thin. Her blue eyes were clear and bright this morning, giving her face an openness the heavy black eyeliner had destroyed. Gone was the weird sinister look. Amused by the difference in her appearance, she privately conceded that it was rather a relief not to have to take so long to get ready. Then she skipped down to the kitchen from where the tantalising aroma of coffee and frying bacon was emanating. Suddenly she realised she was ravenous. She also realised something else too, and that was for the first time in ages she was actually looking forward to the day ahead.

At five o'clock that afternoon, just as Lucy and Poppy had finished planting and raking and weeding the garden, Philip appeared, looking pale and anxious. As soon as she saw him coming out of the back of the house to join them on the lawn, Poppy stiffened and turned away, as if she could not bear to look at him.

'Hello,' Philip said quietly, looking from one to the other.

Lucy met his gaze levelly. 'Hello, Philip.'

'I thought I'd drop by to see you.'

'Would you like some tea?'

'Thanks, Mum.'

Lucy turned to Poppy who was standing with her face averted. 'A cup of tea for you too, darling?'

'No, thanks.' The gleam of unshed tears shimmered in her eyes, and she suddenly looked very lost and vulnerable. Without another word she turned and hurried into the house.

'Did you see how upset she is?' Lucy said. She looked at her son accusingly. 'You do realise that she came home in the middle of you and Camilla . . .'

He nodded wretchedly. 'Camilla told me, that was most unfortunate. We'd no idea she was around.'

'Even so, Philip! The house was still full of servants. If you must carry on like that, at least you could be discreet. I really don't know what you're thinking of these days. Camilla seems to have bewitched you.'

'I love her, Mum. I've never felt like this about anyone before! It's the most wonderful thing that's ever happened to me. Nothing you, or anyone says will make me give her up.' His tone was a mixture of being resolute and yet pleading with her to understand.

Lucy looked back at him, trying to feel sympathetic. Philip was the favourite of her four children, and she tried to tell herself that it was only his happiness that concerned her. But how could he be happy for long with a woman of her age? Someone who was twenty years older and was also sophisticated and worldly? Surely Camilla could be made to see that a young man of Philip's age was impressionable. That a lot of his fascination was to do with her wealth and power. That the chauffeur-driven car and the servants, the expensive restaurants and the lifestyle, appeared incredibly glamorous to him.

'Nothing will make me believe that it's right,' she replied after a moment. 'A situation like this can only end in disaster.'

Philip looked stubborn. 'I don't see why.'

'An age difference like this never works. Not for keeps, darling. Not in the long run. Meanwhile, you're both making Poppy very unhappy, and I can't say your father and I are overjoyed, either,' she added drily.

He shook his head. 'But I don't feel as if she's any older than me. She doesn't feel the age difference, either. I don't know what all the fuss is about.'

Lucy sighed. 'I suppose you think I'm being old-fashioned.'

The hint of a sheepish smile flitted across his face.

'Well . . . a little, Mum.'

'I'm not really, you know.' She spoke earnestly. 'I've seen situations like this before. Everything's rosy at first, and then bit by bit the age difference shows. You'll still be a relatively young man when she's an old woman, darling. How will you feel then?'

'Mum, how can I get you to understand that people are people, and that age doesn't come into it! Camilla was Camilla when she was eighteen, and she'll still be the same person when she's eighty.'

'That's just what she won't!' Lucy cut in angrily. 'That's the whole point.'

Philip dug his hands into the pockets of his trousers and gave the turf an idle kick with his foot. The gesture reminded Lucy of when he'd been a little boy, determined to get his own way.

'Do end it now, darling, for everyone's sake, before it's too late,' Lucy begged.

'I'm not giving her up.'

'But what about Poppy? You saw how she reacted when you arrived just now?'

He gave a slight shrug. 'Camilla will be the first to tell you that Poppy's difficult. She's anti her mother, whatever she does. She'd have found an excuse to be anti-Camilla even if I'd never come on the scene. Don't be fooled into thinking it's all Camilla's fault, Mum. Poppy can be an absolute pain.'

There was a pause and then Lucy said quietly: 'I know there is a problem there, but all the child needs is love and understanding and someone to care for her.'

'Camilla adores her!' he protested hotly.

Lucy shook her head. 'Poppy has become wild because Camilla's too wrapped up in Eaton & Eaton. Until you came along, the company was an obsession with her. She left the house early every morning, didn't get back until the evening, and then either went out to business dinners or entertained at home, almost every night. The house was even filled with her business friends at the weekend. How do you expect a girl of

Poppy's age to react? Her father was dead, and then her grand-father died also. She had no one. That is why she got mixed up with this Danny something-or-other. God knows what she saw in him, but he was obviously giving her something she wasn't getting at home.'

'Sex, I should say.'

'Don't be crude, Philip. Sex isn't the beginning and end of life for all of us, you know. I wish you'd forget Camilla, get on with your studies and really think about the future.'

'That's impossible, Mum.'

Lucy glared at him, seeing that this argument was upsetting him, yet also seeing the obstinate line of his mouth.

'And why is it impossible, pray?'

He spoke simply. 'I love her too much. If you can't accept that, then I'm afraid we're going to have to go our separate ways.'

'What do you mean?' she asked, alarmed.

'I'm not coming to see you and Dad again unless you accept the situation. I'm afraid it's as simple as that.' He still looked distressed but he spoke with as much conviction as ever.

'But, Philip . . .' Lucy felt her heart lurch and sink. She loved her son so much. She couldn't bear a family rift. But neither, in all honesty, could she accept his affair with Camilla. What irony, she thought. Through a disastrous twist of fate she was about to become alienated from her best friend and her own son.

He raised his hand as if to prevent her continuing. 'It's no good. Nothing you say is going to make me change my mind. I can only hope that in time you'll realise how happy Camilla makes me.'

'Poppy won't go home while you and her mother are carry-ing on like this,' Lucy warned. Too late, she realised such an argument was futile. Philip didn't much like Poppy anyway, and might be rather glad not to have her hanging around them all the time.

'That's up to Poppy. Anyway, I must go now.' Philip started to walk across the patchy lawn towards the house.

'Won't you stay for tea?'

He shook his head. 'There's no point. We'd only go on arguing. Give my love to Dad.'

'Philip . . . won't you . . . ?' But it was no good. He'd gone inside and a moment later she heard the front door slam.

Standing alone in the middle of the garden she felt the chilly wind of bereavement flow about her. This was the first serious disagreement she'd ever had with one of her children and she felt hurt and sad about it. What would Anthony say? Would he be able to talk Philip round?

Walking slowly towards the house, following in the steps Philip had taken only minutes before, she felt a sense of rejection. Her beloved son had never turned against her in the past, not over anything. They had always been close. Theirs was a strong united family. She put on the kettle to make some tea and heard Poppy coming down the stairs. A moment later she came into the room, looking around her warily.

'Has he gone?' she asked in a low voice.

Lucy gave a deep sigh. 'Yes, darling. He's gone and right now he's swearing he won't come back.'

'Because . . . because of Mummy?'

'That's right.'

'Oh, dear, and I'm not helping either, am I, by refusing to speak to my mother?' Poppy sat down at the kitchen table, looking disconsolate.

'Darling, I can't advise you what to do. Camilla is your mother, but if she feels as badly as I do at the moment, then I think you should go and see her.' Mechanically, Lucy got cups and saucers out of the cupboard and then put several spoons of tea into a large flowered china teapot.

Poppy shook her head slowly. 'I wasn't getting on with her before any of this happened, and I simply couldn't bear to see her now. I think what she's doing is . . . disgusting!'

Lucy smiled wryly. 'That's a bit strong, isn't it? I don't suppose you and your boyfriend only held hands all the time!'

'Oh, you know what I mean. She's so old for that sort of thing.'

'She's exactly the same age as me, Poppy,' Lucy protested mildly.

'But that's different. Anthony is your husband, and you've been married for years. Anyway, I don't suppose you . . .' Then she paused, blushing.

Lucy smiled broadly. 'Oh yes we do! But perhaps we're a little more discreet about it.'

'Exactly.' Poppy's tone was heartfelt. 'Even Danny and I . . .'

'Quite.' Lucy poured the tea for both of them. 'I'll have to have another talk with Camilla. Things can't go on like this.'

'Well, I for one am not going home with things as they are,' said Poppy firmly. 'Wild horses wouldn't drag me!'

Chapter Twenty

Camilla paused before picking up the phone. Did she really want to speak to Geoffrey? When Jean had said he was on the line she'd automatically asked to have him put through, but then she wondered what she was going to say to him. He'd been on her conscience for weeks now. However, she reflected, she couldn't go on avoiding him forever.

'Hello, Geoffrey,' she said breezily as she grabbed the receiver. 'How are you?'

'I'm fine. I phoned to tell you something interesting. It'll be in the newspapers tomorrow. We're working on it now.'

'It's not something about Poppy's boyfriend, is it?' she asked anxiously.

'No, it's not about Danny Fox. He'll be out of the news until he's tried for the murder of the police constable he battered to death,' Geoffrey replied. 'This is about the gun-running you uncovered in Ardachie.'

'Oh!' Camilla exclaimed, almost in surprise. Ever since she and Philip had returned from Scotland she'd had so much else to worry about that the whole episode had been pushed to the back of her mind. Now it all came rushing back to her with fearful clarity. 'What's been happening, Geoffrey?'

'They've made several arrests, including Hector Ross. He and half the village it seems are to be charged with acts of terrorism, smuggling firearms and terrorist-related offences.'

'So we were right,' Camilla said with satisfaction. 'That *was* what they were doing.' She paused, bracing herself for the next question she felt bound to ask. 'Geoffrey, what about my father's death? Are they going to be charged with murdering him too?'

'So far I haven't heard if the authorities are bringing homicide charges or not. There is a rumour about lack of evidence on that score.'

'Surely not,' she protested, distressed. 'Oh, Geoffrey, I don't want them to get away with it. If I wanted anything avenged, it's Daddy's death.'

'I know how you feel,' he replied sympathetically, 'but with all the evidence they've got, of arms being smuggled over to Ireland by fishing boat, they may feel they've got enough to have these people put away for a very long time.'

'Do you think I'll be called to give evidence?'

'I doubt it, my dear. Intelligence have been gathering information of IRA activities for a long time, and they knew something was happening on the western coast of Scotland. Now they've been able to pinpoint it, thanks to you and Philip Hamilton,' he added. His voice was expressionless. In her mind's eye Camilla could imagine him, eyes down, doodling on a pad as he always did when talking on the phone. Suddenly she wished they could be friends again. Just friends. That was all she wanted. She'd always been fond of him, and for a little while she'd even thought she cared for him, but now she thought how nice it would be if they could meet from time to time with no strings attached.

'It's very good of you to call and tell me all this,' she said warmly. 'The story's coming out tomorrow?'

'Yes. It will be on the television news tonight, but we'll be covering it in detail in tomorrow's *Globe*. That little trip I took to Ardachie on your behalf has proved invaluable.' He sounded enthusiastic and full of energy. 'I've been able to give a first-hand description of the village, and I've even interviewed a few of the people I met, over the phone. Those who are not involved are shocked. They had no idea what was going on.'

They talked for a few more minutes, and Camilla was on the

358

point of suggesting they meet for lunch when Geoffrey made a remark that sent a hot angry flush to her cheeks.

'So how's your young man?'

'If you're referring to Philip, he's very well,' she said shortly.

'Well, that's nice, isn't it?' He couldn't keep the bitterness out of his voice. 'And how is Poppy getting on? Does she like him?'

Camilla decided she didn't want to continue the conversation. It was no business of Geoffrey's what she did. Apart from which she didn't want him to know Poppy had left home because of Philip.

'Poppy's fine. I'm fine, but I'm frantically busy,' she said lightly. 'I must go now, but thank you for giving me a ring with the latest news about Ardachie.'

'And you wouldn't care to have dinner with me one night, I suppose?' She could hear a note of hope.

'I don't think that's a good idea,' she replied candidly.

'You and Philip are really an item, are you?'

'You could say that,' she said, wondering why she suddenly felt embarrassed. ' I must go now, Geoffrey. I've a call on the other line from New York,' she lied.

'I'll talk to you soon. Take care of yourself, Camilla.' He sounded genuinely concerned, and that annoyed her even more. Why was he treating her like a child, as if she wasn't able to take responsibility for her own life?

'Goodbye, Geoffrey,' she said firmly. Then she leaned back in her padded leather desk chair and wondered what would have been happening between Geoffrey and herself if she hadn't met Philip! They would certainly have been having an affair by now. They might have even been engaged. Camilla smiled to herself. Geoffrey was right in so many ways but he was no match for Philip. Her love for Philip was incandescent, like a glowing light from which her very being drew warmth. He was like another part of herself, and only when she was with him did she feel whole. Complete. Utterly fulfilled. No other man had ever made her feel this way. With Philip she could scale the dizzy heights of passion. With him her spirit seemed to soar above the world, so that her feet never seemed to touch the ground. With him she knew what ecstasy was. No, Geoffrey, for all his charm and warmth, could never equal Philip.

'Several arrests have been made in the small scottish village of Ardachie . . .'

The newscaster, reading from the teleprompter, spoke evenly as the TV screen showed pictures of the dockside which Camilla knew so well. Names were given of those charged, including Hector Ross, described as 'the local vet and a lifelong inhabitant of the village' . . . but no pictures of the suspects were shown, and very few details given. For security reasons, she realised, neither she nor Philip would be mentioned for the part they had played. Long after the item had ended, Camilla sat in front of the television set with unseeing eyes as she reflected on what had happened. If only her father hadn't gone to live in Ardachie . . . if only Edith hadn't bred guard dogs . . . if only . . . Her mind lingered sadly on the way things had turned out, and how different life would have been for them all if Malcolm had remained in London.

Poppy, sitting in Lucy's kitchen while she helped prepare supper, watched the same news item on the portable TV set on the dresser with a mixture of fascination and distaste. She thought of her mother and Philip, sharing the danger of discovery, being drawn to each other under the strangest circumstances, finding a mutual attraction as they spied on others, and all the time they'd been . . . falling in love. A swirling fear filled her stomach as she thought of them like that, remembered them writhing on the drawing-room floor. Was it really fear she felt? she asked herself. Whatever it was, it made her feel trembly and sick, and she wished to God she'd never seen them. Nice mothers remained faithful to the memory of their husbands and stayed at home to look after their children. Poppy continued to watch the screen, unaware she was being closely observed by Lucy.

'I just knew the vet was up to something,' Lucy remarked, as she peeled a bowlful of potatoes. 'Thank God they've got him, and all the others.'

'Do you really think Grandpa was killed because he found out what was going on?'

'I think it's more than likely. I wonder if they'll be charged with his murder? I expect your mother and Philip will have to give evidence.' She popped the potatoes into a saucepan and sprinkled salt over them.

Poppy shot her a horrified glance. 'Oh, surely not! God, how awful! Everyone will know about them then.' She looked distressed and her cheeks were pink. 'Christ, how embarrassing! How can she do this to me?'

'I don't think she's aware she's hurting you,' Lucy observed. 'She's so wrapped up in herself these days, she's not really aware of anything. Try not to get upset, darling. Sooner or later I'm sure Philip will come to his senses.'

'You mean he might leave her?'

Lucy hesitated a moment before she spoke. 'I think when the age difference sinks in, he'll realise it's not going to work. She's going to be devastated then. One can't help feeling rather sorry for her.'

'I don't feel sorry for her,' Poppy declared crossly. 'It will serve her right.'

'One must try not to be judgemental,' Lucy pointed out, fairly. 'After all, what about you and your boyfriend?'

'That was different.' Poppy looked stubborn. 'Young people fall in love. That's natural. I wish he hadn't been married, but that's beside the point. But I wouldn't have done it if I'd been my mother's age.' She looked scandalised at the thought.

'. . . one of the suspects has been wanted for some time, in connection with a bomb blast at the army barracks near Windsor. Shane O'Reilly is being questioned . . .'

The words of the TV announcer fell on deaf ears. Both Poppy and Lucy were too busy thinking about Camilla and Philip's affair to pay attention to the news.

Philip came back shortly after six-thirty, looking grave. 'Did you know there was a policeman standing outside the house?' he asked.

Camilla looked up, startled. 'I had no idea. Did you ask him what he was doing?'

'Security, he said. Guarding the premises. He asked to see my identification before he let me come in.'

'Asked you for identification?' she repeated, stunned. 'I'm going to see what . . . Oh, my God! I know what it's about, but I never thought they'd go to these lengths.'

'What is it?'

Camilla looked at him. 'You haven't heard? They've arrested everyone in Ardachie who is suspected of smuggling arms to Northern Ireland. Geoffrey rang to tell me earlier, and it's just been on the news.'

Philip's face lit up with triumph. 'They've got them then? What about Ross. Did they mention him?'

'Yes, he's been arrested too.'

'That's brilliant!' He looked as pleased as if he'd rounded up the terrorists single-handed. He put his arms around Camilla and hugged her close. 'We should celebrate.'

She rested her chin on his shoulder. 'I don't much feel like celebrating,' she said sadly. 'I know it's wonderful they've been rounded up, but it doesn't bring my father back, does it? Or all those wonderful dogs of his.'

'That's true,' he admitted, 'but you must be relieved it's all over, aren't you? I wonder if your stepmother knows? She might come home now, don't you think? It's obvious she stayed away because she was afraid.'

'With good cause,' Camilla agreed. 'After Daddy's death I think her life was in danger, too. My God, imagine having to leave your home because you were too afraid to stay? Poor Edith. What a terrible strain she must have been under!'

'There's no way you can contact her either, is there?'

Camilla shook her head. 'I've no idea where she is.

Meanwhile, I'm going to have a word with that policeman,' she said, rising to leave the room. 'I want to know how long he thinks this is going to go on for. Do you suppose they're going to be standing outside the office every day, too? I'm beginning to feel like *I've* been given a prison sentence.'

'I expect the police are afraid of a revenge attack, now there have been arrests,' said Philip. As he spoke they heard the phone ring. A few moments later Maitland came into the room.

'It's Special Branch on the line, madam,' he announced. 'They want to come round and see you, right away.' He had watched the television news in the kitchen with Mrs Maitland, and his expression was glum.

'Thank you,' Camilla replied. This was an unforeseen development as far as she was concerned, and she didn't like it a bit. Not because she was scared, but because constant surveillance would hamper her activities considerably and make clients nervous. She could lose a lot of business this way. Who would want to be around someone who was a target for terrorists?

'We'd like to come round and see you right away,' a man with an educated voice informed her on the phone. 'It is important we put you in the picture about our activities, and also tell you the measures you should take to look after yourself and your family.'

'All right. I shall be here all evening,' she said with reluctance, before adding, 'I suppose all these precautions are necessary?'

'For the time being, yes.'

'How long do you think this will go on for?'

'It's hard to say, exactly. Until Intelligence has gathered further information about the Ardachie operation. Obviously we will try to avoid intruding too much into your business and private life, but for the moment you will be guarded in much the same way as a Cabinet Minister.'

'Oh, my God.' Camilla could just imagine what the constant attendance of a policeman, probably armed, was going to do to her life.

'We'll be with you shortly, Mrs Eaton. My name is Pritchard, by the way.'

It was only after she'd hung up and was telling Philip what was happening, that she realised she'd never asked for his phone number or the address where he worked. There was no way of checking whether he was genuine or not.

'What a fool!' she exclaimed, 'How could I have been so trusting?'

'I think you can take it he's on the level. Anyway, the chap at the front door will check him out when he arrives.'

The briefing was thorough and the instructions exact. Detective Inspector George Pritchard from Special Branch, accompanied by Detective Sergeant Arthur Duncan, spoke to Camilla and Philip for over an hour, explaining they would require protection until such time as Intelligence, who specialised in IRA activities, said it was safe.

'There has already been an attempt on your life with the explosive device delivered to your office,' Pritchard continued. 'That was a warning that the organisation in Ardachie knew you had prompted the enquiries we were making. Now we have made the arrests, there may be a revenge attack . . . that is a risk we can't eliminate at this stage. And until we can, you must be on your guard night and day . . . particularly you, Mrs Eaton. We have no knowledge that Mr Hamilton, or anyone else connected with you, is on the Wanted List, but I must advise you to take precautions.'

'You've no idea how long this will last?' Camilla asked.

Pritchard shook his head. 'No idea at all. Meanwhile I'd like to talk to the members of your domestic staff. Tomorrow, I will be having a word with everyone who works in your company.'

Camilla cast her eyes to heaven, thinking how this was going to disrupt work. It was also going to prove a logistical nightmare because dozens of couriers rushed in and out of the Upper Grosvenor Street offices every day, delivering or collecting artwork, samples of merchandise, proofs, consignments of printed matter, and the hundred and one things related to a high-powered advertising agency. Was each and every courier to be screened first? Was every letter, parcel, package and container to be examined before it could be opened? Pritchard also wanted to talk to Ferris. As Camilla's chauffeur, he would have the special responsibility of checking her car, especially underneath, every time he took it out.

Camilla asked Ferris, who was having a cup of tea in the kitchen with the Maitlands, to come up to the drawing-room. He marched into the room and stood stiffly to attention in front of the two men from Special Branch. Formerly a driver in the army, his bearing in the face of male authority was military. Camilla wouldn't have been surprised if he'd saluted.

Pritchard turned to her first. 'Do you ever drive the car yourself, Mrs Eaton?'

'On occasions, but only if I'm going on holiday or taking a long trip. In London Ferris always drives me, and if he doesn't I take taxis because of the parking problems.'

'But you have a lock-up garage?'

Both she and Ferris nodded. 'I put it away every night, sir,' Ferris said. 'I live in the flat above the garage, you see, and then I get it out again every morning. No one could get into the garage without my knowledge, sir.'

'Where is this garage and flat?'

'In the mews, round the back of these houses, sir.'

'They're the original stables that went with these properties,' Camilla explained. 'They were converted about fifty years ago.'

'And very nice too,' Pritchard remarked drily. He raised his eyebrows and pursed his thin lips as he made notes.

'Is my daughter Poppy in any danger?' Camilla asked suddenly.

'I have no reason to believe so,' Pritchard replied. 'Why do you ask? Everyone in this house shares a modicum of the danger by virtue of living here.'

Camilla looked relieved. 'That's all right then. My

daughter isn't even living here at the moment.'

The eyebrows were raised even higher. 'Where does she live? Not in Scotland, I hope? We might have to put a special watch on her if she's in the Ardachie area!'

'No, she's in London. She's staying with some friends – in fact Mr Hamilton's mother and father,' she explained, suddenly feeling awkward. 'Mrs Hamilton was with us in Scotland when we first went up to find out what was happening.'

'But it was only the two of you who reported what you'd found to the Glasgow constabulary?'

Both Philip and Camilla nodded.

'Then I don't think we need worry about it,' Pritchard replied, 'unless of course your daughter has anything suspicious to report, in which case she should get in touch with us right away.'

They left soon after, saying they would be visiting her at the offices of Eaton & Eaton tomorrow morning.

'Does there have to be a uniformed policeman outside the office?' Camilla asked anxiously. 'It won't be very good for business.'

He regarded her stonily. 'I presume your life and the lives of your staff are more important than your business, Mrs Eaton?' he asked coldly.

She blushed, hating him for making her look as if she cared more for her flourishing business than for her colleagues.

'Of course,' she replied, smarting. 'But I don't want to make everyone feel as if a bomb was going to go off at any minute.'

When they had gone she turned to Philip, still rattled.

'I don't know what to make of all that,' she said irritably. 'Are we really in danger or not?'

Philip put his arm around her, hugging her close. 'I think they have a duty to warn us what might happen, and they're probably bound to offer us protection, for the time being. As to how much danger we're actually in, it's impossible to say. It all depends on what happens next.'

'When the cases come to court, you mean?'

366

'Yes.'

'That could take months.'

'I know.'

'Oh, my God, Philip, this is going to drive me mad!'

'There's nothing else we can do, sweetheart.'

'I almost wished we'd never gone to Scotland. I wanted to know what the hell had been going on up there, but now it's as if *we'd* been given a sentence! I truly thought all our troubles were over when we told the police in Glasgow what we'd discovered. When Geoffrey said today that arrests had been made, I was really relieved and pleased. I thought, now they'll be put away where they can't do any more harm. I never thought the IRA would put us on their Wanted List, did you?' Camilla demanded.

'I suppose not.' He shook his head.

Camilla sighed deeply.

Philip pulled her closer, kissing her with lips that were hotly ardent, soothing her with whispered words of love.

'I'm going to have a shower before dinner. Why don't you join me?' he whispered.

Camilla looked at him, and as always her heart did a little loop-the-loop when her eyes met his. He was smiling at her in the special way he had when he wanted her, and as she slid her arms round his neck, she felt herself grow weak as he pulled her close.

'I'll ask Maitland to delay dinner by half an hour,' she replied huskily.

Philip was lying on the bed waiting for her when she entered her room a few minutes later. He was naked and at the sight of his strong tanned body, already aroused at the thought of making love to her, she felt her own desire grow and swell so that she ached for him.

'Come here,' he beckoned softly. Their eyes locked and, as in a dream, Camilla walked towards the bed, knowing she could never have enough of this man she loved so deeply. Kneeling beside him, she took his face in her hands, kissing his lips with tenderness, while he slid his hands up inside her skirt, exploring her state of heat, wanting her so much it hurt. The silk of her dress caressed his thighs, billowing around him as she slid over him until she sat astride him. Then slowly and sensuously she started rocking backwards and forwards, while his hands caressed her silk-clad breasts and he voiced the single thought that filled both their minds.

'I want you . . . I want you . . . I want you . . .'

Locked together now, moving in rhythm, they clung to one another as if to life itself, breathing as one, hearts beating as one, moving in feverish unison, as she held him tight, and he offered up to her his love, his life, his heart and his soul. And then she was sobbing, the breath sucked out of her body, the tremors that surged through her so strong he had to hold her fast for fear of losing her.

'Philip . . . Oh dear God . . . I love you,' she cried out at last, sinking onto his chest, eyes closed, cheeks wet with tears. He gasped and, with a final thrust, poured into her the very essence of his being, everything he had to give.

Together they finally lay spent, closer than they'd ever felt before, so much in harmony that words were not necessary. They had become as one, and she'd never known a love like this before.

The next morning the story was front-page news. Neither Camilla nor Philip was mentioned by name, much to her relief, but the tale of the murdered Alsatians had been written about in detail, and the vet in Oban, who had carried out post-mortems on the two bitches Philip had taken to him, made a statement in which he confirmed the dogs had been poisoned.

A large haul of rifles, hand-guns, sub-machine guns and Semtex was also reported to have been found in a lorry on its way to Ardachie from the Clyde. Lookouts posted along the route had followed the vehicle's movements until it reached the port of Ardachie. Then, when half the contents had been transferred into two fishing boats, the police mounted an SAS commando-style operation, arrests were made, and all the arms confiscated.

'It reads like fiction,' Camilla marvelled as she glanced at the newspapers in the office. Jean had laid them all out on her desk and she sat engrossed by the coverage.

'It doesn't mention my father,' she observed. 'I suppose his part in the affair, and his death, is sub judice.' She shook her head. 'God, I hope they get everyone who's responsible.'

'I wonder how long it will be until the trial?' Jean remarked.

Camilla had already briefed her on the security measures that had been imposed on her. 'I don't know, Jean, but the sooner this is all over, the better. I could get quite paranoid thinking there are people out there who might want me dead. It's also pretty awful for the people around me, too.'

Jean nodded, and for the first time Camilla realised her secretary, usually so calm and efficient, was shaking. Her hands trembled as she held one of the newspapers, and her face was pale.

'They're not interested in you, Jean,' she said gently. 'I don't think you've a thing to fear.'

'But as you said, Mrs Eaton, anyone who is connected with you is in the firing line. Isn't Ferris worried?' Her agitation had given a sharp edge to her voice.

Camilla smiled. 'I don't think anything would faze Ferris, do you? He never stops talking about the part he played in World War Two, so I don't think he's going to get particularly upset by the IRA.'

Jean shuddered. 'Nevertheless, it's usually someone's car that gets booby-trapped. I think he's taking a terrible risk every time he turns on the engine. Have you seen what a car bomb can do?'

'He has been fully briefed what to look out for,' Camilla explained. 'Nevertheless . . .' Her voice trailed off and she frowned anxiously. 'I'll talk to him again. I wouldn't want him to carry on working for me if he's not happy.'

Jean didn't say anything, but it was obvious from her distraught manner during the rest of the day that she was disturbed by the presence of the police guarding the building.

At four o'clock she pleaded a headache.

'You'd better go home,' Camilla advised. 'Have an early night. We've got a breakfast meeting here at eight forty-five with the directors of the Diamond Confederation, haven't we? If we get it, it would be an international campaign and the best account we've had so far.'

'I know, Mrs Eaton.' Jean put her hand to her temple and pressed it gently. 'I've left all the relevant papers on my desk. Everything's under control.'

Camilla looked up at her, concerned. 'You will be in though, won't you? You helped prepare our proposal, and no one but you knows as much about it, except for me. As you know, the Confederation is most anxious to reach a larger market, and now that South Africa is releasing more diamonds than ever from their mines, the price is going to be within every woman's reach. Tomorrow could be really important to us, Jean.'

'I know, Mrs Eaton,' she said quietly. Then she turned and without another word left the room. Camilla finished signing her letters, leaving them in a folder for the assistant secretary to post. Jean had never let her down in the past. She was sure that even a migraine wouldn't stop her coming to work tomorrow.

'Lucy, I'm just going back to Wilton Crescent to pick up some of my things,' Poppy announced the following Saturday. 'I need my tennis racquet, and some of my books for school, and I'm running out of clothes!'

'All right, darling. Shall I give you a lift? I have to go to Harrods to do some shopping so it would be no trouble.'

'No, don't worry. I'm going to wait until after lunch anyway because I don't want to bump into Mummy, and she always goes shopping on a Saturday afternoon.' Although she'd been staying with the Hamiltons for only a short while, her face had filled out and her skin had a healthy rosy glow about it. Even her hair, washed and conditioned until it gleamed, looked thicker as it fell to her shoulders.

'Poppy, what sort of clothes were you thinking of collecting?' Lucy began. Then she spoke with her usual firmness. 'Whilst you're staying here, I'd rather you didn't wear the outlandish things you used to go about in, or go back to putting on all that black eye makeup. It really didn't suit you, you know. You're so much prettier without it.' She expected Poppy to explode with defiant anger, but instead the girl grinned impishly.

'I mostly wore it to annoy Mummy,' she admitted disarmingly, 'although of course Danny liked it. I doubt he'd even notice me if he saw me looking like this.' She looked down at the mid-calf culottes that had belonged to Henrietta, and the red silk shirt that went with them. Suddenly she laughed. 'Oh, God, I'm not getting to look like a Sloane Ranger, am I?'

Lucy laughed too. 'Anyone less like a Sloane Ranger I've yet to see! You look fine, Poppy. You needn't worry. You've got a style of your own, and that doesn't mean looking like a scarecrow!' In spite of the bluntness of her words, there was understanding and warmth in her voice.

'You're probably right,' Poppy replied, without taking offence. 'I was so sick of Mummy wanting me to look like a version of *her*,' she emphasised the word in disgust. 'She'd have loved to have seen me in little Chanel suits and dresses. Can you imagine anything worse?'

'Frankly, my dear, I'd die of happiness if anyone offered to dress me at Chanel,' Lucy riposted, 'which just goes to show what the generation gap means!' Then her expression changed. 'That's exactly my objection to your mother and Philip being together. It will cause terrible friction, in time.'

'Well, the sooner the better,' Poppy said crisply.

After a lunch of pasta and green salad, because Lucy had started a new diet, Poppy set off for Wilton Crescent. Halfway there she realised she no longer had a key. She'd left it at Danny's. No sweat, she thought, jumping off the number 9 bus as it stopped at Hyde Park Corner. The Maitlands would let her in.

The first thing she noticed as she walked down the elegant crescent was a policeman standing on the doorstep of her home. He looked as if he were a permanent feature, by the way he stood, feet planted wide, watching everything around him. Then he walked up and down outside for a minute or so before resuming his stance at the bottom of the front steps.

As Poppy drew nearer he noticed her, immediately unclipped his walkie-talkie set from the shoulder holster he was wearing and started speaking into it. She stopped dead and an icy ripple of fear galloped down her spine. This was the final betrayal. For this she would never forgive her mother. It was obvious her home was now barred to her because of the theft of the silver. Screw her! Poppy thought, as hot tears sprang to her eyes. Of all the hurtful . . . beastly . . . cruel . . . She turned away and hurried back the way she'd come, sobs tearing at her throat as she broke into a run. If that policeman had recognised her, and no doubt Camilla had given the police a detailed description of her, she thought, then he might give chase. She glanced back over her shoulder. He was still standing on the doorstep, and he was still talking into his mobile receiver. Panic engulfed her for a moment. Of course he wouldn't give chase. He'd notify police headquarters and a patrol car would pick her up! At the bus stop . . . entering the tube station . . . walking along the pavement.

As if to confirm her suspicions she heard a police siren wailing in the distance. She wasn't going to hang around a moment longer. She must get away. Go somewhere they wouldn't find her. At that moment an empty taxi came cruising along from Knightsbridge. Hailing it frantically, her heart hammering as the police siren drew nearer, she flung herself into the cab the moment it stopped. Slamming the door shut, she fell back on to the bench seat breathlessly.

'Where to, Miss?'

'Seventy-two. Wyvel Street . . . It's off the Whitechapel Road,' she gasped.

* * *

Lucy didn't start worrying about Poppy until nearly half-past seven. After all, Poppy was presumably in her own home sorting through her clothes. She might even have waited to see Camilla after all. But by eight o'clock Lucy decided to ring Wilton Crescent.

'This is Mrs Hamilton speaking,' she said, as soon as she heard Maitland's stately tones. 'Is Miss Poppy still there?'

There was a pause. 'Miss Poppy?' Maitland echoed. 'We haven't seen Miss Poppy today.'

'But she went to the house to pick up some of her things.'

'What time would that be, madam?'

'Early afternoon . . . after luncheon. Are you sure she didn't slip into the house without saying anything?' Lucy persisted. 'I mean, I expect she had her key, and I know she didn't want to see . . . er . . . anyone.'

'It wouldn't have been possible, madam. Every time someone comes to the front door they are questioned by the police. I know they wouldn't let anyone enter, even with a key, without asking me first if they were bona fide.'

'The police?' asked Lucy, stunned. 'What on earth are the police doing there?'

'You will have heard the news, madam, about the arrests in Ardachie?'

'Of course.'

'It seems there may be a revenge attack on Mrs Eaton, and so Special Security are mounting a constant surveillance on this house and the offices of Eaton & Eaton. Mrs Eaton is being guarded night and day and accorded the same degree of protection as a Cabinet Minister.' There was a note of importance in his voice.

'They're what?' said Lucy, appalled. Her first thought was for Philip. If Camilla was in danger then so must he be. Supposing anything happened to him? Regret upon regret flowed through her mind like the waves of an incoming tide. Regret that she'd looked up Camilla again on her return from Hong Kong, regret that she'd suggested Philip come to Scotland with them. Why hadn't she let well alone?

Lucy wasn't listening as Maitland reiterated, using more and more high-flown phrases as he elaborated on what was happening.

'Would you care to speak to Mrs Eaton? Or Mr Hamilton?' he asked at last.

'I think I'd better speak to my son,' Lucy replied. 'It's very urgent, Maitland. Will you tell him that, please?'

There was only the fraction of a pause before he replied: 'Certainly, madam.' A moment later Philip came on the line.

'Hello?' His voice was cool.

'I've just heard about this Wanted List business,' Lucy began agitatedly. 'That's terrible, Philip. I'd no idea you were in danger! I don't think you ought to stay in London.'

'I'm not in any danger,' he reasoned calmly.

Ignoring him Lucy continued: 'I think you should go to the States for a while. You can study architecture just as well in New York as you can here . . .'

'Hey, wait a minute!' Philip cut in. 'I can see what you're trying to do, but it won't work. I'm not leaving England, IRA or no IRA.'

'But don't you realise how serious this is? You know what can happen. I think it's absolutely terrible that a young man like yourself has been put in this dangerous position when . . .'

'Mum! Will you stop going on! I'm not going to run away and leave Camilla to face the music on her own. Is that clear? The police are merely taking precautions. They don't expect a reprisal attack.'

'I still think you should get out of the country before something happens.' Her voice rose on an edge of hysteria. 'And now what's happened to Poppy?'

'What do you mean? Poppy's with you.'

'No, she's not. I mean, she's staying here, but she was going back to Wilton Crescent after lunch today to collect her things and Maitland says she never came. I'm worried about her, Philip, especially now I know about this IRA business.'

'Hang on! I'll ask Camilla if she's seen her.'

Lucy waited impatiently. She had a good mind to phone the police. It was now nearly half-past eight. Poppy hadn't been seen by anyone, as far as she could gather, for seven hours. Anything could have happened to her in that time.

'Lucy?' It was Camilla on the line. 'What's this about Poppy coming back here today? None of us have seen her since she went to live with you!'

Lucy felt herself recoil at the barb. 'And it doesn't sound as if you cared, either,' she shot back. Then she repeated for the third time what Poppy's plans had been for the afternoon. 'No one's seen her since lunchtime,' she added.

'Did she say where she was going?'

'Yes. She wanted to pick up some books and clothes from Wilton Crescent. I presumed she'd come back here afterwards.'

'Oh, my God, I hope she hasn't gone to see any of the people from the riot.' Camilla sounded worried. 'Now that she's due back at Sloane House in a few days, perhaps she's gone to see some of her school friends,' she added hopefully.

'But what about this IRA scare?'

'I know for a fact she's not on their Wanted List, because I specifically asked.'

They talked for a few more minutes, and when Lucy hung up she looked at the clock on the kitchen wall. While Poppy was living with her she was responsible for her. If she hadn't come back by ten o'clock she'd call the police. And she didn't give a damn what Camilla thought.

Chapter Twenty-One

Danny's room had been stripped of all personal possessions. Nothing remained but the double bed, its striped mattress naked of sheets or blankets. Poppy stood disconsolately in the middle of the bare awfulness, which had once been the scene of so many happy nights, and wished she hadn't come. What had she expected? Danny, she knew, wouldn't be there. It was unlikely any of his followers would be around either, and yet in her blind panic to get away from Wilton Crescent, she had sought the familiar, only to discover its strangeness.

One of the black boys who had a room on the floor below had let her into the house, recognising her as soon as he saw her. But he'd gone out now, and so she remained alone in the building wondering what to do next.

'Is anyone else living in Danny's room?' she'd asked him when she first arrived.

The boy had shrugged massive muscular shoulders. 'I dunno.'

It seemed no one had moved in, but she couldn't stay here for long, even if she'd wanted to. She'd had only just enough money to pay for the taxi, and the driver had been scathing about the ten pence tip she'd added to the fare.

'Wot the bleedin' 'ell is this?' he demanded, looking disgustedly at the money in his palm. 'I ain't goin' to get fat on that, am I?'

'I'm sorry, it's all I've got,' Poppy explained.

Now, as she sat on the edge of the bed, she wondered what she ought to do next. She felt totally crushed by Camilla's actions. How could any mother, she asked herself, get the police to guard the family home against her only child? It was the most awful unfeeling action she'd ever heard of. Camilla had done this to punish her, of course, for saying she'd been unfaithful to Daddy. It was her mother who would have told the police about the silver, too, and the forged signature.

Cold and confused, Poppy sat rocking herself to and fro on the mattress, wishing Danny was still here to look after her. But he never had looked after her, had he? That had been the trouble. That was why their relationship hadn't worked. Danny had only been interested in sex, whilst she had wanted love too . . . and closeness . . . and trust! Tears blinded her as she looked out of the window at the familiar view of the council flats across the road, and the one tree that still struggled to survive the atmosphere. How often had she looked out of this window while she was waiting for Danny to come back, alone in this poky room as she was now? And how long should she stay here now? she wondered. Without money she wouldn't survive for long, even if no one came to claim the room.

The house was quiet and still. Getting to her feet, she opened the door a crack and listened. Nothing. If she was quick, she could slip down to the kitchen to make herself a hot drink. There might even be some bread she could pinch. It might be the last thing she'd have to eat or drink for days. Then she'd have to go begging, like those people who lived in Cardboard City. One thing was certain, she could never go home again and she couldn't go back to the Hamiltons' either. The police would be on the lookout for her now, thanks to her mother, and she was quite determined about one thing. There was no way she was going to be caught.

At midnight, Lucy could stand it no longer. Anthony had said she was making a fuss over nothing and that all young people had no sense of time, or that Poppy had probably got caught up with some friends and she'd no doubt turn up when she felt like it. Unconvinced, Lucy stayed up, fretting, listening for Poppy's key in the door.

'She's only got about five pounds on her,' she said worriedly. 'How far can she get on that?'

Anthony tried to soothe her. 'We've no idea who her friends were in the past few months,' he pointed out. 'She may have gone to see them. She probably wanted to hear about Danny and what's happening about his trial. Poppy had a whole life we know nothing about before she came to stay here, you know. She may have friends all over the place. Perhaps she's decided to stay overnight with someone?'

Lucy's face was grey with tiredness and anxiety. 'You mean those people who took part in the riot? The Class Warriors?' She shook her head. 'I think Poppy's changed. She was badly hurt by her boyfriend, you know. The riot frightened her too. I don't think she'd want to go near any of them again.'

'Don't you think you're taking rather a lot on yourself, by getting so involved, Lucy? After all, Camilla is her mother. Let her do the worrying.'

Lucy snorted. 'That's the root of the trouble. Camilla doesn't give a damn! She's too busy seducing our son to care what happens to her own daughter.'

Anthony frowned. 'You're awfully bitter about her, aren't you? I think you're being too hard on Camilla myself.'

'Don't you think I've a right to be?' she demanded. She rose and went over to the phone. 'I don't care what you say, I'm going to ring the police. I wish I'd done it earlier. Anything could have happened to her, have you thought of that? She might even have been kidnapped by the IRA!'

'Now I *do* think you're going too far,' he said, but his smile was tender. He knew Lucy was acting from the best of intentions. She was a maternal woman and she couldn't bear to see Poppy unhappy. Nevertheless, he was conscious of the fact that she wasn't their daughter, and that the responsibility ought to rest with Camilla who was willing and anxious to take it.

A few minutes later Lucy came back and sat down heavily beside him on the drawing-room sofa. 'They're coming round to see us in a few minutes. They're also going to contact Camilla.'

'What? At this hour?' He looked astonished. It was nearly one in the morning.

'Anthony,' Lucy said firmly, 'a young girl has gone missing. I don't believe she decided, on a whim, to stay out all night without letting us know. I think something's happened.'

'Oh, God. What a mess!' he groaned, exhausted. 'I suppose I might as well pour myself a whisky if I can't go to bed.'

Lucy got to her feet again, unable to relax. 'Perhaps I'd better phone Camilla and tell her what's happening, before the police get on to her.'

Her second conversation with Camilla that day was no friendlier than her first.

'Why didn't you phone me first?' Camilla demanded. She'd been sound asleep and now, as she struggled to pull herself together, she was outraged at Lucy's high-handedness.

'What's going on?' Philip asked drowsily.

Camilla cupped her hand over the mouthpiece. 'It's your mother,' she whispered. He was awake instantly. Rolling closer, he leaned towards the phone so that he could hear Lucy too.

'I'm really worried about her,' Lucy was saying. 'I don't know what the police can do, but I won't rest until I know where she is. In view of this IRA business, I think it's quite a sensible thing to have done. Of course, if you don't agree then that's another matter.'

'Lucy, will you stop acting as if I didn't care about Poppy,' Camilla exclaimed heatedly. 'I'll get on to Special Branch right away to tell them what's happened, but I have a gut feeling this has nothing to do with the IRA.'

At that moment Philip grabbed the phone from her hand.

'Mum? Are you there?' he demanded. 'I thought you and Camilla were supposed to be friends? Why are you behaving like this? Camilla's very upset about Poppy, upset that she won't come back here to live and has gone to stay with you instead. How would you feel if Hetty or Charlotte refused to come home? Will you stop punishing Camilla for something that isn't her fault?' Philip had never spoken to his mother so vehemently in his life, and he suddenly discovered he was shaking all over.

Lucy, taken aback, muttered something he couldn't catch and then she hung up. Very slowly, and with great care, Philip returned the phone to its cradle. There was a look of shock on his face.

Camilla put her arms around his bare shoulders. 'I'm sorry about all this, darling,' she said, her voice full of sorrow. 'I've come between you and your family, haven't I? I hate to see you fighting with Lucy.' She shook her head and then dropped her cheek to rest on his shoulder. 'Both your mother and Poppy hate our being together, don't they?' It was more a statement than a question, because she knew the answer and it distressed her.

'I don't enjoy fighting with Mum, either,' he said ruefully, 'but she's being absurd. I don't know what's got into her these days. What are we going to do about Poppy? Do you think she's really gone missing?'

Camilla lay down beside him, snuggling into his side. 'I have to say in all honesty, Philip, that it's not unusual for her to stay away all night. She was always doing it. I was terribly angry at first. I'd always stressed that she must phone me and tell me what she was doing, but for the past few months she's been really rebellious and refused to do as she was told.'

Philip nodded, understanding. 'I know that, darling, you don't have to justify yourself to me. I could see, from the first moment I met Poppy, that she was difficult. It's almost as if she were trying to prove something. What are you going to say to the police about her not returning to Mum's tonight?'

'God knows. I feel humiliated enough as it is without having to explain that I've no idea where she could have got to.'

The thumping came from the far side of the forest, echoing and re-echoing across the sunny meadow. Poppy started running towards it, so that she could tell whoever was making the dreadful noise to stop. The steady bang-bang-bang was spoiling the peace of the pleasant afternoon. But then, just as she reached the edge of the forest, she caught her dress on a bramble bush she hadn't noticed was there. Cursing softly, she turned to the right, but another bush seemed to have sprung up, its cruel tendrils sharp with thorns, catching hold of her, scratching her painfully, tearing her dress. Bewildered, she made a frantic effort to pull away, to go round the edge of the forest to where there were no brambles, to tell them to stop that endless thudding noise . . . but the bushes grew bigger, and the prickles on the branches grew sharper . . . until she realised she couldn't move, couldn't even enter the forest to tell them . . .

Poppy sat up rigid in the darkness, bathed in a cold sweat of fear, as her senses returned and she realised she had been having a nightmare. The thumping was real, though. She hadn't dreamed that. There was someone banging on the door. It was then she remembered she was in Danny's old room.

'Is there anyone in there?' she heard a man's voice shout. Then another voice, a gentler black velvet voice, spoke.

'Ah knows she's in there, man. I saw her go to the toilet earlier on. She's the blond one. She was Danny's girlfriend, y'know, man.'

The first voice spoke again, shouting louder as if she was deaf.

'We have to talk to you, miss. If necessary we'll have to break down the door if you don't open up.'

It was the police. With every fibre of her being, Poppy knew the police had come to get her. The one she'd seen standing on the doorstep of her home had obviously put out a radio call and a description of what she'd been wearing and they'd followed her in the taxi to Wyvel Street. She glanced at the window, wondering if she could make her escape that way, but realised at the same moment that she was more likely to break her neck.

The thumping was resumed, louder and faster this time.

'Come along now,' the voice shouted.

It was no good. She'd have to open the door and let them arrest her. Tears of terror filled her eyes and spilled down her cheeks. In a way this was more frightening than being caught up in the riot where there had been hundreds of police because then there'd also been hundreds of rioters. Her friends, her comrades. And Danny.

Shaking all over, she slid slowly off the bed and, tip-toeing over to the door, turned the key silently. A moment later the door flew open and a large fatherly-looking uniformed policeman almost fell into the room. He was looking at her with a mixture of concern and relief.

'Miss Poppy Eaton?' he enquired in a kindly voice.

'Ah told you she was here, man,' remarked the black boy.

A policewoman emerged from the shadows of the dimly lit staircase. To Poppy's surprise she didn't look much older than twenty.

'You are Poppy Eaton, aren't you?' she asked.

Poppy looked back, terrified. The irony of the situation made her bitterly angry. Having escaped arrest outside Buckingham Palace on the night of the riot she was now to be seized in cold blood, and for no better reason than that she'd helped herself to things she'd inherit anyway in due course, and all because of her damned mother.

'Come along now. There's a car waiting for you outside.' As he spoke, the policeman glanced round the empty room, and sniffed. 'What a dump,' he added.

'Where are you taking me?' Poppy asked in a quavering voice. Her watch showed four-thirty in the morning.

'Well now, where would you like to go?'

'What do you mean?'

'Your ma's anxious to see you, so I thought we'd . . .'

'I bet she is!' Poppy almost spat the words. 'I don't want to see her again, ever!'

The young policewoman spoke, sounding surprised. 'Then you don't want to go home?'

Poppy rounded on her furiously. 'What do you mean? Take me home? You're arresting me, aren't you?' With a defiant shrug, she started walking down the stairs, her head held high.

'Is there any reason to arrest you, miss?' the police sergeant asked blandly.

Poppy turned sharply to look at him, trying to gauge what his intentions were. For God's sake, the police didn't go banging around in the middle of the night, hauling people out of bed, unless their intentions were to arrest them, surely?

'I don't know what you mean,' she replied, playing for time. 'What are you doing here?'

'You were reported as missing earlier tonight by a Mrs Hamilton of seventy-seven Scarsdale Villas, Kensington,' said the policewoman in a cheerful voice as she consulted her note-book.

Poppy started. 'Mrs Hamilton?' she repeated. 'I don't understand.' They had reached the police car now in which a driver sat waiting.

'Get in the back, please, miss.' The policewoman got in beside her.

'How did you know I'd be at Danny's . . . at that house in Wyvel Street?' Poppy asked. 'Did you follow me earlier today? Why didn't you arrest me before? Why did you wait until now?' Confused and angry, she couldn't understand what was happening.

'Arrest you?' The policewoman looked astonished. 'We're not arresting you, and why should we follow you? You weren't reported missing until midnight, then we set out to try and trace you as soon as we could.'

The sergeant turned his head awkwardly from the front passenger seat where he was sitting. He was a large man and his limbs had lost a lot of their mobility over the years.

'Is there something you're not telling us that we should know?' he asked craftily. 'You seem to have been expecting us!'

'No.' Poppy shook her head hurriedly. 'I haven't done anything wrong. I presumed when you banged on my door . . . that, well, I'm not sure what I thought. People do get wrongfully arrested, don't they?'

The policewoman was looking at her curiously now. 'You were reported missing by a Mrs Hamilton who also told us your mother was a Mrs . . .' Here she consulted her notebook, peering at her writing in the semi-darkness of the car as it sped up the

384

Whitechapel Road. '. . . a Mrs Camilla Eaton. When we went to see her at an address in Wilton Crescent . . .'

'Oh, shit!' Poppy groaned aloud.

The policewoman didn't miss a beat. '. . . we asked her who you might have gone to see or stay with. During the conversation the name Danny Fox was mentioned. I believe you used to know him? And as his address is on record we thought it worthwhile seeing if you'd gone there.'

'He doesn't live there any more,' Poppy observed in a small voice.

There was silence in the car except for the crackling of the police radio. The sergeant was reporting to headquarters from what Poppy could gather.

'Yup. We've picked her up . . . on board now . . . We'll inform you when we drop her off . . . Romeo to Delta . . .'

'Are we going back to Wilton Crescent?' the driver asked.

'I'm not going back to Wilton Crescent!' Poppy cut in loudly. 'I don't live at Wilton Crescent any more. I want to go back to Scarsdale Villas in Kensington where I'm staying with the Hamiltons.'

'Is that all right with you?' the policewoman asked the sergeant.

'I suppose so,' he replied wearily. Then he turned and looked at Poppy again. 'It's our duty to inform your mother that we've found you safe and well,' he pointed out. He had a daughter of his own around the same age as Poppy. A good girl she was, though. Never given him or her mother a moment's worry. But then, she hadn't been spoilt something rotten like this little brat sitting in the back of the car, defying them all.

'Okay,' Poppy replied. Her tone seemed nonchalant, but that was because she did not want them to see how relieved she was that she wasn't being arrested.

When they arrived at the Hamiltons' the lights were on in all the windows. A blue dawn was stealing over the white stuccoed houses, and at intervals along the pavement the trees stood dark and trembling as a gust of cool wind freshened the morning air.

Poppy clambered stiffly out of the back of the car.

'We'll see you to the door,' the policewoman said, getting out of the car too, 'and don't go running off again, will you? We'll always find you to bring you back, you know, so it's not worth it.'

Poppy ignored the words as she hurried up the front doorsteps. A moment later the door opened wide and there stood Lucy with dark tired shadows under her eyes but a radiant expression of happiness on her face.

'Poppy darling!' she exclaimed, throwing her arms around her. 'Am I glad to see you safely back! Come in, sweetheart. We've been up all night, worrying about you.'

As Poppy allowed herself to be fussed over, and taken up to her room and tucked into bed, she realised how happy and secure she felt at the Hamiltons'. What a wonderful motherly person Lucy was.

'I'm really sorry to have caused you so much bother,' she said with genuine regret as Lucy brought her a mug of steaming hot chocolate and some digestive biscuits.

'I was frantic in case something had happened to you,' Lucy admitted. 'Why did you run away, darling?'

'I didn't run away from *here*,' Poppy emphasised the word. 'I ran away from the police. As I was arriving at Wilton Crescent I saw a policeman guarding the entrance. I thought Mummy had told them . . .' she blushed a deep red, and then with difficulty continued. 'I thought Mummy had told them I'd taken some silver to raise money for Danny's cause, and that they were there to arrest me and prevent me going into the house.'

'Poppy!' Lucy looked at her appalled. 'How could you think your mother would do a thing like that? My dear child! That's dreadful!'

Poppy looked stubborn. 'Then what was that policeman doing? And why did he start talking into his radio as soon as he saw me?'

'He's there to protect your mother against an IRA attack. How could you imagine the police were there to keep you out?'

'Well, I didn't know. You can never tell with my mother, and I wasn't taking any chances.'

'But you must know that despite your differences at the moment, she really cares for you?' Lucy remonstrated.

'She cares for Philip more.'

'That is a different sort of love, Poppy. Her love for Philip doesn't stop her loving you.'

Poppy shrugged. 'Whatever it is, she thinks more of him than she does of me. Well, that's fine as far as I'm concerned. She can have him.' She pulled the duvet up to her chin and snuggled down lower in the bed. 'I wouldn't let the police take me back to Wilton Crescent, you know?'

'My God, doesn't your mother know you're safe?' Lucy jumped to her feet in spite of her tiredness. 'I thought you had at least gone to see her before you came here.'

'I expect the police have told her I'm here by now,' Poppy said casually.

'They probably have, but I'd better check. Oh heavens, I wish all this unpleasantness would come to an end. Your mother and I used to be such good friends, best friends.' There was deep sadness in Lucy's voice as she hurried from the room.

The breakfast meeting with the Diamond Confederation was due to start in fifteen minutes and Jean still hadn't arrived at the office. Exhausted after a sleepless night Camilla hurriedly gathered together all the papers she'd need.

'Get me some coffee before the meeting starts, will you, please?' she asked Annabel, Jean's assistant. 'I suppose you've no idea why Jean's late?'

Annabel looked cagey. 'Perhaps the tube's broken down?' she suggested.

'If she doesn't turn up in time you'll have to sit in on the meeting instead. I'll need you to take notes. This is the biggest account we've ever pitched for and I don't want anything to go wrong.' Camilla sounded tired and anxious.

'Certainly, Mrs Eaton,' Annabel replied.

Then Camilla buzzed through to Leslie Forbes. 'Ah, at least you're here,' she remarked when he answered.

'Yes, of course,' Leslie said in surprise. 'Why shouldn't I be?'

'I'm just checking. This morning's meeting is important.'

'I know.' He spoke quietly, wondering why Camilla sounded so rattled. 'I'll see you in the boardroom in ten minutes,' he added.

Then Camilla checked with the others who were expected at the meeting: the chief layout and visuals director, the designer, the chief copy-writer, the space buyer. She wanted to make sure they were all ready and assembled. With varying degrees of surprise, they assured her they were. Camilla didn't usually get fussed before a meeting but today she seemed on edge.

'I expect this IRA business is getting to her,' one of them remarked.

'I can't say I'm thrilled to be working with someone on the Wanted List either,' another replied. 'We're all in danger now, but what can we do about it? Quit our jobs and get half what we earn here, from a less successful agency?'

The meeting started promptly with Annabel sitting just behind Camilla, taking notes. But for the first time since she'd taken over the company Camilla found it difficult to concentrate and generate the enthusiasm she usually felt. It was her zeal that had in the past made Eaton & Eaton one of the top agencies in town. David had possessed it, inspiring clients to follow where he chose to lead them, and Camilla had brought the same inspiration when she took over. Clients who walked into the building, wondering if advertising was really necessary for their companies, left in a rosy glow of anticipation at what could be achieved with a carefully planned campaign. But today that vital ingredient was missing from Camilla's performance. She knew it, and yet she could do nothing about it. She felt tired, distracted and irritated because Jean was not at her side as usual.

As the chief designer explained to the client what he had in mind, Camilla found herself thinking about Philip, and about Poppy. Her loyalties, her desires and her feelings had never been more divided in her life, and the conflict was driving her crazy. With every passing day she loved Philip more and more, and yet last night she'd been frantic with worry about Poppy. And hurt too. It seemed that her daughter would rather be anywhere than at home! It also seemed that Poppy was capable of thinking the worst when it came to Camilla. How on earth could she have imagined her mother had asked the police to guard the house so that she could not enter? How could she even think her mother would publicly accuse her of taking the silver? Camilla had refused compensation from her insurance company and had drawn a diplomatic veil over the whole incident, feeling it was better forgotten. And yet Poppy had been convinced she'd told the police the true story. Such lack of trust from a child was damning.

At last the meeting came to an end, and Camilla realised she'd done little to contribute to the presentation. She glanced around the boardroom table, knowing she'd been cruising on automatic pilot, wondering if any of her directors had noticed. Everyone seemed to be smiling, though, and nodding in agreement.

'We'll be getting in touch very shortly, Mrs Eaton,' she heard the chairman of the Diamond Confederation say as he and his colleagues rose to leave. 'I like your ideas and I'm sure there is a lot you can do for us.'

Camilla shook his hand, smiling, glad that it looked as if they had acquired another client to add to their already prestigious list, yet guilty that for once she had played practically no part in securing the account.

'I'll look forward to hearing from you,' she replied. 'If you'd like any further details of the campaign we've designed for you, or if you have any queries, please do not hesitate to give us a ring.'

As soon as they'd gone Camilla hurried back to her office. She buzzed for Jean immediately. It really was too bad of her not to have turned up this morning. Annabel had done a good job, but Camilla relied on Jean's experience.

'She hasn't come in this morning, Mrs Eaton,' Annabel

answered on the intercom from the office she shared with Jean. She sounded nervous and tentative.

'What? No message either?'

'A courier delivered a letter for you during the meeting. Shall I bring it in? It's from Jean . . . I recognise her handwriting.'

Camilla frowned. 'Yes, do,' she replied.

Jean's letter was apologetic but to the point.

It is with deep regret that I feel I must tender my resignation. The stress factor of living with the threat of terrorists who might strike at any time makes it impossible for me to continue working at Eaton & Eaton. I am, as you can imagine, very sad about this and I shall always be grateful for your kindness and consideration over the years. However, the current situation is more than I can bear and so . . .

Camilla stared at the letter with amazement. That Jean of all people, who had been a tower of strength and was the most dedicated personal assistant anyone could wish for, should crack up was nothing short of astonishing. She looked up at Annabel who was standing quietly on the other side of the desk.

'Did you know Jean was resigning?'

Annabel shifted uneasily. 'I . . . well, I sort of guessed . . . she was terrified yesterday with the police and everything here, warning us about what could happen, so I'm not surprised.'

'Well, I am!' Camilla retorted. 'It's me they're after, not Jean.'

'But terrible things can happen, can't they? One's seen pictures in the papers after a bomb's gone off . . . people being blown to bits . . . I don't want to leave, Mrs Eaton, but will this situation go on for a long time?'

Camilla shook her head. 'I don't know, Annabel. The people they arrested in Ardachie will come up for trial in due course, but it seems to me that whether they're sent to prison or not, the very fact that I reported what was going on makes me a target for a revenge killing.'

She spoke in a matter-of-fact way. In the past twelve hours she'd been so worried about Poppy her own safety had been forgotten. In the centre of the storm, in a little niche of numbness, she wasn't fully taking in the enormity of the situation. There must be hundreds of people, she reasoned, who were on a Wanted List, and who learned to live with it. Her method of coping was to push it to the back of her mind and submerge herself in work. That had been her way of coping when David had been killed, and again when her father had died. There was no point in dwelling on a situation. Far better to get on with the job in hand, because nothing was going to change what had happened. Nothing would bring David or Malcolm back; nothing would make Poppy a sweet-natured child again. All she could hope was that, with Philip by her side, she could carve something good and happy and secure out of the future.

'I think I'll give Jean a ring,' she said. 'Maybe I can persuade her to change her mind.'

'Very well, Mrs Eaton.' Annabel withdrew and went back to her own office while Camilla dialled the number of Jean's flat in Baron's Court. It was answered immediately.

'Jean, I've just got your letter and I'm very upset you feel you can't go on working here,' Camilla said immediately. 'Can't I persuade you to reconsider?'

Jean sounded as if she was crying. 'I-I can't, Mrs Eaton. I'm sorry, but I can't work when I'm wondering all the time if we're going to be blown up at any minute. It's too much to expect of anyone.' She gave a little sob. 'You know how I love my work, but I just can't take this strain.'

'Please reconsider, Jean,' Camilla urged. 'Take a month's leave, go somewhere warm and relaxing . . . I'll pay for a trip, but please don't say you're leaving for good.'

'That's very kind of you, but I have a feeling this state of emergency will last a long time.'

'It's hardly a state of emergency. We're not at war!' Camilla remonstrated mildly. 'Don't go over the top, Jean. Even Special Branch who gather Intelligence on IRA activities in Britain look upon these security measures as purely precautionary. Nobody's said my name's on a bomb!' she added lightly.

'I still can't bear it, Mrs Eaton.' Jean was weeping openly now. 'I'm . . . so terrified. All the time. I can't sleep. I can't eat. My heart is pounding . . . I want to get a million miles away in case a bomb is going to explode at any minute!'

'Will you do me a favour?' Camilla asked. 'Will you go and see my doctor? He was wonderful when I was in a state over David's death . . . he'll give you something to help you sleep and calm you down. Then take a trip . . . take as long as you like, but please come back when things return to normal?'

There was a long pause before Jean answered. 'I don't think it would be fair to keep you hanging about when I might never return, Mrs Eaton,' she said at last. 'I've been so traumatised by what's happened, I don't know if I can ever return. Even thinking about it . . .' Her voice broke again and Camilla realised how disturbed Jean had become.

'Let's leave it this way,' Camilla countered. 'I will give you three months' leave of absence on full salary, and I will also pay for you to have a trip, and then we'll review the situation. How about that?'

'I feel terrible,' Jean sobbed, 'letting you down like this. I can usually cope with anything, but somehow . . . this time . . . I don't know, I just feel terrified all the time.'

'Then you must get yourself sorted out, and don't worry! We'll miss you, but we'll manage,' Camilla said stoutly. There was no doubt in her mind now that Jean was suffering from a minor nervous breakdown. 'Let's keep in touch, but what you need right now is a good break.'

Jean sounded doubtful. 'I suppose so. I'm terribly sorry to let you down like this. I feel really awful about it.'

'Let's hope we can all get back to normal soon.'

They talked for a few more minutes, and when Camilla hung up it struck her that everyone around her seemed to be falling apart, and that only she was plodding on regardless.

* * *

But the problems did not go away. A month later, and then two months later, Camilla still found herself under day and night surveillance. Hector Ross, and the others who had been arrested in Ardachie, still awaited trial. But on the plus side, the media had forgotten all about the story. She hadn't heard from Geoffrey in weeks now.

Camilla's other problems hadn't gone away either. Poppy had remained with the Hamiltons, and had resumed her studies at Sloane House. She planned to take her A-levels the following year when she'd be just eighteen, but in the meantime she still refused to have anything to do with Camilla. Lucy had tried on several occasions to get her to go and see her mother, or even to talk to her on the phone, but Poppy was adamant.

Philip was also refusing to have anything to do with his parents, until they accepted the fact that he intended to remain with Camilla. To him she was the personification of all that was kind and good and wonderful. Every night he stayed with her, sometimes making love until the early hours, and he never tired of her passionate warmth and her responsive body. As his mother had feared, Camilla was spoiling him for other women. Young girls now seemed silly and shallow by comparison, but he didn't care. Why should he? he asked himself. He would never want anyone but Camilla. Never find the depths of wisdom and wit that typified her. And yet she still had all the vulnerability of someone much younger. In his feelings of protectiveness towards her he was finding his own manhood and maturity, and nothing was going to make him give her up.

Camilla, basking in the glow of his love, was happier than she'd been for a long time, in spite of her other problems. Philip made her feel young and whole again, and bit by bit the pain and grief of the last few years began to heal, the scars growing fainter every day.

Then she received a letter from Edith.

Chapter Twenty-Two

News has reached me about the gun-running operation in Ardachie. Your father and I were aware what was going on, of course . . . but I expect you know all about that, or at least I'm sure you suspected it. Now that the people concerned have been arrested, I plan to return to Creagnach House, with a view to selling it. I don't think I could bear to live there again, it holds too many sad memories for me. There will be such a lot to do, and there are so many of your father's possessions in the house which you should have, that I wondered if you could spare a few days to help me sort out everything?

Edith wrote in her large spidery hand. The letter heading was a hotel in Switzerland, just outside Lausanne, and it was dated six days before. Edith went on to explain that she intended putting her own possessions in storage while she hunted for another house, this time in Gloucestershire. Meanwhile she would be flying to Paris the following day, where she would be staying for nearly a week. Then she would let Camilla know when she was due to arrive in Scotland.

'I'm so glad she's all right,' Camilla commented as she read the letter aloud to Philip that evening as they sat in the study after dinner. 'Poor woman. She seems to have been on the run ever since Daddy died. I'm glad she's coming back to England for good now.'

'Does she say where she's staying in Paris? You could give

her a ring and find out when you're likely to have to go to Scotland,' Philip remarked.

Camilla picked up the letter again. 'She doesn't say. I don't think she likes to make rigid plans, you know. I wonder why she's staying in Paris, en route for Scotland, anyway?'

'She must be quite rich to do all this travelling.'

'I believe her first husband left her quite a lot of money, and of course Daddy made sure she's well provided for.'

'Are you going to go up to Scotland?'

'Yes. I'd like to help her go through Daddy's things and go back to Creagnach once more, too.' Camilla smiled gently, remembering it was there that she and Philip had first realised they were in love.

'Will it be safe?'

'Probably safer than being in London!'

'How d'you mean?'

'All the IRA suspects have been rounded up in and around Ardachie, whereas we don't know what we're dealing with down here. I'd say Ardachie is the safest place in the United Kingdom at this moment. Everyone knows everyone else up there. Someone new in their midst would stick out like a sore thumb.'

Philip looked thoughtful. 'I won't be able to get away, you know. I'm right in the middle of my studies.' Then he frowned. 'I hate the idea of you going on your own.'

'Edith will be there.'

'Fat lot of good she'll be if anything happens,' he snorted. 'How old is she? Sixty-five? You ought to take someone with you.'

'Darling,' Camilla reached out and took his hand, 'I shall be perfectly all right. I'll check with Special Branch before I go.'

He leaned forward, kissing her gently on the lips. 'I worry about you. We know what they can do . . . it doesn't bear thinking about. And to go back to Ardachie where it all happened strikes me as lunatic.'

'I said I'd tell Special Branch before I went. If they think I need protection, they'll give it to me. What about Edith? She knows as much as I do, if not more. If I'm in danger, so is she.'

'Yes, but she didn't inform the police and you did. That's the difference,' he argued. When he got angry or upset he looked very young and flustered.

'It's going to be all right, sweetheart,' she promised. 'You don't imagine I'm going to run unnecessary risks, do you?' She placed her hands on either side of his face and pulled him closer. 'I love you far too much to do anything stupid. I wish you could come because it would be wonderful to have you with me, but I won't be going into any danger, you know. If the police advise against it, I won't go.'

Philip held her close, his face buried in her neck, his hands stroking her back. Then he swung her legs up on to the sofa where they were sitting, and lay down beside her.

'I'm so afraid of anything happening to you,' he said in a muffled voice. 'I don't know what I'd do without you.'

Camilla, her arms round his neck, pressed closer so that she could feel his hardness. 'I don't know what I'd do without you, darling.'

'My love . . . Oh, God, I adore you.' Then he kissed her, covering her lips with his mouth, pushing his tongue against hers, probing her deeply so that she moaned with pleasure. And as she returned his prolonged kiss, her hands teasingly undid the buttons of his open-necked shirt, and then the zip of his trousers.

'Oh, Camilla! My darling . . .' he murmured as her hands searched him out, cupping him lovingly, stroking and cradling him so that he nearly climaxed. He was pulling her silk skirt up now, sliding his hand inside her satin panties, finding her, feeling her, desiring her with every pounding heartbeat that throbbed through him.

'Oh, I want you,' she gasped. 'I want you so much . . .'

With strong arms, he lowered her on to the floor, gently, tenderly, longing to take her, yet also wanting to prolong the moment when he did. Reaching out for him, Camilla drew him towards her, desperate to feel him inside her, with his weight crushing her into the carpet, and yet also hanging back, knowing the longer they waited, the more exquisite the moment would be when it came.

Bending over, he tore back her silk top and found her breasts naked beneath it, the nipples dark and erect, the soft skin tender to his touch. She shuddered as he sucked gently, holding his head in her hands, her hips rocking to and fro as she waited for him to enter her. Then his tongue travelled to the valley between her breasts and down to her stomach where he lingered, tantalisingly, flicking her skin with soft butterfly touches, driving her demented so that she cried out frenziedly.

'I can't bear it any more . . . take me, for God's sake, Philip, take me!' Writhing beneath him, she clung to him, her eyes closed, her breathing laboured, and then he thrust himself inside her. In unison, crying out in joy as they did so, they stayed locked, moving in harmony, until with a final shuddering spasm they climaxed together.

Afterwards they lay together for a long while, lying on their sides facing each other, both of them delighting in the wonder of their love-making. For Philip it was a revelation. Not even in his wildest fantasies had he imagined sex could be so wonderful. For Camilla it was a re-birth and a re-discovery, just when she'd really thought the joy of love was something she'd never experience again.

Talking gently of unimportant things, laughing from time to time as they shared their thoughts and confidences, learning so much about each other it seemed they would never run out of things to say, they relaxed in each other's arms, until after a while Philip kissed her again and immediately felt a renewed wave of desire. No matter how often he made love to Camilla, there was a fresh sense of excitement about it each time. To satisfy this beautiful woman was such a thrilling experience. The fact that she was as crazy about him as he was about her never failed to enthral him either. Kissing her neck and stroking her tender breasts, he felt her hands holding him again, massaging him in a way that drove him crazy. He had learned so much from her too. If he had all the passion of youth, she had the skill to show him how to squeeze every ounce of feeling from the moment. It was Camilla who had guided him, gently and expertly, into the art of deliciously slow foreplay, curbing his impatience so that when the moment was right, it was all the more intense.

She was running the tip of her tongue over his throat now, and along the ridge of his collar-bone, sending shivers down his spine. Then she stroked the skin behind his ears and raked her nails gently through the hair that grew at the nape of his neck.

Philip could feel his throat contract with desire as he ran his fingers down her neck, echoing everything she did as she had taught him, mirroring each movement so that their mutual desire increased, step by step. For a moment he wanted to break the careful build-up, to free them both but particularly himself from the delicate restraints that she had taught him brought greater delight in the end; he longed to take her with savage abandon, with ferocity, plunging himself into her with the fierceness and impatience that were almost blinding him. For a moment his self-control almost snapped in his over-whelming desire to make her his . . . to hold her forever . . . to possess once and for all this fascinating woman who now lay in his arms ready to be taken. And yet, not quite ready, for she was playing her part in prolonging the act now, by drawing away to gaze into his eyes and run her fingertips slowly down both his forearms, until she paused to entwine her fingers with his so their hands were clasped, and then, still holding him away, leaned forward and kissed his lips tenderly and slowly.

Now it was Philip who could not bear to wait another moment. Now it was he who groaned with longing.

'Please . . . darling . . . please,' he moaned, and there was almost a note of pain in his voice. 'Oh God, I want to take you . . .' The forces that had been building up inside him were on the brink of exploding now; the moment had come when he could no longer hold back, as with a desperation that drove him on to fulfilment he entered her body and found himself in an enveloping molten heat that finally made him lose control.

'Oh, yes . . . Oh, Christ, yes . . . yes,' he gasped, feeling as if he was going to lose his mind as wave after wave of feeling drove him to the edge. 'Oh, Jesus. Camilla!' There was nothing to equal this sensation in the whole world, no one who could turn his body to fire like this wonderful woman. For this moment of pleasure he would gladly die . . . drown in his own juices with the blood pounding in his head, blinding him, deafening him, destroying his mind with sensations that were overpoweringly wonderful.

Gasping for air, heart hammering, senses reeling, he finally lay spent on top of her, and wished the moment could happen all over again.

Camilla saw them before they saw her: Poppy and Lucy looking at clothes in Harrods. It was Saturday morning and Camilla had walked the short distance from Wilton Crescent, intent on buying herself a couple of new outfits suitable for the office. Up on the first floor she walked through the various departments whose display of exquisite garments soon had her reaching for her Gold American Express card. She stopped to glance at the exotic beach wear, tempted to buy brilliantly coloured silk swimsuits and towelling wraps, minuscule bikinis and wraparound sarongs; but then she remembered she wasn't going abroad for the time being and by the time she did, there would be newer and more exciting lines. In the Designer Room she looked at classic suits by Yves Saint Laurent, Umberto Ginocchietti and Valentino, and was just about to ask if she could try on a navy and white skirt and matching three-quarter length jacket, when through the archway to the next department she spotted Poppy, standing by a rail of velvet stretch pants, patterned in soft shades of pink and lilac. Lucy was watching Poppy, head on one side, but Camilla couldn't hear what she was saying.

Slowly she walked over to them, her heart pounding for some unaccountable reason. Seeing Poppy like this, without her garish makeup and wayout clothes, made her long for her daughter. It seemed tragic that they didn't speak now, that she couldn't just go up to Poppy naturally, and fling her arms around her and kiss her.

'Hello,' she said quietly as she reached them. Poppy started as if she'd been shot and Lucy seemed to freeze. 'How are you, darling?'

Poppy turned abruptly away and continued to examine the velvet trousers with deliberate care. Lucy nodded coldly.

'They have such lovely clothes in this department, don't they?' Camilla continued, trying to hide the hurt she felt at the rebuff. She remembered the times when she and Poppy used to have wonderful shopping sprees, indulging in little extravagances and giggling over some of the things on display. They'd both loved pretty things in those days but it seemed a long time ago now.

'Nice but expensive,' Lucy said prosaically. 'We were just looking.' Her tone sounded like a rebuke, shutting Camilla out. Now that Poppy was living with her things were different, she seemed to be saying.

'I don't like any of the stuff, here,' Poppy said arrogantly. 'Let's go, Lucy.'

'Couldn't we have a coffee in the restaurant?' Camilla suggested, her voice wistful.

'Why should we? What have we got to talk about?'

Camilla flinched at the coldness of her words. 'Lots of things, I expect, darling,' she replied as evenly as she could, and smiled.

Suddenly, Poppy seemed to explode with rage. Her pale skin flushed dark red and her blue eyes became bloodshot.

'Well, I've nothing to say to you! I never want to talk to you again! I never want to see you again!' With that, she burst into tears and then ran, sobbing, out of the department in the direction of the lifts.

Camilla turned accusingly to Lucy. 'You're to blame for this.'

Lucy stared steadily back. 'No, Camilla. You're the one to blame. None of this would have happened if you'd paid proper attention to Poppy instead of burying yourself in work. She's felt neglected and unloved for years. And now she feels completely threatened, in the most awful way, by Philip.'

Camilla started to argue, but Lucy raised a commanding hand.

'No, let me finish,' she continued. 'You've put Philip before Poppy ever since you met him, and she's more deeply hurt than you'll ever realise. You're manipulative, Camilla, and very dangerous. You've completely turned Philip's head and, as you know, I strongly disapprove of your relationship with him. Not just because he is my son, but because you've turned your back on Poppy and let Philip take her place in your life, in your home, in your whole existence.'

'That's rubbish!' Camilla shot back. 'I've been begging Poppy to return home . . .'

'To what?' Lucy demanded. 'To share a cosy love nest with you and a man young enough to be her brother? If you want Poppy back, Camilla, the time has come to choose between them. Philip or Poppy. One thing is certain – you can't have both. It will never work and you know it.'

'You're being absurd,' Camilla expostulated. 'You're making them sound like rivals.'

Lucy leaned forward, speaking clearly. 'And in Poppy's mind that's exactly what they are.' Then she turned and walked briskly away, a sensibly dressed woman with low heels and greying hair who thought more of her family's happiness than anything else. Camilla, turning to leave the department too, caught sight of herself in a mirrored pillar; a slim figure in a short skirt, with high heels, shining gold hair, and immaculate makeup. How had she and Lucy ever come to be friends? And then, uncomfortably, the thought crossed her mind. Could it be that Lucy was really a much nicer person than herself? Was she really being selfish in having everything she wanted regardless of Poppy's happiness?

Walking slowly and thoughtfully, without having bought anything, Camilla left Harrods and started making her way home. Lucy's words kept coming back to her, and Poppy's too.

Was she really to blame for the way Poppy had turned out? At least Poppy isn't doing drugs, so I must have done something right, she thought wryly. But could she give up Philip in order to restore peace between the two families? Never in a million years, she thought instantly. Never, no matter what happened. She loved him too much. Right now she could not contemplate ending their affair, but would the pressure brought to bear from Lucy and Poppy prove too strong in time?

It was with sadness that Camilla went up to Poppy's prettily decorated room when she got home, wandering about touching the mementoes of childhood. She longed to turn back the clock to a time when her life had no complications. To the days when Poppy had been a sweet and carefree adolescent. How easy everything had seemed then. A trifle dull at times maybe, a little bit predictable perhaps, but so easy. And so wonderfully secure.

Four days later, as Camilla returned to her office after meeting a client for lunch, Annabel greeted her with the news that her stepmother had phoned.

'Edith?' Camilla said eagerly. 'Thank God for that! Everyone's been trying to contact her. Has she arrived back in Scotland yet? I must phone her right away.'

Annabel consulted her notepad with an air of importance. Since Jean's departure she'd taken over the job of personal assistant and secretary, but she was still having a problem remembering everything the way her predecessor had done.

'Mrs Elliott phoned from her hotel in Paris. She was leaving for Charles de Gaulle Airport a few minutes later. She said she'd be flying to Glasgow. You won't be able to get her on the phone though, because it's been cut off.'

Camilla raised surprised eyebrows. 'Cut off? At Creagnach? That sounds odd.'

Annabel beamed knowledgeably. 'No, not really. As there's been no one living at Creagnach for some months the exchange disconnected the phone for non-payment of the bill.'

'Ah!' Camilla nodded in understanding. 'That figures. So what's the message? Will she phone me again?'

'Yes. She said she'll be staying overnight in Glasgow and then she'll get a car in the morning to drive her to Ardachie. She wondered if you'd be able to join her tomorrow?'

'Tomorrow?' Camilla looked startled. 'What does she think I am? A lady of leisure? How the hell am I going to get away at such short notice? I've a million things to do. I'd better phone her tonight and tell her I can't make it. Which hotel is she staying at in Glasgow?'

Annabel looked crestfallen. 'I'm afraid I didn't ask. She didn't say.'

'Oh, my God,' Camilla groaned. She felt like snapping at the girl, but what was the point? Annabel was underqualified for the job but she was doing her best and to tick her off now would only lead to further lack of confidence.

'Okay,' she said. 'Leave it with me and I'll see what I can do.' The last thing she felt like was rushing up to Scotland at this precise moment, when her workload was so heavy. Next month, or even next week maybe, but not right now. On the other hand, Malcolm would have wanted her to give Edith all the support she could. Her father had loved his second wife, and she owed it to him to be there when Edith needed her.

'As I can't get hold of her on the phone tonight,' she announced, 'I'll drive up to Scotland first thing in the morning.'

'You won't go alone?' Annabel looked astonished.

Camilla thought about it for a moment. She didn't want to have Ferris drive her up, and Philip was deep in his studies. For a split second she thought of asking Geoffrey. He'd find it interesting to go back to Ardachie and talk to Edith again, in view of what had happened, but of course Geoffrey would refuse. She couldn't really blame him either. Then it dawned on her there was no one she could ask, no male or female friend she could ring up and invite. By being with Philip and giving all her time to him when she wasn't working, she had gradually lost touch with most of her friends. Not that she'd kept up with many people since David's death. She hadn't had time. For the last four years, most of the people she'd mixed with had been in some way connected with the business and they were not the type you could ring up and ask to accompany you on a mission to hold your stepmother's hand.

'Yes, I'll go on my own.' Camilla said resolutely. It would be better that way in any case. Edith wouldn't want strangers around when she was having to go through the trauma of selling Creagnach which she and Malcolm had moved into with such dreams and high hopes for the future. 'Now, let's go through everything I have to do by tonight,' she continued briskly. 'We've got our work cut out because I'm going to have to cancel all my engagements for the next week, and you're going to have to make fresh appointments for me.' She also had to inform Special Branch that she would be going back to Ardachie, and she must tell Lucy and Poppy, even if they didn't want to know, that she was going to be away. Last but not least there was Philip. For some reason, quite apart from the fact they'd be away from each other for at least a week, she dreaded telling him most of all.

His face was pale and strained. 'Do you have to go?' he asked hollowly.

Camilla reached out and took Philip's hand. 'Yes, sweetheart. Edith is going to find it hard and I know Daddy would have wanted me to look after her as much as I can.'

'But I don't think it's safe,' he countered. 'Have you informed Special Branch?'

'Yes, and as I thought they said Ardachie is probably the safest place for me to be. All the suspects have been arrested and the police from Glasgow keep a permanent watch to make sure nothing is still going on. I'm much less likely to come to any harm up there where everyone knows who everyone else is, than in a city like London where a terrorist can mingle amongst the crowds.'

'I still don't like it.' He shook his head, worried. 'I wish to

God I could go with you. Can't you delay going?'

'Not really, Philip. Edith wants to go through everything and get away from the place as soon as possible, and frankly so do I. Delaying would only be putting off the inevitable.'

'I'd be free to come with you in a couple of months' time.'

'But Edith wants to move to Gloucestershire as soon as possible,' Camilla pointed out. 'I'll have to go, darling, so don't let's talk about it any more. I hate leaving you, but the quicker I go the quicker I'll be back.' She smiled gently, stroking his hand. 'It will give you a chance to get on with your studies, too. I know I take up all your spare time when you should be working.'

'Who told you that?' Philip demanded. 'My mother, I suppose?'

'She didn't have to, 'Camilla replied quietly. She'd been aware for some time now that he was devoting the minimum amount of time to studying, and it worried her.

'I've got plenty of time to study.' He sounded almost petulant.

'Nevertheless, my being away will give you a chance to catch up. Maybe you can see something of your family, too. With me out of the way, you might be able to heal the rift.'

'That's up to them. If they accept the situation then that's fine by me. I don't actually enjoy having a feud with them, but if they continue to act in an old-fashioned narrow-minded way, then that's their problem. I think their behaviour is ridiculous.'

Camilla looked troubled. Lucy was right. She had come between him and his family, and she hated feeling she was the cause of this split.

'Philip, can't you ignore their disapproval? Your mother still wants to see you and be friends with you, even though we are lovers. It's you who's refusing to be friendly with them,' Camilla reasoned.

'Do you blame me?' He looked hurt, as if she ought to be grateful that he was taking this stand on her behalf.

'How long do you propose to keep up this cold war, for

God's sake?' She felt angry, knowing that as long as he refused to have anything to do with his parents it would affect all their lives. 'You're acting like Poppy,' she accused him. 'She won't have anything to do with me because we're lovers, and you won't have anything to do with your family because they disapprove!'

'How can you say I'm like Poppy?' Philip was suddenly furious. 'Poppy is a spoilt brat . . . I'm sorry, Camilla, it has to be said. She's a spoilt brat who makes a scene if she can't get her own way!'

Camilla flushed. This was the first time they'd quarrelled and she felt instinctively they were treading on eggshells.

'And you don't think you're acting in the same way towards Lucy?' she challenged. 'Acting like a spoilt brat because your mother doesn't like what you're doing? I'm sure we could work out this situation if we could only sit down and talk about it in a civilised way, instead of your refusing even to discuss it further with your family, and Poppy flying off the handle saying she didn't want to have anything more to do with me.'

'When did this happen?'

Camilla shrugged. 'Does it matter? The point is that our falling in love seems to have wrenched our respective families apart, and I think it should stop.'

'I'm not giving in until they see reason,' he said stubbornly. 'They can't tell me what to do with my life! I'm nearly twenty-five, for God's sake, and if they weren't still living in the Middle Ages none of this would have happened. We could have all got along like a house on fire! Think what fun we could all have had together?'

Camilla tried to visualise scenes in which she and Philip and Lucy and Anthony made up a foursome to go to the theatre, or out to dinner, but something about the picture was wrong. It wouldn't gel in her mind. They didn't belong as a foursome and they never would. For a fleeting moment she saw in her imagination a scene in which she and Lucy and Anthony were taking Philip out to dinner . . . for a treat, as they had often done when he'd been very small . . . showing him the sights . . . letting him in on an adult world . . . It was a picture that both sickened and amused her. How could she fail to see the funny side of the situation? That's what they should all be doing – laughing at their own human frailty. Only she knew that with Poppy and the Hamiltons that was never going to be possible.

For a moment she remained silent. When she spoke it was gently, and she realised she was reasoning with him as a mother would with her son.

'This isn't a perfect world, darling,' she said sadly, and her voice was full of regret. 'We have to make the best of things as they are, and if some people cannot accept that, then we have to try and work around it.'

'Isn't that what we're doing?' His face was flushed too now, and for a dreadful moment she was afraid he was going to cry. It was obvious he was upset by the rift with his family, yet he was also being too obstinate to meet them half-way and discuss it reasonably.

'Perhaps when I get back from Scotland we can ask your parents and Poppy to dinner, so that everyone can try and come to terms with the idea of our being together,' she suggested. 'After all, we should all be able to behave like reasonable adults.'

'None of them will ever accept us as a couple.' He was holding her hand in both of his now, and his head was bowed.

'Maybe they can't.'

His head shot up and he looked at her with agonised eyes. 'Then what?'

'But I'm sure they can accept us separately.'

'What do you mean?' he asked alarmed.

'I mean, perhaps Poppy would agree to see me on my own, and perhaps Lucy and Anthony would be happy to see you on your own. If we were to keep our life together as something apart . . .'

Philip jumped to his feet. 'But that's playing into their hands!' he protested.

'It's known as compromising.'

'Compromise nothing! If Mum and Dad and Poppy for that

matter, refuse to accept us as a couple, then I don't want to know!'

Camilla sighed. He was being as stubborn as Poppy and it struck her at that moment that the stance they had both taken was very juvenile. 'Frankly,' she said, 'I think we may have rushed them with the suddenness of it all. To us it was a natural thing to fall in love, but to them it must have been a shock. You must see that, darling. I think we should give them more time to get used to the idea. That's why I'm suggesting we try to see them on our own, as individuals, before we try to force them to accept us as a couple.'

'If they cared a damn they'd accept the fact we're in love,' he said, in a hurt voice.

'I honestly don't think they understand. Maybe, given time, they'll come round to accepting us as a couple,' she continued, but even as she said it, it felt as if a cold hand was being laid on her heart. Lucy would never accept her as Philip's lover even if Poppy eventually did. Their relationship had been damned by the Hamiltons from the beginning, and they weren't going to change their minds now.

'Do you think so?' Philip was asking hopefully.

Camilla forced herself to smile cheerfully. 'We must try to make them understand.'

Suddenly he turned back to her, his expression showing how wretched he felt. 'Darling, I'm so afraid of losing you, of their coming between us,' he blurted out.

She leaned forward and cupped his face in her hands. 'No one can come between us but ourselves,' she said softly. But her heart felt heavy and chilled as he took her in his arms and pulled her close. He's so young, she thought with a jolt. Tonight his youth had shown in the way he'd talked, as if he'd been a young boy complaining that the grownups were giving him a hard time. She yearned to comfort him, gather him to her breast and reassure him that everything was going to be all right; but at that moment, with the shock of realisation, it struck her that she was reacting in a maternal way. He was the child-boy needing to be comforted, and she was the eternal mother figure, there to console him when the going got tough. She cradled his head in her arms and felt very old. Maybe women always became the mother figure sooner or later, she reflected. There had certainly been times when David had leaned on her, appealing to her maternal instincts, but somehow that had seemed different because there had also been times when he'd been like a father figure to her, as well as her husband.

'We're going to be all right, aren't we?' She knew he only wanted to hear her say yes. 'I'll love you till I die, Camilla. I want to spend the rest of my life with you.' His mouth sought hers urgently now and his hands were clutching her feverishly. 'I don't want anyone to spoil what we have,' he murmured between kisses. She kissed him back and felt a tremendous sense of sadness because the more he said, the more she doubted their future. 'You do love me, don't you?' he whispered.

'Of course I love you, darling,' she said, and it was true. She did love him, tremendously, passionately, ardently, with her whole heart. But a small voice echoing in her head asked if their love would be strong enough to withstand the alienation of their families?

Camilla rose at five o'clock the next morning, and, slipping quietly out of bed so as not to awaken Philip, showered and dressed herself in pale slacks and a thick sweater over a silk shirt. Her case had been packed the night before.

Creeping stealthily down the stairs to the kitchen, she made herself a pot of tea and some toast. Thirty minutes later Ferris brought the car to the door, having first carried out what had now become a routine check for hidden explosives.

'The tank's full, madam,' he told her, 'and she's running like a bird.'

Camilla smiled. Ferris loved the Mercedes as if it were a family pet, or even a child. It stood outside the house now, polished so that it gleamed in the dawning light, its bumpers glittering like mirrors.

'Thank you, Ferris.' She'd given him a week off to go and

stay with his son and daughter-in-law in Hampshire while she was away, and now she wished him a good trip. 'Try and have a bit of a rest,' she said as she got into the car. Ferris worked all the hours God gave him, not only driving her around but sometimes the other company directors too. Often he was still working at two o'clock in the morning if they were involved in an evening function entertaining clients.

'Oh, I will, madam,' he beamed. 'My daughter-in-law always looks after me very well. She even brings me breakfast in bed!'

Camilla laughed. 'Good for you, Ferris. Have a lovely time and I'll see you next week.'

'Yes, madam. Thank you.' He closed the car door, bowing to her as he did so. 'Have a good trip.'

A moment later Camilla was speeding away up to Hyde Park Corner, before turning left into the park. It was now nearly six o'clock. By her reckoning she expected to be in Glasgow by lunchtime. The last part of the journey, along the winding roads and through the mountains of the Highlands, would be slow-going and so it would be mid-afternoon before she arrived at Creagnach House. A call from Edith the previous day assured her she would be awaiting her arrival 'with great pleasure', according to Maitland who had taken the message.

Turning on the car radio, she listened to the early morning news and weather forecast. Then she switched to the cassette-player, and the collection of tapes that were always kept in the glove compartment. Soon the strains of Bach filled the car as the miles slipped away, and once outside the suburbs of London the lush greenness of Hertfordshire surrounded her. Ahead of her, like a richly patterned quilt, lay some of the most beautiful countryside in England, and she had seven hours in which to enjoy it while she listened to the soothing music. And seven hours in which to think about Philip and wonder what she should do about their future together. Of one thing she was now certain: changes would have to be made.

Philip, awakening from a deep sleep, rolled to the centre of the king-size bed and reached out for Camilla. The chill empty space made him open his eyes and instantly, with a pang, he remembered. Camilla had left at dawn to drive to Scotland. But why hadn't she woken him to say goodbye? He lay on his back gazing up at the canopy, wondering how he was going to get through the next few days without her. She'd warned him she might be away for as long as a week. Pulling the lacy pillow on her side of the bed towards him, he buried his face in its softness and smelt the fragrance of her hair and skin. Camilla . . . his love. His own. Never had he adored anyone so much. From the first sleepy kiss in the morning, to the last lingering kiss after they'd made love at night, she filled every thought, every dream, every waking moment, and every sleeping moment too, as she curled herself against him in the big bed, her hand cupping his manhood even in slumber. He wished she hadn't decided to go to Scotland. Surely Edith's sister could have helped instead. Not that there was anything to worry about any more, he told himself. They'd been absolutely assured by Special Branch that there was no longer any danger in Ardachie. Nevertheless, for some reason he felt uneasy as he got out off bed and went to shower in her pretty green marble bathroom. He would be going to his own flat while Camilla was away. She'd told him she'd like him to remain at Wilton Crescent 'to keep the bed warm for her', but somehow he wasn't comfortable there without her. The Maitlands, though scrupulously polite and respectful, emanated vibes that told him they really didn't approve and that made him feel embarrassed. When he'd mentioned to Camilla how he felt, she'd laughed and told him not to be silly.

'This is my house and I can have who I like to stay,' she'd said firmly. 'Use it as your home, darling. What is mine is yours, you know.'

But he had decided it wasn't a good idea. Not only did he have a lot of studying to do, but it would be easier to concentrate on his work without the constant reminders of Camilla all around him. He glanced at the glass bathroom shelves and saw bottles of her perfume and bath oil, and delicately scented soap, and almost instantly he was filled with desire. If she had been here now, standing in the shower with him . . . Obsessively he started to fantasise, letting his mind drift to other times when they had made love in the deep jacuzzi bath, on the floor, against the wall . . . Aroused now he turned the shower to cold. There was no point in getting worked up when Camilla was already hundreds of miles away. Ruefully, he dressed and hurried down to breakfast. He'd phone her later. Just to make sure she was all right.

'I'm afraid Mrs Eaton left for Scotland this morning, Mr Hennessy,' Annabel announced brightly. 'Would you like to call back next week, or would you like to leave a message?'

Geoffrey thought rapidly, wondering what had made Camilla go back to Scotland. 'She'll be away for as long as a week?' he enquired, and before he could stop himself he added: 'Did she go on her own . . . or with someone?'

'I believe she went on her own. Can I take a message?'

'No. No, thank you. It's all right. I'll ring back some other time.'

Feeling curiously happy, Geoffrey hung up and then sat at his desk in the offices of the *Globe* wondering if it meant she was no longer with young Philip Hamilton. He couldn't understand what she saw in the boy in the first place, except perhaps a certain virility. Gazing absently at the screen of the word processor on his desk, he cursed himself for ever letting it happen. If he'd only said something to Camilla earlier, some words that hinted of a future for them together! Why the hell hadn't he told her that he loved her? he asked himself. Now it was probably too late.

Geoffrey sighed, causing the Travel Editor, who sat at a desk nearby, to look up.

'That doesn't sound like you, Geoffrey! What's up?'

He shook his head. 'I've been a bloody fool,' he confessed. 'I've been too slow off the mark and now it may be too late.'

'It's never too late with a woman,' chortled his colleague, 'if that's what you're talking about.'

'It is if she's got herself mixed up with a good-looking man who's tall, slim, dresses well, and is also young enough to be my son,' he retorted.

'If you ask me, she's crazy! Show her what experience is all about, Geoffrey! Women like a man who's experienced.'

He shrugged. 'Chance would be a fine thing.'

Chapter Twenty-Three

The first thing Camilla became aware of as she parked her car outside the post office-cum-local store in Ardachie was the difference in the atmosphere of the village. In the few minutes she spent looking up and down the familiar quayside, remembering the night when she and Philip had been chased by the smugglers, she could sense an almost tangible feeling of freedom in the air, as of a dark brooding presence having been lifted. As she looked out to sea, dazzled by the afternoon sunshine reflecting off the water, it seemed unbelievable that so many sinister activities had taken place in this very spot on which she now stood.

Inside the local store it seemed new people had taken over, too. A bright young woman served Camilla as she bought a house gift of some flowers for Edith, and a couple of newspapers. Another young woman was behind the counter of the post office section. Neither showed a flicker of recognition at Camilla's presence, confirming her suspicions that the people who had worked there before had gone. It was as if a clean sweep had taken place, eradicating the reign of terror that had contaminated the district before.

Happy that she would not be facing the horror of the past this time, Camilla got back into the car to drive the short distance to Creagnach. She was looking forward to seeing Edith again and they would have so much to talk about. She wanted to know how her stepmother had come to be friends with Hector Ross, and whether she had realised at first that he was the ringleader of the gun-running operation. She wanted to ask about the young man who had escorted her to Malcolm's funeral, and longed to hear about Edith's recent travels. They had so much news to exchange, and although the next few days were going to be busy, and it would be stressful going through her father's things, Camilla also felt a sense of exhilaration that all the loose ends connected with the whole tragic episode were finally going to be tied up. Then, and only then, could she put everything that had happened at Ardachie behind her, and so be able to get on with the rest of her life with a sense of peace.

There was something else she wanted to talk to her stepmother about, too. Edith was an older and more experienced woman, twice widowed, and from what Malcolm had told her, full of wisdom and understanding. Camilla wanted to talk to her about Philip and ask her advice. Should she end the affair, as everyone wanted? Or should she, for once, let her heart rule her head?

The drive was overgrown and the garden in a terrible state of neglect. As Camilla slowed down and looked out of the car windows, she remembered that afternoon, all those months ago, when she'd walked up this very drive to visit Edith and found the house deserted and all the dogs dead, their bodies strewn about the kennels. The moment came back vividly to her now, sending a shudder through her, and she wondered how Edith had felt when she arrived back this morning. The memories, both good and bad, must have come crowding in as they did with her now. Memories of her father, sitting in the garden looking out to the Firth of Lorne on a summer's afternoon. Memories of the beautiful dogs romping playfully in the kennels. It couldn't have been easy for Edith to have returned today to the place where they had hoped to stay peacefully for the rest of their lives.

Camilla parked the car, reached for the flowers she'd bought, and then climbed the moss-encrusted front steps to ring the bell. The silence of the place was overpowering. She cocked her head to one side, straining to hear a bird singing or the rustling of the wind among the leafladen trees. She leaned forward, so her ear was only a few inches from the heavy oak door, holding her breath for a moment so that she could pick out Edith's footsteps hurrying to let her in. There was nothing. She might have turned stone deaf in those seconds as her other senses told her there was nothing to hear. The place was as deserted as a tomb.

Panic threatened to envelop her for a few seconds as a voice in her head screamed: Oh, not again . . . please God, not again! Breathing deeply, she turned and descended the steps again and stood in the drive, realising that the house still had that dead shuttered look of her previous visit. But it couldn't be like last time, she reasoned, pulling herself together. Everyone involved in the smuggling had been rounded up and arrested. Special Branch had said it would be all right to come to this place. They'd told her they'd even checked it out in the last twenty-four hours. There were no longer dogs to be slaughtered . . .

Common sense overcame her irrational fears as she leaned against her car wondering what to do. First, she must rid herself of the notion that, once again, something terrible had happened. The most likely explanation was either that Edith had missed her flight from Paris or that she'd been delayed in leaving Glasgow. She was probably on her way now, in a hired car as she'd said.

Camilla got back into the Mercedes and reached for the mobile phone which, in spite of her initial reservations, she now found invaluable. Quickly she dialled the number of Eaton & Eaton and asked to be put through to Annabel.

'How are you, Mrs Eaton?' Annabel asked cheerfully, when she came on the line. 'Did you have a good journey?'

'Fine, thanks,' Camilla replied. 'Listen, Annabel, I've arrived at Creagnach and there's no one here. I wondered if my stepmother had been in touch?'

'Not that I know of, but I'll check. Maybe there was a message while I was out at lunch. I won't keep you.' A minute later she was back on the line. 'No, there are no messages from Mrs Elliott.'

'And she definitely said it was today she was arriving here?'

'Absolutely. She was leaving Paris yesterday and flying to Glasgow, where she said she was staying last night, and then she was getting a car to take her to Ardachie today.'

Camilla sighed with relief. 'Then I must have got here before her. She's probably on her way now. Are there any other messages?'

For the next few minutes Annabel filled her in on what had been happening at the office, and when she hung up Camilla decided to phone home in case Edith had left a message there.

Maitland answered. 'I'm afraid we've had no word from Mrs Elliott,' he informed her. 'I'd have rung you on the mobile phone if there'd been a change of plan, madam,' he added with gentle reproof.

Camilla smiled. When it came to competence and efficiency, only Jean equalled Maitland, and Camilla still missed her every day.

'Thank you, Maitland,' she replied. Having checked that everything was all right at home, she decided to let herself into Creagnach. When she and Philip had departed, they'd hidden the spare set of keys in the left-hand pavilion, under a stack of terracotta flowerpots. The keys were still there exactly as they'd left them.

Within a few minutes she'd unlocked the front door and entered the hall. Stale and heavy air permeated the atmosphere with a musty smell. The bunch of heather she'd picked when she'd been out walking with Philip stood dusty and shrivelled where she'd arranged it in a pewter bowl on the centre table.

Moving as if in a dream, and with a strange sense of *déjà vu*, she went from room to room opening doors and those windows which weren't locked to let in the fresh air. When she entered the kitchen her heart nearly stopped. On the kitchen table were the two coffee mugs she and Philip had drunk from before leaving. He was supposed to have washed up but he'd obviously forgotten, and picking up the mugs now she felt for some inexplicable reason like crying. The journey had been long and she was very tired. Finding Edith hadn't arrived yet was an anti-climax, but that was not why she now felt the tears well up in her eyes. It was because when they'd last used those mugs their love had belonged to only them, and they had treasured it secretly. Now everything had become exposed to the criticism of Poppy and the Hamiltons, a lot of the gloss had been stripped away and corners that could seem tarnished had been exposed.

Going slowly to the sink, she rinsed the mugs under the running tap and then remembered she must turn on the hot water so they could have baths. It was now four o'clock in the afternoon. Surely Edith would arrive soon.

Camilla never heard the footsteps coming up the gravel drive, nor was she aware of anyone climbing the front steps and pushing wide the oak door which she'd left open in order to air the hall.

Lucy looked at her watch as she and Poppy sat having lunch in the garden. 'Your mother will have reached Glasgow by now,' she observed. Poppy shrugged. It didn't matter to her where her mother was, or what she was doing. Lucy watched her uneasily, blaming herself in part for Poppy's attitude. 'I wonder how she'll find your grandmother?' she continued conversationally.

Poppy corrected her. 'My step-grandmother!'

'Well, yes. They'll have a lot to talk about.'

Poppy remained silent as she helped herself to Lucy's home-made liver pâté, spreading it thickly on a crust of french bread. She looked almost like her old self these days except for the tight-lipped, slightly petulant expression when her mother was mentioned. Gone was the heavy hideous makeup and trailing greasy hair. Gone, too, were the weird punk-style clothes. Poppy had stopped rebelling because there no longer seemed any point.

'I wonder how long she'll be away,' Lucy remarked, determined to draw Poppy out and get her to talk about Camilla. It was the only way, in her opinion, to clear the air, although of course there could be no major reconciliation until Camilla gave up Philip.

'Who cares! I don't know why she bothered to tell us she was going to Scotland.'

'Poppy, darling, you can't go on being angry with your mother,' Lucy reasoned.

'Yes, I can,' Poppy responded swiftly. 'Why should I care about her when she doesn't give a damn for me? All she thinks about, night and day, is Philip, and I'm sick of it.'

'I'm not very happy about it either, but I've been thinking.' Lucy paused.

'What about?'

'Philip and your mother. I think we've all handled it the wrong way. I think by opposing them we've made them all the more keen on each other.'

'I don't see how?'

'If you do something that everyone disapproves of, doesn't it make you want to do it all the more? Doesn't it make you feel defiant? Like, why shouldn't I do what I want?' Lucy asked.

Poppy took a large bite of french bread, and as she chewed it gazed up at the cloudless sky, deep in thought. At last, when she'd finished her mouthful, she answered somewhat grudgingly: 'I suppose so.'

'Exactly. I was wondering, if we didn't oppose them, might they not realise themselves what a mistake they're making?' Lucy suggested.

'Do you think so?' Poppy didn't sound enthusiastic.

'It might be worth trying. It makes me miserable having this fight with Philip. We've never fought like this, not even when he was a child.' She shook her head in distress. 'We've always been a very close family and I simply can't bear the fact he won't talk to us. I think I'll ask him to supper one night this week, while your mother's away.'

'Ummmm.' Poppy helped herself to more pâté. 'I suppose you could.'

420

'You get on with Philip, don't you? If he's on his own?'

'I hardly know him.'

'Oh, you'd like him if you got him on his own, I'm sure,' Lucy urged. 'We'll have a nice family dinner and see if we can't heal the rift.'

'You're never going to do that while my mother's having an affair with him,' Poppy said shrewdly. 'And now that she's got her claws into him, I don't think she'll ever let go.'

Lucy's brow puckered with worry. 'You don't really believe that, do you, darling? I think she'll suddenly get bored and dump him. My main worry is that he'll get hurt. That sort of thing can have a terrible effect on a young man. I've told her, repeatedly . . .' Suddenly Lucy remembered that she was also trying to bring about a reconciliation between Poppy and her mother. 'Anyway,' she continued lamely, 'the sooner the whole thing blows over the better.'

Poppy shrugged again and continued with her lunch. Her mother was gone for a week, and although she no longer lived at home, it was still a relief to know there was no possibility of bumping into her in Harrods.

Camilla dried the mugs carefully and put them back in the kitchen cupboard, all the time thinking about Philip. He'd been so worried about her when he'd phoned her earlier in the day while she was still on the outskirts of Glasgow. In spite of her reassuring him that everything was fine, his concern was evident and she promised to phone him after dinner tonight. She was missing him too, especially as everything about Creagnach was reminding her of him. Going over to the kitchen window, she looked out at the landscape that had become so familiar to them and wished he was here now to share these last few days at Creagnach with her.

In the hall the intruder had paused to listen, and, hearing a noise coming from the kitchen, made his way quietly across the polished floor. A moment later he flung open the door and Camilla, hearing the sound, spun round ready to greet Edith, wondering at the same moment how she'd managed to arrive so quietly.

But it wasn't Edith who stood there. Startled, Camilla drew in her breath sharply as she found herself face to face with a slim young man with red hair and a pale face. In his right hand he held a revolver. A hundred thoughts, a thousand notions, swam through her bewildered brain for a moment, until with a sickening jolt she realised this whole trip to Scotland had been a trap set to get her up here alone. She knew in her bones, before a word was said, that Edith would not be coming now. Edith had never been coming. She had helped set up this whole thing. Hadn't the letters Camilla had found from Hector Ross to Edith pointed at an existing relationship between them? They had been in it together from the beginning, but Edith had fled to safety before the arrests had been made.

For a moment the room swam before Camilla's eyes as she realised what had happened. But what about Special Branch, set up to gather intelligence on terrorist activities? What about the protection they were supposed to be offering her? She'd told them she was travelling to Scotland. They'd said she had nothing to fear. Would they be coming to her rescue now? She took a deep breath to steady herself and looked more closely at the intruder. He was in his late twenties to early thirties, with a taut face as if the skin had been stretched tightly over the sharp cheek and jaw bones. Small mean eyes glared at her through gold-rimmed glasses. Thin reddish hair, ruffled by the wind, fell spikily around his ears. Camilla was reminded of a fox, cunningly watching its prey. Desperation made her reckless.

'Who are you?' she demanded, raising her chin in a defiant gesture. 'What are you doing here?' The gun was pointing at her chest and his hand was steady. He stood with feet apart and his eyes never left her face. Still he said nothing.

At that moment, with a sudden knowledge so fatal she knew she didn't stand a chance, she remembered when she'd last seen him. Recognition dawned as she remembered the day of her father's funeral. This was the young man who had accompanied Edith, who had refused to let her talk to any of them, who had swept her away immediately afterwards without a word.

'Who are you?' she repeated. She had nothing to lose. He was going to kill her anyway.

The white face gleamed with sweat, the jaw clenching and unclenching. With his gun, he motioned her away from the window. Silently she obeyed. Then he spoke.

'I'm Alastair Ross.'

For a moment her mind grappled with the name. Hector Ross . . . Alastair . . . his son! Her expression was astonished as she looked at the man who stood menacingly a few feet away.

'But you're . . . you're . . .'

'A cripple?' Somehow he managed to convey hatred and bitterness in the one word, so tightly compressed it seemed to explode from his mouth. As soon as she heard him speak she recognised the voice. She'd spoken to him once before when she'd phoned the vet about her father's dogs.

'I d-don't understand,' she stammered, remembering how sorry for him she'd felt when she'd heard he was severely disabled.

'There's a lot you don't understand.' Again he spat the words as if they were poisoned, his Scottish accent pronounced.

'So why not tell me?' she retorted, trying to gather her wits together. What was it they always advised? Talk to your captor? Yes, that was it. Talk to your captor, try to get friendly, play for time while you soften him up . . . Camilla remembered an article she'd read about a woman who had been held hostage for eight days by a psychopath. He'd finally let her go unharmed, and the police had said it was because she'd been co-operative and had got him to talk.

'Tell me what all this is about?' she said, 'Hector Ross is your father?'

He gave a brief nod. 'Bloody old fool! He's where he deserves to be now.'

'In prison?' Camilla longed to sit down, but with the gun still pointing at her chest she didn't dare move.

'Yes.' Suddenly he laughed, a short staccato rasping sound

that sent shivers down her back. 'Thanks to you,' he added.

She remained silent for a moment, watching him closely. He was sweating heavily now, his face glistening with a white waxy look, his breathing heavy.

'You were too clever to get caught, weren't you?' she asked craftily.

He shot her a look with his sharp foxy eyes, wondering if she was being sarcastic. 'They couldn't pin anything on a cripple,' he said boastfully. 'A cripple who never leaves his bed, a cripple who has to be nursed day and night by his devoted wife, Morag.'

Camilla gasped. 'Your wife?'

'Aye. She's more than just my father's housekeeper.'

'Aren't you afraid of being seen now?' In spite of her fear, she felt intrigued. There were so many things she longed to ask him she hardly knew where to begin. 'You're obviously not a cripple,' she pointed out.

'Och, my word, aren't we clever!' he sneered. Then he raised his chin in an arrogant gesture, and the expression in his eyes sent fresh panic pulsing through Camilla. Where were Special Branch now that she needed them? Help must be on its way . . . she wouldn't let herself doubt for a second that in a few minutes someone would come to rescue her from this mad man. Or had Alastair Ross fooled even Special Branch? Had they, when they arrested his father, believed him to be housebound? A harmless cripple who never went out. Who never showed his face in Ardachie, and yet had possessed the gall to escort Edith to the funeral?

'I'm not particularly clever,' she said quietly, 'I just wonder why your father said you were disabled.'

'I told him to,' he said harshly. 'No one suspects a cripple, do they?'

'That's true,' she said nodding. 'So what do you do?' She was desperate to keep him talking until help came, and although the gun was still pointed at her his grip did not look so tight. With any luck she hoped he would begin to talk about the whole operation and she would pretend to know very little, in order to keep him talking.

His eyes were twin beams of searing hatred. 'You don't know? Don't give me that.'

'Of course I know what you do,' she said calmly as she could. 'I just wondered what your particular role was in the . . . the organisation?'

'Particular role?' he mimicked, copying her cut-glass English accent. Then he lapsed into broad Scots, his voice guttural with anger. 'D'you no ken I'm the leader? D'you no ken they were all working under orders from me? M'father had nothing to do with any of it! It was my operation. I run the show in Ardachie. No one else. Certainly not m'father.' He snorted in disgust.

'Had he anything to do with it?' she asked, hardly able to hide her astonishment.

Alastair Ross shrugged, and she noticed he was losing his guarded air. 'He covered for me,' he retorted. 'He carried the can for me. It was him they arrested because I was a bedridden cripple who had to be helped to the bog. How could I be smuggling arms to Ireland?' Still holding the revolver, he moved over to the kitchen window and looked out. 'The others should be here soon,' he commented, as if talking to himself.

'The others?' Camilla said faintly. If there were others, more armed terrorists surrounding Creagnach, she didn't stand a chance. She would be shot and her body disposed of, and she'd never be heard of again. Philip would go frantic when she didn't contact him, and there was Poppy . . . She was sweating now, her heart hammering so she could hardly breathe. Fool! she thought, cursing herself for falling headlong into this trap, believing Edith would be here to greet her. Edith . . . Her mind seemed to spin with horror as fresh realisations hit her with the force of a flying brick. 'Where's Edith?' she whispered. It was her stepmother who had enticed her into this trap . . . who had enticed Malcolm too. Now he was dead, and she was soon to follow! 'Where is she?' If she could have got hold of Edith now, she felt sure she'd have been tempted to kill her. She had brought such grief to them all. Malcolm, herself . . . and Poppy. She had schemed and plotted to get Malcolm to live in Scotland, to be near Hector Ross, no doubt, and when Malcolm had found out too much she had let them kill him . . . in cold blood . . . in his own car. And then she had gone to his funeral, accompanied by Hector's son. Or could Alastair be . . .? The thought was so dreadful she didn't know if she wanted to hear the truth or not, and yet she had to know.

'Was Edith your mother?' she asked.

The look of astonishment on his face was unmistakable. 'Edith? Edith Elliott?' he repeated. 'What in the world makes you say that?' He pronounced it 'wor-rld', drawing the word out so it dominated the sentence.

'I found a letter from your father, saying he was glad she was coming to live here,' Camilla replied. 'It struck me they must have known each other before.'

'They knew each other through the dog world. Crufts and that sort of thing. She sometimes asked his advice on breeding those fucking noisy dogs of hers.'

Camilla frowned. Things weren't adding up. 'But she was involved in . . .' she could hardly bring herself to say it ' . . . in the gun-running operation?'

'Edith?' He shook his head in wonderment, and then he laughed again, that sharp staccato sound that set Camilla's teeth on edge. 'Edith is about as much involved as the fishes in the North Sea.'

'What do you mean?' she countered. 'It was Edith who got me up here today. She must have been acting under orders from you?'

'Those postcards you got from around the wor-rld you mean? Those phone messages inviting you up here, to help sort out your father's things?'

'Exactly!' Camilla pounced on his words with relief. At last he was getting to the point. Out of the insanity of the moment things were beginning to make sense again. A second later her hopes were irreparably dashed.

Alastair Ross paused, and then he said laconically: 'Edith didn't send them.'

Stunned, she gazed fearfully into the mean little eyes. 'Then who did?'

'One of our supporters, acting on my orders. He used to be a master forger. And it was Morag who phoned, pretending to be Edith.'

'Then my stepmother hasn't been staying in Florence . . . and Lausanne . . . and Paris?' The enormity of what she now suspected was too appalling to take in.

'Of course she hasn't.'

'Then . . .?'

He didn't answer but glanced out of the window again, the gun still pointed at Camilla.

Suddenly the atmosphere in the kitchen was deadly quiet. Not even the buzzing of a fly broke the breathless silence as she thought back to that day when she'd arrived and found all the dogs lying dead in the kennels. She and Lucy and Philip had presumed Edith had gone away, fled in terror. Then, when the postcards started arriving in what looked like Edith's spidery hand, they presumed she'd decided to travel. All her clothes had gone, and her personal possessions, packed by her to take on her trip. And yet . . .

'Where is she?' she asked, as her heart beat wildly against her rib cage and she hoped she wasn't going to faint. 'Did she ever leave here?' she asked in a terrified whisper.

There was smug satisfaction in Alastair Ross's voice as he answered, but the deadliness of the words confirmed her worst fears.

'Edith is at the bottom of the North Sea, with all the little fishes.'

The silence in the kitchen intensified. Camilla was sure he would hear the beating of her heart. It seemed as if they were cut off from civilisation; remote, out of reach, and no one could save her now.

'Why?' she asked when she could find her voice. 'What had she ever done to you?'

'She was a meddling old besom,' he snarled with sudden irritation. 'Both she and your father pried in to what didn't concern them. They knew too much!'

'But you went with her to the funeral?'

'It would have caused a hue and cry if we'd got rid of her before,' he retorted. 'And I was able to stop her talking to all of you, telling you what had happened.'

There was one more question Camilla had to ask, one more searching out of the truth, painful though it was. 'Did she know what was going to happen to her?'

Alastair Ross shrugged. 'Not until after the funeral. Then she knew. When we started packing all her stuff, so it would look as if she'd gone on a trip. We shot her that night,' he added flatly.

Camilla gave a strangled cry and covered her face with her hands. He was so cold-blooded she felt as if she were in the presence of an evil force. If they could do that to a defenceless old lady, what could they do to her? An overwhelming wave of nausea threatened to make her throw up as she leaned against the kitchen wall.

'I must sit d-down,' she stammered, groping blindly for a kitchen chair. He didn't answer. The hand holding the gun now hung slackly by his side, as if boasting of his achievements had made him relax. It was obvious to both of them that she was beaten; that her attempts to engage him in conversation had done nothing to bridge the yawning gap of terror that separated her from him. It was just a matter of time now. He would shoot her and drop her overboard into the sea and she'd never be heard of again. She thought of Poppy, her baby, her little girl whom she loved so much, and from whom she'd become so estranged. Her yearning to see her daughter and hold her in her arms once more wrenched at her heart, and her eyes filled with tears. And there was Philip. Not to have a chance to say goodbye to him now was agony.

Suddenly she could bear it no longer. If she was going to be shot, let Alastair Ross do it now. What was he waiting for? The others to arrive, to give him moral support? Was she to be put against a wall and murdered in traditional style by a firing squad?

Recklessly she jumped to her feet. 'Why don't you kill me now?' she demanded, her voice rising on an edge of hysteria. 'Why don't you do it and get it over?' Tears poured down her cheeks and she was racked by sobs. Poppy . . . Philip. She wanted them so much and she was never going to see them again, and they might never even know what had happened to her.

'What's your hurry?' Alastair Ross asked coolly. There was sly amusement in his gimlet eyes now, and his face looked foxier than ever. 'I'm enjoying this.'

Camilla wiped her cheeks with the back of her hand, and tried to control her sobs. 'You're a bloody sadist,' she cried.

'Is that so!' He kicked one of the kitchen chairs away from the table with his right foot, and then sat down on it facing her, 'And what, may I ask, are you?'

'What do you mean?'

'You! You who went blabbing off to Glasgow with your tales!' Suddenly he was filled with anger again, and his Scottish accent thickened. 'You . . . and your fancy man, who came snooping into the village at night, spying on us! M'father told me how you stopped his car and ranted on about ringing the police! Yer meddling besom! Now you're going to pay for what you did! You're going to suffer just like the families of all the men who've been arrested are suffering. Don't think you're going to die quickly. That's far too good for you. We should have finished you off the last time you were here, but you got away, didn't you?' His tone was menacing as he leaned towards her. 'Well, you're no getting away from us this time.'

For a moment Camilla felt a flicker of hope. Perhaps if he delayed in killing her, help would come. Maybe Philip would wonder why she didn't phone him later. Maybe he'd get worried and contact Scotland Yard. Surely, after all that had happened, after the sensational arrests had been front page news, Special Branch couldn't be unaware that the ringleader was free and that he still had supporters?

429

He rose now, kicking back the kitchen chair. 'Get up,' he snapped unceremoniously.

Camilla rose stiffly, drained of energy and emotion. The gun was pointing at her again, and he was directing her out of the kitchen and into the hall. Then he grabbed her arm with his other hand, pushing her past the open front door and into the library. Roughly he shoved her forward.

'Stay in here,' he commanded.

He looked around the room and then nodded to himself, satisfied. 'You'll no escape from here.'

Camilla glanced over to the windows and knew he was right. All the windows of the ground-floor rooms at Creagnach had heavy iron bars on the outside, as protection against intruders. She sank into one of the carved chairs, resting her elbow on the long polished table.

'What are you going to do?' she asked.

'You'd like to know, would you?' He paced around the room, looking at everything as if making a mental inventory. 'This is a job the IRA don't want to admit to, so we're going to have a wee accident, aren't we?'

Camilla gritted her teeth, loathing Alastair Ross more than she thought it was possible to hate anyone.

'A tragic accident, that's what it'll be.'

'How?' The single word hovered in the air between them.

'We're going to torch Creagnach,' he replied simply. 'We're going to remove a few valuable bits and pieces, things we can raise money on, and then we'll make it look like an electrical fault. These old houses, y'ken . . . the wiring's a wee bit decrepit.' He sniggered at his own cleverness.

Camilla felt her throat constrict and her heart squeeze, so she could barely breathe. So that was to be her fate! She was to be burned alive in her father's house, in a 'tragic accident'.

A moment later he turned and left the room, slamming the heavy oak door behind him. Then she heard him turning the key in the lock before removing it. His footsteps sounded loud as he walked away, and then they faded. For the moment he was gone. She looked around the room, seeing if there was any way she could escape, but there was none. The windows were barred. The door was locked and would take three men to lift it off its hinges. She even looked over to the fireplace, but the idea of climbing up the chimney was absurd. The room was built like a fortress. There was absolutely nothing she could do. The house was going to be set on fire, and she was trapped inside it.

Chapter Twenty-Four

At five o'clock Philip decided he couldn't wait until after dinner to speak to Camilla again. He wanted to know if she'd arrived at Creagnach all right. He was interested to know how she was getting on with Edith, but most of all he wanted to hear her voice again and tell her he loved her. Already, after only a day, he was missing her dreadfully, and the prospect of a long evening without her depressed him.

When there was no answer from her mobile phone, he hung up, frowning. Perhaps she'd gone for a walk. Maybe she'd left the phone in the car. No doubt, he reflected, she'd bring it into the house before long because they'd already arranged to speak to each other during the evening. He hoped she wouldn't forget as she became immersed in conversation with her stepmother. Without her he felt lost. Then he tried to settle down to studying, but Bannister Fletcher's *History of Architecture* held little allure for him right now, and when the phone suddenly rang he grabbed it with alacrity, Camilla's name on his lips as he answered.

'How about coming over for dinner tomorrow evening, darling?' His spirits took a dive as he heard his mother's voice. For a moment the anticlimax was almost unbearable.

'Why?' he asked, blunt in his disappointment.

'How do you mean . . . why? We'd like to see you, that's why. It's just the family. I thought of doing a roast with all the trimmings.'

'This is because Camilla is away, isn't it? You never asked

me when she was here.' He sounded hot and cross and deeply suspicious.

'Oh, Philip, don't be like that, darling,' Lucy begged. 'I miss seeing you. Is that so strange? I thought it would be nice to have a quiet family supper with no hassle, no arguments, no fights. Can't we do that?'

'But it doesn't alter anything, does it? You're still against Camilla and me being together, aren't you?' He sounded aggressive in his hurt.

'Oh, Philip! I hate what's happening between us. We've never fought like this before.'

'Well, it's up to you, Mum! If you'll accept Camilla as my girlfriend there's no problem. I don't understand why you find it so difficult. It's not as if you didn't know her and like her. All I ask is that you accept the situation.'

There was a long silence and then Lucy said quietly: 'I don't think I can, darling. I wouldn't be honest if I pretended I didn't mind. I do mind, very much, because I think she's coming between you and your family, you and your studies. You could end up getting really hurt, and the whole thing is miserable for Poppy.'

There was a pause as Philip digested what she'd said. 'Then that's it, isn't it?' he remarked finally.

'But there's no need for you to cut yourself off from us because of this.'

'Mum, Camilla and I are together now. We're a couple. There's no more to be said.'

'Philip, I . . .' But he had hung up and she found herself holding the silent receiver.

Poppy came into the room at that moment. 'What did he say?' she asked curiously, guessing they'd been fighting.

'Oh, God, Camilla's bewitched him!' Lucy wrung her hands in exasperation. 'He won't come. I can't get any sense out of him.'

'Didn't I tell you? Didn't I say my mother was manipulative? If she wants something she gets it. Ever since Daddy died she's been different,' she added, bursting into tears.

'Poppy, darling.' Lucy rushed to her side and put a comforting arm around her shoulders, her own misery forgotten. 'I'm sorry you feel so badly about your mother.'

Poppy continued to weep. 'S-she used to be so nice . . . and such fun. . . and sort of cosy,' she sobbed, 'but now she doesn't care any longer . . . and I miss the mother I used to have.'

Lucy comforted her as if she'd been a small child. What Poppy had said had been very revealing. Camilla *had* changed since David had died, and maybe that explained a lot. Camilla would look upon Philip as her last chance of grabbing a little happiness before it was too late, a final chance to experience the joys of love, and she was going all out to grab that love for herself no matter how many toes she trod on along the way. A part of Lucy could understand how she felt; could appreciate that to be widowed tragically at forty was something few women would emerge from unscathed; understand that sometimes one could not help falling in love, and that occasionally that love was totally unsuitable. But love is blind and ruthless in its seeking, and Lucy wished that her son had not been the person who had become the object of Camilla's last fling. What had happened, she asked herself, to that nice Geoffrey Hennessy who had obviously been crazy for Camilla for years? How preferable an affair with him would have been. A man of nearly fifty, single, successful, charming and interesting. He would have made an excellent husband for Camilla, too. For a wild moment Lucy wondered if she should contact him, take him into her confidence and ask him to try and break up the relationship with Philip. But then, almost immediately, Lucy realised she would certainly be hurting Philip if she did that. If the affair was to be brought to an end, it was Philip who must be persuaded to do it himself.

'Try not to lose heart, Poppy,' Lucy said comfortingly. 'I think your mother is going through a phase, a final fling to prove to herself she's still young and attractive. It will end in time, I'm sure of that.' I pray to God it will, she thought silently.

'Young and attractive!' Poppy exclaimed shrilly. 'How can

anyone her age be young and attractive?'

Lucy suppressed a smile. 'Your mother is the same age as me. While I don't think of myself as exactly young, I hope I'm still attractive!'

Poppy looked at her seriously. 'For someone your age, I suppose you are,' she said with the unheeding cruelty of youth. 'But you wouldn't go running around with a young man, would you?'

Lucy tried to answer the question honestly. She was happily married to Anthony, of course, which made a difference. She tried to imagine herself on her own, wanting love, companionship, someone to share her life with, and she tried to conjure up in her mind's eye a handsome young man, half her age, who wanted to have an affair with her. The prospect was exciting, that she had to admit. But then she thought of what hard work it would be hiding the tell-tale traces of a life already lived to the full. Those greying hairs which showed first at the temples; the bags under the eyes in the morning, and the first signs of a double chin when she looked down; the stretch marks from bearing four children; the wrinkles which showed up in a bright light; the glasses she now needed for reading; the rheumatism in her left knee if she walked too far . . .

Suddenly Lucy burst out laughing, throwing back her head as great gales of mirth filled the room. Poppy stopped crying and looked at her in astonishment.

'What's so funny?'

'I could never do it!' Lucy said, still laughing. 'Never in a million years! Keeping up the appearance of trying to be young would be a nightmare. Far too much like hard work. My God, one would spend one's life on a diet, at the beauty salon, being careful to sit only in a good light. The nights would be worse.' She chuckled as she thought about it. 'No! I'd be so busy hiding the saggy bits of my body, I would never have time to enjoy myself.'

Philip had been phoning Camilla every fifteen minutes since

he'd spoken to his mother, and still there was no answer. At last, unable to bear the worry any longer, he phoned Scotland Yard and asked to be put through to Detective Inspector Pritchard. It was he who had authorised the bodyguards and been responsible for protecting Camilla.

'I'm sorry, Detective Inspector Pritchard isn't on duty this evening,' he was informed when he got through. 'Would you like to speak to his deputy, Detective Sergeant Duncan?'

'Thank you.' When he got through, Philip briefly explained his worry about Camilla.

'I'll look into it, but I don't think you've anything to worry about,' Arthur Duncan told him. 'We've been doing regular checks on Ardachie and there have been no reports of any further gun-running. I think we've cleaned up all the IRA supporters. There have been no more reports from our chaps up there of any suspicious behaviour.'

'Can you check that Mrs Eaton is all right, though? The trouble is the phone has been cut off, but I can give you her mobile number – not that she's answering,' said Philip.

'Okay. Thanks. If there's anything to report I'll get back to you, but it might not be until tomorrow morning.'

'Right.'

It was far from right, far from satisfactory, Philip thought, but it was all he could do. Nevertheless he decided he would continue to try and get hold of her himself, even if it took until midnight.

Terror froze Camilla. She couldn't think. Couldn't move. Panic had immobilised her limbs and her mind screamed in silent anguish. She was trapped . . . *trapped*! Her eyes could see only the iron bars on the windows. Her hearing pick up only the deathly silence of the house. Her reason was gone . . . she was trapped. Nothing else registered. She'd been tricked up here by an organisation that had already killed her father and step-mother, and now they planned to kill her. How long, Oh God, how long was she going to have to wait for the whole ancient mass of oak beams and crumbing masonry to be torched? Daddy, she began praying, please daddy, what can I do? Tears of panic blinded her. Sobs wrenched at her throat. I don't want to die! Why is there no one here to help me? She must get out! She wouldn't sit, locked in this room, waiting for the smoke and the flames to devour her.

And then, quite suddenly, like the answer to a prayer, she remembered her father showing her a strongroom that led off the library by a secret entrance. The previous owners had kept their silver in it for security, but Malcolm had laughed and said he hardly had enough silver to fill one shelf these days, so he wouldn't be using it. But where was it? The flicker of hope that had blazed for a moment subsided. She remembered there was a panel which formed part of the built-in bookcase that took up the whole of the end wall. But which panel? What part of the bookcase? How did it open? Did you pull or push one of the shelves on which rested her father's collection of rare leather-bound books? Or was there a lever? A knob? A button or a switch?

She started rushing to and fro, her hands smoothing along the edges of the shelves, down the battens that divided them, her figures brushing the carved edges. Malcolm had shown her how it worked when he'd first moved in; taken her into the six-foot square strongroom, which was like the inside of a giant lead-lined cupboard. Once inside, he'd pushed a lever down . . . at least she thought it was down . . . and then he'd chuckled and cried 'Hey Presto!' as a further panel opened and they'd emerged into the main hall, through a narrow aperture hidden in the oak panelling on the other side. It was her only means of escape. If she could find the secret door in the bookcase, she could go straight through the strongroom and out the other side, and maybe . . . maybe make her escape! No one else, she was sure, knew of this secret place, and it was her only chance. Sweating, her hands shaking, her mind in a feverish turmoil, she tried to remember what her father had done to open the bookcase. Had he lifted something? Pressed something? She was sure she had the right part of the bookcase because it backed on to the hall, whereas the other two-thirds backed on to the drawing-room.

Suddenly she heard a thumping sound that reverberated from the hall. It was as if someone was dragging a heavy piece of furniture down the stairs, hitting each step with a thud. There were footsteps on the hall floor now, a man's voice . . .

'She's in the library,' the voice shouted as the steps came nearer.

Where, oh God, where was the lever that opened the section in the bookcase?

The footsteps halted right by the library door, and at that moment Camilla felt something under her hand give way. She pulled harder, and as smoothly as a well-oiled gate the secret panel, with its shelves of books, swung gently open. With seconds to spare, as she heard the key turn in the library door, she plunged into the darkness of the strongroom, pulling the secret panel after her. There was a gentle click as it locked. Then angry voices were shouting. Heavy booted feet were stamping around. She could picture their dismay at finding the room empty – the room from which no one could escape, Alastair Ross had boasted.

Camilla stood for several minutes, breathing deeply to calm herself. Her ordeal was far from over. She now had to find the way out of the strongroom on the other side. And when she did, she had to make sure the hall was empty. Meanwhile, she stood listening to the rampaging that was going on all around her. In the hall and in the library, up and down the stairs and all around men were shouting, heavy feet were pounding, furniture was being dragged along the stone-flagged floors and wild oaths uttered. Alastair and his supporters were obviously stealing all they could before they torched the house. If she appeared in the hall now they'd kill her on the spot.

Listening to the din, she stood in the pitch darkness, willing herself not to panic. She still had a chance. As soon as things quietened down – she didn't dare do it a moment sooner – she'd get hold of the lever she'd watched Malcolm push down and open the panel on the opposite side of the strongroom.

It felt as if hours had passed and she could still hear muffled voices and crashes and bangs as they moved things about. It was hot in the confined space, and airless. She was beginning to feel claustrophobic, and yet she knew she must remain hidden. It was too soon to get out of here and yet she didn't know how much longer she could stay. Sweat was running in rivulets down her back and between her breasts. Her hands were wet and it was becoming increasingly difficult to breathe. Maybe she could open the panel just a crack, enough to breathe in some fresh air without giving away her presence? She reached out for the opposite wall, groping blindly in the solid darkness, and her hand encountered a shelf. She ran her hand along the top, feeling the dust but nothing else. Sliding her hand beneath the shelf, she felt for something to push down but there was nothing. And yet she was sure that was how her father had released the catch that opened the panelling into the hall. Breathing heavily and bathed in sweat, she ran her hands all over the wall, bruising them as they encountered more shelves, knocking them on the edge, scratching them until she felt the stickiness of blood seeping from a knuckle; but there was no lever. No catch. Nothing. Fresh waves of panic enveloped her. She was incarcerated in this vault! Whether the terriorists were still around or not, if she didn't get out soon she'd suffocate.

Breathing slowly to try and conserve what air there was, she feverishly renewed her search for the lever. It *must* be somewhere. She'd seen her father flick something . . . Why, she thought with mounting panic, hadn't she paid more attention at the time? Desperately she ran her hands over the reinforced surface of the strongroom, trying the other walls, reaching high above her head and then groping low down, searching all the time for anything she could push or press or pull. Her hands were shaking so much she could barely control her movements. Blood, sticky and warm, ran down her fingers to her wrists. She tried down the wall to her left. Nothing but empty shelves. She tried to her right. A smooth wall, cool to the touch, so it must be made of metal, she thought, gave no response to her probing. Then she turned round to examine the wall behind her and met with more metal lining. But there were no levers. No catches. Nothing. The heat was intense now, the atmosphere stifling. She could still hear thumping and banging in the main body of the house. Petrified, she realised that in the pitch blackness she'd lost her bearings. She couldn't work out which wall she'd come through! The space was square. Was the secret doorway from the library behind her or in front of her? Was it on her right . . . or maybe her left? Which was the wall that held the sliding panel into the hall? Terror-crazed, she banged on first one wall and then another with her fists. If the terrorists heard her even they wouldn't be able to get her out. The whole device was too cunning, unless one was familiar with it.

On the verge of collapse, Camilla sank to the floor, paralysed with terror. And then, most fearful of all . . . seeping through invisible cracks in the panels came the acrid smell of smoke.

Philip, alone in his Pimlico flat, tried to concentrate on his studies, but his mind kept going back to Camilla. He was seriously worried about her now, although he'd been assured there was no cause for concern. He dialled her mobile number once more, but somehow he didn't expect an answer. If she'd been anywhere near her phone she'd have called him by now, so what the hell was going on? He rose from the table in his sitting-room, pushing away his books and papers, and going into his small kitchen put on the kettle to make himself some coffee. Sleep was going to be impossible tonight, in any case, if he didn't hear from her. What could be happening? Over and over again he went through her plans for this trip to Ardachie. But supposing she'd never reached the village? Suppose something had happened to her on the way up? This new reflection, unthought of until this moment, sent a fresh shock of fear pulsing through him. Maybe she'd been involved in a road accident on the way? Maybe she'd run out of petrol on some lonely mountain road, miles from civilisation? Maybe she'd got lost? So many of the roads looked just like each other as they wove through dense forests and alongside jagged ravines, across several mountain passes and down into the valleys. If she'd been delayed, dusk might have fallen before she'd reached Ardachie, and she might have become so lost she'd gone to an hotel for the night.

With fresh impetus, Philip went back to the phone in the living-room. There was something positive he could do instead of waiting around helplessly, hoping by some miracle Camilla would phone him. He'd start phoning hospitals, the police and anyone else he could think of, from London to Glasgow and beyond, in case an accident had been reported. It would help pass the dragging hours, alone, wondering what had happened. It would stop him going crazy.

Two hours later, he'd drawn a complete blank. In between phoning police headquarters and hospitals in major cities and towns on the route she'd taken, he was also trying Camilla's mobile number at regular intervals. There were no reported accidents, but he was told to call the Automobile Association and the Royal Automobile Club as they might be able to put a trace on her car if it had broken down. By midnight he'd still found out nothing. Exasperated, and in the grip of growing panic, he flung himself down on to his bed and lay looking up at the blank white ceiling as if searching for answers. If anything had happened to Camilla . . . he couldn't bear to think about it. And now he blamed himself for letting her go to Scotland alone. If she'd come to any harm he'd never forgive himself. Feeling helpless, he realised he didn't even have a car. If he had he'd have left London by now and started the long drive up to Scotland in search of her. Filled with guilt, and frantic with worry, Philip lay on his bed and wished to God he'd tried to prevent her going. At three o'clock in the morning he was still as wide awake as ever, and it seemed as if the torment of this long night was only just beginning.

The pungent smell of smoke was sharp as it seeped insidiously into the strongroom where Camilla cowered, alone and terrified. It was so airless in the confined space she could only take tiny shallow breaths. If only I could see, she thought, stretching out to the unyielding walls again. To get out of this vault was all she wanted, even if in opening one of the panels she found herself back in the library.

Anything would be better than being incarcerated in this tiny closed-in space, for once the flames took hold she realised she'd be cooked alive, roasted, while the fire destroyed everything around her.

The sounds of banging and shouting had stopped and the silence was eerie. Alastair Ross and the rest of his gang must have fled as soon as they'd torched the house. They'd have left her for dead, of course, whether she'd been locked in the library or trapped in the strongroom, but now she bitterly regretted trying to escape this way. In the library she might have been able to smash a window so that she could have breathed fresh air, even if she couldn't have climbed out. She might have been able to hold on until the fire-brigade arrived, for surely the locals would call out the emergency services when they saw the smoke? Now, no matter how many firemen came, they'd never find her. They wouldn't even know she was in the building. The 'electrical fault' would be blamed for the fire, and everyone would presume the house was empty.

Suddenly, overcome with terror, she started screaming, yelling, as she hammered the walls with her bleeding fists: 'I don't want to die . . . get me out of here!' In the confined space her shrieks were deadened, even to her own ears, and the futility of the situation filled her with despair.

The smell of burning was stronger now. How long was it going to take before it reached her? In a final burst of frenzied fear she flung herself against the sides of the strongroom, lost in the blackness so that she had no idea which way she was facing.

She felt like a blind person sealed in a burial chamber! There was a crackling sound. The flames must be nearer than she thought . . . the smell of smoke was stronger, acrid and pungent as it reached her nostrils. And then . . . Camilla stood still, every nerve prickling with a sharp awareness, her mind spinning as she strained to feel a new sensation. A tiny thread of something freezing cold was blowing across her face. She gasped, sucking the air into her lungs although it was heavy-laden with smoke. It was icy but invigorating. It made her eyes sting and her throat catch, but it was air, and it was fresh.

Camilla reached out in the direction it was coming from but her hands did not connect with anything. Stepping gingerly forward, hands still outstretched, she felt the wall . . . one of the shelves . . . and it moved! She pushed harder and it gave way beneath her touch. The trickle of cold air became a blast. The secret doorway had opened! Somehow she must have touched the right part of the wall, unfastened a catch. Whatever she'd done, the hidden panel had sprung open.

Gulping the air she pushed the opening wider. Would it lead her back into the library where Alastair Ross might well have locked the door again and the windows were certainly barred? As long as she was no longer trapped in the strongroom she hardly cared. Stumbling forward, she tried to get her bearings, but it was dark now and none of the lights in the house had been turned on. It was cold, too. The draught was stronger also, fanning her, freezing the sweat on her face, chilling her body with its icy intensity. And at that moment she realised she was in the hall. As her eyes quickly adjusted, she saw the front door had been left standing open. Beyond it lay her freedom. Then billowing smoke drifted across the darkened hall and she could sense it came from the kitchen. She heard a shout and knew that her captors were still around.

Creeping swiftly and silently to the front door, she peered out cautiously, conscious that she would have to hide in the grounds until they'd left. The drive was empty. They must be round the back of the house. She blinked. The drive was empty!

So what had they done with her car and the mobile phone? Her link with the outside world! The only way she was going to escape now was by hiding as far away from the house as she could. She glanced around quickly, making sure the coast was clear. Then she tiptoed down the front steps, the moss deadening the sound of her feet, and started to run towards the trees and rhododendron bushes that lined the drive. They would provide immediate cover. The crunching of her feet on the loose gravel sounded like pistol shots in the still evening air, but she couldn't stop. She didn't dare stop. She heard a cry.

'What the devil's that?' It was a man's voice with a thick Scottish accent.

'She can no have gang awa'!' another yelled. 'After her, then.'

Camilla reached the grass verge just as she heard the crunching of footsteps on the gravel behind her. Flinging herself into the undergrowth, thankful there'd been no one to tidy the garden for months, she crawled away from the drive as fast as she could, beyond the trees and past the shrubbery, into the thick bracken that grew three feet tall. She was nearing the outskirts of her father's property now. Lying on her side, her heart palpitating, her breathing laboured from the exertion, she kept her head down, laying her cheek on the damp stony soil.

Stamping feet and the sound of rough voices cursing filled the air. Then, through the bracken, she glimpsed the piercing beams of torches being flashed around as they searched for her. Lying still, hardly daring to breathe, she waited and watched. The smell of smoke was everywhere now, penetrating the air with its bitter stench. She could hear crackling, too. The fire was getting a grip and she shuddered as she realised what it would have been like if she'd still been locked in the strongroom. Exhausted, suffering from shock, and chilled by the damp earth and biting wind, Camilla lay shivering. The worst that could happen to her now was that they'd shoot her. It would be an easy way to die compared to being burned alive.

She continued to lie crouched on the ground, shock making her unaware of her aching limbs and grazed and sore hands. She was covered in earth and there were cobwebs from the strongroom in her hair and smears of dirt on her cheeks. But she was safe, for the moment anyway. The men were still hollering at each other as they stomped around waving their torches, and she could tell from their frantic voices that they were all blaming each other for having let her slip through their fingers. If she only knew what they'd done with her car she could try to get away. Without it the wisest thing was to stay hidden in the high bracken; at least until the fire brigade came.

Then she heard a roaring sound as a stiff breeze stirred among the pine trees and swept in coldly from the Firth of Lorne. But it wasn't the wind that was roaring . . . it was Creagnach. As if something had caused an explosion, an inner rumbling combustion, the fire had taken hold with flames shooting into the night sky, belching out of the upper windows, reaching with furious fingers towards the eaves. The sky glowed pink and rich red where the clouds were low-lying. Sparks flew up, hissing and scattering like fireworks. The roaring became louder, punctuated from time to time by the explosion of shattering glass as the heat in the building became intense. Timbers thundered down, collapsing in the inferno. Creagnach was burning with a ferocity and speed that was frightening and Camilla wondered if they had poured some substance around the interior to help ignite the flames. Petrol she would have smelled. Methylated spirits was more likely, clear as gin, and mauve as violets.

Watching, she saw through the bracken her father's home being destroyed. It rattled and reverberated on its foundations while the fire consumed everything in its path. She thought of her father's books, those beautiful leatherbound volumes he'd collected all his life. She thought of his desk and the picture of her mother he always kept on it. She thought of his clothes, so personal to him, and the paintings . . . there was so much. Malcolm's whole life was recorded in the contents of the house. Tears poured down her cheeks. Seeing everything perish in the flames was like witnessing another death. The fire was taking so much with it, wiping out all the treasures of a lifetime, and she felt as if her heart was breaking as she watched. A part of her seemed to be dying in those raging flames. Not her body, that she had saved. But a part of her spirit, her heart and her soul. The past few hours had laid indelible marks upon her, imprinting her mind with truths she hadn't known existed. Truths that would never be erased. Tonight, she had experienced and endured the trauma of nearly losing her life in the most terrible way, and she knew she'd never be the same again. All she longed for now was to get away. She had so much she wanted to do, so much she wanted to say; to Poppy, to Philip. There were a lot of things in her life that needed changing and tonight had shown her what they were. Creagnach seemed to be destroying itself in a last convulsive roaring blaze, and as she watched she knew that parts of herself were also being destroyed as a result of what had happened tonight.

A commotion in the drive by the entrance gates distracted her at that moment, and then she heard the roar of an engine. There was more shouting and she caught the words: 'Gang awa' now!' There was a revving sound, and then the vehicle pulled away and Camilla could hear the sound of the engine fading as it headed for Ardachie.

She was alone now. Alastair Ross and the others had gone. Cautiously, she raised herself to a crouching position and saw that all around her was bathed in a blood red light. Ruby-tipped leaves trembled on the branches and the lawns looked as if someone had thrown a veil of scarlet gauze over the grass. The trunks of the trees were streaked claret, and above, light and feathery, grey ashes were whirling down like powdery snow.

Watching from her hideaway, she knew there was nothing she could do. It would take her ten minutes to walk into Ardachie and then she ran the risk of bumping into Alastair Ross or one of his men. The whole area for miles around must have been alerted by the glow in the sky by now so someone would surely have called the fire brigade. She would wait until they arrived, and only when the fire had been extinguished, and the old stone shell of the house remained, would she leave. There was nothing to keep her here now. Malcolm was gone and so was Edith, and every memento of their lives too. Nothing remained but memories, and nothing could ever destroy those. Malcolm had been a wonderfully loving father who had supported her in all she'd done. To have had a father like him was a blessing for which she would always be grateful. She blinked away tears as she thought how much she missed him. He was someone who had always been there for her. Edith she would remember as a sweet gentle woman, and would always be grateful to her for having given Malcolm at least a brief period of happiness before the troubles started.

As Camilla watched the death throes of Creagnach, feeding upon itself in an inferno of flames, she knew she would never return to this spot. It was time for her to cut clean from the past. All of it. David, her father, and from much that she'd misguidedly been clinging to. Life had to be lived for today, not yesterday, and tomorrow would always take care of itself.

Suddenly she froze, fear chilling her spine. Out of the corner of her eye something was moving among the trees on her right. Straining to see through the smoky haze, she could make out the figure of a man. He seemed to be watching her, and as she stared back he stepped forward, breaking away from the shelter of the trees that lined the drive.

Camilla held her breath, knowing it was useless to run. He was coming straight towards her, and in his hand he held what looked like a gun.

Chapter Twenty-Five

Philip grasped the phone, his senses reeling. He'd been up all night drinking coffee and restlessly pacing his flat until, in desperation, he'd had the idea of phoning the police station in Oban. It was the nearest large town to Ardachie, and if there'd been any incidents in the area they would know about it.

'A fire?' Philip repeated. 'At Creagnach?' He suddenly felt as if he was made of eggshells and the slightest jar or jolt would make him crack and fall apart.

'Aye,' the Desk Sergeant replied. 'The local fire brigade is still there. They've reported to us the place has been razed to the ground.'

'Are there any casualties?' he asked hollowly.

'I dinna ken, but I'll put you through to the Incident Room we've set up.'

'Thanks.' In an agony of suspense Philip waited, dreading the news. He'd known all along that something was terribly wrong and he cursed himself now for not having got on to the Oban police earlier.

'Incident Room. Can I help you?' a woman's voice asked him briskly. She sounded calm and efficient.

'I'm trying to find out if there were any casualties in the fire at Creagnach in Ardachie? My girlfriend and her stepmother were staying there, and I haven't heard from her.'

'We can't be sure. It's really too early to say,' the policewoman replied. 'The fire brigade investigative team are at the scene now, but until we have a report from them we're unable to give out any information.' Her tone was bright and friendly, but firm.

Philip closed his eyes, screwing up his face, imagining them raking through the hot ashes for human remains. How else did they discover if someone had perished or not? But he still clung to the hope that Camilla and Edith might have got out of the house before the flames took hold.

'Do you know who reported the fire?' he asked desperately, his voice cracking. 'If they raised the alarm, maybe they've gone to an hotel or something by now?'

'Can you give me the names of the two ladies please?'

'Camilla Eaton and Edith Elliott – she owns Creagnach.'

'Hold the line please.' There was a click and Philip strained to hear, but she'd switched off her phone while she made enquiries. A thousand nightmarish visions floated before his mind as he waited. Perhaps he should have mentioned Camilla was on the IRA's Wanted List! It struck him then, that the fire must have been started deliberately. Someone from the IRA had found out the two women, who would be key witnesses when the cases came to trial, were going to be at Creagnach and had deliberately torched the house in order to destroy them and any evidence there might be about the place. He should never have let Camilla go to Scotland on her own!

'Are you there?' the policewoman was back on the line.

'Yes.' Philip clutched the phone tighter, and felt sick.

'There are no reports so far of the building in question having been occupied. The fire was reported by someone in Ardachie, but our records show it was a local man. We know nothing of a Mrs Eaton or a Mrs Elliott. Were they actually living in the house?'

As briefly as possible Philip explained the whole story. From the comments he got from time to time, he got the impression the policewoman was taking down everything he said.

'Where can we get hold of you?' she asked when he'd finished.

He gave her his name and phone number. There was nothing more he could do now except wait to hear from Camilla, or the

Oban police, or Special Branch at Scotland Yard. And the hardest part of all was the waiting. It exacerbated all his fears and anxieties, it aggravated his sense of frustration and increased his sense of helplessness. Whilst a part of him longed to fly up to Glasgow and hire a car so he could search for her himself, another part of him knew the wisest course was to remain close to the phone. He would cut his classes today and stay at his flat.

Making himself yet another cup of coffee, he ran a bath, keeping the bathroom door open so he could hear if the phone rang. Then he sank into the hot water, hoping it would ease the tension in his aching limbs. It was now nine o'clock in the morning.

He was old, much older than she'd imagined when she'd first seen him lurking among the trees. His hair beneath the cap he wore was silky white, and in the red glow from the fire his deeply wrinkled face was pale. Camilla stood rigid as he came nearer, waiting to see what he would do. The hand that held the gun hung down relaxed by his side, and then she saw it wasn't a gun but a thick stick. Nevertheless, what was he doing here in the middle of the night, hiding in the shrubbery? Although he might look harmless, she suspected he was one of the men who had helped Alastair Ross empty the house of its valuables before starting the fire.

'What do you want?' she shouted above the roar of the fire, sounding much braver than she felt. If he tried to attack her she had the advantage of being younger and was sure that if she ran he wouldn't be able to catch up with her.

'I've come to see the fire for myself,' he replied, so mildly that she was startled. She'd expected to be threatened again and this old man's gentle manner took her offguard.

'I've called the fire brigade, but they've got a long way to come,' he continued, his soft brogue melodic against the fearful crackling of the burning house in the background.

'You've called the fire brigade?'

'Och, aye. You can see the flames from the harbour. There's

a crowd gatherin'. There'll be more of us here in a minute. There'll not be much sleep for any of us tonight.'

Camilla regarded him with growing astonishment and a deepening sense of relief. After all she'd been through it was amazing to realise that this old man was not going to try and hurt her.

'How soon will the fire engines be here?' she asked.

He shook his head. 'They've got a long way to come.'

'Where from?' She wondered if there'd be anything of her father's house left standing if they didn't come soon.

'Oban,' he replied laconically.

'That'll take ages.'

He shook his head. 'It's the nearest.'

They stood together now, united in watching the destruction of Creagnach. There were a lot of questions she longed to ask him, but he was the one who spoke first.

'D'you ken how it started?'

Camilla shook her head. 'Not exactly,' she replied evasively.

'It's a hell of a blaze, I'll say that for it.'

'Yes, isn't it?' Out of the corner of her eye she looked at him closely, wondering if she could trust him. She had a feeling she could. There was about him a simple country air and she guessed he was a crofter. She also had the feeling that he had no idea who she was. 'Do you know Alastair Ross?' she said carefully.

He turned bleary blue eyes to look at her, and seemed surprised. 'I've not laid eyes on him. He's a cripple, you know. Never goes out. Got a housekeeper looking after him since his father was taken awa' by the police.'

'Ah, yes. I'd heard about that. Does he never go out, even in a wheelchair?' she persisted, watching closely for any reaction.

'I've no seen him since many a year. He was in an accident, so the story goes; never been able to walk since.' He spoke with such quiet conviction that Camilla knew he thought he was speaking the truth.

'It's a lucky thing the house was empty, with everyone gang awa',' he commented suddenly.

'You knew the previous owners?'

'I knew the laird,' he confirmed. 'I didna know the new owner so well, but he seemed a nice enough man. A pleasant woman his wife was, too. Ma niece, Doris, used to help her look after all those dogs of hers.'

Of course, thought Camilla with a start. Doris the kennel maid. Doris whom Camilla had expected to see when she'd come to visit Edith that last time. Doris who had vanished along with Edith and the gardeners. They, she remembered, had been given the sack and were still living in the village, but what had happened to Doris?

She tried to keep her voice steady. 'And what is your niece doing these days?'

The old man shook his head and gave a wistful smile. 'She didna like country life,' he said regretfully. 'I found her the job here, and I thought she'd be suited, but she went back to Glasgow. Told me she preferred working in a shop. The young these days are vurry different to when I was a lad.'

Camilla sighed with relief. 'I'm glad she's all right,' she said thankfully.

'Och, aye. Getting married in a few weeks to a man who works in a garage.' He spoke scathingly. Camilla smiled. Would he ever know the risks Doris had run by working for Edith?

At that moment they heard footsteps coming up the road from the village, and then the hum of voices as the people of Ardachie drew nearer. As he'd said, a crowd was gathering to watch with morbid curiosity the final crumbling moments of the house that had once belonged to their laird. And then, carried by the stiff breeze, she heard the bells of approaching fire engines, clanging through the night. Within a few minutes the grounds of Creagnach were transformed into a scene of frantic activity as the fire engines roared up the drive, followed by police cars whose wailing sirens added to the cacophony of sound. Moments later firemen in fire-fighting gear were swarming all around, uncoiling lengths of hose piping while the police held back the crowds of villagers who had come to see the spectacle. Commands were being shouted, the police were talking into car radios, and the hubbub became as noisy as the blazing building itself.

Camilla moved forward, a dishevelled figure covered in streaks of dirt. She went to the nearest police car and spoke to the driver.

'Are you from Caoldair Police Station?'

He adjusted his peaked cap and looked at her with curiosity. 'No, miss. We're from Oban.'

'In that case I'd like to make a statement.'

Surprised, he picked up his radio receiver. 'What is your name please, miss?'

'I'm Camilla Eaton, and Creagnach . . .' she glanced with sad eyes at the burning house '. . . belonged to my father. I can tell you who started the fire, but first I'd like to be taken to the Ballageich Hotel in Kilninver.' Her eyes suddenly brimmed with tears as she knew what she had to do. 'You see, I've lost more than just my father's house tonight.'

It was after dawn when Camilla finally crawled into bed at the hotel where she'd stayed before with Philip and Lucy. The night staff remembered her, which was fortunate as she had no money or credit cards or means of identification. They even gave her the same large yellow and white room on the first floor, its bay window looking over to the island of Kerrera.

Coffee and sandwiches had been ordered, and as she sat with the two police officers in the deserted hotel lobby, Camilla described the happenings of the night. In an outpouring of emotional words which left her drained but feeling a great sense of relief, she told them about Alastair Ross, and Edith's murder; she described how she'd been tricked into coming up north, and what had happened to her afterwards. It took a long time but in the end it was done, and as she signed her statement she prayed it was really all over.

'Where can we get hold of you if we need to ask any further questions?' the police sergeant asked.

Camilla told him, and then announced she was going to bed.

'I'm really very tired. I left London shortly after five this morning . . . that is yesterday morning.' She felt near to tears again. The strain was getting to her and she felt dizzy and almost sick from lack of sleep.

Assuring her that there was nothing more they needed at that juncture they left, and Camilla climbed the polished flight of oak stairs to her room. She could no longer think. How she was going to get back to London without her car, any money or credit cards, was something she'd have to fix tomorrow. Getting in touch with the office would be the first thing to do. And then phoning Philip – that was the call she was dreading. That was going to be the beginning of the hardest thing she'd ever had to do.

Ferris was at Heathrow to meet Camilla, in a hired car. If he was shocked by her wan appearance he gave no sign. The housekeeper at the Ballageich Hotel had washed and pressed her slacks and silk shirt so that she looked crisply neat, but there was a droop to her shoulders and a grim tension around her mouth as she stepped into the car.

'Thank you, Ferris.' She glanced at her wristwatch. It was two o'clock on Saturday afternoon and she knew Philip would be at home studying.

'Will you take me to Mr Hamilton's flat, please?' she asked. 'And I'd like to keep the car for the rest of the day. Can you make your own way back to Wilton Crescent?'

Ferris looked surprised but was too well trained to show it.

'Certainly, madam. That will be fine.'

'Thank you. I'm sorry about all this inconvenience. They've found the Mercedes, hidden in the same fishing shed where my father's car was kept, but the police want to keep it until they've checked it for fingerprints. I hope we'll get it back in about a week's time, but in the meanwhile are you quite happy with this Jaguar?' Camilla knew how much he loved the Mercedes and how upset he'd been when Annabel had passed the message on to him that it had been stolen.

'It's not the same, madam, but it will do fine for the time being,' Ferris assured her gravely.

As they neared central London, her heart started to hammer nervously and her hands felt icy. They'd be at Philip's flat in twenty minutes and he wasn't expecting her. When she'd phoned him the previous day to tell him everything, she only said she'd be arriving in London during the afternoon. He would presume she was going straight to Wilton Crescent and would call him from there.

Ferris managed to find a place to park the car only fifty yards from Philip's flat.

'The tank is full, madam,' he assured her as he handed her the keys. 'You'll want me at the usual time on Monday morning?'

'Absolutely, Ferris,' she assured him.

Slipping the keys into her trouser pocket, she ran her fingers through her newly washed but dishevelled hair and realised she was without makeup or the perfume she always wore. Not that Philip hadn't seen her before without makeup but suddenly she wished she was wearing one of her immaculate executive suits, with her face and hair beautifully done. It gave her courage to look her best, and that was why she had always made an effort to look good for work. Perfect dressing was a great confidence booster. But then, she thought, what had looking chic and well groomed got to do with anything at this moment? Nothing was going to make her feel better.

Ringing the front doorbell marked 'Hamilton', she waited until she heard his voice on the intercom.

'Who's that?'

'It's me . . . Camilla,' she replied tremulously, starting to shake all over. He sounded delighted.

'Darling! Come in!' She heard the lock buzzing and pushed the heavy black door open. Inside the communal hall she wondered for a moment how her legs were going to carry her. She was drenched in sweat now, and felt as if she'd been injected with lead. I've got to go through with this, she thought desperately. I must, for everyone's sake. She reached the lift, and as she pressed the button the doors glided silently open. Philip was waiting for her on the landing outside his flat. As he opened his arms to greet her she almost fell into them, half fainting, half overcome at the thought of what lay ahead in the next half-hour.

'Please, Philip . . .' she begged, but he took it to mean she was too exhausted to start making love, and so solicitously guided her into his small flat and led her to the sofa in the living-room.

'You must be shattered, my love,' he said sympathetically. 'Can I get you anything? Tea?'

Camilla raised her hand. 'No, nothing thank you, darling. I'm all right. I came to see you because . . . because we've got to talk.'

'What about?' he asked uncertainly.

She looked into his eyes, and inside she died a thousand deaths. She *couldn't* do this . . . she loved him . . . and yet she had to.

'Philip,' she began again, with an effort. 'I've been giving this a lot of thought. This isn't some crazy notion . . . I mean . . .' She was floundering now, unable to say what she'd planned.

He looked at her intuitively, his expression stricken. 'What is it?' he asked in a dangerously quiet voice.

'We have to stop seeing each other . . . it's hurting too many people. Poppy, your family . . . we have to end it, darling.' She was crying now, covering her face with her hands, knowing that if she looked into his eyes she'd falter in her resolution.

'But, Camilla!' He sounded appalled, as if he couldn't believe what he'd heard. 'You can't mean . . .'

'I do! I do . . . don't you understand? There's no future for us together. How can there be, with the age difference? Your family hate the idea of our being together, especially your mother . . . and so does Poppy. I'm worried about her. I feel I've let her down and I must put it right before it's too late.'

'Don't you think you've got a right to your own life?' He sounded angry and bitter now, and deeply upset.

Camilla raised her head to look at him. 'I also have a responsibility to my child,' she replied. 'I think I've been a bad mother since David died, and I need to make it up to her . . .'

'What, by ruining your own life, and mine? How can you do that?'

'Please listen, Philip,' she cried, wiping the tears away with the back of her hand, 'and please don't get so angry. God knows this is the most difficult thing I've ever had to do. Can't you see that? Can't you see it's going to kill me, to say goodbye to you . . .' Her voice broke, and she started sobbing.

'Camilla, you're wrong, darling,' he said, suddenly gentle. He tried to put his arms around her, but she pushed him away. If she once let him touch her she'd give in. She wouldn't be able to resist him. Even looking at him could arouse her, especially when he gave her that steady gaze of his which seemed to penetrate her heart and soul. If he were to try and kiss her . . . She rose abruptly and stood looking out of the window.

'Let's not drag this out, Philip,' she said softly. 'I've made up my mind . . . I've thought of nothing else . . . it's the only solution.'

He jumped to his feet too and stood facing her, every line of his body tense with abject misery. 'You can't do this! God, what are you thinking of? We love each other. Surely that's the most important thing of all?'

She met his gaze, looking straight at him, finding a strength she didn't know she possessed. 'Sometimes the most loving thing one can do is to let someone go,' she said softly. 'I don't want to ruin your life.'

'You will if you leave me,' he shot back. 'What am I supposed to do without you?' He was flushed and his eyes were brimming with angry tears.

'You have your life before you,' she began, but he interrupted her, talking fast as he paced up and down his small living-room.

'My life is you!' he insisted wildly. 'I love you, Camilla. How can I get you to believe me? We belong together. How can you deny that? It's madness to stop seeing each other just because of my mother. She'll come round in time. She'll realise she can't split us up when she sees sense. As for Poppy . . . she's almost grownup. She's got her own life. She's left home.'

'No, she hasn't,' Camilla cut in. 'She's not living at home because she's unhappy. That's not the same thing as leaving home because of studies, or work, or getting married.'

Philip spun on her angrily. 'Poppy's a spoilt brat and you know it! This is all her doing, isn't it? You're pandering to her, Camilla. As soon as she's got what she wants she'll go off and do her own thing, that's what will happen! Poppy is manipulative . . .'

Camilla stood shaking her head. 'Don't you see what's happening?' she asked. 'Already we've begun to say cruel things to each other.' She spread her hands in a gesture of helplessness. 'This is the one thing I wanted to avoid.'

'So you expected to swan in here, tell me blithely it was all over, and have me take it like a lamb?' he demanded.

'No . . . yes . . . no, but I expected you to understand. God knows, if you think this is the most fun thing I've done, then you're mistaken! This is killing me! Can't you see that? I no more want to put an end to our affair than you do.'

'How can you call it an affair? An affair is a cheap little romance with someone you fancy! Have you looked upon this as an affair all along?' he asked and then covered his face with his hands as it it were too painful for him to look at her.

Camilla went to him then, cupping his head between her hands. He slumped against her, sobbing.

'Listen to me, sweetheart,' she said, as she might have to a child. 'This hasn't been just an affair to me. You'll never know how much I love you, or how much you mean to me. But we're being selfish if we think we're the only pebbles on the beach. You don't want to go on hurting your mother, do you? She only has your best interests at heart, you know. Isn't it better to part now, without recrimination, than to go on and finally end up hating each other . . . and alienated from our families?'

'I can't live without you,' he said dejectedly between sobs.

'Oh, my darling, you can, of course you can.' It amazed her how strong she was being now. Perhaps, she reflected, it was because at this moment she was feeling more like a mother than a lover. 'What we've shared has been the most wonderful thing in my life,' she whispered as she held his head in her hands, cradling it against her shoulder. 'I shall probably never stop loving you, either, but it has to end, darling, and it is better to end it now than to wait until we're tearing each other to bits and the whole thing crumbles away in acrimony. Believe me, I do know what I'm saying.'

He drew away from her, blowing his nose, and with tenderness she saw an overgrown schoolboy, his eyes red-rimmed and his hair ruffled.

'I don't think I can bear to let you go,' he said.

'You'll be fine,' she said comfortingly. 'It's going to be tough at first, I'm not sure how I'm going to get through it myself . . .' Keep talking, don't think, keep talking, said a voice in her head. As long as you keep talking and don't think you'll get through this, and then you can go home and howl your eyes out in private.

'I don't know how you can do this,' Philip was saying. 'I can't believe you want to end everything. After all we've meant to each other! After all we've shared! Camilla, are you out of your senses?'

She looked at him sadly. 'Maybe I've just come to my senses. Maybe this has all been a moment of madness . . . I don't know, but I do know that we've got to end it now.'

'I can't accept that,' he protested. 'To hell with what my family think! I'm not a child any more! You talk as if I'd been led astray.' He looked bewildered and rumpled. 'I won't let you go,' he said finally.

'Don't let's go on like this. Please, Philip,' she begged. 'Try to understand, darling. Try not to take it so hard. It's hurting me just as much as it's hurting you . . . more perhaps because there will be other loves in your life, and in time a wife and children. For me this is the end.' She looked at him squarely, her eyes glistening with tears although she tried to smile. 'I shall never love anyone as I've loved you, so don't make it harder

460

for me than it already is. I'm going now, and I won't be seeing you again.' She moved towards the door resolutely, desperate to escape before she was overwhelmed by emotion.

Philip sprang forward, grabbing her by the shoulders, forcing her to stop, twisting her round so that she faced him.

'Camilla darling, for God's sake!' he pleaded, beside himself with grief. 'You don't know what you're doing! You can't leave me like this. Jesus Christ, don't you love me at all?'

She stood still, looking up at him, willing herself not to give way.

'Maybe you'll never know just how much I do love you . . . and that's why I'm doing this,' she said, trying to keep her voice steady.

He launched himself on her in a final embrace, crushing her so she could hardly breathe, burying his face in her neck in a paroxysm of grief.

When he released her she was shaking all over and knew if she didn't get out of his flat quickly she'd collapse under the weight of her own distress. A few minutes later she was in her car driving away, tears streaming down her face, sobs choking her throat. She couldn't go home yet, not like this. Then it struck her how stupid it was to have a lifestyle that wouldn't let her go home when she was upset, because of what the servants might think. How absurd could one get! Was it this sort of pressure that had driven Poppy away? Always having to put on a show? Always dressing to keep up appearances?

She reached into the glove compartment for a tissue, and then remembered it wasn't her car she was driving and swore. She'd asked Annabel to give Ferris some money for her, and so she pulled up outside the next newspaper shop she came to and rushed in to get some tissues. The girl behind the counter looked at her strangely and she realised she must look a mess, with her tear-stained face and dishevelled hair. Not at all the image that the chairman of Eaton & Eaton usually gave, she thought, with a flicker of her old wry humour.

Back in the car she drove on, not caring where she went but

knowing she was not yet ready to go home. Leaving Philip had made her feel as if she'd been wrenched in two; her ribs ached, her stomach felt sore, her arms and legs felt as if they had weights tied to them. If she could only have a few hours' peace, on her own, before she faced the world again!

An hour later, Camilla found herself in the countryside driving along a winding lane overhung with the branches of tall trees, so that it was like going through a green tunnel. Suddenly it grew lighter and the road opened out and the trees grew sparser like curtains parting to reveal a view that was so spectacular she pulled over into a layby and stopped to look. Late-afternoon sunshine cast long shadows from the trees and hedges that bordered the sweep of meadows, lying as far as the eye could see in shades of green and gold, and through the landscape like a winding blue and silver ribbon, a wide stream curled and looped, threading its way through the lush fields and skirting the distant woods in a glittering detour.

Camilla had no idea how long she sat there, breathing in the scented air through the car windows, but when she turned round to head back to London she felt calmer than she had in a long while. With a new sense of resolution she felt she could face the future. The chaos and confusion of the past year were over, and now the madness of love and the fever of desire had subsided she had a feeling she could make a good life for herself. Maybe not as exciting or frenetic, but nevertheless good. Her mouth tilted up at the corners for a moment as she thought how happy Lucy was going to be. And Poppy? She still hoped she and Poppy could be close once again. Philip had changed her life, but now it was over. At this moment she felt as if she'd been reborn and yet was buried and dead; rejuvenated and yet the bearer of a knowledge that made her feel a thousand years old. She'd loved, and from that love she'd learned a lot, maybe more than Philip would ever guess. Now the time had come to put that learning into practice.

Poppy opened the front door and then jumped, startled, when

she saw it was Philip. It was the first time she'd been alone with him since she'd seen him making love to her mother amid the lilies on the floor, and she felt herself grow red and bristle with hostility as he stood uncertainly before her.

'Is Mum in?' he asked diffidently.

'Er . . . yes . . . I think so,' she replied. 'I know Anthony's in.' Then she turned back into the Hamiltons' hall and shouted up the stairs.

'Lucy? Are you there?'

'What is it?' she called back from her bedroom on the first floor.

'There's someone here to see you,' Poppy announced succinctly.

They heard Lucy say, 'I'll be there in a second,' and Poppy turned away, leaving Philip standing in the open doorway alone.

Lucy came hurrying down the stairs, almost tripping in her delight at seeing her son again. 'Come in, darling. What are you doing standing in the doorway like that? Did you ring the bell? Don't you have a key?' She hugged him warmly, kissing him on both cheeks.

'Are you all right, darling? You look . . .' To her horror Philip started to cry. As he clung to the doorpost, swaying as if he was drunk, great sobs racked his body and through the hand that half covered his face tears dripped to land on the lapels of his suit.

'My God! What is it?' she cried, appalled. Her arms went round his shuddering shoulders and she held him as she had when he was a small boy and had fallen down and hurt himself.

'S-she's left me,' was all he could say, and understanding she led him upstairs to her bedroom where she knew they would not be disturbed. Lucy knew better than to ask too many questions, but could guess what had happened. Philip would tell her in his own time, and she would listen, a wise mother, and never say 'I told you so'. And as she sat there comforting him, she felt a sudden pang of sorrow for Camilla. How could she really blame her for falling in love with Philip? If she was honest she'd have to admit that the temptation must have been very strong, and the attraction irresistible. When Philip started talking in a heartbroken welter of words, neither he nor Lucy noticed a shadow fall across the landing outside the bedroom as Poppy stood there to listen.

All Camilla wanted to do now was get home. In what had seemed like the longest day in her life, she had wiped the slate clean and now had to start all over again, building up a life without Philip. Without working so hard either. In the past four years her existence had been that of a workaholic. Everything had revolved around Eaton & Eaton, from seven o'clock in the morning until midnight. Her social life until she met Philip had also been tied up with colleagues and clients and their respective spouses. When had she last had dinner with a friend who was in no way involved in the company, however remotely? Not since the days of David, replied the voice in her head. When had she last had time to spend time lazing around the house, doing nothing in particular? The answer was the same. And since she'd fallen in love with Philip, she'd somehow managed to squeeze him into her frenetic schedule, too.

She had reached Vauxhall Bridge, and as she drove across the Thames she knew that she would be home in fifteen minutes, providing the Saturday evening traffic wasn't too heavy.

Poppy walked briskly up the Earls Court Road. At the top she was lucky enough to catch a number nine bus. She glanced at her watch. It was half-past six. Sitting on the top deck she tried to concentrate on the shops as they flashed by in order to give herself something to do, some distraction that would stop her feeling so nervous. Shoe shops, book shops, chemists and clothing stores, antique shops and chic boutiques displayed their wares in attractive profusion, but she saw none of it. Her eyes were still filled with the sight of Philip's distraught face and her ears still echoed to the sound of his sobs.

Camilla rounded the formal grandeur of Belgrave Square where embassies and residences stood pillared and porticoed in white-painted stateliness. She'd never liked the square much, in spite of the lush gardens in the middle. To her it was too solid and Victorian, too cold and unfriendly. Wilton Crescent, leading off the Square, was much prettier, the buildings more curved and graceful, the whole sweeping crescent delicately executed in pale grey stone. The clock on the dashboard of her hired car said it was twenty minutes to seven. She'd go round the back of her house and put the car in the garage for Ferris on Monday morning. Her plans for the weekend did not include driving anywhere.

Poppy got off the bus, crossed the road and started hurrying down Grosvenor Crescent. Her suitcase seemed to weigh a ton and at one point she had to stop and change hands before continuing. She hadn't realised it was such a hot evening. Her jeans and white shirt were sticking to her, and her blond hair, tied back in a ponytail, seemed to have wrapped itself round the back of her neck. With an impatient movement she lifted it away, thankful she hadn't much further to go.

Camilla rounded the corner of Wilton Crescent, walking very slowly. She was hot and sticky, her cream trousers and shirt wrinkled, her hair hanging loosely down her back making her look years younger. Devoid of makeup, she bore no resemblance to the elegantly groomed woman who stepped into her waiting car each morning, briefcase in one hand, Gucci handbag in the other. She paused for a moment and then, glancing up, saw a figure that was familiar and yet strangely different walking towards her from the opposite end of the Crescent. The flushed young face framed by blond wisps of hair, the slender juvenile body of a girl barely developed, she knew as well as she knew her own reflection, but the smile held a diffident quality and the blue eyes were looking at her with a strange vulnerability.

'Poppy?' she whispered.

Poppy stopped several feet away and stood looking back at

her. It seemed to Camilla as if they were sizing each other up, each astonished by the other's appearance; Camilla so casual, Poppy so clean and without her lurid makeup. It was a wary look they exchanged now, each trying to gauge what the other was thinking, each trying to judge what the other would do next. The last time they'd seen each other they had fought bitterly and the atmosphere between them had been fraught with animosity. They'd been at opposite sides of an unbridgeable gap and it had seemed that they would never be able to forge a bond that would bind them together again as mother and daughter. Both had loved and suffered deeply because of that love, but both had survived and that was what mattered. In time, Camilla hoped, the misunderstanding and bitterness between them would fade. In time, she prayed, they could rebuild their relationship and be supportive of each other. It was something they would both have to work at, and they would both have to learn to forgive.

Camilla took a step forward, but it was Poppy who was the first to speak.

'I'm glad you're home again, Mummy,' she said in a soft voice, reminiscent of the way she'd been as a child.

A moment later they were hugging each other as they stood on the pavement outside their home, Poppy with her arms around Camilla's neck while her mother held her close.

'I'm glad we're both home again, Poppy darling.'

Epilogue

The flattering glow of candlelight illuminated the exquisite dining-room, and across the centrepiece of peachy tulips and white lilies Camilla looked down the table at her dinner party guests. Tonight was almost an exact repetition of a dinner party she'd given over eighteen months before, she reflected. With two exceptions – on that last occasion Philip had been there and Poppy hadn't. Now it was the other way round. There was Anthony, as jocular and rubicund as ever, still trying to catch Maitland's eye to have his glass refilled. There was Lucy, a fraction plumper and a little bit greyer, but once again the placid motherly woman Camilla had known for forty years. Henrietta, back from studying in Paris, looked prettier than ever and talked shyly of the new boyfriend in her life. And Reggie and Charlotte, home for the Easter holidays, were still inquisitive and lively. Only Philip was missing, on an extended trip of the capitals of Europe, studying Renaissance architecture. In his place sat Poppy, blooming with good health yet still with that fragile delicate beauty that typifies the English Rose. She'd passed her GCSE exams better than either she or Camilla had expected and was now studying hard to get her A-levels. There was even talk, much to her mother's delight, of going on to university to read English Literature and Philosophy.

'When does the trial start?' Lucy asked. They'd been discussing Alastair Ross, and how he'd been arrested the day after Creagnach had burnt to the ground.

'Next month,' Camilla replied. 'Did I tell you they'd found

out a third of the population of Ardachie was made up of IRA supporters? Until we exposed what was going on it was the main gun-running operation on the west coast of Scotland.'

'I can't get over the irony of your father and Edith choosing to go and live there, when they could have lived anywhere in the British Isles,' Anthony remarked sagely.

'And only because she'd corresponded with the vet over breeding her blessed dogs,' Camilla added.

'Incredibly bad luck,' Lucy remarked, shaking her head. 'But they'll all be sentenced, won't they? There's no risk of their getting off, is there?'

'They can get Alastair Ross for arson, if nothing else,' Camilla asserted, 'and the men who were with him that night, too. But I think the police found enough evidence to put the lot of them away for a very long time. Except for Morag, Alastair's wife. Apparently she was practically held captive by Hector and his son. She was terrified of them.'

'Looking back,' Lucy observed, 'I can hardly believe any of it happened, you know. Can you? To me it seems like a nasty dream . . . or even a film on television we all watched!'

The two women smiled at each other, all past animosity forgiven and forgotten. Not that they talked much of Philip these days; he was still too delicate a subject to speak of lightly, and so they hardly mentioned him at all.

'I know what you mean,' Camilla agreed. To her too it was as if the madness of last summer had been a dream . . . beautiful, magical, but now gone. Perished in the harsh light of reality. At first the pain had been unbearable as she tried to condition herself to a life without Philip. Her grief was as sharp as when she'd lost David, and there'd been moments when she wasn't sure how she was going to survive. But there had been Poppy to think about, and overcoming the barriers that had grown between them, and working to put their relationship to rights again, had taken up so much of her time and energy that it had helped distract her from her own loss. Now Camilla could look back over the last year and know the worst was over. She was still lonely at times, especially as she'd given up running Eaton & Eaton and was now a consultant to the company, only going in three times a week; but along with giving up Philip, she'd been realistic, knowing the old cliché time being a great healer was true.

'The best thing of all,' said Anthony, breaking into her thoughts, 'must be that you're no longer on anybody's Wanted List!'

'It certainly is! Jean has even come back to work for me, not that I actually need her so much these days, but it is nice to have her around again.'

'What about the girl who took her place?' Lucy asked. 'Wasn't her nose put out of joint when Jean returned to work?'

Camilla laughed. 'As it turned out, Annabel became a first-class PA, so much so that she works for Leslie Forbes who's now chairman.'

'Good for her,' Anthony chortled, looking with pleasure at his full glass. Then he turned to Poppy. 'You must like having your mother around a bit more, don't you?'

Poppy caught Camilla's eye and they both smiled. 'It's great,' Poppy confirmed. 'Just like the old days.'

'What old days?' demanded Reggie.

'The days when Daddy was still alive,' she replied softly.

'We're going to Venice on the Orient Express next weekend,' said Camilla. 'It's something David and I had always planned to do, but never got around to.'

Reggie and Charlotte looked enviously at Poppy. 'Lucky beggar!' Reggie commented. 'No one takes us on trips like that.'

'Oh, you poor deprived children!' Anthony chuckled.

When the evening came to an end, amid much animated chat and laughter, Camilla went into the hall to see them off. It had been one of the most enjoyable evenings she'd spent for a long time.

'You must come again when we get back from Venice,' she promised. 'We'll have lots to tell you.'

Anthony, as he kissed her goodbye, whispered: 'You should

469

be going with a lover to Venice, my dear. It's the most romantic city in the world.'

'I should be so lucky!' Camilla joked, but for a moment her eyes held a sad look and a shadow seemed to flit across her features.

'I'm sure one day you will be,' he said, so softly no one else could hear.

'I wouldn't like to bet on it,' she replied with a wry smile.

When they had all gone, Poppy danced up the stairs to her room in a very good humour. 'Did you hear that Henrietta and I are planning to tour around France in the summer? Won't that be great!'

'Fantastic, darling,' Camilla replied warmly. 'The best way to learn the language is to spend some time in the country.'

Poppy nodded, her fine blond hair swinging silkily about her shoulders. 'Yes, it will be great. I can hardly wait. The thing I'm most looking forward to is the food, though. I'm going to gorge myself for two solid months!'

Camilla looked up, laughing, as her daughter disappeared into her room. A part of her wished it was she who was going to tour France with Poppy, but another part of her knew that she mustn't spoil their newfound closeness by being possessive.

'Goodnight, darling,' she called out.

'Night, Mummy.'

The house was quiet. Maitland had long since blown out the dining-room candles and she'd insisted he and Mrs Maitland retire for the night once he'd served coffee. Alone now, she puffed up the silk cushions on the drawing-room sofa and wished she didn't feel so empty and restless. Anthony had said he was sure she'd have someone to share her life with again, but she didn't think it was likely. Not someone she could love. Not someone who could fill the terrible gap left first by David and then by Philip. She sighed, drawing back the curtains before she turned off the lights. It had been a lovely evening, and she wished now that she didn't feel so lonely. Then she spoke to herself sharply, cursing the stupid self-pity that was about to spoil everything. Count your blessings, said the voice in her head as she went to switch off the chandelier that illuminated the drawing-room.

At that moment the front doorbell rang. Shrugging, she went to answer it. No doubt Reggie or Charlotte had left something behind; Lucy was always chiding them for being so absent-minded. She unlocked the door again, took off the security chain, and opened the door.

'What is it?' she began, but then she gasped and gave a little cry of surprise.

'Is it too late, Camilla? I saw all the lights were on and thought if you were still up I might stop by and say hello. It's been such a long time.'

Camilla stared for a long moment, feeling stunned. Then she smiled, as if this visit was the very thing she had been searching for. She stretched out her hand in welcome.

'Come in, Geoffrey,' she said warmly. 'It's been far too long since we last saw each other.'

A selection of bestsellers
from Headline

LONDON'S CHILD	Philip Boast	£5.99 ☐
THE GIRL FROM COTTON LANE	Harry Bowling	£5.99 ☐
THE HERRON HERITAGE	Janice Young Brooks	£4.99 ☐
DANGEROUS LADY	Martina Cole	£4.99 ☐
VAGABONDS	Josephine Cox	£4.99 ☐
STAR QUALITY	Pamela Evans	£4.99 ☐
MARY MADDISON	Sheila Jansen	£4.99 ☐
CANNONBERRY CHASE	Roberta Latow	£5.99 ☐
THERE IS A SEASON	Elizabeth Murphy	£4.99 ☐
THE PALACE AFFAIR	Una-Mary Parker	£4.99 ☐
BLESSINGS AND SORROWS	Christine Thomas	£4.99 ☐
WYCHWOOD	E V Thompson	£4.99 ☐
HALLMARK	Elizabeth Walker	£5.99 ☐
AN IMPOSSIBLE DREAM	Elizabeth Warne	£5.99 ☐
POLLY OF PENN'S PLACE	Dee Williams	£4.99 ☐

All Headline books are available at your local bookshop or newsagent, or can be ordered direct from the publisher. Just tick the titles you want and fill in the form below. Prices and availability subject to change without notice.

Headline Book Publishing PLC, Cash Sales Department, Bookpoint, 39 Milton Park, Abingdon, OXON, OX14 4TD, UK. If you have a credit card you may order by telephone — 0235 831700.

Please enclose a cheque or postal order made payable to Bookpoint Ltd to the value of the cover price and allow the following for postage and packing:

UK & BFPO: £1.00 for the first book, 50p for the second book and 30p for each additional book ordered up to a maximum charge of £3.00.

OVERSEAS & EIRE: £2.00 for the first book, £1.00 for the second book and 50p for each additional book.

Name ....

Address ....

....

....

If you would prefer to pay by credit card, please complete:
Please debit my Visa/Access/Diner's Card/American Express (delete as applicable) card no:

Signature ....Expiry Date ....